T0391959

The Prosthetic Arts of *Moby-Dick*

The Prosthetic Arts of *Moby-Dick*

DAVID HAVEN BLAKE

OXFORD
UNIVERSITY PRESS

Oxford University Press is a department of the University of Oxford.
It furthers the University's objective of excellence in research, scholarship,
and education by publishing worldwide. Oxford is a registered trade mark of
Oxford University Press in the UK and in certain other countries.

Published in the United States of America by Oxford University Press
198 Madison Avenue, New York, NY 10016, United States of America.

© Oxford University Press 2024

All rights reserved. No part of this publication may be reproduced,
stored in a retrieval system, or transmitted, in any form or by any means,
without the prior permission in writing of Oxford University Press,
or as expressly permitted by law, by license or under terms agreed with
the appropriate reprographics rights organization. Inquiries concerning
reproduction outside the scope of the above should be sent to
the Rights Department, Oxford University Press, at the address above.

You must not circulate this work in any other form
and you must impose this same condition on any acquirer

Library of Congress Cataloging-in-Publication Data
Names: Blake, David Haven, author.
Title: The prosthetic arts of Moby-Dick / David Haven Blake.
Description: New York, NY : Oxford University Press, 2024. | Includes
bibliographical references and index.
Identifiers: LCCN 2024030485 (print) | LCCN 2024030486 (ebook) |
ISBN 9780197780510 (hardback) | ISBN 9780197780534 (epub)
Subjects: LCSH: Melville, Herman, 1819–1891. Moby Dick. | Ahab, Captain
(Fictitious character) | Prosthesis in literature. | Disabilities in
literature. | LCGFT: Literary criticism.
Classification: LCC PS2384.M62 B58 2024 (print) | LCC PS2384.M62 (ebook)
| DDC 813/.3—dc23/eng/20240712
LC record available at https://lccn.loc.gov/2024030485
LC ebook record available at https://lccn.loc.gov/2024030486

DOI: 10.1093/oso/9780197780510.001.0001

Marquis, Canada

So I prophesied as I was commanded: and as I prophesied, there was a noise, and behold a shaking, and the bones came together, bone to his bone.

—Ezekiel 37:7

Coffin! Angels! save me!

—*Moby-Dick*

Contents

Acknowledgments	ix
Introduction: The Ivory Leg	1

PART I. STAGING DISABILITY

1. Ahab, Walking	25
2. Bone to Bone	57

PART II. PROSTHETIC IDENTITIES

3. The Phantom Fedallah	87
4. Ishmael, Salaaming	115

PART III. BODIES POLITIC

5. The Unnatural Stump	143
6. Eternal Hacking	172
Conclusion: Stuck on a Whale	200

Notes	207
Index	235

Acknowledgments

A book like this one requires the support and expertise of many people. For help with images, permissions, and details about the collections, I am particularly indebted to Claudia Triggs of the Mystic Seaport Museum, Erin Hunt of the Berkshire County Historical Society at Herman Melville's Arrowhead, Brianne Barrett of the American Antiquarian Society, and D. Jordan Berson, Michael P. Dyer, and Emma Rocha of the New Bedford Whaling Museum.

My friends at The College of New Jersey's R. Barbara Gitenstein Library have been tremendously helpful in procuring research materials for this work. Special thanks to Dina Carmy in Access Services and Reserves and Bethany Sewell in the Interlibrary Loan Office for their goodwill, creativity, and patience.

I received invaluable support for research and writing from The College of New Jersey (TCNJ) in the form of sabbatical and research awards from 2019 to 2024.

Writing a book about the relentlessly curious Melville is a humbling experience, as each page confronts us with how much we do not know. I am grateful for my TCNJ colleagues who have helped fill in some important gaps, including Jo Carney, Christopher Fisher, Deborah Hutton, Mindi McMann, Consuelo Preti, and, especially, Michael Robertson, who provided crucial advice and commentary at an early stage of this project.

Like Ishmael on the *Samuel Enderby*, I have found a spirited home in the Melville community and have benefited from the conversation and feedback of Timothy Marr, Michel Imbert, and Pilar Martínez Benedí (among many others). David Dowling's early readings of the manuscript were incredibly helpful, as were the comments from the numerous anonymous readers during the review process.

I have enjoyed working with the team at Oxford University Press. Thanks to Jacqueline Norton, Ponneelan Moorthy, Laura Santo, and Hannah Doyle for their interest and expertise. Thanks also to Peter Dougherty, who warmly supported this book from the beginning. Two phenomenal teachers introduced me to Herman Melville: Robert Milder at Washington

X ACKNOWLEDGMENTS

University in St. Louis and Peter Balakian at Colgate University. That I got to share my initial reading of *Moby-Dick* with Scott Dierks and Andy Loesberg undoubtedly contributed to my lifelong interest in the novel.

The germ of this book came from a conversation I had in 2005 with Ameen Ghannam and John Habib in which they shared the ways in which their lives had changed since 9/11. That conversation seems more haunting today than it did nearly twenty years ago.

Ed Schwarzschild has been the steady insightful friend that every book (and person) should have. Not many authors can find the advice of a brilliant novelist, scholar, and singer-songwriter in a single source.

Ralph Savarese and I have been discussing Herman Melville since the fall of 1986. His warm friendship, irreverent humor, and dazzling intellect are unparalleled. I could not be more appreciative of all he has taught me over the years in both his writings and conversation.

Herman Melville has been the fifth member of my household since my children were very young. A Melville scholar in his own right, my son, Eben, has persistently expanded my view of this novel, especially concerning the doctrine of necessity in a complex world. My daughter, Eva, has been this book's medical adviser, supplying insights and clarifications that only a medical professional (with a degree in history) could provide. My gratitude and love for my wife, Julie, knows no bounds.

For nearly forty years my favorite author to teach has been Herman Melville, for his work means so much to so many. I have taught Melville's works to boarding school students, to military cadets, to executives in an MBA program, to neighbors in community book clubs, and to high school teachers under the auspices of the Woodrow Wilson Foundation. I have taught many generations of students at The College of New Jersey—some of whom have married each other, some of whom have gotten whale tattoos, and some of whom have gone on to teach *Moby-Dick* themselves. All of them have taught me something important about Ishmael's "mighty book." I gratefully dedicate this study to them. As always, friends, *We try all things; we achieve what we can.*

Introduction

The Ivory Leg

The Arts of Aggrievement

Amid its many themes and subplots, Herman Melville's *Moby-Dick* (1851) is a meditation on how grief turns into grievance and grievance into the desire for revenge. As even the most casual readers know, the loss of Ahab's leg sets the captain on his hunt for the white whale, a hunt he undertakes to redress "all the subtle demonisms of life and thought."[1] Seconds before he throws his final harpoon, the captain exclaims what we might regard as an epitaph for himself: "Oh, now I feel my topmost greatness lies in my topmost grief" (571). Feeling more than sorrow, Ahab transforms his dismemberment into a sense of aggrievement, a conviction that he has been cheated by a gruesome, conspiring universe. Many characters in the novel suffer extraordinary pain. The captain of the *Rachel* loses his twelve-year-old son. The blacksmith's alcoholism sends his family to the grave. "The universal thump," as Ishmael describes it, passes across the globe, accentuating emotional, physical, and cosmic vulnerabilities (6). Ahab's greatness comes not from his having greater woes than the people he encounters at sea. It comes from the conviction that he has been flagrantly and singularly wronged. Driven by resentment, this American Job rails against the injustice of his loss.

What makes Ahab remarkable, however, is how injury forms the basis of his power. The novel at times depicts the captain as being helpless and exposed, and a series of embarrassments unmask the limits of his pride. But Ahab is most remembered for his dominance over the crew and how he convinces others to identify his revenge as their own. The feeling of perpetual grievance animates the captain's violent path through the world. "I'd strike the sun if it insulted me," he tells Starbuck, warning the first mate that power resides in collecting real and imagined wounds (164). His grief becomes a gift, a topmost quality that separates him from others and yet

---

The Prosthetic Arts of Moby-Dick. David Haven Blake, Oxford University Press. © Oxford University Press 2024.
DOI: 10.1093/oso/9780197780510.003.0001

binds them to his quest. The novel's planetary expanse conveys the magnitude of Ahab's control over other men. For all his suffering and all the potential for revolt, Ahab faces no significant threats from his international crew. Assembled from "all the ends of the earth," they join his effort "to lay the world's grievances before that bar from which not very many of them ever come back" (121). The only justice Ahab can conceive comes in the form of retribution, and the crew pledges to terrorize the globe to execute that judgment. His recklessness goes unchecked.[2]

For generations, Ahab's quest for vengeance has made *Moby-Dick* a thrilling, necessary work. I am particularly interested in Melville's decision to frame that vengeance with images of violence from Muslim-majority regions of the world. In a passage we will revisit later in this book, Ishmael compares the whale's tearing of Ahab's leg first to a mower cutting a blade of grass and then to the villainy of an expert assassin. "No turbaned Turk, no hired Venetian or Malay, could have smote him with more seeming malice" (184). The line reworks a story that Othello tells in his final soliloquy about his killing a "malignant Turk" for beating a Venetian in Aleppo.[3] Adapting Shakespeare's image, the line foregrounds the Turk as being Muslim, establishing at the beginning of Ahab's ordeal an oppressed Christian victim and a Muslim aggressor. Like a playhouse rifle, the image hangs over the pursuit until it is fired in the final act. At the novel's end, when the hunt results in Ahab's sudden death, Melville turns to the Turkish imagery again. He compares the captain's strangulation by the whale line attached to Moby Dick to the way "Turkish mutes" silently "bowstring their victim" (572). Ahab the disabled aggressor becomes Ahab the victim, this time, according to Ishmael's imagination, at the hands of two disabled Muslim assassins.

The Prosthetic Arts of Moby-Dick addresses the problems raised by this puzzling narrative frame and how it combines the seemingly disparate themes of wounding, limb loss, and the projection of American violence onto Muslim-majority societies. Even for a writer with Melville's inventiveness, the comparison demands attention, asking us to consider how the figure of stealthy Turkish assailants could possibly evoke a colossal white whale that dismembers a Nantucket sea captain and later capsizes his ship. Rooted in Orientalist fantasies of the Ottoman Empire, the imagery does more than simply exoticize Ahab's wounds and the battle he wages to avenge them.[4] Melville had a complex understanding of Islamic-based societies and would have rejected attempts to turn *Moby-Dick* into a religious allegory pitting Christians against Muslims. Indeed, he repeatedly uses similar Ottoman

INTRODUCTION: THE IVORY LEG   3

imagery to describe Ahab's command of his men, explaining, for example, how the "certain sultanism" of the captain's brain "became incarnate in an irresistible dictatorship" (147). Ahab and Moby Dick seem locked into a curiously Islamicized conflict in which each reflects a "certain sultanism" in the other. The imagery contributes to the novel's way of estranging the captain from the power it simultaneously incorporates in him. The sultanic American may have found "the world's grievances" in his own severed leg, but his loss seems more treacherous coming from Turks, Venetians, and Malays.[5]

Across novels, stories, and poems, Melville explored the ways that identity could be a form of possession in American democracy, something valuable, deceptive, and subject to volatile change. He knew that in a slave-holding nation in which the status of bodies determined legal and civic rights, a loss such as Ahab's could shake the foundations of individual sovereignty. Ahab rails against his injury as an affront to his being a free, masterless, and self-governing man. Ishmael describes the captain as "receiving all nature's sweet or savage impressions fresh from her own virgin, voluntary, and confiding breast," and like Jean-Jacques Rousseau's man of nature, he is used to being "whole and entire about himself," his fully incorporated body consonant with his assumed superiority (73). Dismemberment reminds Ahab how unstable embodied power can be. The ivory leg disrupts his perceived birthright as a white, American male. It challenges the expectation that, without rank or riches, the democrat can dominate whatever gets in his way. Explicating Rousseau, Bernard Stiegler has remarked, "The prosthesis is the origin of inequality," by which he means that tools such as axes, ladders, and slingshots exteriorize humans from themselves.[6] A central premise of this book is that Ahab perseverates over his ivory leg as if it indicated a fundamental deficit in himself, and yet that perceived deficit ultimately becomes the basis for his "irresistible dictatorship." As much as we might admire his intellect, sympathize with his loss, or respect the white whale's agency, the captain, I argue, is as dangerous a demagogue as critics described him in the aftermath of World War II.

Melville's perspective in *Moby-Dick* diverged from that of many of his contemporaries. In 1840, Alexis de Tocqueville argued that instability was the hallmark of democratic life, spanning everything from the organization of society to the formation of individual desire.[7] Treating dismemberment as a collective loss, numerous nineteenth-century writers turned the fragmented body into the symbol of a fractured, unsteady community. In Catharine Maria Sedgwick's historical novel *Hope Leslie* (1827), Magawisca's

4   THE PROSTHETIC ARTS OF *MOBY-DICK*

severed arm portends the oblivion her Pequod nation will face as white settlers come to dominate the continent. When Walt Whitman describes "a heap of amputated feet, legs, arms, hands" outside a Civil War hospital, he sees the breakdown of American polity.[8] *Moby-Dick* portrays dismemberment not as a volatile collapse in community but as a catalyst for its formation. As if countless afflictions had been ratified in the lost leg, Ahab's wounds become the source of personal power and communal aggrievement. "Is Ahab, Ahab?" the captain asks, highlighting the difficulty of perceiving where his identity begins and ends (545). Only days later, as the crew willingly sacrifice themselves to his revenge, he is metaphorically strangled by Ottoman assassins.

This book sees Ahab as an American dispossessed, not of power but of his sense of who he is. If Ahab's greatness lies in his grief, then his whalebone leg reminds him that his aggrievement has persisted long after his stump has healed. Throughout the novel, he struggles with the question of what his prosthesis means. Is it a stubbornly material object signifying the tragic attrition of self? A sperm whale trophy repurposed as an assistive device? A substitute limb he can regard as *almost* being his? Or almost being *him*? Crudely replicating a functioning leg, the prosthesis conveys the ways in which Ahab's sense of self is mapped alongside his body. He oscillates between cursing the "dead stump" and suggesting that the sound of his "ivory foot" confirms his existence, proving that he is "there" (163, 535). By Ahab's account, the prosthesis announces a relational experience of the world in that he no longer sees himself as the sole master of his body and will. After watching the making of a new whalebone leg, he curses his "mortal inter-indebtedness" to other men. And yet the feeling of "inter-indebtedness" pervades the crew as they continually prop their captain up, offering their bodies, identities, and lives as substitutes for his missing limb (471).

Ahab's prosthesis forms my study's central image (Figure 1), beginning with the material object, sawed from a sperm whale's jaw, and expanding upon the array of emotional, philosophic, aesthetic, and political meanings associated with it.[9] Creating function out of artifice, the whalebone device painfully extends the wounded body and yet never actually replaces the absent leg. The prosthesis becomes the place where trauma meets disability and where past and future coexist, the place where Ahab relives his agony while also plotting his revenge. Melville pays careful attention to how others respond to Ahab's injury: his characters gossip about the ivory leg, wonder what it reveals about his impairments, and fear it as an omen of future

INTRODUCTION: THE IVORY LEG   5

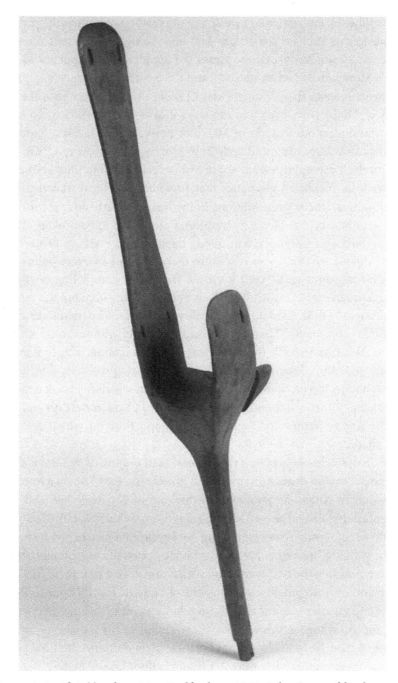

Figure 1 Artificial leg from New Bedford, ca. 1860. Ash, pine, and leather.
Image courtesy of the New Bedford Whaling Museum, Kendall Collection.

6   THE PROSTHETIC ARTS OF *MOBY-DICK*

catastrophe. In a narrative so invested in the reading of bodies, the prosthesis emerges as the site where physical and racial embodiment intersect, where the Nantucket captain assumes the identity of a humpbacked merman, a Mongol ruler, a Grand Turk, and a fire-worshiping Parsee.

When I refer to the prosthetic arts of *Moby-Dick*, I mean both the centrality of Ahab's ivory limb and the ways in which it provides a model for understanding other features of Melville's book. *Moby-Dick* is a "complex, heaving, disorderly, profound text," Toni Morrison has observed.[10] On multiple levels, it exemplifies what Tobin Siebers called a "disability aesthetics," by which he meant an aesthetics that provides "a critical framework for questioning aesthetic presumptions in the history of art" and, accordingly, "embraces beauty that seems by traditional standards to be broken."[11] With its destabilizing metaphors, truncated chapters, and mélange of narrative styles, *Moby-Dick* challenges readers to make sense of an overwhelming, at times incongruous text. "God keep me from ever completing anything," Ishmael proclaims. "This whole book is but a draught—nay, but the draught of a draught" (145). Explaining disability aesthetics, Siebers quotes Edgar Allan Poe's comment, "There is no exquisite beauty without some strangeness in the proportion."[12] In the context of its fascination with brokenness and incompletion, I focus on what I call the novel's prosthetic arts, a term that highlights the mechanisms and devices upon which the book depends. Melville's prosthetic arts encompass not just his characterization and plot, but the improvisatory style and strange proportions in which his story takes shape.[13]

My analysis develops across three parts, each organized around a different perspective on dismemberment and prostheses. Part I offers a historical discussion of Ahab's amputation, the making of his ivory leg, and how, influenced by Shakespeare, Melville envisioned his disability on ship. Following the path from wounding to aggrievement, the first chapter, "Ahab, Walking," recounts Melville's previous portraits of dismemberment before examining the frequency with which the captain dominates his crew, turning others into prosthetic extensions of himself. Titled "Bone to Bone," the second chapter extends this discussion by examining how Ahab's commitment to revenge appears in the construction of his prostheses and the persistent pain from his lost limb. Both chapters demonstrate how prevalent discourses of disability were in the antebellum United States.

Part II moves beyond the medical artifact to understand the prosthetic role that Islamicized powers play in Ahab's revenge. Titled "The Phantom

Fedallah," the third chapter uses the novel's abundant Islamic imagery to contextualize the Parsee's importance in piloting Ahab to his prey and considers whether his mystic powers absolve the captain's responsibility for his reckless quest. In the following chapter, "Ishmael, Salaaming," I explore the often-overlooked fact that Fedallah's death enables the narrator to survive the *Pequod*'s wreck—even as he projects the ship's violence onto Muslim-majority societies. The chapter traces much of the drive to Islamicize the story to Ishmael who, from the novel's iconic opening sentence, regularly uses Islamic culture to define American selves.

Part III extends these inquiries by exploring how disability and the politics of aggrievement apply to the book's critique of American capitalism and its faith in democratic progress. Drawing on work Melville completed after *Moby-Dick*, this section addresses how the themes of dismemberment, Islam, and democracy shaped the author's abiding interest in the American body politic. Chapter 5, "The Unnatural Stump," uses the *Pequod*'s hunt of an impaired whale to articulate the conflict between Ishmael's nationalism and his burgeoning environmental consciousness. The concluding chapter, "Eternal Hacking," turns to whether Melville saw dismemberment as the inevitable state of a body politic founded on racial dominance and othering. To what extent, I ask, did the author see nineteenth-century democracy as endlessly disrupting the body politic? To what extent did that democracy turn others into the prosthetic extensions of an Anglo-American crusade?

Anyone writing a book on Herman Melville has a vast range of sources and approaches from which to choose. Driving this analysis is a lifelong fascination with *Moby-Dick* and how its voluminous details can lead to questions that readers have rarely asked. My preference for a critical style that mixes narration with analysis comes from the conviction that thinking about *Moby-Dick* is more profound and pleasurable when Melville's language appears in the context of his tale. The novel's dramatic structure and Melville's investment in mise en scène have led me to organize my discussion loosely around specific chapters and episodes that showcase Ahab's dismemberment and impairment. This approach comes with the benefit of rooting my interdisciplinary inquiries in the details, conflicts, and verbal energy that these episodes raise in simultaneous relation to one another. Just as important, by emphasizing its social and dramatic context, this approach treats Ahab's disability—not as an isolated thought experiment nor a singularly abnormal condition—but as part of the ship's larger social fabric.

8 THE PROSTHETIC ARTS OF *MOBY-DICK*

In this introduction, I explain my critical orientation in the book's three parts to characterize the balance I hope to establish between focusing on Melville's works in their historical and cultural context and developing insights from multiple schools of thought. The rich critical tradition in Melville studies forces scholars to be selective, but with that comes the opportunity to be wide-ranging and eclectic. These core values shape my book's engagement with disability studies, its meditation on racial embodiment and prostheses, and its exploration of dismemberment as a reflection on the body politic.

Wounding, Disability, and the Use of Prostheses

Ahab has long held a foundational role in disability studies, and many of its leading figures have grappled with his brooding presence. In 1987, Leonard Kriegel critiqued him as an example of the "Demonic Cripple" who "burns with his need for vengeance" and "threatens to unleash a rage so powerful that it will bring everything down in its wake."[14] A decade later, Rosemarie Garland Thomson described Ahab as being "perhaps the quintessential disabled figure in American literature."[15] The following year, Lennard J. Davis noted that Melville "marked" his disabled captain in such negative terms that the novel had to punish him at the end to "consolidate a national norm."[16] In their groundbreaking 2000 analysis, David T. Mitchell and Sharon L. Snyder concluded that, along with Shakespeare's Richard III and Dickens's Tiny Tim, Ahab was among the three most commonly discussed representations of disability in literary criticism.[17] Melville, they explained, practiced a familiar "medicalized determinism" in making the captain's monomania a necessary consequence of losing his leg.[18]

But even as Ahab helps articulate a centuries-long pattern of negative imagery and stereotyping, there are limits to seeing him as being indicative of Melville's vision of disability. From *Typee* (1846) to "Bartleby the Scrivener" (1853) to *Billy Budd* (1924), Melville was preoccupied with what Samuel Otter has described as the stigmatization of "physical or psychic difference."[19] The writer had observed physical impairments while growing up. His sister Helen Maria, older than Herman by two years, was born with a hip dislocation and club foot, a condition that family members rarely mentioned but a surgeon tried to repair when she was in her late teens. Several years later, their brother Gansevoort suffered from such severe ankle pain (theorized by one physician to be reflex sympathetic dystrophy) that he was bedridden for over a year.[20] The impact of these incidents pervades the work. To enter the world of Herman Melville is to enter a place where Tahitian islanders contract degenerative diseases after European ships begin visiting their harbors; where an old blind man is led through the Liverpool streets singing in lamentation that he will never see the sun and moon again; where an impulsive young poet wonders whether he would treat his newly discovered sister differently if she had a hump on her back; where passengers on a riverboat jostle and mock a deaf man who holds a sign urging Christian charity; where, using sticks as crutches, injured soldiers limp from a battlefield to escape the pebble-like faces of the dead; and where, outside the Gates of Zion, an evangelist passes through an encampment of people with leprosy, reminding a shocked seminary student that the figure before him is not just a "trunk of woe" but his "fellow-man."[21]

Moby-Dick is Melville's most sustained and serious meditation on wounds, impairment, and disability. The prophet Elijah has a nonfunctioning arm, and smallpox scars run over his face like a dried-up riverbed. The Spouter Inn, the steward Dough Boy, and the universe itself all seem to be afflicted with palsy. An illustration in a popular natural history book makes the whale look like "an amputated sow," and the white whale reminds Ishmael of an albino who has no actual deformity but seems to the narrator freakishly appalling (262). Frostbite has claimed the blacksmith's toes and arthritis the cook's knees. In *Moby-Dick*, the narrator copes with depression, the weaver gods are deafened, Pip goes mad, and an old whale suffers from flatulence and a damaged fin. A London beggar displays a drawing that accurately depicts a whale crunching his leg, and Ahab meets a British captain who has lost his arm to the white whale. Melville populates *Moby-Dick* with "meanest mariners, and renegades and castaways," many of whom bear physical and psychological differences (117). Even the ebony idol, Yojo, has a humpback, a feature that persists even though Queequeg's penknife could swiftly shave it away.

Like a king with a dreadful scepter, Ahab and his ivory leg preside over these differences and afflictions. Recognizing the broader context of Melville's work helps us see the captain not as Melville's representative of disability but as a character who responds to a disabling injury in a singularly philosophic and incendiary way. While this book has benefited from

10 THE PROSTHETIC ARTS OF *MOBY-DICK*

numerous scholars working in the field of critical disability studies, it neither claims nor critiques Ahab on behalf of that community. Melville regularly gives Ahab's relationship to his body a sense of loss that people with
congenital differences may not experience, and his aggrievement over that
loss almost always reinforces an ableist point of view. When we put Ahab
alongside Samoa from *Mardi* (1849), who is missing an arm, or Don
Hannibal from *Clarel* (1876), who is missing an arm and a leg, he seems
less remarkable for his limb loss than for his reaction to it. The shift in perspective aligns with Melville's allusions to the character's history. The Ahab
who reportedly killed a Spaniard in a Peruvian church before dueling the
white whale seems consistent with the Ahab who insists on "audacious,
immitigable, and supernatural revenge" after their disastrous meeting (92,
186). When it comes to his wounds, Ahab rarely diverges from his "heart-
stricken" rage, but the broader narrative has a different trajectory: from
whales to harpooners, it seems to universalize affliction, showing that being
able-bodied is only a temporary condition (163).[22] Across nationalities,
races, and species, the novel encompasses a rich diversity of somatic experience. Like the scholars who preceded her, Sari Altschuler may treat the
novel as "an urtext of American disability scholarship," but her analysis
showcases what we might regard as the headnote for a new generation of
criticism: "The body speaks not a single word in *Moby-Dick*, but volumes."[23]

I argue that, rather than attempting to punish Ahab for an allegedly rep-
rehensible disability, the novel addresses the establishment of a different
cultural norm: namely, the role that aggrievement plays in sanctioning his
violent will. Kriegel objected to the way Ahab's injury "becomes his selfhood"
and how, in conflict with God and nature, he tries to "bend the world's will
to his own."[24] The condition of limb loss does not animate his defiance,
however, as much as the fierce vindictiveness he exercises in its name.
Injury becomes his selfhood in the way that it does for anyone engrossed in
aggrievement. Perceiving in his lost limb the universe's humiliating scorn,
Ahab swears he will exact revenge on Moby Dick as if the whale had created original sin. The vengeance transforms his wound into narrative, placing it at the beginning of a metaphysical drama that has an uncertain
outcome but a definite end.[25] Once the *Pequod* sails toward Moby Dick,
Ahab's choice gives way to necessity, and the burden of his injury becomes
the burden of his revenge. In the way that a train has no purpose outside
the tracks, the captain requires Moby Dick to comprehend his own lost
limb. As he acknowledges in Chapter 37, "Sunset," "The path to my fixed

purpose is laid with iron rails, whereon my soul is grooved to run" (168). The fixed purpose limits his motion more than the injury that preceded it.[26]

As we will see, the novel keenly envisions Ahab's life on ship, attending to the details of what it would take for him to walk, hunt, and lead a crew at sea. With remarkable perception, Melville contemplates the kinds of assistive devices that would help the captain ascend the masthead or stand in a churning boat—and how the absence of such devices would frustrate and functionally disable him. Ishmael may shrink from Ahab's wounds, but Melville invests considerable energy into imagining how the captain and his crew adapt to the conditions of their work. This attention to detail appears most significantly in Ahab's ivory leg, which, for all its psychological symbolism, is also a material object intimately connected to the captain's daily life. While readers may associate the prosthesis with loss, pain, and grievance, Melville also presents it as a site of medical intervention, functional design, and even the allure of fashion. A study of Ahab's prosthesis requires us to consider both the tangible and the intangible qualities that the author gives the device. As recent work demonstrates, numerous archival materials are available to readers interested not simply in ideas about prostheses but in prostheses themselves.[27]

Knowing the historical context of Ahab's ivory leg can shape the way we think about the extensive scholarship theorizing the nature of prostheses. Sarah Jain has commented that "prostheses are discursive frameworks, as well as material artifacts," and many thinkers have used them to explain technology's role in extending human capabilities.[28] Sigmund Freud saw prostheses in the gramophone, Marshall McLuhan in broadcast media, and Donna Haraway in the camera lens.[29] Some have concluded that these forces diminish, if not destroy, the bodies they seem to augment. "The typewriter tears writing from the essential realm of the hand," Martin Heidegger wrote in lamenting the way that the machine withdraws "writing from the origin of its essence."[30] Regardless of its function, David Wills argues, a prosthesis inevitably implies "the idea of the amputation—or of a lack or deficiency—that would have preceded it."[31] This notion of deficiency has been useful to scholars interested in writing as a form of prosthetic technology. According to the *Oxford English Dictionary*, the word "prosthesis" entered the English language in the 1550s to denote the syllable added to the beginning of words such as *bemoan* and *afar* that do not change their meaning. Eighteenth-century surgeons adapted the term when they began to publish scientific studies of artificial limbs. The link between language

12 THE PROSTHETIC ARTS OF *MOBY-DICK*

and medicine, what Wills calls "philology and orthopedics," found an receptive audience among deconstructionists.[32] The double logic of the prosthesis, the way it amputates and appends, collapses the distinctions between the real and synthetic, the animate and inanimate, the human and nonhuman, and the body and machine. Stiegler has theorized that whether conceived as writing or a mechanized limb, the prosthesis is the supplement that artificially constitutes the human as "human."[33]

The versatility of the metaphor helps explain its appeal, but at the same time, the ever-expanding conceptualization of prostheses can obscure the objects upon which these concepts are built. If one sees prostheses in such diverse items as speech, microscopes, memory, university architecture, and the supervision of factory workers, what becomes of the medical apparatus itself?[34] As Steven L. Kurzman has argued, "the metaphor becomes unsituated" to the extent that the theoretical models are retroactively defined in terms of the physical condition.[35] Theorists might proclaim that prostheses compromise subjectivity or erode the boundaries between humans and technology, but individuals who use such devices understandably reject the idea that they have become less or post-human. To synthesize two of Vivian Sobchack's most powerful points, "the scandal of the metaphor" is that it conceals the reality that people incorporate prostheses into themselves, not the other way around.[36] Neither Kurzman nor Sobchack rejects the conceptualization of artificial limbs, but they dispute the assumption that using them denaturalizes or disrupts the unified body.[37] In a much-cited statement, Stiegler has wittily described the prosthesis as "the end of the human."[38] His reflections display no interest, though, in what it takes to descend stairs with a titanium leg or change a diaper with a silicone hand.

These debates, some of which are decades old, remain relevant to what we value in analyzing characters such as Ahab. My intention is to resituate the discussion around the material experience of prostheses as a meaningful check against what sometimes drifts into an academic obscuring of disability. Wills explicitly turns from a "thematics of the prosthetic in literature" in pursuing his deconstructive analysis in *Prosthesis* (1995).[39] Embracing those themes, however, seems imperative in a study of Herman Melville who brilliantly underscored the ways in which artificial limbs become endowed with material, emotional, cultural, philosophic, and narrative import. Aiming to restore a sense of critical perspective, this book focuses on the historical discourse surrounding Ahab's dismemberment, his organic and artificial legs, and the "oaths of violence and revenge" he and his crew make in their name (179). In Ahab's prostheses, we find pain, loss, and dispossession, but also the potential for embodiment, empowerment, and charismatic leadership. Grounding my analysis in Ahab's wounded, prostheticized body, I explore how, in this novel of topmost grief and greatness, Melville dramatizes the power derived from collecting wounds and plotting vengeance.

Islam as Prosthesis

Among the themes Melville associates with Ahab's quest is that Orientalized violence is both the cause and the cure of his aggrievement. The Ottoman Moby Dick and the sultanic captain feature prominently in this theme, with Ishmael alluding to Islamic powers to characterize an array of human and nonhuman threats. These allusions reinforce the novel's dependence on Fedallah to bring the confrontation to its head. Although considered by many a minor or even forgettable character, Fedallah extends the novel's narrative into a metaphysical realm. His spiritual connection to the white whale and cryptic prophecies give him an important role in Ahab's retribution. Ishmael recoils from Fedallah and joins the crew in speculating about his shadowy presence on ship. But while the ivory leg recalls the continued presence of trauma and aggrievement, Fedallah signals the augmented capacity for revenge. Like the prostheses Heidegger and Wills describe, he encompasses both the amputation that preceded the *Pequod*'s voyage and the extension of that voyage into a supernatural domain. A combination of nineteenth-century gothicism and racial stereotypes, Fedallah possesses the sinister power that Ahab embodies in trying to complete his quest.

My use of prostheses to describe Fedallah's function in *Moby-Dick* builds off several scholars who have applied the concept to understanding narrative content and form.[40] Mitchell and Snyder developed the term "narrative prosthesis" to describe the way that from *Oedipus* to *One Flew over the Cuckoo's Nest* (1962), disability functions in literature "first, as a stock feature of characterization and, second, as an opportunistic metaphorical device." Ahab, in their interpretation, exemplifies the way that "disability lends a distinctive idiosyncrasy to any character that differentiates the character from the anonymous background of the 'norm.'"[41] As the term "narrative prosthesis" would indicate, Mitchell and Snyder see the use of disability as a "crutch upon which literary narratives lean for their representational power,

14   THE PROSTHETIC ARTS OF *MOBY-DICK*

disruptive potentiality, and analytical insight."[42] Whatever deficiency the term implies resides in the lack of imagination that authors bring to characters with impairments.

Displaying only sporadic interest in disability, Peter Boxall's investigation of the "prosthetic imagination" focuses on the history of the novel as a genre. Boxall differentiates the prosthetic from the mimetic in contending that "the history of the novel is also a history of artificial life." The novel, he claims, "is involved in a long struggle to clear a space between consciousness and its material extensions."[43] While Mitchell and Snyder emphasize character and representation, Boxall links the genre's "particular and perhaps strange affinity with the prosthetic" to the idea that narrative "does not refer to the world but produces it, gives rise to it in the form of a prosthetic trace."[44] His association of prosthesis with artifice leads him to celebrate the novel for being "the art form that has achieved the greatest proximity to the difficult junction between mind and material."[45] The novel's development parallels what Boxall sees as an increasingly "prosthetic age."[46]

There are, of course, many ways to conceptualize Melville's interest in Islam. Dorothy Metlitsky Finkelstein's indispensable study, *Melville's Orienda* (1961), focuses on the influence of Islamic books and scripture on the writer. Along with numerous articles, Timothy Marr's *The Cultural Roots of American Islamicism* (2006) presents Melville within the context of nineteenth-century American interest in Muslim societies. The impact of these and other scholars appears throughout my efforts to adapt prosthesis to thinking about Islam's role in *Moby-Dick*. I have manifold reasons for using the term beyond the obvious one that it highlights the centrality of Ahab's dismemberment to his Islamicized battles and tyrannical rule. Mitchell and Snyder understand Ahab's disability to be the prosthetic determinant for his obsession with Moby Dick. But the term does an especially good job recognizing the function of Fedallah and the "five dusky phantoms" the captain enlists as his crew. Acting in synchrony with the wounded body, Fedallah redresses the limits of Ahab's humanity, supernaturally enhancing his knowledge, vision, and power. Called upon to assist avenging the lost limb, he serves the captain as a psychological support, an enigmatic soothsayer, and a metaphysical sonar machine. The shadowy harpooner combines the prosthetic and the prophetic: he notably disappears on the same day that Moby Dick claims the last of Ahab's ivory legs.[47]

The term "prosthetic" brings the additional advantage of articulating Ahab's corporeal relation to the Parsee. Ishmael posits that Fedallah has a mysterious "unaccountable tie" to Ahab's fortunes and wonders about his influence on the *Pequod*'s path (231). A spectral presence upon whom the captain depends, he inhabits the strange supplementary space between being the shadow to Ahab's body and the material substance of his monomaniacal will. Prostheses can be a clarifying concept in explaining the ways that Fedallah is both self and other in Ahab's world, his difference defining how alien the captain has become to himself. Ishmael presents the turban-wearing Parsee as an impenetrable Orientalized mystery; another way to think of him is that he is the racial embodiment of Ahab's quest, the outsider who reveals something definitive about the man who secretly harbors him on ship.

Finally, prosthesis offers an especially revealing way to think about Fedallah's importance in the plot and narration, as Melville relies on the character both to pilot the captain to the whale and to ensure Ishmael's survival after he destroys the ship. Boxall sees the "prosthetic imagination" displayed in the nineteenth-century novel as recognizing that both life and art are artificially composed.[48] My concerns are more focused on Fedallah's artificial presence in the text. Many readers view the character as an unnecessary addition to *Moby-Dick*, a character who never assimilates into the crew and is never realized in the book. The romantic supernaturalism surrounding Fedallah can seem at odds with a novel that finds so much transcendence in the corporeal form. And yet Fedallah produces the result the novel demands, protecting its narrator and ensuring its cosmic conflict. Others might describe the Parsee as Melville's deus ex machina (or *diaboli*, as the case may be), but that minimizes the circumstances upon which Ahab summons him. In a novel about dismemberment, I see him providing a crutch to Melville's storytelling.

The haziness surrounding Fedallah's religion makes his functionality surprisingly clear. Ishmael describes him as a Zoroastrian fire-worshiper and a descendant of the Parsee who fled Iran in the eleventh century. But Fedallah's made-up Muslim name (*Fed-Allah*) contradicts this designation, imparting an Islamicized sense of menace that seems more a conglomeration of fears and stereotypes than a coherent statement about belief. As is the case with Ahab's amputation and disability, having a sense of history will help contextualize the way in which Ishmael confidently joins the pagan Queequeg in his Ramadan observance and yet continually fears the hair-turbaned Fedallah. These conflicting responses reveal a wider divide in the nineteenth-century United States between a fascination with Islamic

16 THE PROSTHETIC ARTS OF *MOBY-DICK*

faith practices and a disdain for Islamic powers that resist Western conquests. Fedallah has a political and aesthetic purpose in *Moby-Dick*, not a theological one.

Melville had an abiding interest in Islamic cultures, and many of his works combine that interest with the experience of disability. His first published work, an 1839 short story titled "Fragments from a Writing Desk," concerns a beautiful deaf woman living in an Ottoman-like harem.[49] The harem setting would intrigue Melville over the decades, as would the wearing of turbans, the history of Islamic leaders, and the appeal of Islam as an alternative to Christianity. Beyond *Moby-Dick*, his novels and stories reflect on the Kabbah stone, recreate a naval battle against the Turks, and describe an ecstatic masthead reverie about Moorish Spain.[50] After his 1856–57 trip to Turkey, Greece, and Palestine, he would write about blind muezzins, looting Crusaders, shepherds bowing toward Mecca, and the attar of the Persian rose. He returned from that trip with a ceramic tile that had fallen from the Hagia Sophia and that a priest had sold him for fifty cents.[51] Meant to commemorate Islam's victory in Constantinople, the tile features a sultan or prince riding a white Arabian horse; above him flies the mythical Huma bird, signifying Paradise (Figure 2).[52]

These works help situate my discussion of *Moby-Dick* and its engagement with Islam as a prosthetic to Ahab's limb loss and the grief that leads to avenging it. Amid the foreboding created by Muslim phantoms, assassins, and despots, Ishmael's fears reveal something far more disturbing about the power of grievance in American society: the greatest threat from Islamic cultures are the terrors they revealed in the nation's psyche. Nine years after *Moby-Dick*, Melville would analyze the vortex of hatred that occupied frontier life, devoting three chapters in *The Confidence-Man* (1857) to what he called "The Metaphysics of Indian Hating." *Moby-Dick* treats the fear of Islam in fragments, offering only brief glimpses into the malice and malady that Islam exposed in the American imagination. Fedallah's fundamental indecipherability attests to the many incongruities the novel makes him signify. The prostheticization of Muslim societies in narratives of American identity forms a fundamental part of US history from the eighteenth through the twenty-first centuries. To ignore the importance of this practice in the iconic *Moby-Dick*, to isolate its Muslim pirates, phantoms, and assassins from its dramatization of dismemberment and grievance, is to perpetuate the belief that Islam cannot be (and has never been) incorporated into the American experience.

Figure 2 Ceramic tile from the Hagia Sophia that Melville purchased in 1856. Featuring the mythical bird Huma, the tile commemorates Islam's victory in Constantinople (Istanbul).
Image courtesy of the Berkshire County Historical Society, Pittsfield, MA.

Dismemberment and Political Bodies

The persistence of trauma can lead us to see prostheses predominantly in relation to the past, to the accidents and treatments before limbs were severed and devices took their place. "Pros-thesis means 'placed-there-in-front,'" Stiegler explains, tying the word's etymology to the idea that "Pros-theticity" indicates "the being-already-there of the world, and also, consequently, the being-already-there of the past."[53] Not only does Ahab perseverate over his accident, but he complains about the haunting pain of his lost flesh. In their very functionality, however, prostheses look forward to a time when the ensemble of organic and inorganic materials allows wearers to grasp, stand, walk, and, in Ahab's case, threaten, lead, and fight. Although conceived in memory and theory, the artificial device ultimately returns its wearer to the body and its anticipated movements through space and time. Prostheses bridge the burden of disaster with the burden of possibility. It is here where their meaning becomes most political, shifting in emphasis from ideas about bodies to the diverse experience of bodies in the world.

The third part of this book looks at the prosthesis in relation to bodies politic, exploring how the intersection of aggrievement, disability, and Islam surfaces in Melville's critique of democratic capitalism. The chapters provide a broader perspective on Ahab's wound, as I turn to the way impairment radiates through Melville's career, touching upon humans and nonhumans alike. The captain responds to his dismemberment as an infringement upon his existential sovereignty, but Melville significantly contextualizes Ahab's individualism in the whaling industry and its role in the antebellum economy. The *Pequod's* violence and its captain's manipulation of other men suggest a more expansive fervor for plundering the environment for economic gain. Ahab's injury may make him willfully "fixed and fearless," but the novel demonstrates that impairment can make others susceptible to exploitation and cruelty (124). Ahab hunts the white whale as fiercely as his countrymen extract resources from the western plains and the South Seas. As Ronald Takaki observed in *Iron Cages: Race and Culture in 19th-Century America* (1990), "Melville perceived death and destruction" in the United States' expansion into the Pacific. "Nearly a half century before the Spanish-American War, he could discern America's dark future in Asia."[54]

Thomas Bender has described Ahab as an "exemplar of the way Americans lived empire."[55] In my analysis, Ishmael also drives this theme. As both a narrator and a guide, he alerts readers to the terror of the whaling industry and its ties to bourgeois society. He sympathetically depicts an old whale whose afflictions and maladies make him vulnerable to being killed. And yet Ishmael repeatedly advances the industry as an imperial enterprise, seeing in its workers not just remarkable courage and skill but an ability to dominate global resources in the name of US democracy. Dennis Berthold has explained that democracy had multiple meanings in the mid-nineteenth century.[56] The term encompassed an egalitarian respect for others; an enthusiasm for opening the franchise to white, working-class men; a rejection of elite institutions and aristocratic rule; a preference for the party of Andrew Jackson; and the conviction that value came not from birth but individual achievement. As he worked to finish *Moby-Dick*, Melville professed to a more organic sense of the term as well, a "ruthless democracy" that, in the words of Jennifer Greiman, included not only "a principle of absolute equality" but also "a process of endless transformation." At once circular, destabilizing, and vertiginous, democracy grew uncontrollably, turbulently pulling at rank and tradition, always seeking new structures to "pluralize, expand, and transform."[57]

Amid these varied meanings, however, Americans such as Ishmael also invoked democracy when they wanted to spread their values and institutions to other parts of the world. The term served as shorthand for the burgeoning nation-state that saw as its mission the expansion of democratic capitalism as a political and economic force.[58] While the transformative spirit of New World democracy could lead to Ishmaelean moments of the sublime, it also resulted in the transformation of different peoples and economies into reflections of an American will. This final section clarifies an obvious but worthwhile point: that Ishmael represents a political and historical type. He should not be considered a stand-in for Herman Melville, and his attitudes about slavery, imperialism, and Muslim-majority societies often conflict with those of other characters in Melville's work. Ishmael's advocacy for the power of New England's whaling fleet intersects with his tendency to treat the sultanic Ahab, the turbaned Fedallah, and the Turkish-rugged sea as threats to American well-being. The narrator may broadly accept other people's customs and faiths, but he repeatedly distrusts the largely Muslim populations who resist the presence of Western imperialists.

The perspective here differs from that of the many readers who praise Ishmael as a champion of democracy while paying little attention to his scattered comments about Turks, Filipinos, and Malays. My entry into

20 THE PROSTHETIC ARTS OF *MOBY-DICK*

these inquiries comes from *Clarel*, the 1876 book-length poem that Melville wrote about a group of Western pilgrims traveling in Palestine. With its portrait of a monomaniacal reformer and identification of the minaret as a "marble mast-head," *Clarel* extends some of *Moby-Dick*'s key themes into a desert landscape. The poem introduces another "wandering Ishmael" (the phrase is Melville's) who levels a devastating critique of how Anglo-American racism conceals its rampant commercialization of "nature's sylvan glade."[59] *Clarel* voices the critique of Anglo-American progressivism that these final chapters entertain: that Western democracies dismember the body politic, that they sever individuals from each other and societies from their history. The section grapples with the opinion that republican embodiment falls prey to the combined forces of democratic capitalism and Anglo-Saxon Christianity. Picking up a theme established in *Moby-Dick*, *Clarel* traces the origins of this belief to the Islamophobia of the Crusades. Bent on violent retribution, the body politic tries to summon power out of its afflictions.

To Dismember the Dismemberer

In Melville's mystical novel *Mardi* (1849), a group of travelers visits a series of allegorical lands looking for an angelic woman named Yillah. (Commentators hear in this name an allusion to Allah and the prayer "La ilaha illa-llah," meaning "There is no God but God.")[60] The travelers come upon what is known as the Isle of Cripples in which the disabled have developed their own system of government and live as "a distinct class of beings by themselves." The visitors are initially shocked by what they see—a person without legs, a man with seal-like flippers, a royal guard with three arms, scores of stammerers—but over time, they begin to recognize that the government works competently, and their legless, deaf leader can communicate with his fingers. The visitors realize that they themselves seem grotesque to the island's inhabitants, that they themselves seem like "monsters." "There is no supreme standard yet revealed, whereby to judge ourselves," the philosopher Babbalanja concludes: "Our very instincts are prejudices." As his biases fall away, the expedition's leader, King Media, grows impatient with the ensuing debate and its reliance on scholarly sources. "Never mind your old authors," he interrupts the philosopher. "Stick to the cripples; enlarge upon them."[61]

We do not know whether that command occurred to Melville as he began to think about *Moby-Dick*. We do know that he would devote considerable portions of the novel to enlarging upon the difficulties a peg-legged sea captain would face in leading his crew against the creature that wounded him. Among those difficulties was a sense of aggrievement that the citizens of the Isle of Cripples do not display. Babbalanja challenges his fellow travelers to contend with their prejudice, to struggle with the fact that no supreme standard can help them judge others or themselves. To Ahab, the only standard is that he has been wronged and that a hostile universe is prejudiced against his claims to himself. When he cries to the heavens that "a personality stands here," when he disputes with the last gasp of his earthquake life anything that assumes mastery over him, he seems dangerous, reckless, and, in many ways, heroic (507). His topmost aggrievement becomes his topmost gift. He is the prosthesis trying to avenge our wounds through his.

One of the epigraphs to this study comes from the book of Ezekiel, in which the prophet describes the resurrection of Israel into an army of rejuvenated men. "So I prophesied as I was commanded: and as I prophesied, there was a noise, and behold a shaking, and the bones came together, bone to his bone."[62] When John Winthrop reflected on this verse in "A Model of Christian Charity," he suggested that Christ's love would knit together the "scattered bones, or perfect old man Adam" in the community he envisioned on the shores of Massachusetts Bay. Ahab rejects the body of Christ for a body of prostheses.[63] When he pledges to "dismember my dismemberer," he envisions a ship ironically brought together around the rendering of bodies under his command (168). Retribution becomes a communal enterprise abetted by one man's ability to dominate. Embedded in Ahab's ivory leg are wounds and healing, destruction and capability, isolation and community. But as the whale and the human bones come together, one crafted to support the other's balance, movement, and weight, we find fellowship built not on love but on a sense of injury.

PART I

STAGING DISABILITY

1

Ahab, Walking

Coffin-Taps

Ahab's shipmates know their captain best by the sound of his walk. Gathered below deck where they work, smoke, and sleep, they hear his "steady, ivory stride" knocking over their heads.[1] The steadiness becomes a source of anxiety and dread. Ships like the *Pequod* typically extended about 106 feet, leaving little room for a sailor to pace.[2] But throughout the novel, Ahab walks, the sound ominously echoing from the forecastle to the mizzenmast. "Hist! above there, I hear ivory," the Black shipkeeper Pip exclaims after Ahab leaves his cabin and resumes his watch on deck (535). Mad, despondent, and afraid, Pip conveys the oppressive gloom that accompanies the captain's movement: "Oh, master! master! I am indeed downhearted when you walk over me" (535).

As a storyteller, Melville is more interested in the sounds of Ahab walking than in his mechanics. That is, while the novel describes Ahab's "quick, side-lunging strides," it pays little attention to the way he must round his leg outwards to plant his prosthesis on the planks or the way his frame must consistently adjust to his hobbling hips (233). Where other novelists might depend on the verb "to limp," Melville never uses the word with Ahab, reserving it for the athletic harpooner Queequeg and the old cook Fleece. What matters to Melville is the dissonance between Ahab's natural and artificial legs and the alternating pattern of living and dead steps. In "The Spirit Spout," Ishmael recounts Ahab's eager pacing when "the silvery jet" of a whale is spotted in the middle of a moonlit night. "While his one live leg made lively echoes along the deck, every stroke of his dead limb sounded like a coffin-tap. On life and death this old man walked" (233). The heavy, reciprocal stride resounds over the course of the book, the crack of the whalebone leg reminding the crew of the wound that Ahab suffered and the original limb that he lost. As the journey goes on, those coffin-taps, heard from below and on deck, come to signify the captain's painful dismembering and relentless pursuit of revenge.

The Prosthetic Arts of Moby-Dick. David Haven Blake, Oxford University Press. © Oxford University Press 2024.
DOI: 10.1093/oso/9780197780510.003.0002

26   THE PROSTHETIC ARTS OF *MOBY-DICK*

As the chapters in Part I demonstrate, Melville repeatedly turned to Shakespeare in depicting Ahab's disability within a broader social context. In transforming the *Pequod* into a stage, he showcased not only the "bold and nervous lofty language" of the captain's soliloquies, but also the dramatic response of others to his ivory leg (73). Even before he mentions Moby Dick, the prosthesis creates tension among the crew as a reminder of their leader's wound and a warning of their own vulnerabilities. Ishmael regularly describes Ahab's physical condition and speculates about his mental state, but spanning the comic and tragic modes, the dramatic structure gives Melville an opportunity to explore the crew's response to the prosthesis.

Melville had come to Shakespeare relatively late in his career. After years of looking into a sun-drenched sea, he regularly complained about the strain that writing and reading put on his vision. On 24 February 1849, he wrote his friend and eventual editor Evert Duyckinck about finding an edition of Shakespeare that was printed in "glorious, great type." "Dolt & ass that I am," he confessed, "I have lived more than 29 years, & until a few days ago, never made close acquaintance with the divine William. Ah, he's full of sermons-on-the-mount, and gentle, aye, almost as Jesus." For the author of two published novels and a third in press, this late encounter with the plays was a bittersweet revelation: "I am mad to think how minute a cause has prevented me hitherto from reading Shakespeare. But until now, every copy that was come-atable to me, happened to be in a vile small print unendurable to my eyes which are tender as young sparrows."[3] The large print edition of Shakespeare's plays would shape Melville's writing of *Moby-Dick*, giving him new ideas about language, style, character, and how he could stretch the novel as a literary form. F. O. Matthiessen wrote that *Moby-Dick* shows "how Melville's sense of life had been so profoundly stirred by Shakespeare's that he was impelled to emulation." With Shakespeare, he continued, "Melville entered into another realm, of different properties and proportions."[4] Melville blamed his late entrance into that realm on his damaged eyes, declaring that "if another Messiah comes twill be in Shakespeare's person."[5] The delay seemed perfectly timed for a narrative about a tragic hero struggling with dismemberment.

In staging Ahab's disability, Melville often emphasized its sound. The crack of Ahab walking pervades the ship, endowing him with such presence that crewmembers have no refuge from his aggrievement. Since the 1970s, activists have commonly differentiated the *impairment* of a medical condition from a *disability*, by which they mean the normative social processes and prejudices that turn those impairments into hindrances.[6] The social model of disability, Matthew Cella explains, "moves the focus away from viewing the impaired mind-body as an isolated phenomenon and instead highlights the mind-body's relationship to the places it occupies."[7] Melville's theatrical use of sound helps construct the captain's disability, for as he walks, his impairment becomes a social condition causing fear, anxiety, puzzlement, and devotion in the people who hear him. Like Macduff and Lennox knocking on the gate in *Macbeth*, Ahab's coffin-tap is a theatrical device that creates tension, foreboding, and what Thomas DeQuincy called a "depth of solemnity."[8] Although it encompasses his accident, surgery, recovery, and revenge, the sound of Ahab walking reminds us that, first and foremost, his prosthesis is a material object: whatever feelings it provokes, its atmospheric effects come from the polished bone of a sperm whale's jaw, attached with leather straps to a severed leg, striking a wooden deck. The constant pacing leaves dents in the deck that look like "geological stones" (160).

By way of introduction, consider how Melville brings these themes together in Chapter 29, "Enter Ahab; to Him, Stubb," the first in a series of Shakespearean scenes that introduce Ahab's command through his walk. Mixing narration with drama, Ishmael tells us that the captain recognizes the effect that his "bony step" has on his shipmates, and at times he exhibits a "considerating touch of humanity" to them (127). "Griping at the iron banister, to help his crippled way," Ahab "usually abstained from patrolling the quarter-deck" so that "the reverberating crack and din" would not disturb his sleeping officers and set them to dreaming about "the crunching teeth of sharks" (127). Such considerations have their limit, however, and one night the second mate, Stubb, hears Ahab lumbering directly overhead. He hesitantly suggests that if the captain wishes to walk, perhaps he could muffle his steps by inserting a ball of yarn into his "ivory heel" (127). The suggestion earns the bleary-eyed mate a heap of abuse. "Down, dog, and kennel," the captain commands, subordinating his officer to the rank of a wayward hound. When Stubb protests, the curses comically escalate: he is a dog, a donkey, and a jackass (127).

The comedy of the Stubb scenes sets a tone different from the "overbearing grimness" Ishmael feels when he first notices the captain's "barbaric white leg" (124). In the cast of *Moby-Dick*, Stubb plays a clown, and his efforts to comprehend Ahab always fall short. And yet the mate's reaction

28   THE PROSTHETIC ARTS OF *MOBY-DICK*

provides insight into the socialization of dismemberment. Citing Erving Goffman, Arthur Frank has written that stigma "is embarrassing, not just for the stigmatized person but for those who are confronted with the stigma and have to react to it." Stigma produces a social contract in which each party is exceptionally aware of the other.[9] That awareness appears in Stubb's response. Stunned by the verbal abuse, he feels physically assaulted: "He might as well have kicked me, and done with it," Stubb says to himself (128). "Maybe he *did* kick me, and I didn't observe it" (128). Contemplating the exchange, Stubb can't get beyond the physicality of Ahab's false leg. The prosthesis takes over the captain's face, his angry brow flashing "like a bleached bone" (128). The encounter seems to have drawn the mate into Ahab's impairment. "I don't stand right on my legs," he admits. "Coming afoul of that old man has a sort of turned me wrong side out" (128).[10]

Stubb struggles to separate Ahab's anger from his whalebone leg, the two creating an insistently physical presence that is expressed in verbal rancor and felt as physical abuse. Of the many impaired men and women who appear in Melville's writings, Ahab most broods upon his condition and gives it a definitive role in his personality. The Black cook, Fleece, feels pain in his knees as he limps around the galley. At one point he even uses his kitchen tongs like a cane, balancing his step as he walks beside the bulwark (294). But when Ishmael marks Fleece as different, he more often alludes to his race than his arthritic legs. The whalebone device sets Ahab apart from his shipmates, but it also prompts him to see himself differently. Both men suffer from impairments that alter their physical activity, but only the white captain sees this as a source of aggrievement. Only he sees it as a violation of his sovereignty. "Ahab is not a self-made man," Rosemarie Garland Thomson has commented; he is "a whale-made man."[11] The image of the bleached bone overtaking Ahab's forehead suggests that Stubb would agree, though by virtue of the power they cede to him, Ahab will claim Stubb and his shipmates as prosthetic extensions as well. As Michael Jonik has written, an "almost universal prosthecity" surrounds the captain's relations with others.[12]

In the sound of walking, Melville balances the metaphorical and physical aspects of Ahab's experience. Stubb insists that "there's a mighty difference between a living thump and a dead thump," but when Ahab walks, the living and dead legs work together in an ensemble of mutual dependence (131). The prosthesis may be a psychological burden, but to borrow from Vivian Sobchack, the crew experience it as "a material but also phenomenologically lived artifact."[13] Stubb wants to dampen the whale-bone's noise, to obscure it to the point that he can regard it as something else, but instead of following his suggestion, the captain transforms it into the more threatening image of a cannon ball (127). The crew can't escape the whalebone leg, just as they won't escape the realization that Ahab, like a mortar, has "burst his hot heart's shell" on the white whale (184). Whether above or below deck, whether seen, heard, or dreamed, the competing experiences of Ahab's prostheses are so burdensome to the crew that they ultimately become whale-made men themselves.

To understand Ahab's prostheticization of others, we need to reflect more carefully on his accident, his wound, his surgical repair, and how he adapts to life on the *Pequod*. Melville contextualizes Ahab's disability with an array of assistive devices, self-conscious social interactions, surgical breakdowns, and bouts with pain. The discussion that follows explains how the ivory leg exists within a system of disabilities and accommodations that Melville creates not just on the *Pequod* but across multiple ships, settings, and books. As central as it is to *Moby-Dick*, Ahab's limb reverberates with history, both the literary example of writers such as Shakespeare and the many voices of Melville's era that addressed amputation and prostheses. Behind the coffin-taps of Ahab's ivory stride lies the prevalence of artificial limbs in nineteenth-century American society.

Amputation Nation

Amputation was embedded in the Anglo-American imagination when Melville was a boy. He grew up at a time when amputees from the American Revolution were widely visible in society, and as that generation passed away, they were replaced not only by veterans of the settler wars, but also by men and women who lost their limbs in agricultural, industrial, and transportation accidents. The stories that received the most attention often raised questions of morality and national identity so that the trauma of limb loss reflected a communal ideology. Ahab had numerous predecessors whose lost limbs were reconciled into cultural narratives about sacrifice, sentiment, and masculinity. Placing his story outside these ideological frames, Melville amplified the captain's personal outrage at his injury.

As a native New Yorker, Melville would have been familiar with Peter Stuyvesant, the Dutch founder of New Amsterdam in 1647. Stuyvesant had

30 THE PROSTHETIC ARTS OF *MOBY-DICK*

lost his right leg during a battle in the Caribbean, and during the eighteen years he presided over the colony, he became notorious for his authoritarian rule and his silver-studded wooden prosthesis. "Pegleg Peter," as some called him, antagonized the settlers who listened to the knock of his wooden leg with equal parts of skepticism and dismay. When British forces arrived in Manhattan harbor in 1664, Stuyvesant tried to rally the settlers for a fight, but having clashed with him on numerous occasions, they declined. He was forced to surrender the colony to British commanders, who then renamed it New York. The defeated governor retired to his extensive plantation, in the area now known as the Bowery, where he died in 1672.

Over the next century and a half, the sound of Stuyvesant's leg would become part of his legend. Washington Irving, who helped launch Melville's career with the American publication of *Typee*, includes the sound of the peg leg in his 1809 book *A History of New York*, a pseudo-history ostensibly written by the Dutch-American historian Diedrich Knickerbocker.[14] Poking fun at Stuyvesant's Calvinist busyness, Irving describes the governor "stumping up and downstairs with his wooden leg in such brisk and incessant motion" that "the continual clatter" sounded like "the music of a cooper hooping a flour-barrel." As Knickerbocker tells it, the old Dutch colonists were infatuated with their fabled leader: "His wooden leg, that trophy of his martial encounters, was regarded with reverence and admiration. Every old burgher had a budget of miraculous stories to tell about the exploits of Hardkoppig Piet."[15]

In later generations, the Stuyvesant legend grew to include the sounds coming from his grave at St. Mark's Church in-the-Bowery, the family chapel he built on what is now the intersection of Tenth Street and Second Avenue. From 1847 to 1850, the newlyweds Herman and Elizabeth Melville lived with family members in a house just two blocks away, where the author wrote *Mardi, Redburn* (1849), and *White-Jacket* (1850) and began *Moby-Dick*. The Melville house was a five-minute walk from the church graveyard where locals reported hearing Stuyvesant's peg leg knocking at night. One story had the ghost pacing the aisles of the church, mourning the loss, not of his limb, but of his colony to the British. Others attributed the sound to Stuyvesant's wooden leg tapping against the lid of his coffin in the dark. There's a trace of the neighborhood legend in Ishmael's comment that the stroke of Ahab's dead limb "sounded like a coffin-tap" (233).[16]

Just as Irving's Dutch colonists revered the peg leg of their founder, eighteenth- and nineteenth-century Americans embraced the image of patriots whose missing limbs affirmed their sacrifice to the new nation. In a highly reproduced drawing from around 1828, the American artist Rembrandt Peale depicted an old soldier displaying his wooden leg and stump to two boys, who shyly inquire about its origins. Like many illustrations from the period, *The Soldier's Birth Right* was adapted from overseas, but the image translated into the American context well (Figure 3). In full uniform, the soldier wears the bicorne, or "cocked hat," most associated with Napoleon, but also favored by American military officers in the early 1800s. Melville's maternal grandfather, the Revolutionary War hero Peter Gansevoort, wore a bicorne hat from 1809 to 1812. (It is now preserved at the Smithsonian Institution.[17])

The illustration focuses on the soldier's wooden leg, which juts out toward the boys' bare feet, a striking visual contrast that the pointing finger, cane, and sword reinforce. Reproductions sold by Boston lithographer John Pendleton explained that the caption on the original French print was "This boy says that you were born with that wooden leg."[18] The caption underscores the soldier's relationship to future generations, for the boys themselves symbolize the soldier's birthright: their intact bodies and open curiosity are the product of his sacrifice. Like the prosthesis that braces and supports the stump, republican patriotism reconciles the broken body with the nation.

In addition to the cane that rests between the soldier's legs, the presence of the children suggests virility and compensates for the crisis of masculinity often associated with amputees. Ahab, of course, feels this crisis with all the talk that Moby Dick has "dismasted" him and reduced him to a "dead stump" (163). He appears a version of the Fisher King when we learn that, before he shipped on the *Pequod*, the prosthesis had nearly pierced his groin.[19] This "sexualized vision of amputation" was common in the late eighteenth and early nineteenth centuries, when even open, bleeding wounds were seen as having feminine attributes. As Jennifer Van Horn argues, "Many equated a man's loss of lower limb to castration," leaving the amputee to appear powerless, unmanned, and impotent.[20] The rhetoric of emasculation suffused US reactions to the Mexican general Antonio Lopez de Santa Anna, who had famously lost his leg fighting the French in 1838. At the Battle of Sierra Gordo in 1847, American forces ambushed Santa Anna while he was in repose and came away not only with his carriage, money, and papers, but also with his highly advanced prosthetic leg featuring a knee joint and foot. The capture of the prosthesis was celebrated

Figure 3 Rembrandt Peale, *The Soldier's Birth Right*, c. 1828. Lithograph. Courtesy Reba and Dave Williams Collection, Gift of Reba and Dave Williams. Image courtesy of the National Gallery of Art.

across the United States. An elaborate lithograph featured a soldier running through the chaos holding the artificial leg in the air (Figure 4).[21] A cartoon sketch depicted the general reduced to a humble peg leg and wearing a diaper-looking loincloth covering his groin. A popular song echoed the castration theme in boasting that "Texas cut off Santa Anna's peg."[22] P. T. Barnum displayed what he claimed was a giant replica of Santa Anna's boot in his New York museum, and in an article that some attribute to Melville himself, *Yankee Doodle* magazine commented that the showman's domain now extended "to all wooden legs lost, as strays on the field of battle, and, as a matter of course, to the boots in which they are encased."[23]

The need to integrate the dismembered into narratives that assert a sentimental, masculine identity informs a story collected in the 1849 annual *Forget Me Not*, a publication meant for women readers in England and the United States. "The Old Boatswain" concerns an aging British naval officer, Boatswain Brace, who has lost his leg during the Napoleonic Wars. When Brace returns home, he ebulliently describes his grandson as "My eyes and limbs," suggesting that whatever body parts he has left behind prosthetically live on in his offspring (292). The homecoming is tarnished by the fact that the boatswain's own son, the boy's father, disappeared years before. Like the amputated leg, he seems forever lost. When a traveling artist visits the home, he shows the family a picture of Lord Nelson at the Battle of Trafalgar, which leads the boatswain to muse about "the brave admiral struck down, and falling in the arms of one of his officers." The publication illustrated the climactic scene when the artist prepares to reveal himself as the lost son and father. (A victim of French impressment, he has spent years trying to return home.)[24] The story has little interest in the return of husband to wife and child to mother. Its emotional and ideological weight lies in the restoration of fathers and sons, especially under the office of Nelson, who, like the boatswain, had famously lost a limb in the Napoleonic Wars.

Of all Ahab's predecessors, Lord Admiral Horatio Nelson was the most significant. Nelson looms over Melville's work as a consummate seaman, an intrepid combatant, a proven leader, a distressingly fervent supporter of slavery, and an amputee. As we will see throughout this book, Melville's characters invoke Nelson with love, humor, and skepticism, using him as a kind of polestar as they navigate nineteenth-century maritime life. In 1793, Nelson lost his right eye while invading French-controlled Corsica and then, in 1797, lost his right arm during an invasion of Tenerife, one of the Spanish-controlled Canary Islands. (As "The Old Boatswain" indicated, he

Figure 4 James S. Baillie, detail from *Battle of Sierra Gordo, April 17th. & 18th. 1847, between Genl. Scott and Santa Anna: Capture of Santa Anna's carriage, cash, papers, dinner & wooden leg.* 1848. Lithograph. Image courtesy of the American Antiquarian Society.

would eventually lose his life at the 1805 Battle of Trafalgar when he was shot through the back while leading the British navy to one of its greatest victories.) A charismatic leader whose victories at the Nile delta and the Cape of St. Vincent captured the imagination of the British public, Nelson did not use a prosthesis and wore his empty sleeve during battle and while sitting for formal portraits. Like Ahab, he knew his own impatience and at one point confessed, "My disposition can't bear tame and slow measures." Like Ahab, he startled his shipmates by taking part in fights that officers of his rank customarily avoided.[25]

Nelson's reputation for fighting through his injuries gave him a larger-than-life stature among the sailors in Melville's world. In *Omoo* (1847), the English cooper Bungs stoutly maintains that Lord Nelson was missing a leg, in addition to an eye and an arm. A heavy drinker, Bungs likes to antagonize a quiet Dane named Dunk by presenting himself as the man who won the Battle of Copenhagen in 1802. As the narrator explains, "He sometimes hopped up to Dunk, with one leg curiously locked behind him into his right arm, at the same time closing an eye."

> "Look you, Dunk," says he, staggering about, and winking hard with one eye, to keep the other shut, "Look you; one man—hang me, *half* a man— with one leg, one arm, one eye—hang me, with only a piece of a carcass, flogged your whole shabby nation. Do you deny it, you lubber?"[26]

In *White-Jacket*, Jack Chase comically boasts that his cannon "brought down the Turkish Admiral's main-mast; and the stump left wasn't long enough to make a wooden leg for Lord Nelson."[27] Ishmael treats Nelson more reverentially. Describing a painting behind the pulpit in the Seaman's Chapel, he compares the image of an angel smiling upon a storm-tossed ship to the silver plate that commemorates where Nelson fell on the *Victory*'s plank (40).

Surgeons at Sea

Melville never identifies which leg Ahab has lost, nor does he define the extent of the damage. While Ishmael offers nuanced discussions of the sperm whale's battering ram, tail, and circulatory system, the details surrounding Ahab's wound, treatment, and recovery are as hazy as his past.

36   THE PROSTHETIC ARTS OF *MOBY-DICK*

Flask claims that Ahab has one good knee and part of another; Stubb doubts that the partial knee exists, and a page later, Ishmael seems to agree, describing the captain's "solitary knee" as it fitted into the whaleboat (230).[28] The only definitive detail we have is that Ahab's peg leg begins with trauma, an experience James A. Berger has argued may be more debilitating than limb loss itself. Ahab's monomania is not linked to his prosthesis, Berger contends, but rather "to the event of his dismembering." The captain's thinking "returns always to that moment of injury: of pain, violation, humiliation, helplessness—in short, of trauma."[29] David T. Mitchell and Sharon L. Snyder see in Ahab's prosthesis "an inescapable destiny" and a disability that serves as a "prescription" for his behavior. Why, they ask, "does a disabling condition unquestionably precipitate Ahab's obsessive and vengeful quest to kill the white whale?"[30] Berger challenges the assumption behind that question in emphasizing a devastating loss. He views Ahab's obsession as a manifestation of his compulsively replaying "the moment of trauma"—as if the repetition were both therapeutic and haunting.[31]

Ishmael's recreation of the first battle with Moby Dick emphasizes the apocalyptic nature of the event. "Suddenly sweeping his sickle-shaped lower jaw beneath him," Moby Dick reaps away "Ahab's leg, as a mower a blade of grass" (184). The strangely pastoral terms conflict with the rage that develops in the months ahead. "When he received the stroke that tore him," Ishmael tells us, Ahab "probably but felt the agonizing bodily laceration, but nothing more" (184). And yet, in the aftermath of that battle, Ahab would come to cherish "a wild vindictiveness against the whale" such that he came to identify it with "not only all his bodily woes, but all his intellectual and spiritual exasperations" (184).

Chapter 3 will return to this scene in looking at the way Ishmael maps this battle onto Muslim assassins, but for now my discussion focuses on the trip home after the "almost fatal encounter" (184). Like biblical lovers "Ahab and anguish lay stretched together in one hammock, rounding in mid winter that dreary, howling Patagonian Cape" (185). The Latin root of anguish, meaning "tightening," expresses the especially sharp, severe, and localized pain arising from the tissue and neural damage.[32] The recovery involves psychological constriction as well, for "Then it was, that his torn body and gashed soul bled into one another; and so interfusing, made him mad" (185). The offspring of physical and psychological pain, Ahab's monomania builds upon this madness and comes *before* the disabling experiences of using a prosthesis or trying to walk on ship. "As in his narrow-flowing-monomania," Ishmael comments, "not one jot of Ahab's broad madness was left behind; so in that broad madness, not one jot of his great natural intellect had perished" (185). As Elijah first intimated, medical trauma had transformed Ahab into a more potent, more ruthless version of himself (92).

Melville had written about amputation in his previous novels, and it is worth dwelling on the knowledge he had accumulated before *Moby-Dick*. At the beginning of *Mardi*, the narrator, who will eventually go by the name Taji, deserts his whale ship in the middle of the night and, with his friend Jarl, strikes out on his own. Rummaging through a seemingly abandoned ship in the South Seas, they spot a bloodstain on deck that leads them to discover the native sailor Samoa and his wife, Annatoo, hiding in the rigging. Samoa recounts how a battle with pirates killed his fellow sailors and left him with such a mangled arm that Annatoo had to amputate it.

Melville's description of what is now called a guillotine amputation explains the centuries-old procedure:

> Samoa's operation was very summary. A fire was kindled in the little caboose, or cook-house, and so made as to produce much smoke. He then placed his arm upon one of the windlass bitts (a short upright timber, breast-high), and seizing the blunt cook's ax would have struck the blow; but for some reason distrusting the precision of his aim, Annatoo was assigned to the task. Three strokes, and the limb, from just above the elbow, was no longer Samoa's; and he saw his own bones; which many a centenarian can not say. The very clumsiness of the operation was safety to the subject. The weight and bluntness of the instrument both deadened the pain and lessened the hemorrhage.[33]

Samoa stops the bleeding and closes the wound by holding his stump in the smoke of the cookhouse fire, a method that goes back at least as far as the fifth century BC.[34] For readers of *Moby-Dick*, Samoa's cool acceptance of his fate sharply contrasts with Ahab's fury. The cultural difference is revealing. "Among savages, severe personal injuries are, for the most part, accounted but trifles," Taji explains. "When a European would be taking to his couch in despair, the savage would disdain to recline" and would not think twice about serving as "his own barber and surgeon."[35] The American Ahab chooses vengeance over despair, but *Mardi* suggests there are multiple responses to limb loss, including those that undermine nationalist

38   THE PROSTHETIC ARTS OF *MOBY-DICK*

narratives. It was easy to forget that Samoa had recently lost his arm, Taji explains, "so Lord Nelson-like and cavalierly did he sport the honorable stump."[36]

Melville addressed medical amputation extensively in *White-Jacket*. Set on a US Navy ship on its voyage home from Peru, the book combines elements of the novel, memoir, adventure story, and political exposé in denouncing an aloof naval bureaucracy that permits the flogging of sailors.[37] Among Melville's many targets was the practice of navy medicine. A series of astounding chapters satirizes the self-satisfied Dr. Cadwallader Cuticle, the decrepit "Surgeon of the Fleet" and a graduate of the Philadelphia College of Physicians and Surgeons. Cuticle has a "peculiar love" for "Morbid Anatomy," and although he professes compassion and refinement, he attaches to his stateroom the plaster cast of an elderly woman's head with a "hideous, crumpled horn, like that of a ram" growing out of her forehead.[38] The woman's face has a sorrowful expression that haunts the narrator long after he has seen it, but Cuticle remains unmoved. He hangs his cap on the horn whenever he enters the room.

Cuticle's indifference surfaces when he eagerly amputates the leg of a sailor who has been mistakenly shot in the thigh. The surgeon's fondness for amputation is well known, and he once confided "that he would rather cut off a man's arm than dismember the wing of the most delicate pheasant."[39] Although they advised him to try to recover the bullet instead, the fleet's junior surgeons assemble to observe the amputation and gossip that Cuticle "can drop a leg in one minute and ten seconds."[40] (A subordinate discretely prepares to time him.) In this dark comedy, however, the withered surgeon seems anything but competent, and he prepares for the operation by removing a series of prosthetics—his wig, his false teeth, and his glass eye. As the patient goes in and out of consciousness, Cuticle reminisces about his medical training and bemoans the lack of interesting operations one can perform at sea. If war breaks out in Texas, he tells his subordinates, join the army because, lacking its own naval forces, Mexico has "always been backward in furnishing subjects for the amputation-tables of foreign navies."[41]

The scene borrows heavily from an article on amputation in the *Penny Cyclopaedia*, a twenty-seven-volume reference set popular in England and the United States. Melville gives Cuticle the same nonchalant faith in medical progress that he found in the article's assertion that "the mere removal of a limb excites in the modern surgeon no degree of anxiety."[42] The article is the source for Cuticle's lecture about the history of amputation and how new methods have improved on the past. When the patient begins to tremble, the surgeon responds with the same banal axiom that Melville found in the *Cyclopaedia* text: "How much better it is to live with three limbs than to die with four."[43] Stretched out on a table, the foretopman looks up at a surgeon clothed "with the attributes of immortality." Who was this "Regenerator of life? The withered, shrunken, one-eyed, toothless, hairless Cuticle."[44]

"No writer ever put the reality before his reader more unflinchingly than [Melville] does in Redburn, and White Jacket," Nathaniel Hawthorne wrote Duyckinck in the summer of 1850.[45] The two novelists had recently met during a hiking party in the Berkshires, and with Duyckinck's encouragement, the author of *The Scarlet Letter* (1850) was reading the younger Melville "with a progressive appreciation" of his talents. Although Hawthorne does not name which scenes he admires, the amputation scene in *White-Jacket* stands out as an unflinching portrait of reality:

> Letting fall the wrist, feeling the thigh carefully, and bowing over it an instant, he drew the fatal knife unerringly across the flesh. As it first touched the part, the row of surgeons simultaneously dropped their eyes to the watches in their hands, while the patient lay, with eyes horribly distended, in a kind of waking trance. Not a breath was heard; but as the quivering flesh parted in a long, lingering gash, a spring of blood welled up between the living walls of the wounds, and two thick streams, in opposite directions, coursed down the thigh. The sponges were instantly dipped in the purple pool; every face present was pinched to a point with suspense; the limb writhed; the man shrieked; his mess-mates pinioned him; while round and round the leg went the unpitying cut.[46]

The passage displays the same attention to detail and technique that would soon appear in the whaling chapters of *Moby-Dick*. Using a combination of participles and parallel phrases, Melville does more than record the visceral details of the moment: he manages to balance the various acts—the dropping eyes, the shaking patient, the quivering flesh—and hold them in suspense as the knife makes its way through the skin. The combination of active and passive verbs has a beneficial effect: Cuticle falls out of the description, and the knife, the sponge, the blood itself all take on their own agency: "Round and round the leg went the unpitying cut."

40   THE PROSTHETIC ARTS OF *MOBY-DICK*

Cuticle abruptly re-enters the narrative when he invites one of the junior officers to saw the thighbone. When the young man begins tentatively, the surgeon snatches the tool from him. "Away, butcher!" he hisses, "you disgrace the profession." And then, ever so briefly, the studied action takes over again:

> For a few moments the thrilling, rasping sound was heard; and then the top-man seemed parted in twain at the hip, as the leg slowly slid into the arms of the pale, gaunt man in the shroud, who at once made away with it, and tucked it out of sight under one of the guns.[47]

Cuticle asks another surgeon to sew the patient up while he windily explains that, rather than a tourniquet, he prefers to have his steward squeeze the arteries during the procedure and then stitch them afterward. With Cuticle discoursing like a schoolmaster, the topman is removed to another room. Moments later, the steward returns with the news: he is dead.

A US Navy ship typically included a physician among its crew, and as Melville explained in *Omoo*, British law required all whalers to carry a physician whose position was wholly dedicated to healing the injured and sick.[48] The US whaling industry only required each ship to maintain a medicine chest of ointments and powders. With such minimal regulations, medical care usually fell to the captain, whom many viewed as the patriarch, or head, of the ship's family.[49] Sometimes in collaboration with well-known apothecary shops, antebellum publishers sold medical manuals, specifically targeted to shipowners and captains, that gave instructions on such matters as how to stock a medicine chest, how to cure jaundice and tropical fevers, and how to treat snakebites. One Nantucket druggist advertised that, upon request, the shop would include amputation instruments, along with instructions for their use, with the purchase of a medicine chest.[50] Most sailors who required an amputation at sea suffered from frostbite or had been involved in an industrial accident—a hand caught in a cable, an arm crushed under shifting cargo, a shattered leg after falling from the main topsail yard. These cases required careful deliberation. Amputation was not always necessary, and many captains were reluctant to perform the surgery.[51] Some cases required immediate attention because gangrene or mortification had set in. Like Ahab, sailors who suffered from bites (usually from sharks and crocodiles) could lose parts of their limbs instantly.[52]

From all accounts, Moby Dick completely severed Ahab's leg, and so the captain would have required surgery to create an even fissure, smooth the remaining bone, and form a stump that could withstand a prosthesis. With the captain down, perhaps the first mate, or even the carpenter, would perform the surgery, though, as one author democratically put it, "any man of common dexterity and firmness" could cut off a leg.[53] Whoever performed the surgery would probably consult a manual such as Dr. Usher Parsons's *Physician for Ships; Containing Medical Advice for Seaman and Other Persons at Sea* (1847), a book that went through multiple editions and was sold in New England, and prominently in New Bedford, through the 1840s.[54]

Surgeons typically tied a tourniquet-like contraption around a patient's leg (a handkerchief wound tighter and tighter with the aid of a stick) and sliced the skin enough inches above the wound to prepare a flap that would cover the stump. Parsons's manual speaks directly to the practitioner, and one can imagine, in a crowded, panicked cabin, someone reading the instructions out loud. "Take the razor and make one straight cut all round the limb, through the skin and fat only," Dr. Parsons instructs. "Then cut these up from the flesh one inch higher, let the assistant hold them back, while you cut through the flesh at one sweep, down to the bone." Using a piece of linen, an assistant should pull "back the flesh from the bone, while you saw as high up as possible without wounding the flesh."[55] If the amputation were above the knee, the sailor performing the operation would then tie up the arteries and blood vessels using a curved needle or pincers before washing the stump and making sure the bleeding had stopped. He would then stitch the flap over the wound, using a dozen separate ligatures, each with a foot of waxed thread. As *The Mariner's Medical Guide* (1860) explained it, a below-the-knee operation required an additional process: before tying up the wound, the surgeon used a small knife to clear away all the flesh between the patient's tibia and fibula.[56]

Patients were awake for the entire process. The first operations using the anesthetic chloroform took place during the Crimean War in 1847, and so, in addition to healing and rehabilitation, they contended with the trauma of both the accident and the surgery. If Samoa represented for Melville the epitome of native resilience, Ahab was the Westerner who experienced dismemberment as an existential crisis, the one who rejected the kind of platitudes that Dr. Cuticle liked to repeat: "It is better to live with three limbs than to die with four."[57] The irony is that, even with an

42 THE PROSTHETIC ARTS OF *MOBY-DICK*

inexperienced surgeon working on his leg, Ahab fared better than the top-man did in the US Navy.

Shakespeare and the Comedy of Normate Thinking

Melville's early fiction suggests a mind fascinated by the medical, social, and philosophical problems raised by limb loss. In adding the structure of Shakespearean comedy to *Moby-Dick*, he broadened the attention that a prosthesis would get on ship. Granting Shakespeare a messianic kind of power, Melville's February 1849 letter to Duyckinck shuttles between his appreciation for the large-print edition of the plays and his attendance at a series of readings performed by Fanny Kemble, a popular English actress who frequently toured the United States.[58] The letter includes some derogatory gossip about the actress's lack of femininity and her husband's desire to be "amputated off from his matrimonial half" (a curious allusion to the couple's much-publicized divorce.)[59] As biographer John Bryant has suggested, though, Kemble's views on Shakespeare may have shaped Melville's own. The novelist seems to have absorbed his "transgressive equation of Shakespeare and scripture" from Kemble, whose readings showcased the plays' "heavenly imaginations" over staged theatrics.[60] Melville elaborated on this theme in his 1850 review of Hawthorne's *Mosses from an Old Manse* (1846). Written concurrently with *Moby-Dick*, the review described Shakespeare as a truth teller who, in a "world of lies," told the truth the only way it could be told—"covertly, and by snatches."[61] The essay memorably praises King Lear's ability to speak "the sane madness of vital truth," a phrase many have connected to Ahab.[62]

Compared to the Duyckinck letter, the essay offers a more nuanced analysis in lamenting how Shakespeare's dramatic efforts had detracted from "the great Art of Telling the Truth."[63] Bryant suggests that the roots of these ideas may also lie in Kemble's public dissatisfaction with the histrionic melodrama of nineteenth-century productions of the plays.[64] Melville's essay nationalizes this critique, for, in elevating Hawthorne, he criticizes his countrymen for appreciating the Bard only through the rants and sword-fights that made up a typical American performance. He differentiates the reader focused on Shakespeare's "quick probings at the very axis of reality" from the common theatergoer who thrills to "Richard-the-Third humps, and Macbeth daggers." "It is the least part of genius that attracts admiration,"

Melville declares, resigning himself to an America that would never appreciate the "deep far-away things" that made Hawthorne and Shakespeare geniuses.[65] Shakespeare wrote for "the tricky stage," Melville explained, which was why he possessed "mere mob renown" in the United States.[66]

Given his aversion to shallow popularity, it is remarkable that Melville would repeatedly turn to "the tricky stage" in depicting a series of unfiltered responses to Ahab's disability. As we saw in the framing of Chapter 29, Melville explicitly bends the form of Shakespearean comedy to Stubb's request that Ahab muffle his prosthesis. The scene initiates a trio of chapters that intertwine Shakespeare and disability: in the first, Ahab's denunciation of Stubb recalls all the comically exasperated barnyard curses and beatings that masters inflicted on servants on the early modern stage; in the second (Chapter 30), Ahab reflects on how his inner turmoil has ruined the satisfaction he used to get from his pipe; and in the third (Chapter 31), Stubb recounts the dream he had after provoking Ahab the previous night. Far from lampooning Ahab's bony step (as many American productions did with Richard III's "deformity"), the comedy focuses on Stubb's tortuously self-aware response to the prosthesis.[67]

Titled "Queen Mab," the chapter follows the three-part dream in highlighting the pitfalls of what Rosemarie Garland Thomson has identified as normate thinking.[68] Talking to Flask, Stubb tries to make sense of his relation to Ahab in his clownishly earnest way. "You know the old man's ivory leg," he tells the third mate, "well I dreamed he kicked me with it; and when I tried to kick back, upon my soul, my little man, I kicked my leg right off! And then, presto! Ahab seemed a pyramid, and I, like a blazing fool, kept kicking at it" (131). Psychoanalytic critics have had much to say about this dream, appreciating the way Stubb identifies Ahab as a father figure who punishes and castrates him for his threatened disobedience.[69] As he left the deck the previous night, Stubb concluded that Ahab possessed "what some folks ashore call a conscience," an apparently painful disorder that the happy-go-lucky mate had no desire to contract himself (128). "I don't know what it is," he mutters, "but the Lord keep me from catching it" (128). From his farm in the Berkshires, Melville could hear laughter coming from the banks of the river Thames.

Folded into this psychological struggle is Stubb's anxiety that Ahab's limb loss might be contagious. On deck, Ahab did not kick the mate; his words only felt like kicks. But in the dream, he worries that if he resists, the captain's condition will spread. Having tried to normalize Ahab by silencing his

44 THE PROSTHETIC ARTS OF *MOBY-DICK*

prosthesis and having mulled over the captain's caustic reproach, he now considers the possibility of losing a leg himself. Ahab exposes a collective vulnerability that Stubb must reconcile with the mismatched power between them.

As the comedy of the dream settles in—with newfound rage, the one-legged mate is somehow kicking the Ahab-like pyramid—Stubb begins to focus on the makeup of Ahab's prosthesis. After taking great offense, he now has second thoughts:

> I somehow seemed to be thinking to myself, that after all, it was not much of an insult, that kick from Ahab. 'Why,' thinks I, 'what's the row? It's not a real leg, only a false leg.' And there's a mighty difference between a living thump and a dead thump. That's what makes a blow from the hand, Flask, fifty times more savage to bear than a blow from a cane. The living member—that makes the living insult, my little man. (131)

Stubb is preoccupied with the question of what constitutes Ahab's body. In contemporary medical scholarship, the issue of embodiment generally concerns "the process by which patients with limb loss come to accept their peripheral device as a natural extension of self."[70] But the process is not limited to artificial limbs. Embodiment also includes how people identify any kind of medical device, form of assistance, or even caregiver as a fundamental part of who they are.[71] Numerous characters raise the question of embodiment in *Moby-Dick*, but Melville first assigns these questions to Stubb as he muddles through his discomfort with the captain's artificial leg.

The mate works from the premise that the peg leg reflects the captain only to the extent that it corresponds to the living limb, and thus the more realistic the prosthesis looks, the more easily it is integrated into the body. Because the whalebone leg is nothing like a foot, Stubb sees the insult as coming from a contrivance rather than Ahab's subjective self. In the way that the whalebone prosthesis narrows into a slender base, the kick is "whittled down to a point only," leaving little cause for offense (132). To the second mate, the question of embodiment depends on the larger question of mimesis.[72]

Stubb is under considerable psychological pressure to relieve Ahab of his imagined offense, and in the third part of the dream, he comically adjusts to the captain's dominating personality. The dream represents Ahab as a timeless power by transforming him into a pyramid, an image that corresponds to the "Egyptian chest" that Ishmael sees in the captain and the pyramid-shaped hump of Moby Dick (185). As Stubb continues with his one-legged kicks, an old merman stuck through with marlinspikes orders the second mate to reflect on Ahab's behavior. "Let's argue the insult," the merman says. Because Ahab kicked him with a beautiful ivory leg and not some "common pitch pine leg," the offense should be received as an honor (132). As others have demonstrated, the encounter helps Stubb not only to rationalize Ahab's perceived abuse, but also to become wiser and more compliant. "*Be* kicked by him," the merman counsels, "and on no account kick back; for you can't help yourself, wise Stubb."[73] In the scrambled contents of his dream, the humpbacked merman, the Ahab-like pyramid, and the looming threat of Moby Dick's "high, pyramidical white hump" all converge as figures to which the mate must submit (183).

Even as he elevates Ahab's authority, Stubb remains fixated on the artificial leg. Carrying lumps of seaweed as if they were his clothes, the merman seems an assemblage of body parts. Badger haired and crouched, part man and part fish, he is a more grotesque version of Ahab and his whalebone prosthesis, his human features taken over by deformity. If the pyramid imagery transforms Ahab into an ancient force, the merman reduces him to a wounded, nightmarish beast. Whatever wisdom he promises seems unnaturally learned. The merman's display of marlinspikes sticking in "his stern" is transposed into Stubb's observation that Ahab was "looking over the stern," shouting his enigmatic instructions about searching for a white whale (132). "Look ye—there's something special in the wind," Stubb says to Flask as the captain strikes his way toward them. "Ahab has that that's bloody on his mind" (133).

Much of the chapter's comedy resides in normate thinking. Rather than using deviant bodies "to shore up the normate boundaries," Stubb comes to understand how much he himself lacks.[74] The theatrical staging foregrounds the process by which Ahab's prosthesis challenges Stubb's identity, and as he comically rambles through his dream, we see him reconstituting himself as the captain's defender, admirer, and humbled subordinate. The sound of Ahab walking on deck surfaces the anxieties, fears, and discomforts of his crew, prompting them to rationalize their own vulnerabilities. The protean nature of Stubb's dream conveys his multilayered reaction to a prosthesis that Ishmael can only regard with dread. The array of responses prompts us to consider whether Ahab's disability resides in his lost leg or in the crewmembers who react to its sight and sound on deck.

46   THE PROSTHETIC ARTS OF *MOBY-DICK*

Melville explicitly raises this question when Stubb and Flask return to the subject of Ahab's leg in Chapter 50, "Ahab's Boat and Crew. Fedallah." When Stubb asks Flask for his thoughts about the dream, his disengaged response underscores the scene's essential comedy: "I don't know; it seems a sort of foolish to me" (132). But after the *Pequod* returns from its first hunt, Stubb and Flask resume their earlier conversation. The sight of Ahab fully engaged in the chase, commanding his own whaling boat with a secret crew of Filipino oarsmen, has left Stubb in awe.

> "Who would have thought it, Flask!" cried Stubb; "if I had but one leg you would not catch me in a boat, unless maybe to stop the plug-hole with my timber toe. Oh! he's a wonderful old man!"
>
> "I don't think it so strange, after all, on that account," said Flask. "If his leg were off at the hip, now, it would be a different thing. That would disable him; but he has one knee, and good part of the other left, you know."
>
> "I don't know that, my little man; I never yet saw him kneel." (229)

Separated by asterisks, this fragment-sized tableau seems more like an epigraph than a fully incorporated part of the chapter. For the only time in the novel, Melville applies the word "disable" to Ahab as the mates clownishly discuss their leader's surprising capabilities.

When Stubb describes Ahab as a "wonderful man," he praises the captain's bravely standing at the steering oar, his arm thrust backward to balance himself as the boat entered "the charmed, churned circle of the hunted sperm whale" (224). The conversation deftly reminds us that Ahab has performed these feats while strapped to his artificial leg. Stubb champions the captain's grit, but Flask seems unimpressed, implicitly raising questions that hang over the ensuing discussion of Ahab's crew and his spiritual guide Fedallah: What exactly constitutes a disability? And who is Flask to make such an assessment? Earlier in the novel, Ishmael had lamented the third mate's "ignorant, unconscious fearlessness" and his lack of reverence for the whale's majesty (119). His response to Ahab's performance is similarly prosaic and glib.

Flask's focus on work echoes nineteenth-century debates about the nature of disability. By the time Melville started composing *Moby-Dick*, the question of what constituted a disability had gained traction in the United States. In 1818, the year before Melville was born, the federal government passed the Revolutionary War Pension Act, which, according to

Kim M. Nielsen, "established disability as a legal and social welfare category." In supporting veterans, the Pension Act defined disability as "the inability to perform economically productive labor." Veterans missing an arm or leg generally had little trouble finding employment in the early nineteenth century, but the growing, industrialized economy of the 1840s and 1850s moved the impaired out of their jobs to standardize the workforce. These changes coincided with the gradual medicalization of society and the emergence of professional training for physicians that emphasized the ability to diagnose norms.[75]

With neither knowledge nor curiosity, Flask takes on the diagnostic role himself, evaluating the captain against an idea of disability that is predicated on economic productivity. Like everyone else, Flask has heard Ahab's "bony step" tap across the *Pequod*'s deck, but he has a different response. Stubb's puzzlement, fear, and wonder prepare him to submit to the captain even before he has learned about the white whale. A symbol of injury, power, and (later) revenge, Ahab's prosthesis requires Stubb to reorient his normate self in relation to the captain's authority. Flask settles for the blunter assessment that Ahab can work. Like an 1840s physician weighing the conditions presented to him, he acknowledges that an above-the-knee amputation would probably limit the captain's performance more than his losing just a shinbone and foot. As a novelist, Melville chose to tell Ahab's story outside the national narratives that were so prevalent in the early nineteenth century. He supplies Flask with the idea that disability places one outside capitalist narratives about labor and efficiency. Chapter 5 will show how dismemberment only becomes important to Flask when it aids or impedes profits.

The Power of Assistance

Pip may be the most obvious product of Melville's intensive reading of Shakespeare, for as generations have pointed out, to Ahab's King Lear the mad shipkeeper plays the Fool.[76] Drafted to join Stubb's crew, the frightened Pip leaps from the boat in the middle of a chase, and as he had threatened, Stubb abandons him to the wide horizon of the sea. Pip's soul descends to wondrous depths, where he learns such mysteries of the universe that when he is recovered and tries to communicate them, his shipmates assume he is speaking gibberish. "So man's insanity is heaven's sense,"

48   THE PROSTHETIC ARTS OF *MOBY-DICK*

Ishmael explains, echoing what Melville and Kemble admired in Shakespeare (414). As a Fool, however, Pip offered Melville a different register than did the stately, but heterodox, Ahab. Clownishly responding to Ahab's leg, Stubb's ignorance makes him the butt of jokes he does not understand. Melville uses Pip's hauntingly perceptive voice to characterize the relationships that will lead to the *Pequod*'s wreck. "Here's the ship's navel," he says of the doubloon, "and they are all on fire to unscrew it." Playing the role of storyteller more than visionary, Pip astutely qualifies his statement: "When aught's nailed to the mast it's a sign that things grow desperate" (435).

Part of Pip's wisdom is that he understands his prosthetic relation to Ahab. As the ship nears Moby Dick, he offers himself as a living replacement for the whalebone that sounds across the deck. "Ye have not a whole body, sir," he says to Ahab when the two are alone in the captain's cabin; "Do ye but use poor me for your one lost leg" (534). As Jonik has argued, Pip is a prosthetic means for Ahab "to draw power from inhuman, impersonal forces."[77] His spiritual capabilities offer the captain a glimpse into the invisible worlds he cannot know. "I do suck most wondrous philosophies from thee!" Ahab says in appreciation. "Some unknown conduits from the unknown worlds must empty into thee!" (529). But Melville, interestingly, never attempts to put those conversations on the page, asking readers to infer the "hoarded heaps" of wisdom that Pip has seen and communicated to his captain (414). What the novel does provide is Pip's voice expressing a desire to become the lost limb. His offer of prosthetic support reveals his simultaneous desire to take refuge in the captain's white body: "Only tread upon me, sir; I ask no more, so I remain a part of ye" (534).[78]

The distinction clarifies the ways that Ahab's human and nonhuman prostheses intensify his powers rather weaken or fragment them. The prosthetic imagery suggests less about Ahab's supposed incompleteness than it does Pip's heartbreaking subservience to him. In "Benito Cereno" (1855), the enslaved mutineer Babo creates a "spectacle of fidelity" when he pretends to serve the captain he secretly controls.[79] Pip wants to be a prosthetic of fidelity, his body offered up to *his* captain's resolve. Although freed from slavery, Pip is the most vulnerable member of the crew. Stubb has reminded the Black teenager that he remains subject to a slaveholding, capitalist marketplace, and because the *Pequod* deems him worth less than a processed whale, the crew abandons him to the sea. Moved by the gods' indifference to his suffering, Ahab folds the shipkeeper into his own sense of aggrievement. Pip regards the relationship as a lifeline. Ever aware of the power differentials separating him from his shipmates, he looks at Ahab's hand in his own and declares it "a man-rope; something that weak souls may hold by" (522). Having known little of love or connection since going to sea, he perceives in Ahab a social relation that could have prevented him from being lost. "Oh, sir, let old Perth now come and rivet these two hands together," he cries, "the black one with the white, for I will not let this go" (522). Alienated from kindness, Pip sees the human hand as expressing the assistance and security of the hemp handrails lowered from the ship.

In staging his disability, Melville showcases how shrewdly Ahab enlists others in his wounds. The captain, as Jonik remarks, may be "suffused and constituted, decomposed and recomposed, by his relations"; he may represent a "mode of transindividuality" that incorporates the human and non-human into his personhood.[80] But he accumulates those prosthetic extensions as an augmentation, not a lessening, of his power. When Pip offers his body to be "tread upon," he suggests that subordination is the most fulfilling position he can inhabit on Ahab's ship. As a Fool, he bluntly articulates the social dynamics that others are unable to perceive. Being Ahab's prosthesis allows him to be safely embodied in the captain's will, to become part of this "anaconda of an old man" whose force, charisma, and occasional humanity draw weak souls into his (178). The man-rope metaphor captures their mutually defining relationship: Pip sees himself as a prosthetic and Ahab as an assistive device.

These scenes dramatize the novel's larger tendency to use embodiment and assistance as expressions of Ahab's ominous command. From boar hunting in *Omoo* to brickmaking in *Israel Potter* (1855), Melville's works are filled with intricate descriptions of characters laboring in the physical world. While obviously famous for its portraits of the whaling industry, *Moby-Dick* pays detailed attention to how the dismembered Ahab not only functions at sea but leads his ship on its vengeful quest. Ishmael joins the crew, for example, in curiously following the captain's modification of a fourth whaleboat to accommodate his prosthesis. Ahab recognizes that the boat needs an "extra coat of sheathing" on the hull "to make it withstand the pointed pressure of his ivory limb" (230). With palpable concern, he adds the reinforcement and then "exactly" shapes the thigh board at the center of the craft so it can better brace his leg while he is stabbing or darting a whale (230). Using the carpenter's gouge, he even carves out a depression in the wood to give his natural leg more support. Anxiety and purpose drive the

50   THE PROSTHETIC ARTS OF *MOBY-DICK*

captain, but by doing this work himself—and in the view of his crew—he communicates his power to shape the world around his ivory leg (230).

Activists have long commented on the ways that built environments disable the impaired, creating obstacles to movement and access through normate design. In his tale of an autocratic captain, Melville imagines how Ahab could transform the built environment to better suit his needs. As he cuts, shapes, and straightens, as he prepares his craft to "go on the whale," we see that, in making the *Pequod* more accessible, the captain makes it a fuller extension of himself.[81] Melville admired this quality in other characters. *Mardi* emphasized the ingenuity of the people who lived on the Isle of Cripples. With its "deformities of calabashes" and "bow-legged stools," for example, the residents' banquet attests to their capacity to design objects to fit their own taste and use.[82] Ahab exhibits a similar resourcefulness, though unlike the outcasts of Hooloomooloo, his motivation centers on revenge.

The same combination of power and performativity appears in Ishmael's description of the auger holes on either side of the *Pequod*'s deck. Instead of detracting from his power, the assistive devices contribute to Ahab's intimidating strength:

> I was struck with the singular posture he maintained. Upon each side of the *Pequod*'s quarter deck, and pretty close to the mizen shrouds, there was an auger hole, bored about half an inch or so, into the plank. His bone leg steadied in that hole; one arm elevated, and holding by a shroud; Captain Ahab stood erect, looking straight out beyond the ship's ever-pitching prow. There was an infinity of firmest fortitude, a determinate, unsurrenderable wilfulness, in the fixed and fearless, forward dedication of that glance. (124)

With his rigid posture and "troubled master eye," he seems as steadfast on his implanted leg as others might be on two (124). Fitted into the assistive device, Ahab's prosthesis gives him "the nameless regal overbearing dignity of some mighty woe"—so much so that, years after the captain's death, Ishmael still associates him with robust vitality and strength (124).

Over the course of the journey, Ahab uses the auger holes as his sanctuary and his stage. They become key to the performance of what David Dowling has called the "ethos of charismatic leadership."[83] In "The Quarter-Deck," for example, Ahab turns to the crew—"half-revolving in his pivot-hole"—to rally them around the search for the white whale (161). In "The Grand Armada," he "quickly revolved in his pivot-hole" to address his men when the ship was being chased by Malaysian pirates (383). As if they granted their own power, Melville contrasts the auger holes with Ahab's difficult movement on ship. In "The Candles," a typhoon inspires Ahab to declare his blasphemous defiance of God. Amid intense thunder and lightning, however, he first appears in the dark "groping his way along the bulwarks to his pivot-hole" (505). These devices, in Cella's words, create an environment in which the captain "is part of, and not separate from, the places [he] inhabits and moves through." The "dialectic between embodiment and emplacement" becomes one of the ways in which Ahab consolidates his leadership.[84]

Melville's focus in these scenes is not on disability as a general condition but on Ahab's singular capacity to involve others in his sense of injury. The captain who modifies the *Pequod* to his purpose employs the same resourcefulness in manipulating its crew. As we have seen with Pip and Stubb, people are part of the built environment that Ahab alters to his will. He is the "cogged circle" that makes their "various wheels" revolve (167). In their painfully self-aware comments, the Fool and the clown see the locus of that power in the ivory leg and their own strained relationship to it. That both readily subordinate themselves to the captain says as much about their social condition as it does the strength of Ahab's command. In the Shakespearean conception of their characters, they supplement his presence and storyline.

A more complex case comes from Starbuck. Although significantly more tense, the balance of power between the captain and first mate unfolds along the same axis of prosthetic embodiment and assistance. Ahab rails against Starbuck's moral independence. When they disagree about fixing a leak in the main hold, he points a loaded musket at the insistent mate, telling him, "There is one God that is Lord over the earth, and one Captain that is lord over the Pequod" (474). The shocking act may distract readers from Ahab's actions when Starbuck leaves the cabin. "Unconsciously using the musket for a staff," Melville writes, "with an iron brow he paced to and fro in the little cabin" (475). The image conveys the latent violence in Ahab's prostheticized walk and the lethal message his snow-white leg comes to represent: he will coerce the crew until it assists and embodies his revenge. The authoritarian power he lords over his men consistently returns to their becoming his emotional or bodily extensions. He is a match to the sailors'

52 THE PROSTHETIC ARTS OF *MOBY-DICK*

"ant-hills of powder" (168). He sees in Starbuck's eyes his own wife and child (544).

Stubb's dream revealed his fears that Ahab's dismemberment would spread from the captain to the rest of the ship. Ahab returns to the image of contagion in "The Quarter-Deck" when he reflects on how he has elicited Starbuck's reluctant acquiescence. Speaking to the first mate, he masterfully combines solicitude and flattery with a portrait of the crew's longing for Moby Dick's death:

> The crew, man, the crew! Are they not one and all with Ahab, in this matter of the whale? See Stubb! he laughs! See yonder Chilian! he snorts to think of it. Stand up amid the general hurricane, thy one tost sapling cannot, Starbuck! And what is it? Reckon it. 'Tis but to help strike a fin; no wondrous feat for Starbuck. What is it more? From this one poor hunt, then, the best lance out of all Nantucket, surely he will not hang back, when every foremast-hand has clutched a whetstone? (164)

The first mate begins to relent, and like a Shakespearean villain, the captain turns aside and exults: "Something shot from my dilated nostrils, he has inhaled it in his lungs. Starbuck now is mine; cannot oppose me now, without rebellion" (164). Ahab sees himself as acting upon the rest of the crew, but as if he were a biological host, Starbuck draws the virus of Ahab's power into his system. Contagion prepares the way for embodiment.

The metaphor gives us a good way to think about how the captain dominates the first mate by getting inside his system. Pip offers to become Ahab's prosthetic, to become a living replacement limb. Starbuck is taken over from within. Although he challenges Ahab openly, he faithfully follows orders because, as the captain predicted, to refuse them would constitute rebellion—not just against his leader but against his own sense of self. As the *Pequod* enters the hunting grounds, Ahab develops a contraption to bring him to the top of the royal mast. Attaching a basket to a system of ropes, he asks Starbuck, the man he had threatened with a musket days before, to watch over his ascent, effectively turning him into another assistive device. Up the basket goes, and "with one hand clinging round the royal mast, Ahab gazed abroad upon the sea for miles and miles,—ahead, astern, this side, and that,—within the wide expanded circle commanded at so great a height" (538). On deck, Starbuck suffers the humiliation of being trusted.

My Arms and My Legs

The final chapters of *Moby-Dick* present Ahab with a changing roster of prostheses and assistive devices, all of which suggest a shifting sense of power. The coffin-taps that haunted the *Pequod*'s deck are now accompanied by the sound of weapons clattering alongside the captain's living and dead limbs. As Ahab successively steadies himself on a gun, harpoon, and lance, we see the violence of his intentions. But Melville also exposes the limits of his pride.[85] The ring of Ahab's walk mixes in with the sound of Pip's "strange mummeries" and "wretched laugh," both mocking "the black tragedy of the melancholy ship" (490). The theatrical language fits the dramatic structure that Melville has used to depict the varied responses to Ahab's leg, but Pip's laughter now suggests that this performance of power will be inadequate. When Moby Dick flips a whaleboat during the first day's chase, Ishmael observes Ahab immersed in the churning sea, "half smothered in the foam of the whale's insolent tail, and too much of a cripple to swim" (551). The captain who has so diligently altered the ship to fit his needs remains, in the end, functionally impaired. Ahab can prostheticize the *Pequod*, but he cannot prostheticize the sea. The next day brings the point home when the whale destroys the boat, the ivory leg snaps off, and Ahab is left with "one short sharp splinter." He is "helped to the deck" and "instead of standing by himself he still half-hung upon the shoulder of Starbuck" (560). The ivory leg was an ominous, but triumphant trophy. Supplied from his boat's broken keel, the wooden replacement signifies past and future wrecks.

Ahab makes a strong case for seeing the loss of his prosthesis as a kind of disembodiment. Admitting to Starbuck that it is "sweet to lean sometimes" and that "old Ahab" should have "leaned oftener than he has," the captain seems to accept a sense of interdependence that he has rarely displayed on ship (560). The shift corresponds to a newfound identification with the material device. Exhibiting his customary concern about the captain's body, Stubb asks about broken bones, and Ahab speaks about his splintered prosthesis as if it were barely distinguishable from his natural leg:

> But even with a broken bone, old Ahab is untouched; and I account no living bone of mine one jot more me, than this dead one that's lost. Nor white whale, nor man, nor fiend, can so much as graze old Ahab in his own proper and inaccessible being. (560)

54   THE PROSTHETIC ARTS OF *MOBY-DICK*

Ahab strangely embodies the whalebone in its loss. His inaccessibility rests in what he claims is his transcendence. The captain who accused the world of covering for invisible, malignant powers dispenses with his broken flesh in claiming an indomitable soul. "Ye see an old man cut down to the stump; leaning on a shivered lance; propped up on a lonely foot," he tells the crew. "'Tis Ahab—his body's part; but Ahab's soul's a centipede, that moves upon a hundred legs" (561). The captain distances himself from a corporeally defined self, but Starbuck has no such luck. The next day, he will realize the burden of being an extension of Ahab's physicality. "My legs feel faint," he says, as he watches the battle from ship (567).

The more disembodied Ahab becomes, the more he inhabits the bodies of other men. This line of thinking receives its fullest expression when, during the third day's chase, Ahab threatens to harpoon his crew and then shouts, "Ye are not other men, but my arms and my legs; and so obey me" (568).[86] The crew are both his prey and prostheses, and whatever interdependence he seemed to promise was simply a means to further his domination. The master who walks over his crew turns out to be the master who wants to destroy their autonomy and animate their limbs. As we know from Samoa, Melville did not see an inescapable link between dispossession and dismemberment, and from battlefields and whaleships to train tracks and farmyards, amputation was relatively commonplace in the nineteenth century. The tragedy of *Moby-Dick* centers on Ahab's ability to turn the feeling of dispossession into a means of emotional and corporeal control. The contagion that Stubb and Starbuck should fear is not limb loss but authoritarian aggrievement. Chapter 6 delves into the politics of this aggrievement, arguing for the continued relevance of the tyrannical Ahab that dominated Melville criticism during the Cold War. For now, however, it is important to recognize how Ahab builds power out of his wound. His ivory limb reciprocally matches the limbs of others, as well as the gun and harpoon.

In *The Wounded Storyteller* (1995), Frank addresses the ways in which "shared corporeality" impacts who we are to—and for—each other. "The shared condition of being bodies becomes a basis of empathic relations among living beings," he explains. "Albert Schweitzer expressed this concern in his phrase, the 'brotherhood of those who bear the mark of pain.'"[87] It is tempting to see this "other-relatedness" in Ahab's devotion to Pip and his eventual decision to leave Starbuck on the ship during the third day's

AHAB, WALKING 55

hunt. But ultimately Frank's comments illuminate how treacherously Ahab exploits the brotherhood of men in convincing them to bear the burden of his woes. As the penultimate chapter indicates, the crew become one body unified under Ahab's will:

> They were one man, not thirty. For as the one ship that held them all; though it was put together of all contrasting things—oak, and maple, and pine wood; iron, and pitch, and hemp—yet all these ran into each other in the one concrete hull, which shot on its way, both balanced and directed by the long central keel; even so, all the individualities of the crew, this man's valor, that man's fear; guilt and guiltiness, all varieties were welded into oneness, and were all directed to that fatal goal which Ahab their one lord and keel did point to. (557)

The passage beautifully celebrates collective work, and with good reason, C. L. R. James praised its portrait of men "freely subordinated to the excitement of achieving a common goal" and "moved by feelings common to all humanity in its greatest moments."[88] But as James admits, such is the false promise of autocratic rule. The unity originates in the crew's being embodied into Ahab's pursuit. If he is the keel of their ship, they are his new limbs, the individual arms and legs that coordinate under his command (568). The passage touts the brotherhood of whalemade man, each of them subordinate to the grievance represented by the ivory leg.

Ahab, of course, can only embody others if they are willing to submit. For all their fears and misgivings, no one on the *Pequod* mounts a meaningful resistance. Being captain gives Ahab significant authority, but his extraordinary power comes from the fact that his wound-collecting has become the source of collective meaning and collaborative work. Whether made of whalebone or wood, the peg leg suggests a sense of dispossession that differentiates Ahab from other amputees and yet binds him closer to his men. Among the elements that make up the *Pequod*'s final assault—the iron, pitch, pine, and hemp—Melville gives us a leader who embodies in his wounds a sense of cosmic wrongs. Like many nineteenth-century amputees, Lord Nelson's empty sleeve signified his sacrifice to the nation. Ahab's prosthetic leg signifies the sacrifice that others will make on his behalf.[89] The crew's sacrifice to his tyranny compensates for his loss. Dismemberment

56 THE PROSTHETIC ARTS OF *MOBY-DICK*

threatened antebellum Americans as economic producers and self-defining agents. Ahab expands on that threat, seeing injury itself as an affront to the democratic dream of being "the prophet and the fulfiller one" (168). Ironically, his wounds become the site of both power and dependence as the captain relies on others not only to support his quest, but to make the devices that allow him to stand, walk, and hunt.

2

Bone to Bone

Trauma and Prosthetic Time

Among the many lessons Herman Melville learned from Shakespeare, one was how to embed stage directions in a character's lines.[1] The presence of this lesson appears in Chapter 108 of *Moby-Dick*, "Ahab and the Carpenter," in which Melville dramatizes the making of an ivory leg. Interspersing conversation and soliloquy, the chapter dismantles one of the novel's central symbols by presenting it as screws, pads, slabs of ivory, and leather straps. The captain approaches the carpenter, who is simultaneously filing the whalebone and sneezing from the bone dust floating up around him. "Just in time, sir," the carpenter says. "I will now mark the length. Let me measure, sir." Noting that he has stood for such measurements before, Ahab agrees, but when the carpenter proceeds, the captain interjects himself into the process. "There, keep thy finger on it," he commands.[2] The line tersely gestures toward the handling of an unmentioned measuring rod that the carpenter holds to the captain's side. The invisibility of this prop, and the reader's need to infer that it is there, captures the complexity of the carpenter's task. His measurement must encompass the natural leg of the past, the empty space of the present, and the bony prosthetic the captain will wear into the future. The construction of Ahab's prosthesis begins with material parts, but it ultimately traverses the immeasurable experiences of trauma, memory, and time. Like the missing leg, this nod to Shakespeare has the presence of a ghost.

Earlier in the novel, Tashtego reported that the captain shipped with a "quiver" of ivory legs, but that detail must have faded into the background when Melville recognized the rewards in staging the construction of an ivory limb (124). The scene informs us that when we speak of Ahab's artificial leg, we refer to at least four distinct prostheses mentioned in *Moby-Dick*. Chronologically, the first device became "violently displaced" while Ahab was home in Nantucket, leaving him wounded on the ground, his groin nearly pierced by the stake-like ivory joist (463). After an extended

The Prosthetic Arts of Moby-Dick. David Haven Blake, Oxford University Press. © Oxford University Press 2024.
DOI: 10.1093/oso/9780197780510.003.0003

58   THE PROSTHETIC ARTS OF *MOBY-DICK*

recovery, both onshore and at sea, Ahab appears on deck wearing "the barbaric white leg" that shocks Ishmael with its grimness and appears in Stubb's dream (124). Ahab wears this prosthesis until it cracks upon his return from the *Samuel Enderby*, where he visits with Captain Boomer, the English captain who lost an arm to Moby Dick. Dutifully crafted by the carpenter, the replacement is the "ivory" that Pip ominously hears on the quarterdeck as he waits in Ahab's cabin, feeling downhearted while his master walks above him (535). As we have seen, Ahab loses this third prosthesis during the second day's battle, and on the next day, he dies while wearing a simple wooden peg leg made from his boat's shattered keel.

The devices are distinct objects—fashioned, fitted, and attached to the captain at specific moments in time. In contrast to his Greek predecessors Oedipus and Philoctetes, whose wounds remained part of their swollen, oozing flesh, Ahab's severed limb is replaced by prostheses that are so haunted by the original that he often refers to them simply as legs. To borrow a term from Sarah Jain, the physicality of these prostheses, their composition of iron, leather, wood, and bone, conveys "the material differences of absences."[3] Cobbled together from available substances, the devices cast the captain across time, their presence as objects summoning a lost limb, a prior injury, an ominous warning, and the promise of future vengeance. Time itself is condensed in each prosthetic, and each prosthetic marks the passage of time. A conspicuously wishful example of metonymy, the phrase "Ahab's leg" acknowledges that the wound remains present in the apparatus that succeeds it.

Moby-Dick has little regard for the calendar. Except for the *Pequod*'s Christmas Day departure and the intriguing passage in "The Fountain" when Melville records the precise moment of composition—"(fifteen and a quarter minutes past one o'clock P.M. of this sixteenth day of December, A.D. 1850)"—time on the *Pequod* sweeps over months, weeks, and days (370). When Ishmael mentions the calendar, he almost always does so to blur it. "Days, weeks passed," he tells us in "The Spirit Spout" (232) as if no one had thought to make a precise calculation. "It was a week or two after the last whaling scene recounted," he remarks in "The Pequod Meets the Rose-bud" because, to sailors on a years-long voyage, the difference would hardly matter (402). Homer's Odysseus describes his adventures with notable precision: ten days drifting in the ocean, seven full years on Calypso's island, eighteen days sailing to the Phaecians.[4] The *Pequod* follows a looser accounting, one that suits an open-ended voyage across a cosmic sea. "Time and tide flow wide," Starbuck says, using a phrase that could also characterize Ishmael's narration (169).

Amid this watery sense of time, the scene with the carpenter marks the end of an unusually identifiable and prolonged day. Ahab compares whalebone prostheses with Captain Boomer, feels the exigency of revenge, and then, upon returning to the *Pequod*, supervises the nighttime construction of his new artificial limb. The day's events carry across nine chapters (100–108), though in four of those chapters, Ishmael ponders the whale's skeleton and its appearance in the fossil record. What ties these chapters together is the primacy of bone. Sturdy, dusty, and resistant to time, bones are the harvested material of a whaler's life in passing from backbone to trellis, from tooth to scrimshaw, from vertebrae to billiard ball, and from jawbone to artificial shin. Frozen in ice, buried in soil, and imprinted in clay, they are a record of geologic history and a testament to the whale's longevity as a species. "Ahab's harpoon had shed older blood than the Pharaohs,' " Ishmael writes, pitting his nineteenth-century captain against an ancient and noble foe (457). When enslaved persons on an Alabama plantation discover the skeleton of an extinct whale, they pronounce it "the bones of one of the fallen angels" (457). As everyone on the *Pequod* knows, however, bones are also fragile and vulnerable to contusions, fractures, and breaks. In Ahab's battle with Moby Dick, Ishmael sees the collision of human and tertiary time.

In examining this single day on the *Pequod*, we turn our attention to the making and meaning of Ahab's prosthesis. The previous chapter discussed how Melville uses the socialization of Ahab's ivory leg and the prostheticization of the crew to characterize the brutal extension of his power. Reducing others to his arms and legs, he transforms prosthetic embodiment into an instrument of autocratic rule. Chapter 2 focuses on what the construction of Ahab's prosthesis reveals about his conception of himself. My concern in this chapter has less to do with the crew's response to Ahab's disability than it does with the ontological problems raised by his prostheses. The staging of the carpenter's work prompts a Shakespearean dialogue about how Ahab's wounds, limbs, and vengeance have altered his sense of being. The scene's comedy explores the way dismemberment seemingly extends his physical self into another realm, spreading identity across different species, conditions, and time periods.

Part of this inquiry involves the proliferation of artificial limbs in the mid-nineteenth century, for the scenes on both the *Pequod* and the *Samuel*

60 THE PROSTHETIC ARTS OF *MOBY-DICK*

Enderby consider the various forms that prostheses can take and the medical situations they seek to remedy. Melville offers the carpenter as our clownish, soliloquizing guide to the way prostheses represent the combined forces of technology, medicine, capital, and fashion. Humble in design and form, the whalebone contraptions exist in a broader social sphere of elaborate commercial limbs sold in international markets. Melville invokes the history of this industry (and the medical discourses adjacent to it) in positioning the *Pequod*'s carpenter and the *Enderby*'s surgeon in implicitly dueling roles, each one reflecting on the prostheticized body from their comically distinct perspectives.

As much as Ahab cares about selecting the "stoutest, clearest-grained" bones for the carpenter's work, his vision of the ivory leg remains mired in the long "ancestry and posterity of Grief" (464–465). The captain hints at the longevity of his trauma when he describes the pain he experiences in his missing leg. Years ahead of medical science, Melville was interested in the phenomenon of phantom limbs, and in Chapter 108 he contemplates the spectral pain of amputees. To a certain extent, the crushing feeling in Ahab's lost leg encapsulates the afterlife of his injury. "Trauma," Cathy Caruth has explained, "is not locatable in the simple violent or original event in an individual's past."[5] Instead, as Robert Stolorow has commented, "In the region of trauma all duration or stretching along collapses, past becomes present," and, other than repetition, "future loses all meaning."[6] For Ahab, trauma does not amount to the collapse of time as much as the condensation of time into the event itself and the life that is lived thereafter. His anguish may be "the direct issue of a former woe," but it is through that anguish that the past remains alive, ever present and defining (464). The inexplicable feeling leads him to wonder about the origins of pain and whether invisible powers inhabit the body, ensuring that suffering and punishment continue even though the flesh itself has gone away. In "The Quarter-Deck," Ahab questioned whether dark spirits control Moby Dick. The riddle he poses to the carpenter is whether a similarly unknown, presumably malicious force has supernaturally bridged his artificial and phantom legs.

The posterity of Ahab's grief inexorably leads to aggrievement and the feeling of resentment that demands his future action. Even as the carpenter's work prompts questions about embodiment and being, the prosthesis explicitly anticipates the moment of the captain's revenge. In a detail that barely registers in Melville scholarship, but this chapter explores in depth, the carpenter incorporates into the ivory limb a highly polished oval slate. Ahab uses this slate to calculate the *Pequod*'s position in relation to the summer feeding grounds where he expects to kill Moby Dick. This synthesis of slate and prosthetic leg establishes an intriguing counterpoint to Ahab's reflections on the never-ending trauma of bodiless pain. *Moby-Dick*'s day of whalebones and missing limbs positions the material exigency of revenge alongside what David Wills has called "the ghostly space of the prosthetic."[7] These chapters grapple with the spiritual and material worlds, inviting readers to consider how shadows inhabit bodies, ghosts inhabit prostheses, the past inhabits the future, and transgressors inhabit the transgressed. Ahab's planning for revenge—his calculation of time, space, and maritime conditions on his artificial body part—establishes a direct narrative arc in which the past will remain present until he violently cancels his obligation out. What eludes the carpenter and mystifies Ahab is the extent to which the prosthesis embodies his sense of dispossession, as well as his empowerment.

Making Prostheses

As he did with Stubb and Flask, Melville makes comedy out of the carpenter's interaction with Ahab's artificial leg. This was not a sign of disrespect to the dismembered. Shakespeare had shown Melville how to engage serious topics through the humor of misunderstanding, and accordingly the scene brings the captain into conversation with a "pure manipulator" who, with his "old, crutch-like, antediluvian, wheezing humorousness," takes on a prosthetic relation to the ship (467). Like Sheffield contrivances with their folding screwdrivers, scissors, and tweezers, the carpenter can address a wide range of tasks, from building a birdcage to pulling teeth to drilling holes for shark bone earrings (468). Ishmael spends all of Chapter 107 struggling to identify the carpenter's distinctive neurodiversity, questioning whether his "impersonal stolidity" and "all-ramifying heartlessness" betrayed "a sort of unintelligence" in him (467). Intimately connected to the "infinite of things," the carpenter seemed almost to work by "a kind of deaf and dumb spontaneous literal process," Ishmael recalls, suggesting that sensation for him was a form of thinking. "His brain, if he ever had one, must have early oozed along into the muscles of his fingers" (468).[8] The carpenter's skills make him a uniquely mismatched counterpart to "a man of greatly superior natural force, with a globular brain and a ponderous heart" (73).

62　THE PROSTHETIC ARTS OF *MOBY-DICK*

This emphasis on materiality suffuses the dramatic setting of "Ahab and the Carpenter." From the beginning, the stage directions highlight the labor of construction. Surrounded by "*Slabs of ivory, leather straps, pads, screws, and various tools of all sorts lying about the bench*," the carpenter is "*busily filing the ivory joist for the leg, which joist is firmly fixed in the vice*" (469). Ishmael's fear of Ahab's "barbaric white leg" pervades *Moby-Dick*, but as he "hummingly soliloquizes" to himself, the carpenter offers a crucially different perspective, treating the prosthesis as a materials-based problem (468). His repeated sneezing replaces Ishmael's dread with frustration over the differences between bone and wood:

> Drat the file, and drat the bone! That is hard which should be soft, and that is soft which should be hard. So we go, who file old jaws and shin-bones. Let's try another. Aye, now, this works better (*sneezes*). Halloa, this bone dust is (*sneezes*)—why it's (*sneezes*)—yes it's (*sneezes*)—bless my soul, it won't let me speak! This is what an old fellow gets now for working in dead lumber. Saw a live tree, and you don't get this dust; amputate a live bone, and you don't get it (*sneezes*). (469)

Melville's comedy cuts against the somber quality of the task, effectively subordinating the medical emergency of amputation to the mechanical emergency of an unstable prosthesis.

The setting reworks Hamlet's conversation with the gravedigger in putting a rustic, plainspoken workman alongside a more philosophical counterpart who speaks to him in riddles. Melville gives the carpenter Hamlet's role of handling the dead bone, but instead of reflecting on the impermanence of life, he diligently fits it to Ahab's waiting stump. Quizzing a manmaker, rather than a grave-maker, Ahab pines to be remade as a less vulnerable, Titan-like man, picturing himself as standing fifty feet high, with a chest "modelled after the Thames Tunnel," "legs with roots to 'em," "about a quarter of an acre of fine brains," and "no heart at all" (470).[9] Hamlet wonders how men such as Alexander the Great could be reduced to dust and then ultimately become the clay plugs used to stop up barrels of beer.[10] Surrounded by dust, the carpenter envisions Judgment Day as the moment when "the resurrection fellow comes a-calling with his horn for all legs, true or false, as brewery-men go round collecting old beer barrels, to fill 'em up again" (472). Until that day, however, the craftsman (who grudgingly makes a life buoy out of a coffin) trusts in the temporary redemption of man-made limbs that help the dismembered walk again.

The chapter's dramatic structure reinforces the carpenter's alternating attention between the missing and artificial legs. Lit by lanterns, the workbench and forge promise that a craftsman can provide a serviceable restoration if the captain will accept a physical substitute. As the blacksmith makes the ferrule (cap) to prevent the piece from splitting and the buckle that will attach the leather straps to the captain's waist and thigh, the carpenter feels lucky that "there's no knee-joint to make." His task is to create "but a mere shinbone," which he says is as easy as crafting a gardener's hop-pole (469). Making sure the bone is long and slim enough for such a tall, heron-like man, the carpenter both measures and materializes absence. "For most folks one pair of legs lasts a lifetime," he later muses. "But Ahab; oh he's a hard driver. Look, driven one leg to death, and spavined the other for life, and now wears out bone legs by the cord" (472). Amid the cutting, filing, and sneezing, the carpenter looks on his production with a craftsman's pride: "What a leg this is!" he says. "It looks like a real live leg, filed down to nothing but the core; he'll be standing on this to-morrow" (472).

Melville knew about many of the new prostheses being developed in England and the United States, and although faraway in the South China Sea, the carpenter reflects on the shops and gadgets he has seen on land. Wanting "to put a good finish" on the piece, he laments the lack of time to make Ahab "as neat a leg now as ever (*sneezes*) scraped to a lady in a parlor." "Those buckskin legs and calves of legs I've seen in shop windows wouldn't compare at all," he privately boasts. "They soak water, they do; and of course get rheumatic, and have to be doctored (*sneezes*) with washes and lotions, just like live legs" (469). Although extensive innovations would come during the Civil War, the antebellum period featured numerous developments in the creation of more elaborate prostheses than the highly finished wooden limbs that wealthy eighteenth-century Americans preferred because they blended in with the furniture. A delegate to the Continental Congress, the New York statesman Gouverneur Morris was well known for his oak prosthesis that recreated the tapered legs of an upholstered armchair.[11]

Prosthetics in the 1840s often included limbs that could be manipulated at the elbow or knee. The development of footlike protrusions at the end of artificial legs permitted amputees such as General Santa Anna to wear boots that furthered the perception that, underneath their clothes, they had natural legs. Stephen Mihm has described the pressure on nineteenth-century manufacturers to produce and purchase naturalistic artificial limbs to help amputees appear in public without offending others' sensibilities. "In higher social positions and at an age when *appearances are realities*," Oliver

64 THE PROSTHETIC ARTS OF *MOBY-DICK*

Wendell Holmes wrote, "it becomes important to provide the cripple with a limb which shall be presentable in society." Holmes wanted to eradicate disability from public view, expressing sentiments that would later result in the banning of the physically disabled in cities across the United States.[12] The carpenter speaks as more of a craftsman than an ableist when he regrets that, in his haste, he can't make a prosthesis that is good enough for the parlor or, as Holmes would put it, that could be "tolerated under the chandeliers."[13]

These class-based concerns resulted in a wide variety of products in Europe and the United States (Figure 5). Developed in England, the Anglesey leg was popular due to its association with Lord Uxbridge, the Marquess of Anglesey, who had lost his leg at the Battle of Waterloo. With its system of cogs and gears, the leg became the standard among wealthy amputees through the first decades of the nineteenth century. When the Palmer leg appeared in the United States in the 1840s, it employed a system of catgut tendons that allowed for movement at both the ankle and knee. Supporters on both sides of the Atlantic widely praised the Palmer as the successor to the Anglesey, and the company's promotional materials claimed that the marquess himself was going to order one.[14] The Palmer Leg Establishment was headquartered east of Melville's Arrowhead in Springfield, Massachusetts, but with its renowned College of Physicians and Surgeons, Philadelphia provided an especially vibrant prosthetics market. The makers of the Palmer, Salem, and Bly legs published pamphlets (Figure 6) touting the value of their wares, often filled with tips for amputation surgery and testimonials from physicians and patients as to their natural movement and appearance.[15] Edgar Allan Poe satirized the industry in his 1839 short story "The Man That Was Used Up," in which a war hero is wholly formed by artificial parts.

The construction of the ivory leg foregrounds the problem of conceptualizing a body of natural and replacement limbs. In one sense Ahab makes it easy on the carpenter by having such physically simple expectations. Making a version of the peg leg that the poor had worn for centuries, the carpenter avoids the problems of trying to imitate human flesh. The captain's bone legs may wear out by the cord, but they don't absorb water or require special oil or ointments. Holmes had applauded the ability of the new products to disguise disabilities and thereby appeal to polite norms. But Melville, like the carpenter, strips the prosthesis to its core, a "mere shinbone" that would fit in a garden better than a dining room. And yet, the

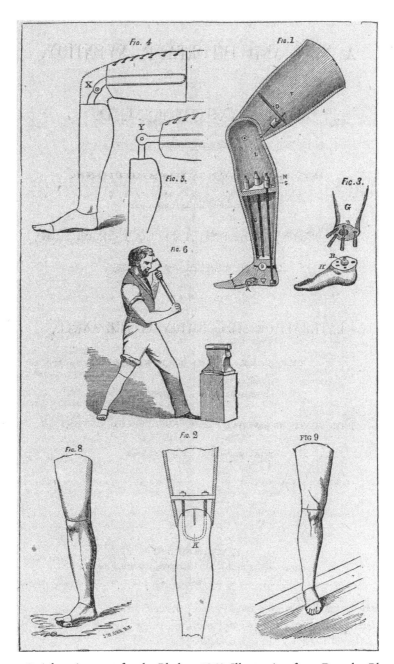

Figure 5 Advertisement for the Bly leg, 1862. Illustration from Douglas Bly, MD, *A New and Important Invention* (Rochester, NY: Press of Curtis, Butts & Co., Union and Advertiser office, 1862), an advertising pamphlet.
Image courtesy of the American Antiquarian Society.

Figure 6 Advertisement for Yerger and Ord, mechanical leg, from *Rae's Philadelphia Pictorial Directory & Panoramic Advertiser*, 1851.
Image courtesy of the Library Company of Philadelphia.

process of embodying the leg and fitting it to Ahab's mind is quite complex. The carpenter's sneezing is his own somatic response to a cross-species transference in which the whalebone becomes the locus of trauma for the nameless donor whale as well as the vengeful recipient who, even before it has come out of the vise, has already identified the object as being his own. Comfortable with things, the carpenter trusts that artificial limbs are pragmatic on earth and equally worthy in the eyes of the Lord. But like Hamlet, Ahab perceives in these bones a sense of loss that the workman does not.

Phantom Pain

Attempts to allegorize the scene, or to see it as a purely philosophic meditation on corporeality, do it a disservice when they neglect its explicit physicality.[16] The carpenter's repurposing of whalebone brings not only excessive dust, but also a sense of history, irony, and violence that a wooden prosthesis would not contain. The prosthetic arrangement of species to species, and bone to bone, establishes an indispensable setting for Ahab's reflections on embodiment and the unexpected legacies of dismemberment. Melville puts the material and the spectral on the same stage when, as the sneezing carpenter files the two ivory brackets that will run up either side of the captain's thigh, Ahab reflects on what we now call phantom limb pain. "When I come to mount this leg thou makest," he tells the carpenter, "I shall nevertheless feel another leg in the same identical place with it; that is, carpenter, my old lost leg; the flesh and blood one, I mean. Canst thou not drive that old Adam away?" (471). We know that Ahab continues to suffer, that he wakes with his sheets in knots and that he walks the deck to escape his cabin's tomb-like solitude (128). The problem Ahab poses to the carpenter is whether corporeal experience is so strong that it remains after the body has been severed into pieces. To what extent will a new prosthesis help him shed his former appendage and cease feeling its original pain?

The carpenter is no philosopher, but he has heard of such pains and is eager to draw the elliptical captain into further discussion:

> Truly, sir, I begin to understand somewhat now. Yes, I have heard something curious on that score, sir; how that a dismasted man never entirely loses the feeling of his old spar, but it will be still pricking him at times. May I humbly ask if it be really so, sir?

68   THE PROSTHETIC ARTS OF *MOBY-DICK*

> It is, man. Look, put thy live leg here in the place where mine once was; so, now, here is only one distinct leg to the eye, yet two to the soul. Where thou feelest tingling life; there, exactly there, there to a hair, do I. Is't a riddle?
>
> I should humbly call it a poser, sir. (471)

In recounting his dream, Stubb differentiated between real and artificial legs, concluding that the peg leg was too unnatural to be associated with the captain himself. Ahab and the carpenter are more open to the puzzle of embodiment, wondering whether amputated limbs continue to have a presence in their original bodies. The eye recognizes only the flesh and blood, but "the tangibility of sensation," as Leslie Katz writes, suggests two limbs to the soul.[17] If the leg is a poser, as the carpenter wonders, how do we differentiate it from the amputee? Or is it the presence of some original soma-spiritual connection that cannot be severed by the surgeon's knife or whale's teeth? Or, as some nineteenth-century physicians speculated, is it a connection that amputation creates? The exchange dramatizes the idea that "when one suffers chronic pain," as Michael Snediker puts it, one "is ontologized... by the very thing one can't see."[18]

Ahab does not compare his ivory leg to the limb he lost. Rather, he draws the carpenter into his experience, suggesting that his phantom leg is as real and responsive as the live one positioned in its place. This blurring of self and other corresponds to the experience of some amputees, as Pilar Martínez Benedí and Ralph Savarese have explained. Ahab, they argue, exhibits the symptoms of mirror touch synesthesia in which amputees come to feel their phantom limbs in someone else's body.[19] The sociologist Cassandra Crawford indicates a similar condition when she uses the term "phantom occupation" to describe the sensation of lost limbs occupying objects as well as other persons.[20] "Where thou feelest tingling life; there, exactly there, there to a hair, do I," Ahab says, pointing to the carpenter's leg and claiming that neurologically he feels it as his own. "All I am sure of," the philosopher Babalanja says in *Mardi*, "is a sort of prickly sensation all over me, which they call life."[21] In an echo of Ahab's command about the measuring rod earlier in the scene, Melville lyrically indicates that Ahab points to the carpenter's leg—"there, exactly there, there to a hair"—but of course the *there* encompasses what can and cannot be seen. Ahab's description of phantom pain suggests the possibility that he can embody not only the carpenter's handiwork, but also his tingling limb—an ironic outcome for a character whose impersonal stolidity, according to Ishmael, shades off "into the surrounding infinite of things" (467).[22]

The problem of phantom limbs has occupied philosophers, spiritualists, doctors, and patients since at least the tenth century. When the French doctor Ambroise Paré reported the phenomenon in 1552, he felt compelled to acknowledge how fantastic the stories seemed:

> Verily it is a thing strange and prodigious, which will scarce be credited unless by such who have seen with their own eyes and heard with their own ears, the patients, who have many months after the cutting away of the leg, grievously complained that they yet felt exceedingly great pain of that leg so cut off.[23]

Melville most likely read about limb pain in James Fenimore Cooper's 1823 novel *The Pioneers*. (His uncle Peter Gansevoort's copy is now at the New York Public Library.) The novel includes an anecdote about an amputee whose severed leg had been buried in such a narrow box that he could feel its pain shooting through the surviving limbs.[24] Melville found a similar tale in Nathaniel Hawthorne's "The Unpardonable Sin," which he read in *Dollar* magazine the summer he was feverishly writing Hawthorne about his frustrations with *Moby-Dick*.[25] The story includes the soap-boiler Giles, who could feel "an invisible thumb and fingers" after losing his hand in a steam-engine accident. "Though the corporeal hand was gone," Hawthorne wrote, "a spiritual member remained."[26]

The Civil War produced approximately sixty thousand amputations, and with them came a new concern about the problems of rehabilitation and adaptation.[27] American neurologist Dr. Silas Weir Mitchell coined the term "phantom limb" in 1871, five years after he introduced the idea in a widely read short story in the *Atlantic Monthly* about a Union veteran who, in attending a séance, is momentarily reunited with his amputated legs.[28] Mitchell's research concluded that the problem was neurological and stemmed from divided nerves during the amputation that gave the sensation of an entire limb. The presence of this "unseen ghost of the lost part" seemed tragic to Mitchell, who envisioned "thousands of spirit limbs haunting as many good soldiers" and painfully reminding them of their loss.[29]

Researchers now believe that phantom limb pain is a consequence of the brain's adjusting its map or image of the amputated body. Every brain contains a map of its neural parts, but as neurologist V. S. Ramachandran has

70   THE PROSTHETIC ARTS OF *MOBY-DICK*

discovered, when amputation deprives some of those parts from their usual stimulus, stimuli from other parts of the body will satisfy the neural need. In one series of experiments, for example, the sensations a patient felt in his amputated hand stemmed from specific touch points on his face.[30] Malcolm MacLachlan explains that "while the neural 'image' of the amputated limb remains on the somatosensory strip, it is actually stimulated by inputs from elsewhere." The reorganization of the cortex occurs rapidly after amputation as the brain adjusts to its new neural environment.[31] Phantom limb pain is the cortex's way of compensating for the neural stimuli it previously received from the missing limb.

Although he proposed that nerve damage was the source of such pain, Mitchell employed a spiritualist language to convey what amputation meant to his soldier-patients. Melville includes an analogous scene in *Mardi* when Samoa treats his removed arm with great care. Having admired his steely acceptance of amputation, the American Taji derides the islander's reverent view of his lost extremity:

> But shall the sequel be told? How that, superstitiously averse to burying in the sea the dead limb of a body yet living; since in that case Samoa held, that he must very soon drown and follow it; and how, that equally dreading to keep the thing near him, he at last hung it aloft from the topmast-stay; where yet it was suspended, bandaged over and over in cerements. The hand that must have locked many others in friendly clasp, or smote a foe, was no food, thought Samoa, for fowls of the air nor fishes of the sea.[32]

Taji's tone reflects his ambivalence toward Samoa's culture. The sacramental treatment of the limb comes from the belief that, because they are intimately connected, the destiny of the part will surely affect the whole. Samoa's belief may have seemed quaintly nonsensical to Melville's nineteenth-century readers. The nation that delighted in the symbolism of US troops capturing Santa Anna's wooden leg had responded with mockery when, nine years earlier, the Mexican general had held an elaborate funeral for his real leg after it had been blown off by a French cannon. In a highly popular book, George Wilkins Kendall commented that with all the processions and "great pomp and ceremony" surrounding Santa Anna's limb, "I have little doubt that the leg, in pickle, is of infinitely more service to him than when attached to his own proper person."[33]

These responses betray a prevailing sense of ethnic, political, and religious bigotry. What they don't reflect is any thought about how such customs might help reconcile amputees to their violently altered bodies and, in the process, ease or eliminate phantom pain.[34] The more Taji thinks about it, the more Samoa's amputation suggests a problem of identity as he projects his own sense of the body onto the islander's experience. Was Samoa "the dead arm swinging high as Haman? Or the living trunk below?" "The residual part of Samoa was alive," Taji asks, "and therefore we say it was he. But which of the writhing sections of a ten times severed worm, is the worm proper?"[35] After pushing readers to consider whether our limbs are ourselves, the American reinforces the belief that anything but the normative, fully functioning body is less than human. The severed arm, like the Persian king Haman, hangs high above the deck, an enemy of the faith that Adam was made in God's image. "For myself," Taji comments, "I ever regarded Samoa as but a large fragment of a man, not a man complete." He argues that some of the greatest warriors in history came home as only partial men—including Lord Nelson, who, after the Battle of Teneriffe, found himself "but three-quarters of a man."[36]

Taji anticipates the argument that the Civil War veteran would make in Mitchell's 1866 short story, that a man "is not his brain, or any one part of it, but all of his economy, and that to lose any part must lessen this sense of his own existence."[37] In the world of Herman Melville, however, that sentiment proves to be inadequate, and Taji's perspective on dismemberment undergoes multiple revisions in the books and stories ahead. In *Moby-Dick*, Ahab's discussion of phantom limbs speculates on the soma-spiritual connection between the body part and the self. Like Ahab, Lord Nelson complained of phantom pain, the two men feeling "the ghost of the lost part" as they went about their post-trauma lives. Long after his arm had been amputated, Nelson could feel fingers digging into the palm of his missing hand, and although surgeons told him the sensation came from a nerve being accidentally stitched into an artery, he settled for a different explanation.[38] To Nelson, the phantom limb was "direct evidence for the existence of the soul." "If an arm can exist after it is removed," Ramachandran explains, "why can't the whole person survive physical annihilation of the body?" Nelson saw the pain as proof "for the existence of the spirit long after it has cast off its attire."[39]

Ahab viewed his phantom limb in similarly metaphysical terms, though he understood the torment to be proof not of salvation but of doom. In a

72 THE PROSTHETIC ARTS OF *MOBY-DICK*

wicked moment of projection, he includes the carpenter in his thoughts about damnation. "If I still feel the smart of my crushed leg, though it be now so long dissolved; then, why mayst not thou, carpenter, feel the fiery pains of hell for ever, and without a body?" (471). If the absent body still feels pain on earth, then surely it can continue to feel its due punishments in hell. He predicates these questions on the feeling that phantoms inhabit us at any given time. Ahab previously speculated that he was occupying the carpenter's leg. Moments later he presents the phantom as having invaded his own body, challenging the carpenter to consider whether "some entire, living, thinking thing may not be invisibly and uninterpenetratingly standing" where he stands (471). The question is reminiscent of the captain's wondering whether an invisible force secretly operates behind the pasteboard mask of Moby Dick. Now he asks whether "eavesdroppers" inhabit corporeal space, taunting the body from within (471). His suspicions lead to an unsettling paradox: he has not simply lost a body part; his lost limb has been occupied by an unknown spectral force.

As the maker of whalebone legs, the carpenter is the most likely crewmember to rid the captain of his pain. Researchers today try to help amputees by reversing the reorganization of the cortex, using mirrors and trick photography to deceive the brain into thinking the limb continues to provide stimuli and still exists. The fit of a lifelike prosthesis can help this process. Some researchers contend that as long as the pain can be eliminated, phantom limbs themselves can benefit patients. According to neurologist Oliver Sacks, "All amputees, and all those who work with them, know that a phantom limb is essential if an artificial limb is to be used." The phantom limb, he argues, is instrumental in helping the mind accommodate the prosthesis and in convincing the wearer that it can function like a leg. Sacks quotes a fellow neurologist who concludes that "no amputee with an artificial lower limb can walk on it satisfactorily until the body image, in other words, the phantom, is incorporated into it."[40] Although his treatment focused elsewhere, Mitchell anticipated such a relationship when he noted that a movable prosthesis with a visible foot reduced the common sensation of a shortened (or "reverse telescoped") phantom leg. The act of walking seemed to trick the brain as the remaining muscles acted "in locomotion with the acquired member."[41] As Crawford puts it, the artificial limb "coaxed" the phantom into place.[42]

Melville had neither research nor terminology to draw upon, but he sensed a kinship between phantom body parts and their material replacements.

BONE TO BONE   73

Ahab asks the carpenter whether his craftsmanship will drive the "old Adam" of his phantom limb away, and like Hamlet, the captain initiates a theological conversation for which the workman is ill prepared. The blacksmith is "Prometheus," hell is probable, and as a "manmaker," the carpenter should exchange his bone for clay (470). The carpenter, of course, doesn't understand this level of discourse, and he doesn't recognize the comedy in which he unknowingly participates. Immersed in material process, he works the whalebone with a pragmatic devotion to craft, effectively stripping it of the history and myth the previous chapters had provided. In the carpenter's world, bones produce dust rather than metaphysics, and phantoms only produce pain.

Comparative Anatomies

Near the beginning of *The Confidence-Man*, Melville includes a stunning scene for any reader of *Moby-Dick*. A Black man with seemingly deformed legs asks for alms on a steamboat traveling down the Mississippi River. Going by the name Black Guinea, he encourages the white travelers to toss him coins, which, in an act of humiliating showmanship, he catches in his mouth, and then cracks his beat-up tambourine. To use Melville's word, the scene is "grotesque." And then a white man with a wooden leg steps out of the crowd and accuses Black Guinea of being a sham. "He's some white operator, betwisted and painted up for a decoy," the wooden-legged man croaks, casting doubt on the performance of both racial subservience and disability.[43] The crowd chastises the wooden-legged man for his lack of faith in humanity, but the accusation sets the tone for a novel that mistrusts appearances and undermines charitable thought. As the confidence tricks pile up, readers can conclude that Black Guinea was, perhaps, a fraud, especially after they encounter another alms-seeker who deceptively claims that *his* legs were damaged at the Battle of Contreras during the Mexican War.

While no one in *Moby-Dick* doubts Ahab's condition and the story of his injury, the novel acknowledges that the disabled face routine skepticism and scrutiny. In a series of chapters describing the difficulty of visually representing whales, Ishmael recalls "a crippled beggar (or *kedger*, as the sailors say)" from the Tower Hill neighborhood of London who displays a "painted board before him, representing the tragic scene in which he lost his leg" (269). The painting features three whales and three boats, one of

74   THE PROSTHETIC ARTS OF *MOBY-DICK*

which is being smashed to pieces by leviathan jaws. For ten years, the crowds have doubted the man's dismemberment and story, but based on the accuracy of the painted scene, Ishmael vouches for both. To the "incredulous world," he praises the Tower Hill artist, proclaiming, "His three whales are as good whales as were ever published" in his dockside neighborhood. The painting leads Ishmael to conclude that the artist has an "unquestionable" stump (269).

Like the Tower Hill artist, Ahab is largely left alone in "ruefully contemplating his own amputation" (269). While his authority and authenticity are never challenged, he remains utterly isolated on the *Pequod* as a leader and an amputee. Crewmembers fear and discuss the ivory leg, but rarely do they talk about it with the captain himself. The isolation of the Tower Hill artist and the man with the wooden leg provides a useful context for thinking about Ahab's meeting with Captain Boomer of the *Samuel Enderby*. Both having encountered Moby Dick, the captains recognize in each other a fellow victim and amputee, but the sense of mutuality proves to be short lived. A prelude to the carpenter's construction of the artificial leg, Chapter 100, "Leg and Arm," introduces a study in contrasting temperaments, nationalities, modes of maritime leadership, and whalebone prostheses. Emerging as an explicit alternative to Ahab's aggrievement, the jovial English captain accepts his limb loss as a natural consequence of hunting the "noblest and biggest" whale he had ever seen (438). Boomer's presence suggests both the singularity of Ahab's vengeance and the extent to which he rejects the self-knowledge that might come from interacting with someone similarly impaired. With an almost proprietary interest in exposing the scam, the wooden-legged man exposes Black Guinea as a fake. "You fools!" he cries to the credulous passengers, "you flock of fools, under this captain of fools, in this ship of fools!"[44] By the end of their visit, Ahab has similar feelings about the *Samuel Enderby*, but his fallout with Boomer occurs not from distrust, but from the inability of others to comprehend his aggrievement.

From its beginning, the gam with Captain Boomer alternates between fellowship, frustration, and the promise of bonhomie. As the *Pequod* and *Enderby* pull close, Ahab asks the English captain, who is "carelessly reclining" in his whaling boat, whether he had seen the white whale (436). Boomer spies Ahab's "plainly revealed" ivory leg and cries out, "See you this?" as he unwraps his own artificial limb, "a white arm of sperm whale bone, terminating in a wooden head like a mallet" (436). Within a minute,

Ahab's boat is on the water and rushing to the *Enderby*'s side, but once there, this "king of the sea" realizes that he has no way of climbing aboard (129). In the previous chapter, I discussed how carefully Ahab controls his environment, installing assistive devices on the *Pequod*'s decks, customizing his whaleboat, and using his crew to help him stand and walk. In "Leg and Arm," Ishmael pays attention to the way the *Enderby* reduces the captain "to a clumsy landsman again" (437). "Hopelessly eyeing" the "rocking bulwarks," Ahab grows angry when the English officers swing him a pair of ropes, not considering that "a one-legged man" might be "too much of a cripple to use their sea bannisters" (437). The struggles with inaccessibility continue until Boomer recognizes the problem and has a blubber hook lift him onto the *Enderby*'s deck. He exhibits the "sympathy in common misfortune" that, according to the travelers in *The Confidence-Man*, the wooden-legged man lacks.[45]

Face to face and prosthesis to prosthesis, the two captains take pleasure in sharing their unlucky fate:

> With his ivory arm frankly thrust forth in welcome, the other captain advanced, and Ahab, putting out his ivory leg, and crossing the ivory arm (like two sword-fish blades) cried out in his walrus way, "Aye, aye, hearty! let us shake bones together!—an arm and a leg!—an arm that never can shrink, d'ye see; and a leg that never can run." (437)

As the two men "shake bones," we see the solidarity of their loss and yet also the mirroring of their totem-like prostheses. The ease and familiarity are unusual for Ahab, whose hearty "walrus way" seldom interrupts his charismatic defiance and morbid self-absorption. Feeling empowered in the presence of the mallet-handed Boomer, he envisions their whalebone limbs as bodily enhancements not deficiencies. The arm that does not shrink, the leg that does not run, the two prostheses seem more steadfast in battle than human flesh and bone.

The captains are part of a long line of Melvillean characters with missing or injured limbs. If Captain Boomer descends from *Mardi*'s Samoa, the islander who nobly wears the stump of his amputated arm, Ahab recalls Tommo, the hero of Melville's first novel, *Typee: A Peep at Polynesian Life*, whose leg mysteriously swells on the South Seas island Nukuheva and leaves him "almost a cripple."[46] Among the extended family of Melville's limb sufferers, Ahab and Boomer are brother amputees, forever joined by

76   THE PROSTHETIC ARTS OF *MOBY-DICK*

their common antagonist and whalebone prostheses. The resemblance ends there. The warm fellowship that Boomer has established on his ship diverges from the hellish atmosphere of Ahab's *Pequod*. It is little wonder that Ishmael would admire the *Samuel Enderby* on a later visit, as the vessel exudes the Ishmaelean values of humor, storytelling, and sociability. Having been orphaned by Ahab's "monomaniac revenge," he finds in the *Enderby* "a jolly ship; of good fare and plenty; fine flip and strong; crack fellows all, and capital from boot heels to hat-band" (187, 445).

Boomer displays this collaborative spirit when he invites Dr. Bunger to participate in his storytelling.[47] A dry and quiet "professional," Bunger serves as a reminder that British whalers were legally required to include a full-time surgeon in their crews (439). Part of the chapter's comedy is that as the doctor soberly narrates his decision to amputate, Boomer interrupts, irrepressibly engulfing him in outrageous jokes and asides. He claims that the teetotaling surgeon had served him hot rum toddies on the nights following the amputation, the two getting so drunk they could hardly put on the bandages. Bunger counters that the captain swings his mallet hand in "diabolical passions" and drolly points to a minor indentation in his head as proof (440). "Bunger, you dog, laugh out! why don't ye?" the captain cajoles. "I'd rather be killed by you than kept alive by any other man" (439–440). Eight chapters later Melville counters these "tall-talking clowns" (as John Bryant memorably described them) with the more Shakespearean comedy of Ahab's denouncing the carpenter for not following his ontological queries.[48]

Melville invests more in the surgeon than the teasing might indicate. With a marlinspike in one hand and a pillbox in the other, Bunger has the divided attention of a sailor and physician (439). Though he casts "a critical glance at the ivory limbs of the two crippled captains," the doctor makes it clear that prosthesis-making is not his responsibility. "I had no hand in shipping that ivory arm there; that thing is against all rule," he tells Ahab, fixating on its departure from convention. Referring to the "club-hammer" attached to the end, he clarifies "that is the captain's work, not mine; he ordered the carpenter to make it...to knock some one's brains out with, I suppose" (440). Bunger's differentiating his work from that of the *Enderby*'s carpenter may reflect professional sensitivity to the period's association of surgery with manual labor.[49] Amputation was a form of "medical carpentry," the physician-turned-satirist Percival Leigh wrote in Charles Dickens's weekly magazine, *Household Words*.[50] Before the *Pequod*'s carpenter appears on stage, the professional distancing has already taken effect.

Bunger is not a man-maker. He reads and amputates bodies; he does not replace them.

Compared to the "unreasoning," soliloquizing carpenter, his brains oozing into his hands, Bunger possesses an expert's confidence in his ability to elucidate the natural world. The novel repeatedly satirizes the limitations of his scientific perspective. When Boomer says that Moby Dick "doesn't bite so much as he swallows," the young surgeon intervenes and, "very gravely and mathematically bowing to each Captain in succession," proceeds to correct him:

> Do you know, gentlemen, that the digestive organs of the whale are so inscrutably constructed by Divine Providence, that it is quite impossible for him to completely digest even a man's arm? And he knows it too. So that what you take for the White Whale's malice is only his awkwardness. For he never means to swallow a single limb; he only thinks to terrify by feints. (441)

With words such as "inscrutable" and "providence," Bunger applies language the novel associates with Ahab and Ishmael to physiologic design. The "grand programme of Providence" may have compelled Ishmael to go to sea, leading to his encounter with Moby Dick's "predestinating head" as it prepared to sink the ship (7, 571). As Bunger presents it, however, providence lies not in the actions of men and beasts but in the makeup of species. He ludicrously concludes that because whales know they cannot digest human flesh, they would not bite with cruel intent. "What you take for the White Whale's malice is only his awkwardness," he counsels, "for he never means to swallow a single limb."

It would be easy to read Bunger's comment as an insightful rebuke of Ahab's quest, but Melville actually satirizes the argument's premise. Since when do acts of oral malice depend on the ability to swallow or digest? Whales may use their teeth and jaws as instinctual forms of defense, as Starbuck argued in "The Quarter-Deck," or they might possess the intention of hurting the forces that antagonize them, as Ishmael explains in "Schools and Schoolmasters." When Moby Dick sinks the *Pequod* with his battering ram, he does so with "retribution" and "eternal malice" (571). In giving the whale agency, Ishmael echoes Owen Chase's popular 1821 account of a bull whale that purposefully struck the whale ship *Essex*.[51] Bunger's reasoning, which he supports with an irrelevant tale about a sword

78   THE PROSTHETIC ARTS OF *MOBY-DICK*

swallower spitting out tacks, cloaks his specious logic in the aura of explanatory fact.

Bunger has no need to convince his captain that he should refrain from hunting Moby Dick. Since losing his arm, Boomer has twice seen the white whale and has not lowered for him. "Aint one limb enough?" he asks the increasingly impatient Ahab. "'What should I do without this other arm?...No more White Whales for me...he's best let alone; don't you think so, Captain?'—glancing at the ivory leg" (441). Boomer names several reasons why one might knowingly hunt the white whale. The most obvious is the "ship-load of precious sperm" that Starbuck and the *Pequod*'s owners expect (441). To be one of the "Quakers with a vengeance" is to fight for "Heaven's good gifts," as Bildad earlier put it (73, 105). Another motive in hunting Moby Dick would be the distinction that would come from slaying him. Ishmael touts the glory of whaling, but Boomer is the only character to suggest that "great glory" would come from battling such a legendarily destructive beast (441). Viewing the whale as a noble, worthy combatant, one that would bring honor to the men who killed him, Boomer echoes countless literary heroes who believed glory would redeem their suffering.

The prospect of revenge remains notably absent from the Englishman's thinking because injury does not leave him feeling dispossessed or in need of identifying an antagonist. While Ahab personalizes his missing limb, Boomer describes Moby Dick as the "cause" of his injury, not the perpetrator (438). Bone for bone, arm for leg, the captains look upon alternate versions of themselves, with Ahab's recklessness coming into greater focus. Melville's portrait of disability has been criticized for being overly deterministic in suggesting that dismemberment dictates Ahab's maniacal pursuit of revenge.[52] As Harriet Hustis has argued, however, Captain Boomer demonstrates that disability does not "indicate a predetermined end."[53] "Ahab's character and destiny are not intrinsically fixed by the loss of limb," Sari Altschuler writes; "rather, Ahab's obsessive mania has fixed its energies on the missing limb, and that obsession is the root of his troubles."[54] With all its good humor and hospitality, the visit to the *Samuel Enderby* illustrates that, in the aftermath of catastrophe, there are appealing alternatives to Ahab's violent, all-consuming quest. Rather than wealth, glory, or fellowship, he summons meaning from purpose: he will avenge his wounded self.

Readers often see the surgeon as a source of sober wisdom amid Ahab's monomania, but Bunger's failure to understand his motivation introduces a surreptitiously powerful discourse into the encounter. When Ahab

BONE TO BONE   79

announces his continued search for Moby Dick, the doctor tries to examine him:

> "Bless my soul, and curse the foul fiend's," cried Bunger, stoopingly walking round Ahab, and like a dog, strangely snuffing; "this man's blood—bring the thermometer!—it's at the boiling point!—his pulse makes these planks beat! Sir!"—taking a lancet from his pocket, and drawing near to Ahab's arm. (441)

As if the intense desire for revenge could just be reasoned away, Bunger is shocked by Ahab's refusal to heed the *Enderby*'s warning. Captain Boomer wonders whether Ahab is "crazy," but the surgeon seeks a more medically based diagnosis (442). Unlike the carpenter, he interprets Ahab's passion as a pathology.

Though Ishmael presents it comically, Bunger predicates his response on "the calibrating gaze," a term Samuel Otter coined to describe nineteenth-century craniologists but one that applies equally well here.[55] Flask breezily declared that Ahab could not be disabled because he still had one and a half knees. Bunger makes a more professional statement in viewing the captain as a subject for scientific inquiry. As the doctor prepares to monitor his temperature and pulse, Ahab the metaphysical warrior becomes Ahab the patient, or, in Michel Foucault's terms, Ahab the "medicalizable object."[56] The surgeon likely thinks that the captain suffers from hypertension or fever, and thus he rushes to give him a venesection to relieve the blood pressure he feels pounding on the *Enderby*'s deck.[57] Calling for a thermometer and pulling out his lancet, the normally dry Bunger fervidly declares his medical intent. In the nineteenth century, ship's thermometers were cumbersome, footlong objects. With Ahab eager to depart, Bunger improbably wants to remove his coat, vest, and shirt and then place the thermometer underneath his armpit for a period of ten to fifteen minutes. Meanwhile the surgeon hopes to use his spring-loaded lancet to puncture a vein in Ahab's arm and rapidly release some of his blood. As it was with *White-Jacket*'s Dr. Cuticle, the comedy is both rich and serious. Armed with such tools, Bunger aims to cure Ahab's defiance by giving it a biological cause.

Bunger's pathology-driven response recalls what Lennard Davis has described as the "hegemony of the middle."[58] Dedicated to the process of norming, the surgeon identifies Ahab as being unfit, not because of his missing leg, but because of his extraordinary commitment to killing Moby

80 THE PROSTHETIC ARTS OF *MOBY-DICK*

Dick. Bunger's reference to blessed souls and cursed fiends reminds us that he trained as a clergyman before becoming a ship's surgeon, and with his government-mandated position on the *Enderby*, he represents a remarkably consolidated voice of British institutional power. According to Jonathan Schroeder, Ishmael applies a psychiatric term to Ahab when he sees him suffering from "monomania," a diagnosis that had significant impact on legal proceedings in France and the United States.[59] Bunger takes the pathology to another level in seeing Ahab as a medically abnormal individual who, like the mallet-headed prosthesis, must be accommodated to an industrial labor force.

The doctor's measurements have no way of illuminating moral injury and aggrievement. Meeting the "ungodly, godlike" Ahab, he concludes that his motivation is connected to his temperature and pulse (79). When Ishmael measures the length of the whale's skeleton on the island of Tranque, he invites the indignation of the local priests who cannot abide the thought that he would dare to measure their god (450). But Ishmael's measurement is to appreciate the magnitude of the whale rather than to correct its behavior against an agreed-upon norm. The dimensions he tattoos on his right arm only remind him how insufficient his comprehension of the whale will be. Bunger, who even bows mathematically, tries to reduce Ahab's Promethean spirit to a set of medical controls and biological data points. The surgeon's nineteenth-century medicine was laughably inadequate to the task of relieving Ahab of his will, though with the rise of psychopharmacology, we know that over subsequent centuries, the bio-power he represents would grow in both scope and efficacy.

Bunger's talky jokes and proclamations can distract us from the medical determinism of the British ship. Indeed, the *Samuel Enderby* emerges from the chapter as a materialist's paradise, brimming with sperm and looking toward a century of forced logic, misleading statistics, and scientific analyses. Although it has Ishmaelean appeal, the ship is a predecessor to the geologist Margoth in *Clarel*, who descends from the Mount of Temptation, where Jesus resisted Satan's offer to give him the kingdoms of the world, and teasingly declares that every spur of the mythic site was Jura limestone.[60] Pain haunts the *Pequod*, with Ahab's ancient feud reminding crewmembers that malignant forces guide the world in ways they cannot understand. The *Enderby* seems to have banished pain and naively replaced it with a mallet-handed prosthesis, perfect for discipline and repetitive work.

In cherishing the memory of his catastrophe, Ahab never openly contemplates what the completion of his quest might look like, nor how he would reconcile himself to a world without the white whale. Moby Dick does not destroy meaning for Ahab as much as he creates it. Glory descends upon traditional heroes at the completion of their battles, but for Ahab, the whale's significance exists only as long as the two of them remain locked in their mutually defining relationship. Boomer can offer his cautionary tale, but as Ahab replies, Moby Dick "will still be hunted." The passive construction conveys how Ahab has come to see revenge as a task thrust upon him. "What is best let alone, that accursed thing is not always what least allures. He's all a magnet!" (441). Ahab exhibits the fatalism of a man who has wholly submitted to his choices.

The captain's hatred, Peter Boxall writes, "is such that his material form cannot contain it."[61] The gam with the *Enderby* reveals that Ahab nurses his desire for revenge as if it were the cherished product of woe. The ivory leg symbolizes to the captain not just the whale that dismasted him but the value of aggrievement. Ahab continues to feel his severed leg, for out of trauma, retribution has become his animating mission. Vengeance has transformed his natural and artificial limbs into the totalized sum of his purpose. The poet W. H. Auden once voiced the perspective of romantic avengers who identify so strongly with their vengeance that, like Ahab and Hamlet, they think of it as a vocation. My injury "is not an injury *to* me, it *is* me," he wrote in *The Enchafèd Flood* (1951). "I cannot live without it."[62]

Figuring Revenge

It is fitting that Ahab breaks his prosthesis in returning from the ship that disables him—both in impeding his arrival on deck and in regarding his resolve as a physiological disorder. Arthur Frank has written that in seeking professional care, the wounded agree to "*a narrative surrender*" in which their story becomes framed in "medical terms."[63] Ahab's visit to the *Enderby* illustrates his resistance to the narrative Bunger wants to construct. On board the *Pequod*, he will torment the carpenter with his own concerns, weaving his pain into a narrative that attests to the breadth of his embodied self. Whether it is spavined on the deck or dusty in the vice, his prosthesis exists in synchrony with both the ghostly leg he has lost and the natural leg

82   THE PROSTHETIC ARTS OF *MOBY-DICK*

that survives. His wounds encompass the physical and spirit worlds. But what about its relation to time? The data Bunger seeks would only account for the moment Ahab rants on the *Enderby*'s deck, but in the captain's narrative, his past injury and future revenge are intertwined. Dismemberment has not reduced him to "a large fragment of a man." It has expanded him.

The image that perhaps best conveys the temporal dimensions of Ahab's identity is easy to overlook. Using a pencil, the captain likes to write on the ivory leg, and thus the carpenter supplies it with a polished slate. Melville makes the detail so incidental that he dramatizes the carpenter's almost failing to include it. "Halloa!" he exclaims at the chapter's end. "I almost forgot the little oval slate, smoothed ivory, where he figures up the latitude. So, so; chisel, file, and sand-paper, now!" (472). Chapter 34, "The Cabin-Table," describes Ahab "mutely reckoning the latitude on the smooth, medallion-shaped tablet...on the upper part of his ivory leg," but the feature takes on new significance in the context of the carpenter's labor (149). The prostheses that enable ambulation and inspire commentary also provide a surface for Ahab to write. The word *prosthesis* never appears in *Moby-Dick*, but whether polished or dusty, the oval slate evokes the word's surgical and linguistic meanings. A supplement to Ahab's identity, the prosthesis is both the object and subject of interpretation: the carpenter and Ishmael collaborate on a device that can be written upon as well as written about. It is a text that invites future text.[64]

And yet Ahab sets down numbers rather than words, turning the carefully measured limb into the site of his own measurement. Captain Boomer requests a club-hammer for his terminal device. Ahab requests a flattened surface where he can calculate his position at sea. The distinction says a lot about his incorporation of aggrievement, as he literally plots his revenge on the site of his absent leg. Ahab's figures are analogous to Queequeg's tattoos, erasable markings that contain not the secrets of the universe but where he is in relation to the southern feeding grounds favored by Moby Dick. A companion to the chart, the compass, and the quadrant, the prostheses become the captain's way of navigating his body's distance from avenging its lost limb. John Kerrigan has explained that, in balancing historic wrongs with impending retribution, revenge narratives establish "equilibrium-through-action."[65] From Orestes to Hamlet to Ahab, the avenger manipulates a "fluid and contingent world" in seeking a newly just and settled state.[66] The scenes with the carpenter put pressure on the ivory limb as a theatrical prop, a medical artifact, and the material embodiment of loss, pain, and grievance. The prosthetic slate adds to the complexity in looking toward a future conflict that, in the avenger's eyes, will cancel the relational burden he has with Moby Dick. In the circular logic of retribution, the desire for vengeance consumes the captain and leaves him dispossessed, but he believes that vengeance alone will restore him to that settled state. Dismembering the dismemberer is built into his prostheticized self.

Ahab's comments about phantom pain leave the carpenter perplexed and feeling the need to "calculate over again" as he recognizes that there is more to this captain, and more to prosthesis-making, than he originally thought (471). And Ahab, who wants skylights that would illuminate his interiors rather than eyes that can see out, curses the "mortal inter-indebtedness" that checks his pride (471). Susan McWilliams has described Ahab as an American isolato because he exemplifies a culture "in which the idea of human interdependence seems disgraceful."[67] If democracy threatens to "shut up" man "in the solitude of his own heart," as Tocqueville writes, then Ahab resembles his countrymen and women who "form the habit of thinking of themselves in isolation and imagine that their whole destiny is in their own hands."[68] "Here I am, proud as a Greek god," he laments, "and yet standing debtor to this blockhead for a bone to stand on!" (471). In Ishmael's telling, *Moby-Dick* both celebrates and laments an American willingness to wound, terminate, and dismember whatever threatens the imagined autonomy of the nation and its citizens. As McWilliams comments, the only joint action the isolato accepts is one that produces violence.[69] In the name of democratic sovereignty, the most violent missions seem theologically righteous and communally just. The power of Ahab's prosthesis to extend, to support, and to be the surface for calculating revenge becomes the power of the *Pequod* to hunt Moby Dick and to kill other whales as a source of American dominance and wealth. What sanctions such violence is the belief that interdependence is a threat. The living soul in Ahab's phantom leg is the haunting reminder that his vaunted individualism may ultimately be prosthetic. He is an individual only to the extent that other people are his arms and legs.

Ahab desires a more powerful sense of embodiment, a learned synchronicity between phantom and substance, than the carpenter can supply. The oval slate can help the captain calculate his position at sea, but as I explain in the next section, he ultimately relies on the stowaway Fedallah to bring him to Moby Dick. Pacing across the decks, his legs alternating between dead and living steps, Ahab enlists Fedallah in his crusade to conquer the white whale who is at once an inscrutable symbol of creation and an infidel who nullifies belief. Fedallah's mysterious, Islamicized presence transforms the captain's will into a metaphysical quest, promising to redeem his loss with a climactic act of violent, blasphemous revenge. Fedallah is the racially embodied counterpart to Ahab's ivory limb, and it seems anything but coincidental that Moby Dick claims him on the same day he destroys the last of the whalebone legs.

Shakespearean drama provided Melville with the impetus to stage the crew's interaction with Ahab's disability and how the construction of his prosthesis inevitably involved the construction of both his and their identity. As so frequently happens with Melville's work, however, the materiality of these scenes quickly turned to ontological problems about invisible spheres and the pain that surfaces in lost legs. Fedallah may provide prosthetic service to Ahab's revenge, but he haunts Ishmael's narrative like a phantom limb, inhabiting the space between spiritual power, plotted vengeance, and wrecked flesh.

PART II
PROSTHETIC IDENTITIES

3

The Phantom Fedallah

A Muffled Mystery

The character Fedallah plays an instrumental role in the prosthetic arts of *Moby-Dick*. As we have seen, the dismembered Ahab treats his shipmates as prosthetic extensions of himself. Whether Starbuck, Flask, Pip, or the carpenter, the men on the *Pequod* become Ahab's arms and legs, extending his physical power on deck and at sea. Ahab may aspire to be as bodiless as the wind, but until that happens, he will weaponize their bodies against Moby Dick (564). What makes Fedallah so exceptional is that he encompasses the qualities of the book's many prostheses, propping up Ahab's body, elevating his vengeance, and mystically tracking the white whale. Melville shrouds the character in such secrecy that when Captain Boomer asks if the *Pequod*'s captain is crazy, he simply puts "a finger on his lip" and disappears over the bulwark.[1] The wordlessness conveys Melville's meaning. An agent of metaphysical knowledge, the Parsee extends Ahab's quest into the spiritual realm, hinting at more intangible powers than maritime dictatorship. Fedallah's relation to Ahab, his capacity to facilitate and augment the quest, corresponds with his relation to the novel itself. As hackneyed and underdeveloped as the character might be, he ensures the survival of the narrator and the text. Part II aims to move Fedallah out of the shadows by recognizing the assistance he lends the storied hunt for Moby Dick. In a novel about grief and dismemberment, Fedallah functions as the prosthesis upon whom Ahab, Ishmael, and Melville himself depend.

Following the lessons of many nineteenth-century writers, Melville found in gothic fiction a way to endow Ahab's rebellion with cosmic significance. (What is the point of railing against the gods if the gods don't exist?) Fedallah personifies the gothic energy in *Moby-Dick*, an energy that Ishmael consistently associates with racial and religious difference. The narrator who plumbs the depths of Ahab's monomania and learns to accept nearly everyone on ship remains aghast at the Parsee's shadowy presence. Of the many phantoms haunting Ishmael, Fedallah and the Manilla oarsmen

The Prosthetic Arts of Moby-Dick. David Haven Blake, Oxford University Press. © Oxford University Press 2024.
DOI: 10.1093/oso/9780197780510.003.0004

88 THE PROSTHETIC ARTS OF *MOBY-DICK*

represent the dark, unknowable dimension of Ahab's aggrievement. To Ishmael, their race underscores the captain's eagerness to accept demonic assistance in avenging his lost limb.

Ishmael alerts readers to Fedallah's difference as soon as he appears on deck. A tall, swart-skinned man dressed in black Chinese clothing, he and his companions enter the novel amid the commotion of the first lowering. Although they hail from "the ends of the earth" and grapple with their own diversity, the crew fixate on the strangers' exotic clothes and "dusky" skin (121, 216). Speculation turns to Ahab's relationship to the "phantoms," a relationship so familiar that he calls Fedallah by name. The shock carries over to when Ahab's boat appears in the water with five "tiger-yellow" natives at the oars (217). Standing erect in the stern, his ivory leg braced against the modified thigh board, Ahab orders the other boats to spread out, but "with all their eyes again riveted upon the swart Fedallah and his crew, the inmates of the other boats obeyed not the command." "Captain Ahab?" Starbuck meekly responds, too astonished to formulate a complete thought (218). The crewmembers sense that, in the face of their own "horrible oath" to hunt the white whale, the strangers have a secret connection to the captain's revenge (416).

Although he has long accepted Queequeg's matrimonial clasp, Ishmael never moves beyond his fixation on the Parsee's religion and race. His introduction of the Manilla oarsmen is shockingly offensive, and in a line to which we will frequently return, he describes their coming from "a race notorious for a certain diabolism of subtilty, and by some honest white mariners supposed to be the paid spies and secret confidential agents on the water of the devil, their lord" (217). Ishmael eventually modifies this statement, assuring us in a subsequent chapter that these "aboriginal natives" partially assimilated into the crew (217). His dread of Fedallah, however, does not change. The Parsee remains "a muffled mystery to the last," a cipher the other characters are never able to comprehend (231). In their clownish way, Stubb tries to convince Flask that Fedallah is "the devil in disguise," the two wondering where he hides his tail and how his cloven feet fit into boots (325). As the *Pequod* prepares for its final battle with Moby Dick, Starbuck refers to Fedallah as Ahab's "evil shadow," reinforcing the image pattern that Ishmael initiated when he glimpsed dim figures creeping onboard the ship in Nantucket (561).[2]

Ishmael's physical description of Fedallah turns him into an amalgam of sinister omens and racist stereotypes. Fedallah has thin, steel-like lips, and his voice seems "half-hissed" (217). "One white tooth evilly" protrudes from his mouth, a "tusk," as Flask describes it, that "is a sort of carved into a snake's head" (217, 325). Most notably, Fedallah has long white hair that he has braided and "coiled" around his head, an arrangement that looks like a "glistening white plaited turban" against his ebony skin (217).[3] "One cannot sustain an indifferent air concerning Fedallah," Ishmael warns, before readers can really judge him themselves (231). For all the qualifiers he employs, Ishmael wants us to see the silent, shadowy character as being unmistakably linked to "Ahab's peculiar fortunes" and exerting "some sort of a half-hinted influence" or even "authority" over the captain and his vengeful quest (231).

Like Stubb and Flask, multiple scholars have searched for the whereabouts of Fedallah's tail. He fills the role of Mephistopheles to Ahab's Faustus and the three witches to Ahab's Macbeth.[4] Scholars have described him as an "avenging angel," a "bad angel," a "diabolic infidel mystic," a "shady genie," a "Gothic symbol" for Ahab's inner darkness, and a "duplication of self that never threatens the self's integrity." Others have seen him as "the spectre of barbarism," "a hateful figure to both Islam and Muslims," and a turban-wearing "handler" who keeps his leader "on task."[5] And yet for some readers Fedallah is merely an afterthought, a stock supernatural figure with a minor, if predictable, role. Describing the character as a "terrible bore," Ray Bradbury eliminated Fedallah from his screenplay for John Huston's celebrated 1956 film of *Moby Dick*.[6] Amid a lengthy analysis of the Faustian Ahab, Franco Moretti dismissed the Parsee mid-sentence—and in the bluntest terms. "(Melville's Mephistopheles, Fedallah, is an insignificant figure)." The parentheses were the point.[7]

Dismissing Fedallah is shortsighted, however. The character seems closely aligned with Ahab's inner demon, and Ishmael identifies him as a spectral presence in the captain's vindictive soul. Such imagery presents the Parsee as the incarnation of a psychological force, a phantom indicating how far Ahab has wandered from reason in pursuing the white whale. "Human madness is oftentimes a cunning and most feline thing," Ishmael writes. "When you think it fled, it may have but become transfigured into some still subtler form" (185). Fedallah can represent the transfiguration of Ahab's monomania or the objectification of his lunatic "hidden self" (185). Stubb understands Fedallah in humorously literal terms. The shape-shifting devil has offered Ahab an irresistible exchange: Moby Dick for the captain's "silver watch, or his soul, or something of that sort" (325). Ishmael and

90   THE PROSTHETIC ARTS OF *MOBY-DICK*

Starbuck imply a more psychologically nuanced version of that swap: Fedallah is the product of Ahab's bargain with himself.

This book adds to these interpretations by looking at Fedallah as one of the many prostheses that Ahab has incorporated into his quest. The captain receives physical and emotional assistance from the likes of Stubb and Pip, but he turns to the Parsee for a more sustained and elaborate kind of support. In the aftermath of dismemberment, Fedallah provides the kind of cunning, supernatural aid Ahab believes will lead him to the white whale. Like the phantom leg, he seems to haunt the injured body, a spiritual member that exists in the interstices between lost and artificial limbs. David Wills has suggested that every prosthesis implies the amputation that preceded it.[8] If so, we might see Fedallah as the embodiment of both Ahab's wounds and his will to avenge them. The captain can manipulate Starbuck into assisting a plan he repeatedly rejects, but Fedallah inhabits powers that are simultaneously more familiar to Ahab and more distant from anything on ship. Like the ivory leg, he expresses the legacy and exigency of Ahab's aggrievement.

In *Civilization and Its Discontents* (1930), Sigmund Freud argued that man had become a "prosthetic God" to himself, remarking on the technological advancements that had augmented humanity's natural sensory abilities. Functioning like "auxiliary organs," the telephone had enhanced human hearing, the microscope human sight.[9] Thinking of Fedallah as an auxiliary organ can help clarify his singular role in the hunt. Like the compass and the quadrant, he is a mechanism by which Ahab locates the white whale, but in the cosmic narrative of *Moby-Dick*, the power he offers the captain seems preternaturally derived. The Parsee's moonlight meditations and cryptic prophecies amount to more than gothic coloring and more than the mystification of an ethnic group. They become Melville's way of bringing the hunt to a climax and of transforming one man's personal hatred into a metaphysical battle that blends the spirit and natural worlds. Freud saw prostheses as progressively giving humanity the status of gods.[10] Summoned as an assistive device but then accepted as an instrument of fate, Fedallah is the apotheosis of Ahab's will and the prostheses that supplements his capacity for revenge.

The German sociologist Erich Fromm can be useful in thinking about the implications of Fedallah's role. His 1941 book, *Escape from Freedom*, analyzed the rise of "authoritarian personalities" at a moment when humanity had encountered more freedom than it ever had before. Publishing the book as fascism was threatening much of Europe, Fromm contended that authoritarian personalities are not revolutionaries so much as they are rebels who thrill to the act of defiance. Rather than engage the prospects ahead of them, they long to succumb to forces much larger than themselves. "The authoritarian character loves those conditions that limit human freedom," Fromm explains; "He loves being submitted to fate."[11] Whether it is an ethical, religious, or philosophical concept (as in "duty," "the will of the Lord," or "destiny of man"), authoritarians appeal to powers outside the individual, powers to which they "can do nothing but submit."[12] To the autocratic Ahab, Fedallah represents this higher power. The captain can command Stubb like a dog and dare Starbuck to let him drop from the royal mast. In each case, he fears no consequences. But the captain eerily depends on Fedallah as the force that will deliver his fate. Fedallah, not monomania, leads Ahab to claim that his battle with Moby Dick was "immutably decreed" (561).

In a novel that repeatedly contemplates inscrutability, Fedallah inhabits the peculiar prosthetic space in which his body is deemed radically other and yet, by virtue of its association with Ahab, not entirely his own. He emerges from Ishmael's narration as an assortment of Orientalist influences and stereotypes that ultimately define the depths of Ahab's resolve. The contradictions surrounding his character reinforce the "explicitly racialized form of embodiment" he represents.[13] Ishmael describes Fedallah as a Zoroastrian, an ancient religion that may have contributed to the monotheism of Judaism, Christianity, and Islam.[14] As a Parsee, he descends from one of the ancient Persians who were driven out of Iranian lands in the seventh century and subsequently settled in India. But Melville gives Fedallah an Islamic name, which seemingly contradicts his Zoroastrian roots. The Parsees fled their home to escape the Arab Muslim conquest. With his religious name and white hair coiled like a turban, Fedallah embodies and complicates the novel's larger network of Islamic ideas and imagery.[15] Part of the mysteriousness comes from the way he crosses continents, traditions, and centuries. Although it sounds like an oxymoron, we might view Fedallah as the spectral embodiment of the violence that Ahab wants enacted upon the world. His indecipherability makes him one of the "ghosts" that Wai Chee Dimock has found in mapping US literature alongside "hemispheric Islam."[16]

Moby-Dick is a revenge narrative that imagines retribution not for a malicious killing but for the trauma of limb loss. In structuring his tale,

92 THE PROSTHETIC ARTS OF *MOBY-DICK*

Melville does not rely on the female Furies who tormented Orestes through ancient Greece, nor does he resurrect the kind of aggrieved family member who charged Hamlet with prosecuting his will. Adapting the genre to the United States, Melville shifts the revenge narrative away from the clan and toward the wounded individual. As Rosemarie Garland Thomson has commented, Ahab sees in his disabled body a devastating threat to his self-determination and autonomy.[17] Ahab, George Schulman argues, suffers an attack on his "democratic dignity" and the masculine fantasy of Jacksonian individualism.[18] The captain stands alone in his explicitly American sense of injury, and yet because his nemesis lives in the sea, he requires others to identify with that injury for retaliation to take place. Filtered through misunderstanding, racist stereotypes, and, yet also, cosmopolitan intrigue, Melville creates an artificially sinister Asian man who both supports the dismembered captain and characterizes the dark recesses of his soul. Following the history of Islam in the New World will help us understand that such mysteries are not Fedallah's own. They stem from a long-established Euro-American practice of using Islam to blur the lines between what is other and what is self.

The Islam of Democracy

The prostheticization of Muslim societies in narratives of American identity originated in the eighteenth century. Members of Melville's social class perceived Islamic culture to be fascinating, alluring, and suspiciously extreme. The Founders made regular use of Islam in their personal and political writings, alluding to the religion to convey their openness to other faiths. Writing in his *Autobiography* (1791), Benjamin Franklin recalled that in helping the community design an open worship house in Philadelphia, he argued that the structure should not favor any sect, "so that even if the Mufti of Constantinople were to send a missionary to preach Mahometanism to us, he would find a pulpit in his service."[19] Although it met stiff opposition in the Virginia State Assembly, Thomas Jefferson wrote his Bill for Establishing Religious Freedom to protect, as he later put it, "the Jew and the Gentile, the Christian and the Mahometan, the Hindoo, and Infidel of every denomination."[20] At the turn of the century, hostage taking by North African pirates brought the United States into closer contact with the region and produced a handful of popular literary works about so-called Barbary captivity.[21] Reflecting on his boyhood, Melville's semi-autobiographical character Redburn was enchanted by such tales and longed to tell his own stories about traveling in "remote and barbarous countries." The boy stares with wonder when a man who recently returned from "Stony Arabia" attends his local church. Redburn had already read the man's "arid-looking book" about his adventures; after the Sabbath encounter, the traveler's weather-beaten face appears in the boy's dreams.[22]

Melville benefited from a thriving literary marketplace for books and articles about Asian history, culture, and religion. His teenage enthusiasm for the *Arabian Nights* was matched on both sides of the Atlantic. In addition to illustrated editions of specific stories, New York publishers brought out two versions of the book in 1847–48, and with them came a series of articles in the *Literary World*—the magazine edited by Melville's friend and editor Evert Duyckinck—about the tales' origins.[23] Critics eagerly awaited Washington Irving's multivolume biography of Muhammad, though at least one wrongly expected the author to treat Islam as "a gigantic scheme of fraud and imposture." "The life of Muhammed by Washington Irving!" the *United States* magazine proclaimed in 1847. "What visions of delight flood the mind at the thought!" When the biography appeared in December 1849, the *Literary World* devoted a lengthy two-part article to it.[24] Since the late 1830s, articles and poems on Zoroastrian fire worship had been appearing in US periodicals, including Nathaniel Hawthorne's *American Magazine of Useful and Entertaining Knowledge*.[25] Hawthorne returned to the "Parsis" in the story "Fire-Worship," which he included in *Mosses from an Old Manse*. Melville glowingly reviewed the collection in the summer 1850, and as their friendship deepened, Hawthorne's interest in the subject may have rubbed off on the younger writer.

In addition to travel narratives and his own experience at sea, Melville read novels that offered a sensationalist look at the Near and Middle East. In Paris in 1849, he purchased a "fine copy" of Thomas Hope's picaresque novel *Anastasius: Memoirs of a Greek* (1819), which told the adventures of a young Greek protagonist in the seductive and dangerous lands of the Ottoman-controlled Levant. Melville was "enraged" when English customs officials confiscated the book, claiming it was "food for fire."[26] In London, he received a new copy of *Anastasius* and William Beckford's *Vathek, an Arabian Tale* (1786), probably as gifts from his British publisher.[27] Melville joined Lord Byron, John Keats, and Edgar Allan Poe in admiring *Vathek*, a steamy novel that combined power struggles, Islamic devil worship, and

94   THE PROSTHETIC ARTS OF *MOBY-DICK*

gothic supernaturalism in a licentious Arab court. Notably, the main character, the Caliph, sells his soul to a devil-like genie referred to as "the Giaour."

In the summer 1850, as Melville struggled with the "strange sort of a book" he was writing about sperm whales, William Starbuck Mayo's novel *The Berber, or, The Mountaineer of the Atlas* (1850) was popular among Berkshire vacationers.[28] Flush with the excitement of hosting Duyckinck, meeting Hawthorne, and starting his review of *Mosses from an Old Manse*, Melville attended a neighborhood costume party in the flowing robes and turban of a Turk. The party was raucous enough that Melville's brother Allan was ejected from the premises at midnight, but Herman remained, in the company of his wife, Lizzie, his sister Sophia, several unmarried women, and the hostess, Mrs. Sarah Morewood, with whom he had a close, flirtatious relationship.[29] In such a context, Melville's costume played upon the reputed power and debauchery of harems in the Turkish royal court. Westerners saw the harem as "nothing but a fantasm," Ali Behdad observes, "a purely fictional construction onto which Europe's own sexual repressions, erotic fantasies, and desire of domination were projected."[30] The Morewood party allowed the writer to imagine that fantasy playing out.

We can see something of Melville in the imagery Ishmael creates out of a bull whale swimming amid a "harem" of females in the "Schools and Schoolmasters" chapter. Whether written before or after the Morewood party, the portrait of this "luxurious Ottoman" or "Grand Turk" swimming among his "concubines" reproduces a widespread Orientalist fantasy (391–92). Six years later Melville peered through the latticed window of a real-life harem in Constantinople. A journal entry registers his admiration for the harem's decorum and lack of flirtatious ogling, though such high-mindedness did not stop him from twice remarking on the shape of the women's breasts.[31]

The "Schools and Schoolmasters" chapter is one of the few passages in *Moby-Dick* that identify Arab and Ottoman culture with exotic sensuality. As Edward Said pointed out, despite its "allusions to the Orient," *Moby-Dick* largely avoids those common motifs; in the novel's bachelor world, there are no sailors talking about harems and "no gardens of sensual delight."[32] Melville employed such imagery in other works, and *Redburn* offers an extended portrait of opulence when the young sailor visits a London establishment called "Aladdin's Palace."[33] With its bowing waiters, "Moorish looking tables," and "Persian carpeting" so thick it feels like "a bower in Babylon," the Palace seems as confining as it is plush. Even the "oriental ottomans" are cunningly "wrought into plaited serpents" that flash out into "sudden splendors of green scales and gold." The exotic atmosphere makes Redburn profoundly anxious, as if an assassin were stalking him in a gothic novel. "The whole place seemed infected," he concludes, "and a strange thought came over me, that in the very damasks around, some eastern plague had been imported."[34]

The scene reflects the period's tendency to collapse distinct ethnic groups into a single "eastern plague." Some of this could be attributed to the isolation of nineteenth-century Americans, but it also reveals how Europeans and European-Americans saw Muslims in the context of other subjugated ethnic groups. Spanish conquistadors in South America routinely called the native population "Muslims" and referred to their temples as "mosques."[35] As early as 1570, Native Americans were pressed into playing the role of Moors in a Peruvian pageant celebrating Spain's liberation from Moorish conquest.[36] In *Clarel*, the reclusive character Vine compares the Muslims he sees in Palestine to Native Americans in the United States.

> Clan of outcast Hagar,
> Well do ye come by spear and dagger!
> Yet in your bearing ye outvie
> Our western Red Men, chiefs that stalk
> In mud paint—whirl the tomahawk.[37]

"To Vine," Malini Johar Schueller writes, the vision of an Arab man on horseback "represents an ontological puzzle" that "defies clear definition," a puzzle he tries to solve by reading him through the New World.[38] Like both Vine and Irving (who once compared a Creek Indian to "a wild Arab on the prowl,") Melville was drawn to the idea that Arabs practiced the noble, athletic violence he associated with other peoples of color.[39] Although he does not share in the harpooners' fraternity, the Asian Fedallah complements the racial mix of the African Daggoo, the Native American Tashtego, and the Pacific Islander Queequeg.

These examples convey the ways in which European settlers artificially incorporated Islam into their colonial engagements, using Muslims and Muslim societies as an extension of a wide range of political experiences. Antebellum Americans inherited the European practice of using the fear of Islam to attack their political or religious enemies. After a century of sectarian Christian violence, European intellectuals deployed anti-Muslim

96   THE PROSTHETIC ARTS OF *MOBY-DICK*

rhetoric to advance a surreptitious political agenda against Protestants, Catholics, and Jews. Denise Spellberg has traced the way Voltaire's 1742 play *Le Fanatisme, ou Mahoumet le Prophète* initially used the mask of Islam to level a biting critique of state-sanctioned violence against French Protestants. Two years later, a British adaptation of the play employed the life of Muhammad to praise the openness of Anglo-Protestantism against the grip that Catholicism held on France. When a Baltimore theater presented Voltaire's work in 1782, the story became a parable about the dangers of British tyranny.[40]

The American version of the play suited a political climate that, as the harem did with sex, projected fantasies of arbitrary violence onto Islamic societies. The Ottoman Empire's reputation for brutal political rule made it a convenient symbol of despotism during the American Revolution, and numerous pamphleteers and politicians attacked Britain as a corrupt, Ottoman-like power. (Melville echoes this practice in his novel about the Revolutionary War, *Israel Potter*. After the British capture the character Ethan Allen, he describes himself as a Christian oppressed by the English Turks.)[41] Uprooted from scripture, creed, and place, Islam became a phantom image in Europe and the Americas, with Muslims serving as substitutes for an array of threatening persons or groups. Thus, at the end of the eighteenth century, John Quincy Adams could accuse Jefferson of adhering to the "*Islam* of democracy" in following the false prophet of Thomas Paine.[42] Decades later, the false prophet, or "Mohammed of America," could be Joseph Smith, whose Mormon followers were accused of building a version of Islam in the western United States.[43] Thus, while the Founders invoked it as a sign of religious tolerance, Islam began to emerge in other rhetorical settings as the externalization of an internal threat. When Adams attacked Jefferson, he aimed to estrange his well-known adversary by comparing his politics to a mythically feared faith practice. In the process, however, he made the figure of Islam part of the nation's cultural discourse. Attached to the body politic, it represented the burgeoning United States as well as an extreme and inscrutable antagonist.

Such images tapped into anxiety about Islam's geopolitical influence even as it turned the faith into a ready-made substitute for Christian wounds. As Timothy Marr has commented, Islam threatened Christianity's assumption that it was the culmination of world religions. "Unwilling to view Islam as a legitimate religious dispensation," he explains, Westerners "have imagined it as a post-Christian provocation to which they have responded by devising an archive of ideological fictions aimed at defusing" what they perceived to be a "heretical rivalry."[44] Islam represented what Said has called the "'*original* cultural effrontery.'"[45] Despite his own religious doubt, Melville gave his characters ample room to voice their fears that Islam was eclipsing the Christian world. In the dreamscape narrative of *Mardi*, the travelers sail past Africa (Hamora) and are confronted by Islam's rise as a force competing with European Christianity. "Hamora's northern shore gleamed thick with crescents," Taji reports, "numerous as the crosses along the opposing strand."[46] The philosopher Babbalanja cryptically notes that lies and truths run in parallel lines that never intersect.

Melville returned to these themes in *Clarel* with the pilgrims struggling to make sense of the three Abrahamic religions vying to coexist in Ottoman-controlled lands. ("Three Sundays a week in Constantinople," Melville observed. "Friday, Turks; Sat, Jews, Sunday, Romanists, Greeks, & Armenians.")[47] In Jerusalem, Clarel observes a Turkish guard who "permits" the Jews to gather at the Wailing Wall. He later notes that a palm-like minaret rivals the belfry of a Christian church.[48] When a traveler sees a group of shepherds bowing their turbaned heads toward Mecca to pray, he feels dismayed that they turn their backs to nearby Bethlehem. An Anglican priest responds with a more cosmopolitan view. "Yes, for they pray / To Allah. Well, and what of that?" Melville's journal records a similar scene without comment. In *Clarel*, though, the priest explains that "Christ listens, standing in heaven's gate— / Benignant listens, nor doth stay / Upon a syllable in creed."[49] Although the priest is overly sanguine in the text, his ecumenical vision and non-dogmatic belief suit Melville's distaste for the Zionists and Christian missionaries who come to the Holy Land to convert Muslim souls to their faith.[50]

Weary of Christian theology, Melville admired not only Islam's vibrancy but also the solemn unity of its call to prayer, which he translated in *Clarel* as "Prayer is more than sleep."[51] Compared to the spiritual turmoil of the West, Melville found something ancient and calming in Islam as if the newest of the Abrahamic religions had tapped into the beginnings of time.[52] Vine speculates that the Arabs "show a lingering trace / Of some quite unrecorded race."[53] The head guide, Djalea, exhibits the kind of "passive self-control" that comes from generations of belief. "No god there is but God," he modestly explains when questioned about his faith: "Allah preserve ye, Allah great."[54] The poem reinforces the perspective of Thomas Carlyle, whose famous 1840 essay on the Prophet praised Islam as a "religion heartily *believed*."[55]

98 THE PROSTHETIC ARTS OF *MOBY-DICK*

To Ishmael, however, that sense of ancient time becomes fearsome and unsettling in the person of Fedallah. The Parsee's age and race take him back not to the world of prophets and revelation but to the sinister origins of the universe:

> He was such a creature as civilized, domestic people in the temperate zone only see in their dreams, and that but dimly; but the like of whom now and then glide among the unchanging Asiatic communities, especially the Oriental isles to the east of the continent—those insulated, immemorial, unalterable countries, which even in these modern days still preserve much of the ghostly aboriginalness of earth's primal generations, when the memory of the first man was a distinct recollection, and all men his descendants, unknowing whence he came, eyed each other as real phantoms, and asked of the sun and the moon why they were created and to what end; when though, according to Genesis, the angels indeed consorted with the daughters of men, the devils also, add the uncanonical Rabbins, indulged in mundane amours. (231)

Tying Fedallah to the "ghostly aboriginalness" of the earth's first inhabitants, Ishmael straddles the Mesopotamia of Genesis with "the unchanging Asiatic communities" of the eastern islands. In this formulation, however, Fedallah is less the dark-skinned Parsee from India than a "tiger-yellow" Muslim from the Philippines.

The lack of clarity arises from the same mindset that the conquistadors had in linking Muslim practices to the indigenous people they encountered in Peru. Ishmael critically substitutes a group of ill-defined others into a single, artificial construct that is explicitly not Euro-American and yet helps define life in the "temperate zones." The mythic, dreamlike quality of Fedallah and his companions puts them outside the progressive sense of history at the heart of the Jacksonian era, and yet they remain enough a part of the national psyche that even the "civilized" have nightmares about them. To adapt David Mitchell and Sharon Snyder's phrase, Fedallah becomes a crutch upon which the novel's geopolitical narrative leans.[56]

American Turks

Understanding the prosthetic logic of this exchange can guide the way we read the extensive Islamic imagery in *Moby-Dick*. The novel regularly compares whale hunting to the Crusades, the series of religious wars from AD 1095 to 1291 in which Christian soldiers sought to wrest the Holy Land from Muslim control. Ishmael compares each mate on a whaling voyage to a "Gothic Knight of old" who is accompanied by a harpooner ready to provide a "fresh lance" during the fight (120). Although he understood the Crusades' lingering prestige, Melville perceived how the chivalric veneer glossed over plunder, carnage, and cruelty. In *Clarel*, he writes that the age combined "belief devout and bandit rage."[57]

Ahab also identifies the Crusades as a model for motivating the *Pequod*'s pursuit of Moby Dick. In a passage in which Ishmael communicates the captain's inner thoughts, Ahab presumes that to control his crew, he must appeal to humanity's fundamental "sordidness." The white whale may incite the hearts of "my savage crew," he thinks. And their "savageness" may breed "a certain generous knight-errantism" in the pursuit, but one must still feed their baser appetites:

> For even the high lifted and chivalric Crusaders of old times were not content to traverse two thousand miles of land to fight for their holy sepulchre, without committing burglaries, picking pockets, and gaining other pious perquisites by the way. Had they been strictly held to their one final and romantic object—that final and romantic object, too many would have turned from in disgust. I will not strip these men, thought Ahab, of all hopes of cash—aye, cash. (212)

The passage briefly sets up the *Pequod* as a crew of venal idealists who have committed themselves to a battle against that greatest of infidels, the white whale. Whatever thievery takes place, whatever mercenary crimes occur in pursuit, all will be redeemed if they claim the whale's corpse, the holy sepulcher of the captain's aggrievement.

Melville's well-known resistance to allegory should caution us from extending such a reading across the novel. Writing to Sophia Hawthorne in 1851, he delicately suggested that her "allegoric construction" of the novel revealed more about her "spiritualizing nature" than it did his text.[58] Ishmael was not as polite in "The Affidavit" when he warned against interpreting the white whale "as a monstrous fable, or still worse and more detestable, a hideous and intolerable allegory" (205). The admonition pertains to the military symbolism as well. Ahab may compare his crew to Crusaders fighting Moby Dick, but Ishmael joins a series of characters in applying similar imagery to the captain himself. Using a wide range of

100 THE PROSTHETIC ARTS OF *MOBY-DICK*

historical references, he repeatedly associates Ahab with Islamic forms of power. From Stubb to Archie to the carpenter, crewmembers refer to Ahab as "Old Mogul" or "Old Mogulship," imagining their captain as one of the Mughal rulers that descended from Genghis Kahn and Islamicized much of Asia in the thirteenth century.[59] Such images exoticize and amplify Ahab's power, turning the "weather-stained" *Pequod* into a grand conqueror's vessel engaged in a transhistorical quest. The desire to elevate the journey knows no religious bounds. Ishmael compares the ship's wrinkled deck to "the pilgrim-worshipped flag-stone in Canterbury Cathedral where [Thomas] Becket bled" and then, fourteen chapters later, describes Ahab as a "Khan of the plank, and a king of the sea" (69, 129).

The imagery helps Melville build his epic not around allegory but around an extraordinary, but nonetheless common man. As Chapter 33, "The Specksynder," explains, the captain represented a kind of hero different from the "highly renowned and prosperous" characters that had populated Aristotelian tragedies.[60] "But Ahab, my captain, still moves before me in all his Nantucket grimness and shagginess," Ishmael laments, "and in this episode touching Emperors and Kings, I must not conceal that I have only to do with a poor old whale-hunter like him" (148). Denied "all outward majestical trappings," the storyteller must find his character's greatness in the contours of his mind rather than fortune or illustrious background. "Oh, Ahab! what shall be grand in thee, it must needs be plucked at from the skies, and dived for in the deep, and featured in the unbodied air!" (148).[61]

As if underscoring the point, Melville follows this passage with Chapter 34, "The Cabin-Table," which presents Ahab as a sultan ruling over his three emirs, Starbuck, Stubb, and Flask. The setting is a dinner table, and all eat the same modest dish. But as each mate shortens his meal to accommodate the officer who ranks above him, the ship's rituals subtly confirm and convey Ahab's rule. Ahab has no interest in pomp and grandeur, but as Ishmael phrases it, the "certain sultanism" of his brain leads him to embrace maritime conventions that embody his "irresistible dictatorship" (147). The supreme ruler of the nineteenth-century Ottoman state, the sultan (meaning "authority" in Arabic) supervised lesser dignitaries who submitted to his political and cultural power.[62] The chapter's sole majestic trapping, the sultanic allusions underscore the scene's shaggy poverty, while also suggesting that dinner with Ahab could equal the machinations of an Ottoman royal court.

Like many of his contemporaries, Melville identified the Turks with ruthless, unchecked power. During the Renaissance, Turks had replaced Arabs as the "dominant symbol of Islam," and over four centuries of imperial rule, that view had become solidified in the eyes of Europeans who regarded the Ottomans as a threat to their own culture and sovereignty.[63] Cemil Aydin has explained that, in the nineteenth century, the Greek War of Independence helped catalyze the impression that Christian subjects were oppressed by an aggressively Muslim tyrant.[64] "The Ottomans have been 'encamped in Europe for centuries,'" the New Hampshire congressman Daniel Webster warned in an 1824 speech to the US House of Representatives. "The religious and civil code of the state being both fixed in the Koran, and equally the object of an ignorant and furious faith, have been found equally incapable of change."[65] Webster's comment reflects a practice that would become prevalent in the nineteenth century: treating the Ottomans not as a rival imperial power but as a religiously defined enemy to Christian civilizations. As Carl W. Ernst pointed out, the idea that Islam positioned itself against the West was the product of European colonialists and the scholars who paved their way by explaining the religion. Like many, Webster notably associates the Ottomans with the same refusal to change that Ishmael linked to Fedallah and the Muslim-majority societies of the "Oriental isles." His anti-Ottoman rhetoric thinly disguised Christian ambitions for its territories. In fact, as Ernst points out, between Napoleon's invasion of Egypt in 1798 and the dismantling of the Ottoman Empire after World War I, nearly 90 percent of the world's Muslim population had been under colonial rule.[66]

Melville's 1856–57 trip to the Holy Land gave him opportunities to see the Ottoman Empire himself. His journal records his resentment over the Turkish exercise of power in Jerusalem. Visiting the Holy Sepulcher containing the reputed Tomb of Christ, he remarked on the Turkish policemen who disdainfully looked over the pilgrims entering the church. Melville found the ruined sepulcher disappointing as both a tourist and a spiritual site. "All is glitter & nothing is gold," he wrote. "A sickening cheat." But he repeatedly visited the site to witness "the spectacle of the scornful Turks on the divan, & the scorned pilgrims kissing the stone of the anointing." Like much of the journal, the entry records Melville's frustration with the "mildewed" nature of Christianity, but it is also political.[67] In recoiling at the policemen, he recoils at the arrogance of a declining imperial power.

102   THE PROSTHETIC ARTS OF *MOBY-DICK*

Melville's earlier writings tended to use Ottoman imagery in commenting on the cultivation of despotic power in the United States. When Ishmael refers to Ahab as the Grand Turk in "The Cabin-Table," he echoes a prominent theme in *White-Jacket*: how the leadership practices of the American navy imitate the excesses of sultanic rule. The narrator repeatedly collapses the distinction between democratic and Ottoman power, suggesting that democracies cultivated the authoritarianism that Americans scorned in the Turks. In one chapter, he compares the elaborate etiquette surrounding the sultan of Constantinople to the custom of forcing sailors to stop rowing so that they can doff their hats to officers in a passing ship. Other comparisons focus on the abrogation of human rights. The American navy, he argues, operates by a "Turkish code" in granting officers the right to punish "others with a judicial severity unknown on the national soil." As the source of law and punishment, an American commander wields an explicitly Islamic power: "With the Articles of War in one hand, and the cat-o'-nine-tails in the other, he stands an undignified parody upon Muhammed enforcing Moslemism with the sword and the Koran."[68]

But Islamic societies were not simply a convenient reference point in Melville's critique of tyrannical rule: they were a haunting reminder of America's failure to live up to its purported ideals. *White-Jacket* invokes Muhammad as did the different renditions of Voltaire's play, using the Prophet as a rhetorically flexible image to attack both internal and external adversaries. The figure of prostheses is especially enlightening here. Repeated over multiple texts, the image of American Turks extends the discourse surrounding national identity in externalizing a practice that Melville views as being part of democratic life. "We talk of the Turks, and abhor the cannibals," the young narrator of *Redburn* asks, "but may not some of *them*, go to heaven, before some of *us*?"[69] The Ottomans help Melville characterize the authoritarianism that lurks in the United States' political and military affairs.[70] An 1836 article in *The Knickerbocker* contended that moral motives "seem to lose their force" when Turks ascend "in the scale of despotic power." The Turk believes that "when an action highly criminal in itself flows from high, irresponsible authority, that there must be some great end in view, by which it is redeemed and sanctified."[71] What is the Grand Turk Ahab but a "high, irresponsible authority" emboldened by the thought that his pursuit is "redeemed and sanctified"? Melville's imagery rejects allegory in turning the Islamicized Ahab into an image of an American willingness to wreak violence in the name of power.

Phantoms, Prophets, and Assassins

Fedallah's conflicting ethnic and religious traits suggest that Melville had difficulty deciding who precisely this shadowy character should be. A fitting disclaimer comes from Pierre Bayle, one of Melville's favorite sources, who introduced his *Encyclopedia* entry on Zoroaster by warning readers "not to expect here any thing besides a heap of uncertainties, and an odd medly of stories."[72] Melville's Fedallah significantly adds to these uncertainties. Not only does the Parsee worship fire, and not only does he have a made-up, incongruously Muslim name, but his physical description changes considerably. When Fedallah first appears, Ishmael describes him as a dark-skinned Persian from India whose companions have the "vivid, tiger-yellow complexion peculiar to some of the aboriginal natives of the Manillas" (217). Fedallah's Chinese clothes seem to align him with the "Manilla men," however, as if he came not from Pakistan or India but from the islands of the South China Sea (442). Flask reinforces this impression when he refers to Fedallah as a "gamboge ghost" whose skin has the same color as the yellowish resin of the Cambodian Garcinia tree (325). Melville seems conflicted about how much to differentiate Fedallah from his companions and how much to have him share in the description that, in their time at sea, they were covertly serving "the devil, their lord" (217). With all these opposing traits, Fedallah emerges as a "cosmopolitan concatenation of oriental tags," as John Bryant has put it, "a stereotype and yet a parody of stereotyping."[73] No matter how scrambled they seem, the tags and parodies have a fundamental utility in prosthetically extending and externalizing the will to kill Moby Dick. Fedallah's embodiment of racial difference is inextricable from his embodiment of Ahab's aggrievement.

Amid the contradictions, we can identify at least two versions of Fedallah. In one version, Fedallah is a dark-skinned Parsee who bows before the blacksmith's forge and recognizes the eternal battle between good and evil. In "The Candles," he dramatically kneels in prayer as the ship lights up in flames and Ahab claims that despite having once been a fire-worshiping Persian himself, he now defies God's "speechless, placeless power" (507). In the other version, Fedallah is a saffron-skinned Muslim with a hair turban, one of the phantoms who haunt the dreams of people in the earth's northern ("temperate") regions, but periodically "glide among the unchanging Asiatic communities, especially the Oriental isles to the east of the continent" (231). A representative of the Global South, he ties the hunt to prehistoric

104   THE PROSTHETIC ARTS OF *MOBY-DICK*

times and a sinister threat to Christian civilization. Melville saw two possibilities in Fedallah, and in his rolling approach to characterization, he chose both.[74]

Fedallah is "the gothic extreme" of Melville's "dark Islamicism," as Marr has argued, and the central figure in what Spencer Tricker has called "Melville's Pacific Gothic mode."[75] His shadowy, dreamlike presence (in addition to the crew's suspicious response to him) makes him a fitting addition to the gothic characters of Hawthorne and Poe. Emerging as a critique of enlightenment rationalism, the gothic often dramatized moments of racial and gender difference. The Ottoman Empire featured prominently in two of the genre's most enduring narratives, Mary Shelley's *Frankenstein* (1818), in which the doctor creates his prosthetic monster out of graveyard body parts, and Bram Stoker's *Dracula* (1897), in which a monstrous contagion sweeps across Europe. Although less enthralling to later generations, Beckworth's *Vathek* introduced Melville and his contemporaries to what Sophia Rose Arjana has called one of the most notorious "monsters of Orientalism" to come out of the romantic period (Figure 7).[76] A despotic, cruel, and pleasure-seeking sultan, Vathek fills his harem with women, men, and children; he blasphemes constantly; and naked himself, he lures fifty naked boys to their deaths (or so it seems at the time). Melville was intrigued by the grotesque Indian sorcerer who embeds himself in Vathek's court with promises of the "palace of subterranean fire." This dark-skinned genie, whose supernatural power bewilders and astounds, persuades the sultan to "abjure Mahomet" in favor of "devoting himself to the worship of fire" and gaining "the treasures of the pre-adamite sultans."[77]

The prevalence of Asian stereotypes in the eighteenth and nineteenth centuries appears in the multiple sources that scholars have identified for Fedallah, from a story about a Persian king named Fadlallah in *The Spectator* to a group of Arab devil worshipers in Hope's *Anastasius*.[78] One could say that, like the monster in *Frankenstein*, Fedallah emerges from the gothic tradition as a combination of exotic but ill-fitting parts. A compelling source comes from Thomas De Quincey's *Confessions of an English Opium-Eater* (1822), which Melville purchased in London for one pound, six shillings in the winter of 1849.[79] The novel had such an impact on the young writer that he proudly opened his journal as soon as he completed it. "Have just this moment finished the 'Opium Eater,'" he wrote on 23 December at 3:30 p.m. "A most wondrous book." When he sailed home on Christmas Day, his novel about a white whale was already taking shape in his head.[80]

THE PHANTOM FEDALLAH   105

Figure 7 Richard Westall, illustration from *Vathek* by William Beckford: The "Giaour" and Caliph Vathek. Late eighteenth to early nineteenth century. Watercolor.
Image courtesy of the Dyce Collection, V&A Museum, South Kensington, London.

Melville's granddaughter, Eleanor Melville Metcalfe, first suggested that a scene in the novel influenced the writing of Fedallah and his Manilla men.[81] Holed up in the English mountainside, the opium-addled De Quincey meets a mysterious Malaysian man who appears at his cottage door. With "his turban and loose trousers of dingy white relieved upon the dark

106 THE PROSTHETIC ARTS OF *MOBY-DICK*

paneling," the "tiger-cat" Malay seems the physical inspiration for Ahab's stowaway crew.[82] Narrating his own story, De Quincey emphasizes the contrast between the white skin of the English servant girl and the "sallow and bilious skin of the Malay," with his "small, fierce, restless eyes, thin lips, slavish gestures and adorations."[83] We can hear Ishmael in the narrator's belief that a terrifyingly ancient presence has appeared in his hallucinatory dreams. "The causes of my horror lie deep," he recounts. "Southern Asia in general is the seat of awful images and associations. As the cradle of the human race, it would alone have a dim and reverential feeling connected with it."[84] The narrator's racial anxiety compels him to believe that civilized men have more to fear from the "ancient, monumental, cruel, and elaborate religions of Indostan, &c." than they do the barbarisms of Africa. Like Ishmael, he fears "the mere antiquity of Asiatic things, of their institutions, histories, modes of faith," especially as they persist through "immemorial tracts of time."[85] In changing the Hindu Malay to the Muslim Parsee, Melville adapted the "monstrous scenery" of De Quincey's "Oriental dreams" to Ishmael's fear that Fedallah retained the "aboriginalness" of the earth's first days.[86]

Ishmael repeatedly presents the Parsee as an extension of Ahab's consciousness. As if they were governed by the same neural network, the "potent spell" joining Ahab with Fedallah allows the two men to communicate without "the slightest verbal interchange" (537). The crew may move "like machines" under Ahab's "despot eye," but they secretly notice Ahab and Fedallah "fixedly gazing upon each other" as partners in a "mystic watch" (536–38).[87] The more incorporated Fedallah becomes into Ahab's will, the more disembodied he becomes. "A gliding strangeness, began to invest the thin Fedallah now," Ishmael reports in Chapter 130, "The Hat." "Such ceaseless shudderings shook him; that the men looked dubious at him; half uncertain, as it seemed, whether indeed he were a mortal substance, or else a tremulous shadow cast upon the deck by some unseen being's body" (537). In Ishmael's conception, it is Fedallah, not the Westerner, who shudders at what he finds in the other man, but committed to mystifying the Parsee's already ethereal presence, the narrator turns him into the shadow of both Ahab and an unnamed spectral force. When Ishmael later describes Fedallah as looking upon Ahab and seeing the "abandoned substance" of himself, he effectively turns him into a twice-cast shadow that once took substantive form (538). As flesh and spirit, the two form parts of a prosthetically defined whole: after Ahab laughs in derision in "The Whale Watch," "both were silent again, as one man" (499).

Like the slate on Ahab's ivory leg, Fedallah's ability to find the whale ultimately brings about the novel's final sequence. In "The Spirit-Spout," Ishmael describes the dark moonlit nights in the waters south of St. Helena when Fedallah climbs the masthead and mysteriously stands watch. The seamen's wariness grows as they behold the "old Oriental perched aloft at such unusual hours; his turban and the moon, companions in one sky" (232). One serene and silvery night, Fedallah spies a "silvery jet" ahead of the *Pequod's* bow. "Lit up by the moon," Ishmael intones, "it looked celestial; seemed some plumed and glittering god uprising from the sea" (232). The more superstitious crewmembers identify the spout with Moby Dick, who seems to beckon them elusively toward a battle "in the remotest and most savage seas" (233).

The chapter positions Fedallah at the point at which Ishmael turns the *Pequod's* physical journey into a transcendental hunt. A strong breeze behind the stern gives the impression that "two antagonistic influences" were "struggling" in the ship—"one to mount direct to heaven, the other to drive yawingly to some horizontal goal" (233). The silvery jet temporarily disappears, but the image of the ship—simultaneously rushing forward and rising above—encapsulates Fedallah's prosthetic role in the quest. Whatever his theological angst, Ahab seeks his revenge in physical space. He can chart currents, read the sun, and navigate from the South Atlantic to the Solomon Sea. His knowledge and monomania are the most dependable winds rushing the *Pequod* to the promise of revenge. The gothic Fedallah spiritualizes the narrative, lifting the *Pequod* toward heaven or plunging it toward hell. Ahab may walk on death and life, his "dead limb" sounding like a coffin-tap across the deck, but Fedallah crosses between the physical and spirit worlds, "his turban and the moon, companions in one sky" (232). With Fedallah on the masthead, spouts are celestial, whales glitter like gods, and the cry "There she blows" awakens the crew as if it were a Judgment Day trumpet (233).

Melville couches much of this gothicism in superstition and prejudice, but the narrative confirms Fedallah's metaphysical insight when he prophesies the three conditions necessary for Ahab's death. The conditions are so deceptively reassuring, of course, that the captain naively gloats about his immortality, but the accuracy of Fedallah's prophecy adds another dimension to the text. Like the witches in *Macbeth*, he is a soothsayer who sees beyond the limitations of human time, and his vision lifts Ahab's quest out of monomania and into a realm in which spiritual forces intercede in human affairs. The anxious chart reader who later throws his quadrant to

108   THE PROSTHETIC ARTS OF *MOBY-DICK*

the deck relies upon Fedallah as his metaphysical guide, a prosthetic prophet who can extend his mortal abilities and know what the future holds. Unlike the novel's other prophetic voices, Elijah and Gabriel, Fedallah provides the captain with the intimate, unnatural power that helps him avenge his missing leg. With his terrifying, relentless will, the captain seeks prosthetic assistance. That assistance, we later learn, is as compromised as the ivory leg that splinters in the same wreck that kills the Parsee.

Fedallah does not use the word "prophet" to describe himself, but in prophesying Ahab's death, he underscores his own supplemental relation to the hunt. "I shall still go before thee thy pilot," he tells the captain, offering an image that Ahab finds so comforting he repeats it twice (499).[88] The image comes from the Greek word for blade or oar (*pēdon*), and in maritime usage, it refers to the smaller boat (and, in some cases, simply a steersman) that helps larger ships navigate a harbor's currents and shoals. Captains Peleg and Bildad pilot the *Pequod* out of Nantucket harbor on Christmas Day, but once the Spirit Spout appears, the stowaway Fedallah becomes Ahab's guide, the pilot who will lead him to his catastrophic battle with the white whale. Ishmael subtly foreshadows this duplicitous role when he describes Fedallah's "living hair" turban as being "braided and coiled round and round upon his head." As Tricker points out, the image resembles the rope that will serpentine through the crew and catch Ahab around his neck (217).[89]

The biblical King Ahab had a similarly external presence in his court. The king had continually angered the Lord for worshiping the idol Baal and refusing to heed the prophets who tried to correct his evil ways. In a remarkable passage, Micaiah reports that the Lord has sent a lying spirit into the mouths of the false prophets Ahab has gathered around him, and they entice the king into a battle against the Syrians that he will fatally lose.[90] The dogs, as Ishmael recalls, lick the blood of his corpse (79). When Fedallah appears on the chase's final day, his "half torn body" lashed and pinioned to the hearse of Moby Dick, the captain understands that he has been deceived (568). Fedallah, as Peter Szendy has written, "is above all the voice of Ahab's fate," a fate that necessitates his going before his captain as if his prophecy were a "pro-thesis and prosthesis" at the same time.[91]

Fedallah's corpse reminds us that images of Islamic violence converge around Ahab's quest. As a narrator, Ishmael emphasizes bulk and power when he describes the whale severing Ahab's leg like a mower cutting a blade of grass. But when he characterizes the whale's intentional cruelty, he compares it to an assassination. "No turbaned Turk, no hired Venetian or Malay, could have smote him with more seeming malice" (184). The line recasts Othello's final soliloquy as he implores the assembled officials to represent him fairly after he has murdered his wife, Desdemona. He wants them to know that he is wracked with grief and that his eyes "Drop tears as fast as the Arabian trees / Their med'cinable gum." But even more importantly, Othello wants the men to remember his military service in a hostile Ottoman state. "In Aleppo once," he tells them, "Where a malignant and a turbaned Turk / Beat a Venetian and traduced the state, / I took by th' throat the circumcised dog And smote him—thus."[92] Othello fatally stabs himself, for in his mind, he is both the avenger of innocent Venetians and the Muslim assailant whose brutality must be avenged.

The allusion captures the ways in which *Moby-Dick* repeatedly implicates Ahab in its Orientalist portrait of violence. By adding the hired Malay and the Venetian to the "turbaned Turk," Ishmael compares the whale to a series of assassins at the edges of the Islamic world. Starbuck has told Ahab that it is "blasphemous" to credit the "dumb thing" with an act of will, but as Ishmael presents it, the whale acts with the same deliberate cruelty as a stereotypical Turk (164). Othello may have recognized the beast within, and as a Moor, he is closer to the turbaned Turk than his fellow Venetians. But the American Ahab externalizes the threat. He does not avenge the mistreatment of his countrymen or insults to the state. He avenges the loss of his leg by a force so furious and inscrutable that Ishmael conjures the figure of Islam to convey it.

The Islamic theme continues when the whale appears in the "Turkish-rugged waters" of "the mysterious, divine Pacific" (548, 483). The turbaned Turk, the hired Venetian, and Malay all carried the threat of an ominous and exotic influence stalking its Nantucket prey. But with Fedallah as his pilot, Ahab dies not as a Christian Crusader at the hands of a foreign assassin. He dies as a member of a Turkish imperial court:

The harpoon was darted; the stricken whale flew forward; with igniting velocity the line ran through the groove;—ran foul. Ahab stooped to clear it; he did clear it; but the flying turn caught him round the neck, and voicelessly as Turkish mutes bowstring their victim, he was shot out of the boat, ere the crew knew he was gone. (572)

110   THE PROSTHETIC ARTS OF *MOBY-DICK*

Melville was hardly the first Western writer to mention "Turkish mutes," a term referring to the deaf, illiterate guards often employed in Ottoman palaces and seraglios. Shakespeare references a "Turkish mute" in *Henry V*, and numerous travel narratives recount how rulers found their disability useful because they could neither hear nor communicate state secrets.[93] As executioners, they were unlikely to report their acts.[94] The quest for revenge begins with Ahab's dismemberment and ensuing rage. It ends with secrecy and silence.

In bowstringing their victims, Turkish guards would loop a cord around someone's neck and pull the opposite sides. The strangulation of enemies was a recurrent feature in Orientalist tales, and *Vathek* includes a gruesome scene in which the Caliph's mutes adjust "their cords" to fit the necks of multiple victims. ("Never before had the ceremony of strangulation been performed with such facility," the narrator cheerfully reports.)[95] Ottoman law prescribed multiple forms of the death penalty. Highway robbers were impaled, criminal soldiers cut into two, and corrupt mine supervisors thrown into the pits. Judges who failed to inform the sultan about oppressive local officials were pounded to death in stone mortars. But the bowstring was the traditional "instrument of execution for members of the royal house in order to avoid shedding their blood."[96] Moby Dick ultimately claims the "poor old whale-hunter" as a royal Turk.

The association seems ironic only if we fail to recognize that Ahab generates the same authoritarian violence that Ishmael repeatedly ascribes to other governments and societies. From its first appearance on deck, the ivory leg suggests that the captain defines himself by the species that dismasted him. Ahab's execution makes clear that Ishmael extends that relation from the shared substance of wounded bodies to the shared (and overdetermined) figure of geopolitics: in the Turkish rugged waters, the Grand Turk captain dies connected to the Turkish assassin Moby Dick. As we saw with Fedallah, the only other turbaned character in the novel, the imagery that isolates the whale as an exotically fearsome other ultimately binds him closer to his vengeful antagonist. The attempt to portray this threat as being vaguely (and yet treacherously) Muslim ultimately underscores the willfulness of Ahab's power. In this way, the novel undermines the comfortable distinctions Adams and Webster tried to raise between democracy and Ottoman rule. As Ishmael reminds us, at the heart of the Jacksonian era was the drive to subjugate the western frontier and own the seas. The idea of self-determination, which Tocqueville saw as the central

THE PHANTOM FEDALLAH   111

promise of popular sovereignty, created imperial desires as brutal and prone to autocracy as a sultanic regime. With grievance rather than scripture as his spiritual core, Ahab yearns to conquer the infidels by force.

The Prosthetics of Fate

Debates about Fedallah's name have obscured the work that the character performs in Ahab's assault against the heavens and seas. In her 1961 book *Melville's Orienda*, Dorothee Metlitsky Finkelstein argued that Fedallah means "the Sacrifice [or Ransom] of God."[97] As Finkelstein saw it, the root *Fed* comes from the Arabic term *fedai*, which means "'the devoted one' or 'he who offers up his life.'"[98] Connecting Fedallah with the Ismaili mystic assassins who targeted religious enemies, she viewed Fedallah as "Fate's devoted 'assassin' sent to 'assassinate' Ahab the heretic."[99] In this reading, Fedallah serves the dark purpose of bringing Ahab to justice, similar to the role that the false prophets played in leading the Hebrew king to his battlefield death. Many commentators have described Fedallah as "the sacrifice of God" without endorsing Finkelstein's belief that his pledge to Ahab—"hemp only can kill thee"—alludes to the alleged Ismaili practice of smoking hashish to prepare for their missions against Christian Crusaders.[100] Other critics have rejected Finkelstein's etymology, claiming that Fedallah derives from Fadlallah, the protagonist in *The Spectator* story that Melville may have encountered as a schoolboy.[101] Derived from *Fazl*, Fadlallah is a common Arabic name that means "Generosity or Effusion of God." This interpretation may be difficult to reconcile with Ahab's demonic hunt, but it brings the advantage of avoiding the dubious legends about Muslim assassins that date from the days of Marco Polo.[102]

The precise meaning of Fedallah's made-up name is less significant, however, than what his presence suggests about the novel's climactic scenes. Stubb's final lines explicitly insert the assassination theme into the final chase and, notably, are the only time the word appears in the book. "Look ye, sun, moon, and stars!" Stubb shouts from the *Pequod* as he and Starbuck see the whale coming down on them. "I call ye assassins of as good a fellow as ever spouted up his ghost" (571). Starbuck wonders if this is the end of his "bursting prayers" and "life-long fidelities" (570). When he beseeches God for help, he knows he is facing more than a "dumb brute" acting out of "blindest instinct" (163–64). Stubb believes something more sinister has

112   THE PROSTHETIC ARTS OF *MOBY-DICK*

occurred, accusing the heavens of conspiring in the assassination of every-one on ship. The narrative momentarily undercuts the gravity of the accu-sation when Stubb begins to disrobe, determined to die wearing nothing but his drawers. But Ishmael returns to the idea when he describes the white whale "strangely vibrating his predestinating head" as he barrels toward the ship. "Retribution, swift vengeance, eternal malice were in his whole aspect, and spite of all that mortal man could do, the solid white buttress of his forehead smote the ship's starboard bow, till men and timbers reeled" (571). Ishmael gives Moby Dick a timeless, metaphysical agency. Reversing the expectations that the novel has done so much to create, he turns the indom-itable beast into a force of retribution infinitely greater than anything the avenger Ahab could attain.[103]

The Parsee prepares readers for this role reversal. The more Fedallah looms over the novel's final chapters, the more Ahab seems to distance him-self from the quest.[104] Ahab may seem "an independent lord" and the Parsee "his slave," but the captain comes to shun the sight of Fedallah as if he rep-resented a fatal, unfulfilled task (538). Amid his appeals to the devil and blasphemous attacks on the gods, Ahab begins to think of vengeance as a burden imposed upon him by a powerful, external force. Fedallah might lead us to ask whether he was serving Ahab's vengeance or Moby Dick's.

In "The Quarter-Deck," Ahab tells Starbuck that he sees "inscrutable malice" in Moby Dick, and "that inscrutable thing" is what he chiefly hates (164). But communing with the first mate in "The Symphony," he concludes that another power controls his will. Seeing his own family in the first mate's eyes, the captain asserts that an "inscrutable, unearthly thing" drives his commitment to revenge:

> What cozening, hidden lord and master, and cruel, remorseless emperor commands me; that against all natural lovings and longings, I so keep pushing, and crowding, and jamming myself on all the time; recklessly making me ready to do what in my own proper, natural heart, I durst not so much as dare? (545)

Amid this crisis of responsibility, the captain suffers from personal doubt and begins to extricate himself from the conflict he has done so much to create. "Is Ahab, Ahab?" he asks Starbuck. "Is it I, God, or who, that lifts this arm?" (545). To borrow his metaphor for Moby Dick, Ahab wonders whether he himself is a pasteboard mask. Is he the physical agent of a larger controlling principle? Does a "hidden lord and master" imperceptibly shape what we mistake as individual will? Looking back at him in the sea, Fedallah's eyes suggest that, in the end, Ahab has no choice: an external power has determined his fate.

Although it may seem paradoxical, the captain is startled by his lack of agency even as he takes solace in it. Eric Fromm identifies a similar phenomenon in authoritarian personalities. "The feature common to all authoritarian thinking is the conviction that life is determined by forces outside of man's own self, his interest, his wishes." Although we might think they subscribe to a world that is wholly made of their will, authoritarians such as Ahab treasure the "powerlessness of man," viewing themselves as the product of larger forces and circumstances that have summoned them into being.[105] They carry out their will convinced that they are sanctioned by a higher order. "Not only the forces that determine one's identity directly," Fromm writes, "but those that seem to determine life in general are felt as unchangeable fate."[106]

With Fedallah missing and the captain standing on his fractured prosthetic limb, Ahab and Starbuck return to their conversation about sailing home for Nantucket after the chase's second day. But while Ahab felt confusion and despair in "The Symphony," he now resolutely submits to an "unchangeable fate" that gives him no freedom to make a different choice. "Ahab is for ever Ahab, man," he tells Starbuck. "This whole act's immutably decreed. 'Twas rehearsed by thee and me a billion years before this ocean rolled. Fool! I am the Fates' lieutenant; I act under orders" (561). The monomania of his iron purpose gives way to his deference to a predetermined end.

The change is even more stunning than Ahab's claim to have worshiped the "clear spirit of clear fire" since his days in ancient Persia (507). Having absorbed part of Fedallah's identity, he asserts that one cannot escape the past, that it looms over the present and eradicates the individual will. Such is the promise of the escape from freedom. "The authoritarian character worships the past," Fromm explains. "What has been will eternally be."[107] Ahab offers a sacralized vision of history in which the laws of the past do not allow for revelation, choice, or change. At the moment when Starbuck urges Ahab to most assert his will, the captain claims he is powerless to deviate from a providential decree. Pointing to his "lonely foot," he foregrounds the very impetus for his revenge, only to proclaim that he will complete the mission that eternity bequeathed to him (561).

114 THE PROSTHETIC ARTS OF *MOBY-DICK*

The transformation provides multiple interpretive possibilities. Throughout the novel, Ahab has expertly staged his leadership, knowing that with his outlandish demands and missing leg, he must periodically amaze his crew to keep them subservient. His magically fixing the compass needle, his railings against the gods, and his pursuing an eternal, supernatural fight are all examples of a theatrical leadership style meant to fortify his control of the ship. But we can also conclude that these final chapters illustrate the evolution of monomania into megalomania: in the pressure of the hunt, the captain's feline madness has become delusional and overtaken his sense of self. Ahab, by this account, clings to symbols and meanings that endow his revenge with a cosmic significance that matches his self-regard. Armed with the belief that he is fated to defy God, the captain absolves himself of responsibility for the crisis he has produced.

Fedallah facilitates this transformation in sanctioning the violence that Ahab yearns to inflict. The novel's final chapters reveal how Ahab shifts responsibility for that violence, and the catastrophe it will produce, to the ancient, shuddering Parsee. As they do in "The Symphony," Ahab's humanities become more pronounced the more Fedallah prosthetically pilots the *Pequod* to its catastrophic end. An important psycho-cultural transaction happens here. Fedallah emerges from *Moby-Dick* less as Ahab's dark shadow than as an image of American violence as it has been projected onto an Asian man with an explicitly Islamic name. The novel's gothic orientalism mirrors a cultural practice, as ubiquitous as the white whale, of situating Western violence in the character of savages, barbarians, and infidels. Melville understood how Americans racialized difference in advancing their geopolitical goals, justifying their own violence as democracy's right to sovereign conflict around the globe. Exuding triumphalism, this logic parades across the twenty-first-century news, though in 1851, Melville glimpsed it as one of American democracy's many self-delusions. Like the *Pequod*'s owners, Ahab might be a Quaker with a vengeance, but he depends on Fedallah to execute and complete his holy war of revenge. What the next chapter will explore is the role that he plays not just in Ahab's quest, but in the narrative telling of *Moby-Dick*. Crucial to the plot, survival, and voice of the text, Fedallah is the prosthetic upon which both Ahab and Ishmael depend.

4

Ishmael, Salaaming

The Prosthetic Structure of *Moby-Dick*

A passage from Chapter 44, "The Chart," raises some valuable questions about Islamic imagery in the narrative of *Moby-Dick*. Ishmael compares Ahab's search for the white whale, among the hundreds of thousands of whales swimming in the sea, to a hunter looking for a specific Islamic legal scholar on Constantinople's crowded streets. The pauses and shifts in the phrasing merit attention:

> But granting all this; yet, regarded discreetly and coolly, seems it not but a mad idea, this; that in the broad boundless ocean, one solitary whale, even if encountered, should be thought capable of individual recognition from his hunter, even as a white-bearded Mufti in the thronged thoroughfares of Constantinople? No. For the peculiar snow-white brow of Moby Dick, and his snow-white hump, could not but be unmistakable.[1]

The passage offers a more complicated version of the needle-in-a-haystack problem. As a narrator, Ishmael expects his readers to be skeptical that such a hunt could be successful—"seems it not but a mad idea"—and with his characteristic hyperbole, he compares the futility of seeking Moby Dick with the futility of seeking a specific, white-bearded mufti in a city teeming with white-bearded, turban-wearing men. Answering his own question, he assures readers that "No," finding the white whale would not be implausible. A captain such as Ahab *could* recognize Moby Dick's snow-white brow and hump. As Samuel Otter tells us, the chapter alludes to well-known nineteenth-century whaling charts in trying "to convince readers that the search for one whale in the world's oceans is grounded in actual data and practice."[2] Ishmael raises the mufti comparison only to shift from it. Science and experience win out over improbability.

And yet Melville's manuscript presumably answered the rhetorical question with "Yes," as that is the response that appears in the novel's first British

The Prosthetic Arts of Moby-Dick. David Haven Blake, Oxford University Press. © Oxford University Press 2024.
DOI: 10.1093/oso/9780197780510.003.0005

116   THE PROSTHETIC ARTS OF *MOBY-DICK*

and American editions. The correction comes from a team of twentieth-century scholars who determined that the logic of the paragraph would dictate a "No" and that Melville simply got "mixed up" when he wrote "Yes."[3] I have no interest in disputing this editorial decision, but the confusion is worth exploring in greater depth. In plotting his novel, could Melville have been concerned that the central premise of his narrative would strike some readers as being far-fetched? Seems it a mad idea that a captain could both find and recognize a single whale among all the whales in the sea? "Well," the hasty and, at times, self-doubting writer might have thought, "Yes."[4]

As the paragraph continues, the flat declaration of "No" seems less convincing. As Ishmael describes him, Ahab certainly has his doubts:

> And have I not tallied the whale, Ahab would mutter to himself, as after poring over his charts till long after midnight he would throw himself back in reveries—tallied him, and shall he escape? His broad fins are bored, and scalloped out like a lost sheep's ear! And here, his mad mind would run on in a breathless race; till a weariness and faintness of pondering came over him; and in the open air of the deck he would seek to recover his strength. Ah, God! what trances of torments does that man endure who is consumed with one unachieved revengeful desire. He sleeps with clenched hands; and wakes with his own bloody nails in his palms. (201)

Ahab tries to soothe himself by rehearsing the whale's physical qualities, but that does not eliminate the anxiety that despite the hours charting currents and tallying his prey, the whale could escape. Articulating Ahab's private worries, Ishmael wonders whether Moby Dick could disappear in the ocean like a white-bearded mufti in a crowded Ottoman street.

The last chapter explained how the mysterious Fedallah helps address these concerns. By establishing a mystical structure to the narrative, the addition of Fedallah oddly makes the climax more convincing. Fedallah emerges as a counterpart to the chart, a prosthetic extension not just of Ahab's knowledge but of Melville's plot. His secret powers make him an agent of narrative design, a spectral force that pilots the avenger to the predestinating head of the captain's similarly vengeful adversary. Other scholars have discussed the ways in which "The Chart" chronicles the birth of Fedallah as a disembodied version of Ahab's self, a devilish fiend who comes out of Ahab's dreams and yet, like his purpose, is a "self-assumed, independent being of its own" (202).[5] To these psychoanalytic readings, I would add that the birth of Fedallah is equally important to Melville's plot. Three chapters after Ishmael compares Moby Dick to a Turkish mufti, three chapters after the text raises the possibility that the whale might never be found, Tashtego sees flukes, and Fedallah and his "dusky phantoms" appear on deck, seemingly "fresh formed out of air" (216). It's as if Melville had smuggled them aboard the *Pequod* to brace a wobbly part of his book.

This chapter turns to a related aspect of Fedallah's prosthetic function in *Moby-Dick*: how he both protects and assists the narrative mode. Readers often forget that Ishmael owes his survival not simply to the coffin life-buoy, decorated with the image of Queequeg's tattoos, but to the Parsee's vanishing during the second day's hunt. As he explains in the "Epilogue," *"It so chanced, that after the Parsee's disappearance, I was he whom the Fates ordained to take the place of Ahab's bowsman, when that bowsman assumed the vacant post; the same, who, when on the last day the three men were tossed from out the rocking boat, was dropped astern"* (573). The Fates create the need for Ishmael to leave Starbuck's crew and join the "dusky phantoms" Ahab had first hidden in the steerage (216). Already crucial to Melville's plot, Fedallah becomes crucial to the narration as well. Moby Dick's pulling him into the sea allows for Ishmael's singular escape. The teller and the tale float upon the coffin life-buoy only after Fedallah has resurfaced, his "half torn body" lashed around the whale's back (568). "To any meditative Magian rover, this serene Pacific, once beheld, must ever after be the sea of his adoption," Ishmael writes, hinting that the Pacific was where, as the book's final sentence discloses, the *Rachel* brought him onboard (482). Fedallah expands and supplements Ahab's rage. He and Ishmael have a more subtle, but equally important, relationship: the Parsee's silent disappearance enables the survival of the rover's voice.

Speaking to an audience in New Delhi, Gayatri Chakraborty Spivak commented on the importance of seeing "how the master texts need us in the construction of their texts without acknowledging that need."[6] Often quoted in the scholarship of wounds and disability, the statement helps articulate the line of inquiry this chapter pursues: how Fedallah is necessary to the construction of *Moby-Dick* and how the novel avoids acknowledging that need. I argue that, as narrator, Ishmael both covers and reveals his debts to the Parsee, and that the context of this survival is filled with significance. Like a phantom limb, Fedallah haunts the telling of *Moby-Dick*, his discredited figure quietly positioned at the axis of its plot and narration. The character's structural importance (as inconspicuous as it might be) aligns with the fear he awakes in the *Pequod*'s American crew members.[7] Even as he promises to avenge the captain's injury, Fedallah awakens in Ishmael a conflation of narrative and racial anxieties, a psychic wound he claims to share with the "civilized, domestic people" of the northern hemisphere (231). The narrative depends on a curious transfer of power in which the Jacksonian proponent of empire arises from the death of a harpooner he repeatedly foregrounds as a supernatural and Asian threat. In this master text, we need to acknowledge that Ishmael's hatred of Fedallah not only contradicts his vaunted cosmopolitanism, but also undergirds it.

Amirhossein Vafa has explored these details in depth. In a stunningly creative analysis, Vafa asks us to imagine Fedallah in an "alternate universe" in which he and his "untold story" occupy their own "cultural zone."[8] As we have seen, from the moment he appears in "The First Lowering," Ishmael dehumanizes the Parsee, persistently pushing readers to dread his "unearthly voice" and the multiple regions he is made to represent.[9] What Vafa sees in that characterization is a sustained attempt to eclipse and silence Fedallah's story so that Ishmael can "better articulate that of his own."[10] The "deliberate effacement of Fedallah's voice" ultimately pits its voracious American narrator against the silence of the Parsee.[11] In liberating this "West Asian drifter" from the margins of *Moby-Dick*, Vafa hopes to liberate "the proleptic narrative" that Ishmael has tried "keeping...at bay."[12]

My aim in this chapter is not to give Fedallah his own story (Vafa has already demonstrated what a vital story that would be) but to explore how the novel prosthetically incorporates him into Ishmael's narrative. From his naming himself at the novel's beginning to his unlikely survival at its end, Ishmael's story repeatedly bears the trace of an influence he condemns. The character who metaphysically extends the captain's powers, who seems the insubstantial shadow to his grievously abandoned body, is also the crutch upon which the narrator explicitly leans. Ishmael may compulsively demonize Fedallah, but the Parsee is as much a part of the narrative as he is a part of Ahab's quest—ethereally present, impossibly contrived, and reflective of identities not his own. His increasingly immaterial body aligns with a voice that is both scarcely heard and crucially misunderstood. As Spivak might have predicted, there are consequences to acknowledging the supplementary role Fedallah plays in a narrative that represents him as a racial and spiritual threat. The character introduces a peculiar politics into *Moby-Dick* in which Ishmael vilifies Fedallah and the Manilla men and yet uses the other harpooners to promote his fascination with Islamicized religious experiences. In recognizing Fedallah's importance from the margins of the text, we see what Ishmael gains from this prostheticized relationship, as well as his hostility to the peoples he perceives to be American rivals in the Asia Pacific.

The introduction of this book discusses how scholars have applied the figure of prosthesis to such dissimilar topics as human memory, the cinema screen, and religious faith.[13] The advantage of applying the figure to Ishmael's narration is that it underscores the connections between storytelling and dismemberment. As Christopher Castiglia reminds us, the depression Ishmael announces on the novel's first page establishes a context for his own fixation on disability, limb loss, and the physical condition of others.[14] The sense that Ahab's limbs have been wasted by fire, that he walks across the deck in coffin-taps, and that his whalebone leg is "barbaric" is indicative of an Ishmaelean consciousness that recoils especially from dismemberment (124). Ishmael prefers permeable bodies over broken ones, and while his most sublime moments express a desire for absorption and melding, his storytelling is haunted by the fragmentation of body parts. In their incomplete, piecemeal fashion, the prosthetic arts of *Moby-Dick* work to reconcile its orphaned parts, bringing dislocated chapters and limbs into coordinated alignment. When Melville commented that he would have to take the "Whale" "by his jaw...and finish him up in some fashion or other," he was inadvertently suggesting that writing the novel involved its own version of dismemberment and prostheses building.[15]

The Phantom Hand

Writing to Hawthorne in spring 1851, Melville complained that he would seldom obtain "the silent grass-growing mood in which a man *ought* always to compose." Feeling "bluely" about his prospects, he confessed, "What I feel most moved to write, that is banned,—it will not pay. Yet altogether, write the *other* way I cannot. So the product is a final hash, and all my books are botches."[16] Melville had numerous frustrations that day—money, rain, blisters, three weeks farming instead of tending to his manuscript—but he could not foresee how botched his novel would seem when, nearly six months later, it was published in London without the "Epilogue." An unauthorized decision by the publisher Richard Bentley, the exclusion of these

120   THE PROSTHETIC ARTS OF *MOBY-DICK*

pivotal sentences gave reviewers something obvious to complain about, as they struggled to reconcile the narrator's survival with the *Pequod*'s sinking into the sea. Accusing him of ad-libbing, the *London Spectator* demurred, "It is a canon with some critics that nothing should be introduced into a novel which is physically impossible for the writer to have known. Mr. Melville hardly steers clear of this rule."[17] *Dublin University* magazine more directly challenged the narrator's viability. If "he was present when the whale smashed the ship to pieces, capsized the boats, and drowned every mother's son among the crew, how does it happen that the author is alive to tell the story?" The reviewer seemed to poke the novelist in the chest: "Eh! Mr. Melville, answer that question, if you please, Sir."[18]

While the response was not uniform, other reviewers characterized the book as a catastrophe. The *London Athæneum* dismissed the novel as "absurd" and lumped Melville among the "incorrigibles" who, amid tantalizing genius, "summon us to endure monstrosities, carelessnesses, and other such harassing manifestations of bad taste as daring or disordered ingenuity can devise." Ahab's theological protests provoked some of this hostility, but like other publications, the *Athæneum* emphasized the monstrosity of Ishmael's narrating a voyage that had apparently killed him off. The novel was "so much trash belonging to the worst school of Bedlam literature," the journal charged, especially because its author seemed "disdainful of learning the craft of an artist."[19] Taking a lighter tone, the *Literary Gazette* observed, "How the imaginary writer, who appears to have been drowned with the rest, communicated his notes for publication to Mr. Bentley is not explained." Alluding to the opening festivities at the famed London circus, it drolly concluded that "the whole affair would make an admirable subject for an Easter entertainment at Astley's."[20] Melville, readers might reasonably have concluded, had tried to ride two horses at once.[21]

The botching of the British edition accentuates how Melville explicitly avoided the narrative wreck that some reviewers accused him of producing. If Ahab resembles Job, whose grief can neither be explained nor soothed, Ishmael becomes the lonely servant whose escape delivers the tragic tale. Melville, of course, had innumerable options for saving his narrator's life, but he explicitly designated the Parsee's disappearance as the originating event that left Ishmael "*floating on the margin*" of everyone else's death (573). Fedallah's bloated corpse lacks the redemptive symbolism of Queequeg's coffin life-buoy, but as plot devices, they share credit for preserving the telling of *Moby-Dick*. There's a trace of Fedallah's posthumous contribution in

Ishmael's decision to name himself after the "wild man" described in the book of Exodus, the son who was born in affliction to the bondwoman Hagar, rescued from abandonment by an Angel of the Lord, and whose lineage, by tradition, led to the Prophet Muhammad.[22] The relationship between Ishmael and Fedallah is more complex than it might initially seem in that the force that persistently haunts the narrator has a vital function in his tale. In the logic of Melville's text, the wordless, hair-turbaned Parsee enables the emergence of Ishmael's multiple identities—the character, the imaginary writer, and the compendium of narrative voices, styles, and modes.

Ishmael's expansiveness clarifies how significant Fedallah's assistance becomes. Andrew Delbanco has commented that *Moby-Dick* "is simply too large a book to be contained within one consistent consciousness subject to the laws of identity and physical plausibility."[23] We might think of Ishmael as the name of the narrative presence that pervades the book, a presence that crucially inhabits spaces and conversations from which a more conventional novel would exclude him. On this point, the *Spectator* was correct: Melville blatantly supplied his imaginary writer with information he could not have known. Like "Pantheistic ashes" that are sprinkled in a stream and ultimately reach "a part of every shore the round globe over," Ishmael's narration travels across the *Pequod* and its environs, occupying perspectives beyond his own (159). Thus, it is Ishmael who reports Ahab's message to Pip in the captain's cabin and Ishmael who details Starbuck's struggle whether to kill Ahab while he sleeps at his desk. His narrative presence extends to Ahab's meeting with the *Samuel Enderby*'s Captain Bunger, though Fedallah was the only crew member to accompany him on that gam.[24] And then, of course, there are the soliloquies, staged dramas, tall tales, short stories, and disquisitions on marine biology and natural philosophy, none of which violate laws of identity but nonetheless exhibit an astonishing range. "Ishmael is less a character," Denis Donoghue writes, "than the trajectory of one style displaced by another and yet another."[25] The question I want to explore is how Fedallah's wordless gestures and cryptic prophecies are incorporated into the discourses, styles, and modes garrulously organized under Ishmael's name.

A passage from Chapter 4, "The Counterpane," can explain the prosthetic logic of this structure more fully. In a novel known for its experiments in character, the chapter includes the kind of detailed childhood memory that readers would associate with a traditional first-person narrator.[26] Waking in

122 THE PROSTHETIC ARTS OF *MOBY-DICK*

the Spouter Inn with Queequeg's arm hugging him, Ishmael feels the same, strange sensation he experienced as a child when, as a punishment for trying to climb up the chimney, his stepmother sent him to bed mid-afternoon. After hours of agonizing daylight (it happened to be the summer solstice), he woke in darkness to feel a mysterious presence holding his hand:

> At last I must have fallen into a troubled nightmare of a doze; and slowly waking from it—half steeped in dreams—I opened my eyes, and the before sun-lit room was now wrapped in outer darkness. Instantly I felt a shock running through all my frame; nothing was to be seen, and nothing was to be heard; but a supernatural hand seemed placed in mine. My arm hung over the counterpane, and the nameless, unimaginable, silent form or phantom, to which the hand belonged, seemed closely seated by my bed-side. For what seemed ages piled on ages, I lay there, frozen with the most awful fears, not daring to drag away my hand; yet ever thinking that if I could but stir it one single inch, the horrid spell would be broken. I knew not how this consciousness at last glided away from me; but waking in the morning, I shudderingly remembered it all, and for days and weeks and months afterwards I lost myself in confounding attempts to explain the mystery. Nay, to this very hour, I often puzzle myself with it. (26)

The memory confirms that from an early age, Ishmael was haunted by the invisible spheres, and whether formed by love or fright, they took the shape of bodies and body parts that ruptured the "mannerly world" (231).

The passage has inspired a rich tradition of commentary. For decades, scholars have used psychoanalysis to explore this evocation of childhood guilt, phallic hands, and maternal chimneys. In recent years, attention has shifted to how the scene melds sensation and perception, deepening the correspondence between Ishmael, Queequeg, and their material environment. The passage revels in the mixing of categories: arms seem like counterpanes; hands grasp across a metaphysical divide; and the bedding itself provides a sensory and aesthetic experience.[27] "The mystery of the phantom hand is never solved, but it also never leaves the psychic scene of the novel," Peter Boxall writes, connecting the passage to the many nineteenth-century novels that include spectral or deadened hands. *Moby-Dick*, he explains, joins works by Mary Wollstonecraft, George Eliot, Charles Dickens, and others in juxtaposing "the narrative imagination and the experience of handedness" as if these lost, disconnected members reflected the artifice of storytelling.[28] It is worth remembering from Chapter 2 that Melville read about the phantom pain of a severed hand in Hawthorne's "The Unpardonable Sin," a story he praised, even as he complained to its author that four blisters on his palm had soured his mood for writing.[29]

I propose the supernatural hand as a metaphor for the novel's narrative design. One's "hand," of course, can refer to the way penmanship reflects individual identity, and the mysterious, phantom-like grasp aptly conveys Fedallah's nearly invisible role in enabling the text. The passage provides ample reason to entertain this idea, as the descriptions of Fedallah regularly echo the "nameless, unimaginable, silent form or phantom" that appears at the boy's bedside. If Moby Dick is the "grand, hooded phantom" and the Manilla oarsmen "subordinate phantoms," Fedallah is the pilot-phantom who Ishmael repeatedly shuns but remains a mystery to the end (7, 230). Like Fedallah, the "silent form" arouses "the most awful fears," and Ishmael seems so paralyzed by this contact that he cannot withdraw his hand. When he recalls that he "knew not how this consciousness glided away from me," he uses a word he twice applies to the Parsee, who fatalistically "glided away" after Ahab trampled the quadrant "with his live and dead feet" (501).[30] What Ishmael discovers under the Coffins' counterpane is a confusing mix of bodies, identities, mental states, and time periods. "Whether it was a reality or a dream," his consciousness of the phantom hand had remained such a strong sensation that he re-experiences it in New Bedford as the *winter* solstice nears (25). To continue the thought experiment, Fedallah could rightfully be considered the phantom narrator of *Moby-Dick*, the spectral figure whose disembodied hand haunts Ishmael's text. In the image of one hand grasping another, we can see (or, to use Spivak's phrasing, we can *acknowledge*) a partnership between the chatty democrat and the silent Parsee.

Part of the prosthetic arts of *Moby-Dick* is Melville's way of making his story work among competing narrative modes. Castiglia has commented that "replete with digressions, false starts, halting plots, and unsteady narrative rhythms, *Moby-Dick* becomes in its narrator's telling, a significant example of what Tobin Siebers and others have called an aesthetics of disability."[31] Melville gestured toward this aesthetic when he wrote Hawthorne that he was working on "shanties of chapters and essays" as he prepared the novel for its fall publication.[32] These were not highly finished pieces, he warned, but makeshift products cobbled together from available (and often scavenged) materials. The sense of incompletion pervades the text, reflecting an

124   THE PROSTHETIC ARTS OF *MOBY-DICK*

aesthetics that, according to Castiglia, "keeps disability ubiquitous in the novel, even when the narrator is not addressing it directly."[33] To Tara Robbins Fee, the lack of coherence reflects Ishmael's condition as an unhealed trauma victim. "The fissures in the narrative do not obscure the story," she writes, but "are the means by which the story can be understood."[34]

One of the hallmarks of this style is that in telling his story about limb loss, Ishmael frequently signals paths that he has chosen not to explore. "The Lee Shore," for example, is widely admired for its conviction "that all deep, earnest thinking is but the intrepid effort of the soul to keep the open independence of her sea" (107). But even as it expounds on this theme, the "six-inch chapter" calls attention to the abandonment of Bulkington as a character and plot point. The dead-end aesthetic only increases its thematic power. When Ishmael describes the chapter as Bulkington's "stoneless grave," he gives the missing mariner what we might call an absent presence in his book. ("Bulkington! Bulkington! where's Bulkington?" his *Grampus* shipmates cry, hailing a comrade who has already left the scene [16].) The paean to independent thinking celebrates possibilities that "The Lee Shore" both raises and aborts. Rendered bodiless and invisible, Bulkington supplements the novel's correlation of truth-seeking with disappearing at sea.

Something similar happens with Fedallah, though on a much larger scale. Neurologists tell us that the sensation of a phantom limb is essential to a functioning prosthetic.[35] Whether through reawakening the cortex or reorganizing the brain's map of itself, the two operate as partners in making dismembered bodies work. Although they register as the sensation of a traumatically separated part, phantoms exist within the brain, and as Ramachandran explains, they arise from an abundance of neuronal activity, rather than a lack.[36] Fedallah, I argue, is both the prosthesis and phantom of *Moby-Dick*. Like Bulkington, he empowers Ishmael through his disappearance. Psychologically, the Parsee exists in the ironic state of reflecting the needs of the individual characters who dread him. Although never accepted by the crew, he remains a presence in their consciousness, stirring each of the mates to reflect on his mysterious identity. As it is with Ahab, Fedallah's relationship with Ishmael is more unsettling. He both haunts and abets the text, rescuing the novel from the wreckage that the British reviewers accused it of producing. His supernatural presence grasps the narrator from the introductory sentence to the fateful last paragraph. As much as Ishmael shuns it, that hand prosthetically adjoins his own.

The centrality of Queequeg in "The Counterpane" both complicates and clarifies Fedallah's opposing role. The chapter recounts one of the most rapid transformations in US literature when Ishmael accepts the tattooed cannibal as his "intimate and confidential" bedfellow (18). Exhibiting the variable tones of a disability aesthetics, the narration fluctuates between the comedic and gothic modes. Comedies traditionally end in marriage, but Ishmael announces the resolution up front, informing us in the chapter's second sentence that, to Queequeg's affectionate husband, he played the role of cuddled wife. Against this matrimonial backdrop, he recalls that he first associated Queequeg with the phantom of his youth. "Now, take away the awful fear," he writes, "and my sensations at feeling the supernatural hand in mine were very similar, in their strangeness, to those which I experienced on waking up and seeing Queequeg's pagan arm thrown round me" (26). Forged in the gothic past, the memory obstructs Ishmael's perception of the comic present.

That Ishmael mistakes the phantom body with a real one suggests a larger transition as Queequeg moves in his consciousness from a peculiar specter to a "Bosom Friend" (49). The transition says less about Queequeg than it does Ishmael's evolving values. "Better sleep with a sober cannibal than a drunken Christian," he concludes, famously signaling his openness to a multiethnic, multireligious world (24). The pressure of Queequeg's arm momentarily tests that decree, but the "horrid spell" and "awful fears" of childhood give way to the security of an ecumenical embrace. The passage effectively strips Queequeg of any supernatural meaning that Ishmael had imposed upon him, presenting the head-peddling "savage" as a customary part of maritime life. (As Geoffrey Sanborn points out, Ishmael discovers in these opening chapters that *he* is the exotic, not his "pagan friend.")[37] In retrospect, the confusion of Queequeg's tattoos with the Coffins' counterpane emerges as a moment of genuine insight. Like the hair-turbaned Fedallah, "the silent form or phantom" remains a terrifying puzzle years after it appears. In the early morning light, Queequeg seems indistinguishable from New Bedford's parti-colored, patchwork society.

Furthering the opposition, Ishmael attributes radically distinct somatic experiences to Queequeg and the novel's phantom characters. The childhood recollection emphasizes the isolation of limbs with the various hands and arms disassociated from an organizing consciousness or body. The supernatural hand may "belong" to the "silent form or phantom," but it does not seem part of a coordinated, embodied whole. The boy feels the phantom in his hand, but, "wrapped in outer darkness," that sensation is detached from the kind of visual and auditory stimulus that would help him process what he is feeling. The threat of fragmentation animates much of

126   THE PROSTHETIC ARTS OF *MOBY-DICK*

Ishmael's thinking, from the phantom whale that dismasts Ahab to the single-toothed Parsee.[38] Describing him as more shadow than substance, the narrative gives almost compulsive attention to Fedallah's eyes, as if they overwhelmed his body with secret powers and intrigue. As we have seen, the threat of emasculating dismemberment reigns over the comic scenes. Wary of his kidnapping Ahab, Stubb promises to give the turbaned "devil in disguise" such a "wrenching and heaving that his tail will come short off at the stump." The humiliation makes this an appealing punishment. "When he finds himself docked in that queer fashion," the second mate boasts, "he'll sneak off without the poor satisfaction of feeling his tail between his legs" (327).

Queequeg represents a wholly different trajectory in Ishmael's mind, one in which the bosom friends experience a kind of protean mutuality. Rather than disassembling itself, the body takes on an almost liquid form. Only hours after mistaking the islander for a supernatural presence, Ishmael describes a stormy night in which "phantoms" gathered outside the windows, gazing upon a cozy scene they had seemingly once haunted from within (51). "I began to be sensible of strange feelings," Ishmael comments as he looks at Queequeg across the room. "I felt a melting in me. No more my splintered heart and maddened hand were turned against the wolfish world" (51). The desire to melt into others, to retain bodily cohesion in a variable form, leads to the vision of sublime companionship in "A Squeeze of the Hand." The chapter, as even first-time readers note, represents the culmination of the homoerotic feelings that Queequeg first inspired in "The Counterpane." With his hands in a tub of spermaceti, Ishmael experiences not detachment but the pleasure of commingling and metamorphoses. "My fingers felt like eels, and began, as it were, to serpentine and spiralize" (415). Within minutes, he is squeezing the hands of his shipmates and desiring to squeeze spermaceti until he himself "almost melted into it" (415). This "strange sort of insanity" bears little resemblance to the "strange sensation" he felt waking up alongside Queequeg in the Spouter Inn (416). Possessed by "an abounding, affectionate, friendly, loving feeling," he begins looking in his shipmates' eyes and wishing they could dissolve into each other. "Come; let us squeeze hands all round; nay, let us all squeeze ourselves into each other; let us squeeze ourselves universally into the very milk and sperm of kindness" (416). As Ishmael's fingers "weave him into a malleable continuum of bodies in elements," the scene exemplifies what Branka Arsić has described as a moment of ambiental cogito, a state of porousness and total sensitivity that eliminates boundaries between Ishmael, the whale, and his fellow crewmembers.[39] But the sensation is short-lived, and by the chapter's end, he returns to the Ahabian terror of dismemberment in which "blubber-room men" risk slicing off their toes as they process pieces of the blanket (418).

If *Moby-Dick* establishes an aesthetics of disability, then we might think of the "Epilogue" as a prosthesis that brings the narrative to the page. Compared to an envoy that effectively sends the audience away, an epilogue provides additional speech, language that is distinct from (but also related to) a more coherent formal entity. (In literature, an epilogue's power resides in supplementing the textual body that precedes it.) Melville designates the account of Ishmael's rescue as being crucially extra, two paragraphs that prosthetically explain the contingencies that helped him avoid his shipmates' fate. Fedallah's disappearance and Queequeg's coffin feature prominently in this subjoined text, as throughout the narrative the two have occupied parallel spots in Ishmael's consciousness. Both characters embody racial difference in extravagantly complicated (and often contradictory) ways. One affirms Ishmael's openness to other peoples and faiths, his redemptive coffin swiftly incorporated into Christian theology. The other haunts Ishmael's dreams, introducing him to cultural fears he struggles to name. Compared to the "soothing savage," the ghostly Fedallah suggests eternal conflict between races, civilizations, and metaphysical beliefs. And while Queequeg, like all the harpooners, eagerly supports Ahab's revenge, the Parsee makes that revenge happen, extending the captain's capabilities into unknown realms. In their broken, fragmented experience, Ishmael and Ahab depend on Fedallah to locate their position in the world—the narrator in relation to his voice and the captain in relation to his prey. A pilot to both text and quest, he exercises a power that neither character could muster on his own. To acknowledge Fedallah's prosthetic utility is to acknowledge the difficulty of defining where he begins and where both Ahab and Ishmael end.

Ishmael's Islamic Moods

Part of Ishmael's receptiveness to Queequeg stems from his home in Kokovoko, an imaginary Pacific island that gives him a more symbolic, comic presence than if he had come from Fiji or the Marquesas Islands. The

128   THE PROSTHETIC ARTS OF *MOBY-DICK*

fanciful nature of his "savagery" makes him less a representative of a specific colonial experience than a register of Ishmael's evolving attitudes toward people of different races and faiths. Embedded in Ishmael's evolution, however, is his assumption that Queequeg, too, will adapt to his new setting. The islander may feel disillusioned by the misery and wickedness in Christian life, but Ishmael trusts that, with guidance, he will learn how to use a wheelbarrow or understand the purpose of books. "His education was not yet completed," Ishmael states, expressing confidence that the savage behaviors will change (27). Such patronizing expectations do not surface with Fedallah, for Ishmael associates the phantom and his subordinates with cultures that are "insulated," "unalterable," and intransigent to the influence of Europe and the United States (231). Ishmael would never describe the Parsee as "an undergraduate" or "a creature in the transition stage," for his gothic powers and ancient culture make him static, threatening, and opaque. Queequeg may be "neither caterpillar nor butterfly," but Ishmael finds comedy in the awkwardness between those states (27). The contrast heightens a peculiar similarity that this section explores in depth: how among the multiple racial signifiers applied to his tattooed and turbaned shipmates, Ishmael loosely associates each of them with Islamic traditions and faith practices.

Sanborn has brilliantly traced the origins of Queequeg to George Lillie Craik's nonfiction book *The New Zealanders* (1830). Craik's volume includes a biographical account of a Maori man named Te Pehi Kupe who joined a British whaling ship and, in the process, became a devoted friend of its captain, Richard Reynolds. Queequeg, Sanborn demonstrates, shares numerous qualities with Te Pehi Kupe (whose name Craik spells as Tupai Cupa). Like Te Pehi Kupe, Queequeg wears a poncho-like coat and signs his name by copying one of his tattoos. Both characters follow the traditional Maori practice of acknowledging moments of understanding by pressing their foreheads together. In the course of their narratives, Queequeg and Te Pehi Kupe steal onboard a whaling ship, sell Maori heads in a Euro-American market, and save someone from drowning.[40] Although Queequeg's Maori background is unmistakable, Sanborn argues that by making him a native of Kokovoko, Melville created a character who ultimately resists being absorbed into Western customs and values. Unlike Te Pehi Kupe, Queequeg has no desire to establish trade between his island and the Global North. He plans to return to his pagan island once he is cleansed of Christian life.

ISHMAEL, SALAAMING   129

Nowhere in *The New Zealanders* does Craik mention Te Pehi Kupe fasting or practicing a form of Ramadan. And nowhere does he suggest that the Maoris "salamed" before idols in the way that Ishmael describes Queequeg bowing before Yojo. The absence of these details underscores the strangeness of Ishmael's using Islamic terminology to describe Queequeg's pagan observance. Scholars differ on how to interpret these passages, suggesting that, with his tomahawk and Congo baby, Queequeg is either a "composite nonwhite figure" who represents "all darker races" subjugated by the West or that, by virtue of his travels, he has assembled a collection of global religious practices.[41] A more pertinent question comes from acknowledging that Melville imported these details into *Moby-Dick*, embroidering Te Pehi Kupe's story with incongruously Islamic references. In the context of Ishmael's fear of Fedallah and the Manilla men, the Islamicization of Queequeg creates a puzzling inconsistency. Ishmael associates Fedallah with a terrifying metaphysics, and as we saw in the previous chapter, he regularly invokes the image of sultans and moguls to characterize menacing power and violence. And yet, in a sign of tolerance and magnanimity, he joins Queequeg in an Islamically themed pagan observance.

It will be helpful to contextualize Ishmael's references before delving deeper into this problem. Idol worship, of course, is profoundly antithetical to Islam, which, in many sects, forbids representation of the Prophet Muhammad, let alone Allah. But there is little doubt that, no matter how unsuitably applied, Ishmael's imagery signifies Muslim customs. In the 1840s, English usage of the word *salaam* was almost universally applied to "Mussulmen." Memoirs by travelers and missionaries referred to the way Muslims salaamed before each other, the bow (with or without a raised palm) providing a memorable detail about cultural cohesion and respect for hierarchy. Handbooks for travelers to India, Persia, Africa, Greece, Hindustan, and the Indian Archipelago included the variously spelled phrase "Salaam" or "Salaam Aleikoom," though they largely discouraged Jews and Christians from returning such a greeting.[42] Ishmael seems uncertain what to call Queequeg's fast, referring to it as his "Lent or Ramadan" in Chapter 16 and then, two chapters later, his "Ramadan, or Fasting and Humiliation" (69, 81). He ultimately settles on "Ramadan," not only using it as a chapter title, but once he has offered the alternatives, employing it another ten times. Public fasting had been a regular part of colonial American culture since the seventeenth century, and until 1894 Massachusetts recognized 19 April as an official Fast Day.[43] Ishmael alludes to the practice when

130   THE PROSTHETIC ARTS OF *MOBY-DICK*

he wonders whether Starbuck had been "born in some time of general drought and famine, or upon one of those fast days for which his state is famous" (115). In using the word "Ramadan," then, Ishmael was not grappling with a way to describe a largely unknown practice in North America. He meant to exoticize Queequeg and, in the process, give his paganism the stability of a well-established religious tradition.[44]

The point of such references was not to characterize Queequeg as an authentic believer, nor to describe Kokovoko with the level of detail that Melville supplied the imaginary islands in *Mardi*. The contradictions simply signify Ishmael's interest in other peoples and faiths. The racist greenhorn becomes a cosmopolitan, democratic laborer at sea. Ishmael encourages this view when he describes his salaaming before Yojo in Chapter 10. "Now, Queequeg is my fellow man," he self-consciously explains. "And what do I wish that this Queequeg would do to me? Why, unite with me in my particular Presbyterian form of worship. Consequently, I must then unite with him in his; ergo, I must turn idolator" (52). Ishmael's Ramadans and salaams convey his willingness to experiment with his own faith and accept that of others. George Shulman has argued that Ishmael spends the book in "ethnographic humility," but we can't forget that this humility comes with a heavy dose of cultural superiority.[45] In Chapter 17, he proclaims that he cherishes "the greatest respect towards everybody's religious obligations, never mind how comical," stating that he would never undervalue "a congregation of ants worshipping a toad-stool" (81). Ishmael's tolerance comes with limits, though, and he questions any religion that becomes "a positive torment" to its practitioners and "makes this earth of ours an uncomfortable inn to lodge in" (84–85). His pragmatism recalls the Enlightenment-era statesmen who used Islam to signify their acceptance of disparate religions. Franklin said he hoped that even missionaries from the mufti of Constantinople would find a place to preach in Philadelphia.[46] Such speakers would find a welcoming, engaged audience in Melville's narrator.

The descriptions of Queequeg are consistent with Ishmael's tendency to give the religion of Islam an honored place in his own system of spiritual value. (The novel finds a way for Ishmael to salaam, but it does not offer him the opportunity to attend a Quaker meeting, a Roman Catholic mass, or a Narragansett Nikommo feast.)[47] Even as he invokes Turks and sultans to characterize ruthlessly violent power, he welcomes Islam itself as a sign of inexpressible truths and visionary mysticism. A good example appears in

ISHMAEL, SALAAMING   131

"Cistern and Buckets." The chapter is most remembered for Queequeg's rescue of Tashtego, who, while baling nearly ninety buckets of spermaceti, falls into the whale's head and crashes it into the sea. Armed with "his keen sword," Queequeg dives into the water to cut the Gay Head Indian out, a rescue Ishmael comically compares to a birth (343–44). The scene builds around a steady stream of comparisons, with Ishmael likening the head to an old house, a water well, a giant cask of wine, and the seductive idealism of Platonic thought. The whale's head, one might say, is a womb of tropes.

As if he were preparing for this effusion of language, Ishmael opens the scene with an Islamic image. Tashtego walks along the yardarm ("nimble as a cat") and then swings onto the decapitated head that rises above the deck. Perched above the crew on yet another dismembered body part, the Gay Head Indian reminds Ishmael of a devout Muslim beckoning the faithful from a minaret. "There—still high elevated above the rest of the company, to whom he vivaciously cries—he seems some Turkish Muezzin calling the good people to prayers from the top of a tower" (341). The image presents the head as the source of both religion and profit, its intoxicating, perfumed substance recalling, in the phrasing of *White-Jacket*, both "Mohammedan sensualism" and the rewards of the Nantucket market.[48] The passage evokes the historical descriptions of "savage" Muslims and tribal "mosques" that we encountered in Chapter 3. It also introduces a more particular context in that the athletic Tashtego devoutly calls his crew members to the sperm whale's head. Far from being a snaky-limbed pagan (as Ishmael once described him), he becomes a believer and a laborer, a beacon of devotion to Allah and wealth (120). Suffering a near fatal industrial accident, the Gay Head muezzin is almost smothered in spermaceti, "coffined, hearsed, and tombed in the secret inner chamber and sanctum sanctorum of the whale" (344). In Ishmael's restless imagery, that "sanctum sanctorum" is momentarily Muslim.

Melville's contemporaries used Islamic imagery to a similar effect, often linking visionary Islam with creative possibility. Poised on top of the whale head, in fact, Tashtego exemplifies a sentiment from the Qur'an that appealed to the novelist and poet Lydia Maria Child: in calling from a minaret, the muezzin invites the faithful to turn the whole world into a place of prayer.[49] Other mid-century writers saw in the teachings of Muhammad a reflection of their own romantic idealism. Although he repeatedly compared it to Christianity, Carlyle detected a truth in Islam, which seemed to be "of Nature herself; equal in rank to Sun, or Moon, or

132 THE PROSTHETIC ARTS OF *MOBY-DICK*

whatsoever thing Nature had made."[50] The prophet functioned like "lightning out of heaven," igniting "blazes heaven-high from Delhi to Grenada!" "The rest of men waited for him like fuel," he concluded, "and then they too would flame."[51] In her lengthy discussion of "Mohammedanism" in *The Progress of Religious Ideas* (1855), Child appreciated how the Qur'an's poetry went beyond human expression, imparting the authority and force of a celestial source. She recounts the story of "four unbelievers, most eminent for eloquence," who tried "to produce a book equal to the Koran." After encountering one of its most sublime verses, they gave up "in despair." Child reports that others reacted similarly. "After that verse was revealed to Muhammad," all the poets removed the lines they had hung from the Kaaba's walls in Mecca, so inferior were they to the verses from the Qur'an.[52]

Ralph Waldo Emerson was especially drawn to the visionary aspects of Islam, and as Jeffrey Einboden has shown, he employed two Islamic aliases in his journals that, dating from his college years, became fertile ground for his lectures and published work. The practice went well beyond his fondness for copying passages from the Qur'an or translating fragments of Persian poetry. Emerson used these alter egos as vehicles for self-reflection, effectively mirroring himself in his entries and stories about these Muslim personae.[53] The idealized character of "Osman" appears in the essay "Manners" (1844), in which he is celebrated for having "a humanity so broad and deep" that the kingdom's sufferers rushed to his side.[54] Emerson would gradually replace "Osman" in his journals with the character "Saadi," an artist whose name alludes to the thirteenth-century Persian poet Saadi Shirazi. The 1842 poem honoring this Persian predecessor was first published in *The Dial*, but it closely reflects personal concerns Emerson raises in his journals. Saadi loves "the race of men," but the Muse instructs him to write his poems in solitude. Only there will he earn a glimpse of heaven "where unveiled Allah pours / The flood of truth, the flood of good."[55] Emerson curiously inserts a phantom shadow into Saadi's room that guides the poet to this transcendent moment. Einboden suggests that the phantom acknowledges the role that Muslim aliases played in Emerson's developing work.[56]

As the Islamicized alias for the narrator of *Moby-Dick*, Ishmael uses Queequeg, rather than Fedallah, to signify the redemptive aspects of his broadminded faith. The desire to bring others into his theological and narrative orbit appears in Ishmael's tribute to an ancient African temple that used whalebones for its rafters and beams. Described in Chapter 104, "The Fossil Whale," the story comes from the sixteenth-century Berber diplomat al-Hasan ibn Muhammad al-Wazzan al-Fasi, whom Europeans knew as "Johannes Leo Africanus" and Ishmael calls "John Leo, the old Barbary traveller." Africanus was writing about three Moroccan villages that for centuries had made religious use of the whalebones that had washed up on their shores. "They keep a Whale's Rib of an incredible length for a Miracle, which lying upon the Ground with its convex part uppermost, makes an Arch, the Head of which cannot be reached by a Man upon a Camel's Back" (458). Ishmael explicitly invokes the Abrahamic tradition in characterizing the sanctity of this place. "Their Historians affirm, that a Prophet who prophesy'd of Mahomet, came from this Temple, and some do not stand to assert, that the Prophet Jonas was cast forth by the Whale at the Base of the Temple" (458). Like the muezzin Tashtego calling the faithful from a severed head, the whalebones evoke Islamic forms of worship that reach beyond Christian pieties.

Melville quotes Africanus's account almost verbatim from the collection in which he found it.[57] He follows the quotation, however, with a crucial sentence in which Ishmael directly addresses his audience. "In this Afric Temple of the Whale I leave you, reader, and if you be a Nantucketer, and a whaleman, you will silently worship there" (458). As a narrator, Ishmael enjoys the rhetoric of his storytelling mode, directing readers to remember specific details or prompting them toward self-reflection. Here he instructs readers how to honor the holy site in which he has deposited them. Whitman's famous conclusion to "Song of Myself"—"I stop somewhere waiting for you"—avoids stating how or where readers will re-encounter the poet they have accompanied through the poem.[58] Ishmael does not leave things so open-ended. He firmly situates his readers not just "somewhere," but in an African place of miracles, prophecy, and spiritual durability. The sentence associates worshiping at the temple with reading Ishmael's "mighty book," emphasizing that whether we are real or imagined whalemen, our observance will be grounded in Islamic legend and lore (456). As he did with Yojo in Nantucket, he expects readers to salaam before the temple as if it were our own.

Ishmael and Racial Aggrievement

So how, then, do we understand Ishmael's relation to Fedallah and the Filipino oarsmen who operate Ahab's boat? If he applies Islamic imagery to

134 THE PROSTHETIC ARTS OF *MOBY-DICK*

Queequeg in an admiring way, why does he become so ugly when describing the people from Muslim regions who physically support the captain in his quest? Ishmael both racializes and vilifies the difference these men represent. As cloudy as his response to Islam may be, we can detect a somewhat discernible pattern in his commentary. First, there are the traits that readers most often associate with his democratic voice. He conveys his Franklinian pragmatism in respecting all religions so long as they don't harm their adherents or harm others who don't have the same beliefs. He urges "good Presbyterian Christians" to "be charitable" toward people of other faiths and not hold themselves "so vastly superior to other mortals, pagans and what not" (81). And he demonstrates a cosmopolitan openness to other customs and beliefs—not just welcoming but actively seeking the meaning that Islam, Catholicism, and paganism can add to his spiritual life. But then there are the more troublesome traits. Ishmael's religious tolerance belies his tendency to demonize the race of people who oppose Euro-American progress at sea. The populations he targets for such vilification come from Maritime Southeast Asia: the combination of oceanic trading routes extending from Sumatra and Java in the west to Malaysia in the north and to the Philippine Islands in the east.[59]

Chapter 3 has already discussed the mystery of Fedallah's origins and how, despite his being named a Parsee, the text regularly aligns him, in dress, skin color, and racist caricature, with the "tiger-yellow barbarians" in Ahab's boat (566). Ishmael does not see savagery in Fedallah as much as an alarming devotion to an inscrutable metaphysical force. On the *Pequod*, of course, the Parsee serves his captain's aggrievement, but Ishmael insinuates that he and his fellow stowaways serve another master as well. According to "some honest white mariners," they are "the paid spies and secret confidential agents on the water of their devil, the lord" (217). Putting the question of devil-worship aside, I want to focus on the "honest white mariners" that Ishmael so carefully invokes. The line may be the most offensive phrase in *Moby-Dick*, for he frames his racial stereotype in reference to the alleged integrity of whiteness. Ishmael is calculating in both distancing himself from the accusation ("some" sailors) and yet also creating a racial divide that authenticates the bigotry of the accusation. The phrase does not just attribute superiority, it bestows the transnational, racial category of whiteness upon Ishmael and his kind. This ancient race consorted with phantoms at the beginning of time: "when the memory of the first man was a distant recollection, and all men his descendants, unknowing whence he came, eyed each other as real phantoms, and asked of the sun and the moon why they were crested and to what end" (231). Ishmael refers to these people as aboriginals, but he sees them as being radically different from Tashtego, Daggoo, and Queequeg. The product of metaphysical couplings, they haunt northern dreams.

Ishmael's characterization of the Manilla men is as sloppy as his characterization of the Parsee.[60] The stowaways themselves quickly recede into the text, though the qualities they represent remain racially terrifying to him. By the 1840s, the Philippine Islands had been a Spanish colony for nearly three hundred years. With Manilla as the capital, Spanish priests and bureaucrats struggled to control the islands' diverse population, which included, at that point, numerous indigenous tribes, Spanish-speaking Catholics, and Muslims whose contact with Arab and Malaysian traders had introduced them to Islam in the fourteenth century. The Spanish called this population the Moros, a name that continues today but hearkens back to the Moors of North Africa who, of course, had conquered the Iberian Peninsula in the eighth century and departed the continent in 1492.[61] Ahab's oarsmen most likely come from the Moro population that (compared to the mountain-dwelling tribal peoples) had frequent contact with American whaling ships.[62]

An 1859 account of this Muslim population by Sir John Bowring, the former British governor of Hong Kong, can illuminate the qualities that Ishmael attributes to the "Manillas" in Ahab's boat and (as the next chapter explains) to others who sailed in these seas. Bowring describes the frustration of the Spanish colonialists who wanted to open ports, mine for iron, sulfur, and gold, promote trade with the Spice Islands, and increase the number of converted Catholic souls. As Bowring presents it, the Moros regularly challenged these efforts and had little "recognition of Spanish authority."[63] The colonial attempt "to undermine or depreciate the authority of the Koran," he writes, "has wholly failed," and he postulates that "the enmity between the Mahomedan races (Moros) and the Spaniards may be hereditary."[64] Try as they might, he concludes, the Augustinian friars "have never been able to maintain themselves against the fanaticism of the Moros."[65] The Spanish had come to view them "as a fierce, faithless and cruel race."[66]

Bowring pays particular attention to the heavily Islamic region of Zamboanga, which the Spanish had permitted to remain organized under the Sultanate of Sulu. In this region he encountered people "familiar with

136   THE PROSTHETIC ARTS OF *MOBY-DICK*

the Arabic formula of Islamism" and people with names "such as Abdallah, Fatima, and others" that were "common to the Mussulmans."[67] Zamboanga was a preferred destination for American whaling ships, which beginning in the 1820s used the harbor to replenish their supplies.[68] Until 1880, American and British whaling ships hunted in the Mindoro and Sulu Seas, both off the coast of heavily Muslim regions in the southern Philippines.[69] Melville never visited the Philippines and was thus dependent on the stories and perceptions of other Euro-Americans who had traveled (or read about) the region. Bowring was a deep believer in Western expansion into Southeast Asia and wondered if the Irish could emigrate to Australia and America, why had more Spaniards not emigrated to the Philippines, where they would improve the native race. "The noble and higher axiom," he wrote, "is that 'progress' is the law of Providence, which never fails."[70]

Although he lacks Bowring's administrative ambitions, Ishmael applauds whaling's role in opening the Pacific to American trade. In *Typee*, Tommo repeatedly condemns the misery that Westerners had brought to the island kingdoms of Polynesia and Hawaii, lamenting how colonial contact had created "diseased, starving, and dying natives." Visiting Honolulu after years of missionary control, he learns "that the small remnant of the natives had been civilized into draught horses, and evangelized into beasts of burden."[71] Ishmael presents the Polynesian situation differently, claiming that the islands not only owed their survival to the whaling industry, but that they "do commercial homage to the whale-ship, that cleared the way for the missionary and the merchant, and in many cases carried the primitive missionaries to their first destinations" (110). When he regards the seafaring communities of Southeast Asia, he sounds like the colonialist who is threatened by a population that resists foreign rule. His response to the Islamicized stowaways clashes with his response to other racial and ethnic groups. Fierce, faithless, cruel, fanatical—the traits he sees in Fedallah and his Filipino crew are the traits invaders associate with peoples who refuse to submit. Ishmael presents that intransigence as a form of metaphysical depravity.

Ishmael's hostility leads us to reassess his beautiful paean to collective work when he describes the crew's becoming "one man, not thirty" during the second day's chase (557). The union here does not rival the erotic squeezing of hands that Ishmael celebrated in Chapter 94, but it does represent the unity of individual bodies merged into Ahab's violent will. "All the individualities of the crew," he rhapsodizes, "this man's valor, that man's fear; guilt and guiltiness, all varieties were welded into oneness" (557). Considering the present discussion, however, we might ask whether that vision depended on Ishmael's laboring with the familiar Queequeg in Starbuck's boat.

On the next day, seated among the "subordinate phantoms," he seems driven to separate himself from his boatmates, to isolate his story from the men who looked to Fedallah as much as Ahab as their leader (230). When Ahab's boat hits the water, sharks immediately surround it, maliciously snapping at the oars and yet allowing Stubb's and Flask's boats to go unimpeded. Ishmael uses this unusual occurrence to make an insulting point about racial difference.

> But these were the first sharks that had been observed by the Pequod since the White Whale had been first descried; and whether it was that Ahab's crew were all such tiger yellow barbarians, and therefore their flesh more musky to the senses of the sharks—a matter sometimes well known to affect them,—however it was, they seemed to follow that one boat without molesting the others. (566)

Reading that sentence closely clarifies how Ishmael never states an alternative to his theory. Although grammatically sound, his "whether" syntactically hangs in the balance, a fragment waiting for an opposing statement that never comes. The phrasing detaches the crew from the world federation he has recently praised. "Rendered mute, hidden, and demonized, anonymous, unindividuated, and inscrutable," Elizabeth Schultz observes, the phantoms are deemed "separate from 'the common continent of men.'"[72] Ishmael's comment takes this social isolation further in suggesting that the sharks express—not hostility to Ahab's quest—but a state of naturalized racial difference. The passage refers to Baron Cuvier's racist comments that, because of their scent, sharks killed more Black men than white. Explicitly changing Cuvier's statement to designate the Filipino boatmates (rather than African sailors such as the harpooner Daggoo), Melville accentuated the pattern of prejudice that Ishmael has repeatedly displayed.[73]

These lines prepare us to see how Ishmael indirectly credits his whiteness as the reason for his being the *Pequod's* lone survivor. Three oarsmen were cast into the shark-infested sea, but only Ishmael was found alive. Were the other two eaten by sharks? The "Epilogue" suggests that explanation as a possibility. As Ishmael explains, Queequeg's coffin buoyed him for days,

138 THE PROSTHETIC ARTS OF *MOBY-DICK*

and he loses neither his limb nor his life. "*The unharming sharks, they glided by as if with padlocks on their mouths*" (573). Compared to his boatmates, the narrator's race seems to be the source of his power. The Manillas, he assures us, eventually assimilated into the crew, but in the end, it is only their otherness that survives.

The Narrator's Prosthesis

Emerson used "Osman" and "Saadi" as prosthetic extensions of himself, Orientalized characters who helped him reconcile the competing demands of his private and public manuscripts. As literary devices, these personae mediated between self-reflection and professional speech, and, in the process, they redressed the alienation he suffered in his personal, theological, and vocational capacities. What began as the private costuming of an undergraduate evolved into a constituent part of his literary performance— the alternate, exoticized selves becoming a mechanism for expressing spiritual aspiration. Emerson's texts incorporated these identities as a way of defining discourses and experiences that were not typically available to New England clergy.

Melville's Ishmael represents a more submerged version of this practice. Avoiding the Islamicized cultural performance in which Emerson periodically engaged, he adopts a biblical name that expresses both a sense of exile and a desire for religious experience outside the Presbyterianism in which he was raised. Grounding himself in Islamic lore, the narrator conveys Melville's humor, love of metaphor, personal history, theological struggles, and intellectual range (to name just a handful of traits). He also demonstrates a mindset as distinct from the author's as Ahab's would be, and we would be wise to remember Dennis Berthold's warning that "many of Melville's narrators and characters make political statements clearly opposite to the author's personal views."[74] Indeed, while Emerson wove his Islamic aliases into his poems, lectures, and essays, Melville's fictive persona was an end itself, not a platform for future creativity. As the next section explains, when he returned to Islam, dismemberment, and revenge in his later writings, Melville challenged some of the political values that Ishmael articulates.

Moby-Dick, according to Peter Szendy, depends on a constantly circular process in which "the writing of the end is presented both as the end of writing and as its beginning anew. Or its beginning period."[75] Like the circle of Ixion, the narrative cycles over itself as the sinking of the *Pequod* generates the need to both save and name the narrator repeatedly. The "Epilogue" may showcase Ishmael as the only survivor, but what makes him an especially interesting narrator is that Fedallah haunts his telling of the story. Shoshana Felman has described testimony as being "composed of bits and pieces of a memory that has been overwhelmed by occurrences that have not settled in the understanding or remembrance, acts that cannot be constructed as knowledge nor assimilated into full cognition, events in excess of our frames of reference."[76] Traumatic events produce speech acts, she argues, not "totalizable" statements. Amid the wreckage we find at the end of *Moby-Dick,* Fedallah appears in the bits and pieces of the narrator's memory. He never assimilates into the crew and never assimilates into Ishmael's consciousness, continually escaping his cognition and frames of reference. In this novel of dismembered and prostheticized parts, he destabilizes Ahab's quest and any effort to provide a comprehensive account of its subsequent tragedy. He is the Osman that Ishmael did not choose, the silent phantom who both makes the narrative work and troubles it with uncertainty.

In the end, Ishmael's racial grievance matches the literary structure he employs. His colonial vision of history depends on the silencing of figures such as Fedallah and his fellow stowaways so that his ever-expanding consciousness can dominate their verbal and physical space. Reduced to being phantom narrators and shipmates, these crewmembers exist outside the providential laws of history that contend (as Bowring put it) that Western progress never fails. As Ishmael salaams with Queequeg and admires the athleticism of Tashtego and Daggoo, he establishes a plot that welcomes populations who do not resist the historical narratives proposed by the West. In this respect, the shark-infested waters surrounding Ahab's boat have an ideological as well as narrative purpose. The prosthetic structure of the novel reinforces this colonial logic, leaving Fedallah wrapped around the white whale and Ishmael floating among the *Pequod*'s pieces.

PART III
BODIES POLITIC

5

The Unnatural Stump

Cruel as a Turk

Herman Melville had a darker vision of imperialism than one might conclude from reading Ishmael's comments in *Moby-Dick*. Comparing its whalers to Alexander the Great, the narrator famously celebrates Nantucket as a key player in the nineteenth-century race for global expansion. "Let America add Mexico to Texas, and pile Cuba upon Canada," Ishmael cheers in his paean to the Massachusetts island; "let the English overswarm all India, and hang out their blazing banner from the sun; two thirds of this terraqueous globe are the Nantucketer's."[1] Filled with the swagger of Jacksonian America, Ishmael's digressions and outlandish claims can sometimes negate the very propositions he advances.[2] Knowing Melville's early attacks on imperialism in the South Pacific, some readers might conclude that Ishmael meant the opposite of what he was expressing: that Nantucket whaling was a problematic attempt to claim the world's seas and that, through this irony, we could reconcile the gaps between Ishmael and other Melvillean characters on the issue.[3]

In Part III, however, I argue that the substance of Ishmael's remarks is consistent with comments he makes elsewhere in the book. Across an array of discursive styles and moods, Ishmael regularly ties whaling to the expansion of American interests around the globe. In "The Advocate," for example, he touts the economic development that whaling brought to the colonies of Australia and Polynesia. He then turns to Japan, which, despite its long-standing hostility to foreigners and foreign trade, looms on his horizon as an even bigger prize. "If that double-bolted land, Japan, is ever to become hospitable," he explains, "it is the whale-ship alone to whom the credit will be due; for already she is on the threshold" (110). Ishmael's advocacy for whaling as a literary subject and an economic benefit often merge. Melville's vision was known to be more complex. Three years after the publication of *Moby-Dick*, American gunboats would follow American whalers into Japanese seas and force the Tokugawa shogunate to begin trading with

The Prosthetic Arts of Moby-Dick. David Haven Blake, Oxford University Press. © Oxford University Press 2024.
DOI: 10.1093/oso/9780197780510.003.0006

144   THE PROSTHETIC ARTS OF *MOBY-DICK*

the United States. The lead negotiator was Commodore Matthew Perry, a hero of the Mexican American War. When Nathaniel Hawthorne proposed that Melville assist in writing Perry's memoirs of the Japanese voyage and treaty, the commodore rejected the idea, seeming to resent Melville's well-known criticism of Pacific imperialism and the US Navy.[4]

Decades after Ishmael expressed these opinions, Melville used another wanderer to denounce English and American imperialists for terrorizing the globe. In *Clarel*, a character named Ungar flatly contends that Islamophobia was deflecting attention from the treachery of Christian capitalists. Conversing with the travelers outside Bethlehem, Ungar, who is part Native American, attacks the hypocrisy of the expression "*As cruel as a Turk*," an adage he claims is as "old as the Crusades":

> The Anglo-Saxons—lacking grace
> To win the love of any race;
> Hated by myriads dispossessed
> Of rights—the Indians East and West.
> These pirates of the sphere! grave looters—
> Grave, canting, Mammonite freebooters,
> Who in the name of Christ and Trade
> (Oh, bucklered forehead of the brass!)
> Deflower the world's last sylvan glade.[5]

A refugee from the American Civil War, Ungar is the most problematic in the series of monomaniacs that Melville introduced in *Clarel*.[6] An antislavery southerner who served as an officer in the Confederate army, he meets the travelers while working in Palestine as a Turkish mercenary. His censure of nineteenth-century progressivism chafes against the travelers who do not see the world in the same chilling way. Ungar's estrangement from his countrymen coincides with his estrangement from the times. C. Vann Woodward memorably commented that, in creating the character, Melville may have "penned the blackest commentary on the future of his country ever written by an American in the nineteenth century."[7]

Ungar's Confederate background and hatred of democracy would make him a lousy ally of progressives today, but like many of Melville's characters, his flaws lead him to speak bitter truths. His comments display stunning prescience about where the next centuries would lead. Building on the pillars of capital, commerce, religion, and race, the Anglo-Saxons herald a new kind of crusade: they uproot indigenous peoples, destroy the environment, and subject others to their commerce and Christianity. Describing his "Anglo brain, but Indian heart," Melville endows Ungar with an intellectual independence that sees through the self-congratulatory cant of his Anglo-American contemporaries.[8] Ungar's grievances would not have mesmerized the crew on the *Pequod*'s quarterdeck, but in this instance, what he stands for is less significant than what he sees: the way "progress" in capitalist democracies ultimately means the conquest of both nature and foreign territories. Stretching from the North Atlantic to the Pacific Oceans, this new Anglo-Saxon empire honors profit as its sultan, emperor, and king.

Ungar's criticism comes from the reactionary right, and as Jennifer Greiman comments, he directs his rage against "the reconstructed United States." Racist, skeptical, and fiercely aggrieved, he "quarrels explicitly with democracy as the name for all that he hates in the modern and secular world."[9] Hilton Obenzinger observes that among the many conflicting perspectives Melville included in *Clarel*, Ungar "delivers scathing denunciations of liberal religion, democracy, capitalism, notions of progress, and New World exceptionalism."[10] This defiance reflects the character's family history. As "the descendant of both Cherokees and English Catholics," Brian Yothers argues, Ungar not only "stands outside the Protestant mainstream" but has experienced the Puritan "errand into the wilderness" from the perspective of its most significant adversaries.[11] He draws upon a reservoir of resentment in denouncing institutions that, to many Americans, proudly differentiated the New World from the Old. As a mercenary for the Turks, he actively defends a faltering monarchical empire that Melville's journals rail against and that, from Greece to the Balkans, numerous liberation movements opposed.

Described as a "wandering Ishmael of the West," Ungar shares little in common with the narrator of *Moby-Dick*, but his comments illuminate how environmental destruction intersects in the novel with disability, capitalism, and the representation of Islamic peoples.[12] Amid his promotion of the whale fishery, Ishmael laments how, in the name of energy and profit, American "pirates of the sphere" heighten the violence inflicted upon these "monsters of the sea" (156). Although it would be anachronistic to call him an environmentalist, he seems keenly aware of how capitalists exploit the differing abilities of human and nonhuman species. And yet what makes Ishmael so complex is that in the international battle for energy, his

146 THE PROSTHETIC ARTS OF *MOBY-DICK*

episodic concerns about the violence of his industry rarely moderate his ambitions for the nation-state. Ungar provides a useful interlocutor for Ishmael's imperial and environmental politics, for despite their mutual regard for nonhuman life, Ishmael's faith in progress leads him to fear and, in some cases, villainize the forces that resist Western trade.

Part III explores the tensions in *Moby-Dick* between imperialism and the violence done to both individual bodies and bodies politic. Using his later writings, and especially *Clarel*, these chapters discuss the frequency with which Melville employed wounded bodies to think about the fate of democratic capitalism as it expanded across the nineteenth century. Images of dismemberment pervade Melville's works from Tommo to Samoa to Ahab. As Parts I and II explained, Ahab's ivory leg tangibly conveys the depth of his aggrievement and the novel's narrative design. In Part III, I explore how these images cross not only continents, but also species as Melville's characters contemplate the progress of Western nations in conquering oceans and earth. Reading *Moby-Dick* with the aid of future texts helps clarify Melville's interest in the rapacious treatment of humans and nonhumans alike. Dismemberment reflects the condition of imperial societies in which some characters use prostheses and others are effectively turned into them—the dispossessed (in Ungar's words) being forced to support economies from which they do not benefit. In the last decades of US slavery, Melville explored how the wounds of others became integral to the expansion and prostheticization of the American body politic.

If prostheses are the origins of inequality, as Bernard Stiegler has remarked, then we need to recognize that they also involve questions of power and capability.[13] These chapters consider the politics of Melville's prosthetic arts, positioning him alongside figures such as Benjamin Franklin, who viewed dismemberment as an image of both empire and revolt.[14] Challenging the Stamp Act of 1765, Franklin engraved, printed, and distributed a highly influential cartoon that pictured the American colonies as Great Britain's amputated limbs (Figure 8). Britannia, he explained, had dismembered itself in favoring "*one* part of the nation, to the prejudice and oppression of *another*."[15] By the middle of the nineteenth century, the perspective on national identity had changed, and Melville faced the different problem of how to represent nations that artificially connected disparate territories into imperial versions of themselves. Rather than showcase an empire maimed by its own mistakes, he reflected on the bodies wounded and prostheticized in the name of political and economic gain. Ishmael, we

Figure 8 Originally disseminated during the winter of 1766, Benjamin Franklin's *Magna Brittania or the Colonies Reduc'd* was reproduced widely in colonial America and used for a variety of political purposes.
Image courtesy of the Library Company of Pennsylvania.

will see, emerges as a remarkably ambivalent narrator on this theme, for he both sympathizes with the bodies mutilated for economic progress and yet disparages the populations who resist his country's imperial claims. Whaling's significance as an economic, political, and diplomatic force makes it an important precursor to the looting, Islamophobic empires that Ungar disdains. The question this fifth chapter contemplates is how these powers disguise themselves as forms of prosthetic aid.

In training his eye on what he called the "whale fishery," Melville promised readers a philosophic reflection on the combined forces of capitalism, imperialism, and the development of new technologies (395). The industry employed seventy thousand people at its height in the 1850s and drew over $70 million in capital investment.[16] By one estimate, it was the fifth largest industry in the nation.[17] While countries such as Great Britain and France also possessed substantial whaling fleets, the United States far exceeded their numbers. Out of the 900 whaling ships at sea during 1846, 735 of them came from the United States. When New York senator William Seward praised whaling as a "source of national wealth," he could have been referring to both the ships' profits and the range of commercial occupations

148 THE PROSTHETIC ARTS OF *MOBY-DICK*

surrounding the fishery such as sail-making, oil distribution, and the production of supplies.[18] The industry produced sperm oil for candles, ambergris for vitamins, perfume, and soap, and oil for the lubrication of industrial machinery such as trains, printing presses, and textile looms.[19]

In "The Advocate," Ishmael praises American whalers not simply for the dollars they were bringing into the national economy but also for their role in bringing democracy to colonies around the world (110; Figure 9). As his portrait of the *Pequod* attests, whaling ships employed an extraordinarily international group of sailors who transported their experiences and customs to new lands. In voyaging to distant oceans and seeking provisions in far-off ports, the ships helped establish new maritime trade routes, and from lubricants to candles, the products themselves were in high demand in both European and American markets. Anthropologist John D. Kelly has playfully responded to one of Walter Benjamin's most famous essays by calling New Bedford, not Paris, "the capital of the nineteenth century," for New Bedford candles lit the city's famous arcades.[20] The New Bedford fleet, which alone was valued at $6.2 million, harvested an astonishing $7.7 million worth of oil and baleen in 1845. *Moby-Dick* arises from the few crucial decades when whaling was arguably driving the growth of the mammonism that Ungar would later denounce.[21]

Ishmael's advocating for the industry does not prevent him from describing its fundamental brutality and the toll it took on laborers and the environment. Amid his appreciation for the sailors' skill, Melville disparaged the would-be capitalist who focused only on profits. The satire of the owners Bildad and Peleg—with their hypocritical regard for the "widows and orphans" who invested in the voyage—exemplifies one approach to the theme (77). The metaphysical quality of Ahab's vengeance over Starbuck's anxious duty to the "Nantucket market" exemplifies another (163). But it is the third mate, Flask, who bears the brunt of Melville's critique, the "small and short" officer who is "full of a large and tall ambition" (221). Flask has little regard for the men in his boat, but in an industry built around violence, he displays exceptional cruelty toward the whales themselves.[22]

Chapter 1 discussed how Flask's limited understanding of Ahab's impairment echoes antebellum views about the body's capacity to do meaningful work. An equally profound image comes when Flask stands on the shoulders of the majestic Daggoo so he can peer across the waves as the *Pequod* lowers for its first hunt. The image, as several scholars have argued, visually captures the oppressiveness of the antebellum economy with the privileged

Figure 9 An 1864 dollar bill from the Whaling Bank of New London, Connecticut. Whaling had become so ingrained into New England's economy that, as early as 1846, it became a part of local currencies.
Image courtesy of the Mystic Seaport Museum.

150 THE PROSTHETIC ARTS OF *MOBY-DICK*

white master supported by a powerful African body.[23] Looking like a "snow-flake" perched atop the mountainous Daggoo, Flask stamps impatiently on the Black harpooner who coolly props him up. As Ishmael drily observes, "The bearer looked nobler than the rider" (221). Flask and Daggoo reflect the global ambitions of the whaling industry in which the "native American," as Ishmael describes a white New Englander, "liberally provides the brains, the rest of the world as generously supplying the muscles" (121). Harpooners outranked common sailors, of course, and Queequeg's ninetieth lay far sur-passed Ishmael's three hundredth. But the image makes the structural imbalance clear. With its myriad bankers, investors, suppliers, buyers, and officers, the industry produced a summit of New England snowflakes atop a mountain of international laborers. "Mounted upon gigantic Daggoo," "little Flask" epitomized how the combination of racial and financial capital dominated the international business of whaling (221).

Amid the incessant killing and rendering of bodies, it is also helpful to recognize that Flask turns Daggoo into his personal prosthesis. Ahab, of course, has done the same with his crew, and figures such as Pip and Stubb offer themselves as replacement legs or props upon which the captain can lean. But Flask's demands reveal that his power depends on a hierarchy of bodies based on birth, race, and species. Compared to the monkey rope that temporarily binds Ishmael to Queequeg, the prostheticization of Daggoo avoids any pretense of mutuality or a shared fate. No matter how cordially the African offers his assistance, there is no "Siamese ligature" between the two men (320). Flask's stamping foot declares that this relation is about dispossession and control. As this chapter explores, the third mate exemplifies the freebooter that Ungar would later deplore, for he regards the domination of bodies as a birthright transcending his own character and form.[24] Extending its biopolitical rule to other continents and species, the *Pequod* produces disability as part of a capitalist crusade against its Islamicized enemies. Part of Melville's wisdom was that he situated his cri-tique in the third mate, whose "pervading mediocrity" surfaces not just in his indifference, but in his attraction to others' suffering (187).

The Value of a One-Armed Whale

Flask's mediocrity appears in the peculiar offense he takes from the whale's perceived inferiority. Ishmael tells us that, although periodically

THE UNNATURAL STUMP   151

waggish and jolly, the third mate "seemed to think that the great Leviathans had personally and hereditarily affronted him" and that it was "a sort of point of honor with him, to destroy them whenever encountered" (119). Captain Boomer acknowledges the "great glory" that would come from killing Moby Dick, the "old great-grandfather" who was "the noblest and biggest" whale had ever seen (441, 438). Flask's conception of honor stems from the indiscriminate joy he feels in exterminating a pestilent species:

> So utterly lost was he to all sense of reverence for the many marvels of their majestic bulk and mystic ways; and so dead to anything like an apprehension of any possible danger from encountering them; that in his poor opinion, the wondrous whale was but a species of magnified mouse, or at least water-rat, requiring only a little circumvention and some small application of time and trouble in order to kill and boil. (119)

That Flask's vision stands apart from Ishmael's and Boomer's is not surprising, but even Ahab, with all his anger, sees a secret wisdom in the whale's "vast and venerable head" (311). When Flask battles a whale, he foolishly believes he is punching down, rather than up.

In a novel that regularly contemplates the difficulty of reading both human and cetacean bodies, Flask stands out for being a legible text. To Ishmael, the mate's short, compact physique signifies how fundamentally ordinary and mundane his violence could be. Ahab's scar may terrify the crew. Queequeg's tattoos may tantalize and mystify. And, of course, Moby Dick's whiteness dissolves all meaning into nothingness and makes a "leper" out of the "palsied universe" (195). But like a wrought nail, Flask is built to last, his body and character clinched tight around the simple, transparent fact that he was "very pugnacious concerning whales" (119).

Flask's capitalism takes center stage in "The Pequod Meets the Virgin," a chapter in which the American-led ship overtakes an incompetent German crew in capturing an old bull whale that promises to yield many barrels of oil. Consumers did not use whale oil for locomotion, and across its many varieties (sperm, spermaceti, and baleen), the oil bears no relation to the petroleum-based machine fuel that emerged later in the nineteenth century. But the whaling industry was partially built on the promise of providing clean burning radiant energy. Amid its many uses, consumers preferred sperm oil over other illuminants because it "burned brightly" in lamps and

152   THE PROSTHETIC ARTS OF *MOBY-DICK*

"did not thicken in the cold." To meet demand, in 1845 New Bedford produced 274,616 candles and 1,230,439 gallons of sperm oil for domestic and international use.[25] The same year, the quest for efficient, reliable light led British physicist Michael Faraday to conduct experiments comparing the brightness of rapeseed (colza) and sperm oil lamps.[26] Melville highlights the need for energy when the Germans, who have yet to catch a single whale, must accept the humiliation of beseeching Starbuck for enough oil to light their lamps. A strangely persistent presence during the pursuit, the empty German lamp-feeder foregrounds the fact that, despite the chapter's comedy, whaling was ultimately an international competition for energy.

The chase turns on the question of impairment, for as the *Pequod*'s boats near the "venerable" leviathan, the crew observe his many ailments. The bull's spout comes out in short, choke-like gushes; his skin is covered in yellow scabs; and he suffers from foul smelling, underwater flatulence. "Lord, think of having half an acre of stomach-ache!" muses the ever-colorful and body-aware Stubb. "Adverse winds are holding mad Christmas in him, boys" (352–53). Most significantly, the whale swims erratically, moving from side to side. When the boats get closer, the crew discovers "the cause of his devious wake in the unnatural stump of his starboard fin" (353). Like Captains Boomer and Ahab, the bull whale is missing one of his limbs.

Just as Melville's ships contain a range of bodies, minds, and abilities, so, too, does his sea. The activist and artist Sunauro Taylor has argued that animals with physical impairments challenge cultural assumptions about "what makes a body valuable, explainable, useful, or disposable."[27] The normate thinking that shapes the way humans see the disabled appears in the way they treat animals as well. Exposing the brutality of animal-based capitalism, Melville's chapter offers a contiguous perspective on Taylor's concerns. Flask is so immersed in the industry and so invested in the selling of animal commodities that the unnatural stump increases the whale's value, for the crew can extract the same profit while investing less labor into the hunt. Melville highlights Flask's perverse sense of power when the third mate first spots the missing fin. "Only wait a bit, old chap, and I'll give ye a sling for that wounded arm," he cries, "pointing to the whale-line near him" (353). There's more than cruelty in this anthropomorphic joke. Mocking expressions of sympathy, Flask uses the image of an immobilizing prosthetic to characterize the rope that will fasten the old bull to the boat. Dripping with irony, the statement articulates the premise behind the emergent empires that the third mate represents: that the power to wound hides behind the promise to prostheticize and assist.[28]

Compared to Moby Dick, there is little majesty in the old bull, and throughout the chapter Ishmael seeks the right language to explain his wounds. With the *Pequod*'s three harpoons firmly lodged in him, the bull sounds deep under the surface, leaving the boats to contemplate the hidden torment of this "utmost monster of the seas" (356). Even amid agony, the old bull retains its massive power, and his "life and death throbs" vibrate through the water, trembling beneath the oarsmen in their wooden seats (356). When Ishmael refers to the great leviathan invoked by the book of Job, the comparison seems inadequate, for the biblical creature who "laugheth at the shaking of a spear" shares little with the one who writhes in pain "under the mountains of the sea" (356). Indeed when he surfaces, Ishmael observes, the whale cannot see. "His eyes, or rather the places where his eyes had been, were beheld. As strange misgrown masses gather in the knot-holes of the noblest oaks when prostrate, so from the points which the whale's eyes had once occupied, now protruded blind bulbs, hor- ribly pitiable to see" (357). Far from exalting the whale, the references to Job magnify the extent of his decline.

The passage repeatedly describes the whale's impairment in human terms. Ishmael says the whale has "one arm," rather than one fin, and when he descends, he has "the strength of a thousand thighs in his tail" (356). Presented as an odd collection of body parts, the bull whale resembles the hump-backed, marling-spiked merman that haunted Stubb's dream in the "Queen Mab" chapter. But if the merman helped Stubb rationalize his sub- servience to Ahab, the bull whale rises from the sea like the surfacing of an unconscious fear. Leaking profuse amounts of blood, wallowing in pain, and suffering from blindness, ulcerated skin, and a missing limb, the whale graphically represents the vulnerability of bodies across species and time. Although occasionally helpless, Ahab has transformed his collection of wounds into the source of his ruthless power, turning the crew into the prosthetic arms and legs that will bear his aggrievement. The bull's com- pounded suffering comes closer to the experience of any species in the wild. The atrophying body isolates him from the pod, exposing him to compet- ing predators.

The "Jungfrau" chapter raises the question of what Ishmael's anthropo- morphism accomplishes in an industry built around the commodification

154   THE PROSTHETIC ARTS OF *MOBY-DICK*

of whales. Numerous eco-critics, of course, have demonstrated how poetic techniques from personification to pathetic fallacy foster an anthropocentric vision of the planet. "The rhetoric of nature's personhood," as Lawrence Buell has explained, can "deflect back into narcissism" and center the natural world on human life.[29] The scene's portrait of disability can certainly feed into an anthropocentric view, with the whale's "unnatural stump" becoming an auxiliary image of the captain's "dead" leg (353, 163). The *Pequod* hunts a gruesome version of itself, and as the crew comes face to face with the destruction involved in its quest, it can gain a different perspective on the toll of dismemberment. Though he briefly interrogates one of the *Jungfrau's* officers about the whereabouts of Moby Dick, Ahab neither participates in the hunt nor acknowledges the bull whale. As Philip Armstrong has argued, *Moby-Dick* oscillates "between apparently opposed attitudes to the whale: wonder and contempt, mundane nonchalance and transcendent awe, humanized fellow-feeling and the calculus of market value and profit."[30] Keeping the captain, Fedallah, and the Manilla oarsmen on ship allows Melville to focus on the whale's suffering and not engulf it in Ahab's narcissistic brooding.[31]

Like the doubloon, the scene reveals a lot about its participants. As soon as he notices the whale's wounds, Flask wants to exploit them. Thinking of sperm whales as nothing more than water rats, he acts with neither awe nor compassion when confronted with the bull's might. Ishmael grows alarmed by the suffering whale with his "continual tormented jet" and "his one poor fin beat[ing] his side in an agony of fright" (354). The rapacious Flask responds with a gruesome exercise of power. His cruelty exacerbates this "terrific, most pitiable, and maddening sight" (354). When the whale surfaces in distress, the third mate eyes "a strangely discoloured bunch or protuberance, the size of a bushel, low down on the flank" and resolves to "prick him there once" (357). The humane Starbuck tries to stop him, but the third mate sends his dart into the sore anyway. The malice goes beyond an inability to see the whale as a worthy adversary or a reflection of human frailty. Flask exemplifies what William James called "the pleasure of disinterested cruelty." Writing in *The Principles of Psychology* (1890), James used the phrase to explain a sensation that had aroused the interest of his contemporaries: the intense gratification that some people experience from inflicting pain on animals. "Human bloodthirstiness is such a primitive part of us that it is so hard to eradicate," James drily observed, "especially where a fight or a hunt is promised as part of the fun."[32] Flask's cruelties may come from the hunt, but they signify something more than its primitive lure. The fact that James's contemporaries saw the need to explain and debate such viciousness suggests that the sadistic Flask was a particular historical type.[33]

After characterizing the impaired fin in human terms, Ishmael ultimately recognizes the whale as an independent, suffering being. His gruesome description of the bull's death underscores the mate's gratuitous violence:

> At the instant of the dart an ulcerous jet shot from this cruel wound, and goaded by it into more than sufferable anguish, the whale now spouting thick blood, with swift fury blindly darted at the craft, bespattering them and their glorying crews all over with showers of gore, capsizing Flask's boat and marring the bows. It was his death stroke. For, by this time, so spent was he by loss of blood, that he helplessly rolled away from the wreck he had made; lay panting on his side, impotently flapped with his stumped fin, then over and over slowly revolved like a waning world; turned up the white secrets of his belly; lay like a log, and died. (358)

Flask's boat turns over, dropping the cheering crewmembers into the sea, but not before they are bathed in the gore they have created. Dripping with blood, the crew cannot escape Flask's sadistic dart. In a novel that revels in "the pornography of violence," the death of the old bull stains the crew with their own brutality.[34]

It seems absurd that the ignoble Flask has killed such an ancient beast, especially because he is so eager to extract pain and profit from the process. But the mate's violations earn a fittingly ironic reward when the whale proves to be so heavy that it nearly tips the ship into the sea. Dead sperm whales usually float alongside a ship for days, buoyed by their blubber and bones, but as Ishmael notes, some corpses mysteriously sink. The bull whale's age and infirmity seem to haunt the *Pequod*, and the strain of being bound to his weight literally begins to pull the ship apart. In a foreshadowing of Moby Dick, the whale threatens to capsize the *Pequod* unless the crew can disentangle themselves from Flask's handiwork. A study conducted by the National Bureau of Economic Research estimates that, on average, sperm whales yielded about thirty-four barrels of oil.[35] Caught up in the chase, Flask guesses that the whale contains one hundred barrels, and the commerce-driven Starbuck tries desperately to hang onto the wealth. When Queequeg finally breaks the fluke chains binding the carcass to the ship, the ancient mass sinks, its precious sperm escaping the *Pequod*'s materialists.

Flask and the Capitalist Crusade

Ishmael's attention to the whale's death does not take the form of a polemic, and it coincides alongside passages that capture the excitement of a chase, the power of communal labor, and the mythic grandeur that comes from fighting dragons, giants, and sea beasts. What the scene unequivocally reveals, however, is that in a book filled with impairments and disabilities, Flask stands alone in grotesquely exploiting them. Presented with numerous bodies and bodies politic, he seeks weakness and vulnerability. He is the realization of what Eric Fromm said about the man who thrives under authoritarianism:

> Powerless people or institutions automatically arouse his contempt. The very sight of a powerless person makes him want to attack, dominate, humiliate him. Whereas a different kind of character is appalled by the idea of attacking one who is helpless, the authoritarian character feels the more aroused the more helpless his object has become."[36]

Elizabeth Schultz has observed that the chapter tries to humanize the old bull, and in appealing to the reader's sympathy, it shrewdly employs the rhetoric of sentiment and sensationalism that was popular in the mid-nineteenth century.[37] Narrating the episode, Ishmael checks his customary use of literary and historical allusion, thus forcing readers to comprehend the whale's pain without the buffer of intellectual analogy. The figurative language tends to reinforce the natural setting, variously likening the dying whale to a fountain, a river, a log, and a fallen oak. The imagery temporarily removes the afflicted body from "the universal cannibalism of the sea" and transports it to a more familiar terrestrial landscape (274). Whether he was born with his "stumped fin" or was injured in battle, the whale's disability realizes the somatic vulnerability that formed the heart of Stubb's dream. The anthropomorphism acknowledges that all species experience physical difference and that human and nonhuman animals confront their own version of bloody spouts, ulcerous skin, and atypical fins.[38] This egalitarian vision was more progressive than it might initially seem. Schultz demonstrates that Melville actively rewrote his sources to emphasize the "cetacean-human kinship" that Ishmael's narration displays.[39]

Of course, Flask is not alone in perpetrating horrible violence on whales. The Germans and the Americans pursue the bull because he is old and slow, and both intend to harpoon, dart, and kill him for their gain. Three chapters later, Ishmael will describe Stubb's dexterity with the pitch pole as he pierces a whale forty feet away. Stubb's exaltation when he produces a gushing spout of blood suggests a peculiarly American capacity to produce these deaths on the high seas. "That drove the spigot out of him!" cries Stubb. "'Tis July's immortal Fourth; all fountains must run wine to-day!" Stubb exhibits a frontier mentality when he wishes the blood were "old Orleans whiskey, or old Ohio, or unspeakable old Monongahela!" (368). But it is Flask's dual focus on the whale's wound and profitability that captures his approach to disability. The third mate does not view the whale as a noble, or even sentient, opponent but a commercial resource that should be converted into a commodity as quickly and contemptuously as possible. When Starbuck says there is no need to prick the dying whale, he is trying to obscure the ruthless system he himself serves.

The scene typifies how Melville uses the episodic nature of *Moby-Dick* to develop a larger consciousness about the economic foundations of the industry. As John Levi Barnard comments, "The localized hunt cannot be separated from the global systems that both demand and justify it." The killing of the bull whale occurs "not in isolation but in relation to the traffic in animal commodities that drives them."[40] The particulars of this scene illuminate the larger dynamics of an extractive industry that mines the sea to produce consumer goods and, more importantly, to keep its lamps lit and its machinery functioning smoothly. Although an industrial accident produces Ahab's aggrievement, he responds by seeing his dismemberment as a cosmic affront that turns the hated Moby Dick into a metaphysical opponent. Ishmael's emphasis on pity creates a space for intersubjectivity in which the whale becomes part of his interiority—so much so that he laments that, without a voice, the bull cannot express the fear that is "chained up and enchanted in him" (355). Richard J. King notes that, in an unusual move for *Moby-Dick*, Ishmael takes readers inside the whale's consciousness, asking them to consider the hunt from a different perspective: "Who can tell how appalling to the wounded whale must've been such huge phantoms flitting over his head!" (356).[41]

In multiple ways, the rhetoric of Ishmael's narration explicitly counters the actions of the third mate. Flask follows the logic of his industry, seeing the old bull as he does the other whales the *Pequod* kills on its voyage: an object meant for profit. He epitomizes the capitalist practice of reducing the environment to the foundation for continual trade, or as his twenty-first-century

158 THE PROSTHETIC ARTS OF *MOBY-DICK*

counterparts might say, the source of a global supply chain. Whether he is mounted on Daggoo's back or darting a suffering whale, Flask represents an antebellum American economy that turns both humans and nonhumans into object commodities. The practice takes a tremendous toll, and although he concludes that the whale will never grow extinct, Ishmael senses that environmental decline is inevitable. "We account the whale immortal in his species, however perishable in his individuality," he later writes, but the story of the old bull catches him in a darker mood (462). The bull's vulnerability comes to signify a general fear and weakness at the heart of human interactions with nature. Ishmael refers to more than girth when he describes how the whale "impotently flapped with his stumped fin, then over and over slowly revolved like a waning world" (358). The hunt goes beyond how the destruction of individual whales could endanger the entire species. In that slow revolution, we can see the image of a dying planet, exhausted by the search for energy.

Even as the crewmembers lose their riches, Ishmael underscores the unseemly, financial motivations of the hunt. Because the corpse sinks so rapidly into the sea, its treasures go "unrifled," and the crew miss their chance to have "rummaged" through its "monstrous cabinet" looking for hidden jewels (358). Schultz points out that the imagery aligns the *Pequod* with a gang of housebreakers going from room to room.[42] But the language also recalls Ishmael's early description of the crew as Crusaders who, amid their romantic quest to gain the Holy Land, enrich themselves by "committing burglaries, picking pockets, and gaining other pious perquisites by the way" (212). With Flask as its relentlessly callous leader, the crew intends to plunder the sea's riches and dominate its creatures.

Melville made the connection to the Crusades explicit in Ungar's diatribe about Anglo-Saxon "pirates of the sphere." Armed with the phrase "*As cruel as a Turk*," the Anglo-Saxons are willing to disparage people of other faiths, while disguising their mammonism in the mantle of evangelical Christianity.[43] The old bull scene exemplifies the global piracy of the whale hunt. Worshiping the false god of profiteering, the crew are literally "grave looters" as they ransack the whale's ulcerated corpse. Rob Nixon has written about the "slow violence of environmental catastrophe" and the way that toxic chemicals, contaminated water, and climate change are gradually destroying the earth and further dispossessing the poor.[44] These subtler forms of planetary aggression are predicated on centuries of venomous acts committed by men such as Flask. "Through this layering of human history

THE UNNATURAL STUMP   159

and nonhuman bodies," Barnard argues, the *Pequod* "registers the destruction of cultures and ecosystems that has attended the extractive and expansive course of US empire."[45] In his arrogant disregard, Flask thrives as he administers the sanctioned violence of nineteenth-century England and America. For good reason, commentators have repeatedly identified Ahab with the power of Big Oil, but Flask may be a more revealing analogue. On a broader historical canvas, we can see him somewhere between the brass-helmeted Crusader pillaging Jerusalem and the hard-hatted Aramco manager drilling the Persian Gulf.[46]

Reservoirs of Oil

While Starbuck wrestles with his conscience and Stubb his awareness of other bodies, Flask sees the world through the lens of commerce and trade. From Ahab to Queequeg, from the Manxman to Pip, his fellow crewmembers develop complex readings of the golden doubloon that Ahab has nailed into the main mast. Starbuck sees an image of a rising sun that shakes his faith; Stubb sees a zodiacal accounting of the stages of human life. Flask sees only "a round thing made of gold," which, in its way, is as revealing as anything his crewmembers have disclosed. "So, what's all this staring been about?" he asks. "It is worth sixteen dollars, that's true; and at two cents the cigar, that's nine hundred and sixty cigars" (433). Flask's transactional vision rarely goes beyond material price.

As the boats from the *Pequod* and the *Jungfrau* race toward the disabled whale, Stubb and Flask exhort their men to overtake their German competitors and fasten onto him first. Stubb promises a "hogshead of brandy" to the oarsman who most helps him beat the "Yarman" Derick and his crew (353). Flask exalts in the possibility of monetary gain. He calls the whale a "sogger," meaning that he is drenched in profitable oil (354). C. L. R. James remarked that instead of helping their men, the *Pequod*'s officers demoralized them. This seems especially true of Flask, whose focus on commercial value would mean more to owners and investors than sailors with a three hundredth lay.[47] "Don't ye love sperm," he shouts to his crew. "There goes three thousand dollars, men!—a bank!—a whole bank! The bank of England!" (354). Not only monetizing the kill, Flask also foregrounds its connection to capital, comparing it to the royal government's principal banker and debt manager. From his 1849 visit to London, Melville knew

160 THE PROSTHETIC ARTS OF *MOBY-DICK*

that five years earlier the government had awarded the Bank of England sole responsibility for issuing paper notes.[48] Spotting Moby Dick may represent a handsome payday to Flask, but extracting the old bull's spermaceti suggests the control of money itself.

As Melville constructs the scene, however, he spreads responsibility for the whale's gruesome death beyond the third mate. The gore that splatters Flask's crew ultimately splatters all those domestic consumers eager for the light the processed whale would bring. The bull's condition may have been pitiable, Ishmael remarks:

> But pity there was none. For all his old age, and his one arm, and his blind eyes, he must die the death and be murdered, in order to light the gay bridals and other merry-makings of men, and also to illuminate the solemn churches that preach unconditional inoffensiveness by all to all. (357)

Although William James would see it as a primitive instinct, Flask's cruelty reflects the rise of industrial capitalism and its growing contribution to environmental ruin. Ishmael warns that the extraction of the resource cannot be separated from its appearance as a consumer product. As if he were channeling Friedrich Engels on the family and Karl Marx on religion, he places the whale's killing at the heart of bourgeois society. The whale's sickness and dismemberment underscore an industrial system that profits from the debilitation of other peoples and species.[49]

Ishmael invoked these themes before. Early in the novel, he guides his readers through New Bedford, pointing out whaling's overwhelming impact on the economy. "The town itself is perhaps the dearest place to live in, in all New England," he writes. "Nowhere in all America will you find more patrician-like houses, parks and gardens more opulent, than in New Bedford" (32). From the owners' mansions on County Street to the elegant captains' homes on Cottage Street, the wealth was widely admired. Having settled in New Bedford after escaping slavery, Frederick Douglass also touted the town's prosperity: "From the wharves I strolled around and over the town, gazing with wonder and admiration at the splendid churches, beautiful dwellings, and finely-cultivated gardens; evincing an amount of wealth, comfort, taste, and refinement, such as I had never seen in any part of slaveholding Maryland."[50] Like boats on a rising tide, coopers,

THE UNNATURAL STUMP   161

dockworkers, hotel owners, craftsmen, builders, and foundry workers were all lifted by the nation's first global industry. As Douglass explained, labor seemed more dignified in New Bedford than it had in the slave city of Baltimore, for knowing that there was money to be made and no threat of abuse, workers went about their business "with a sober, yet cheerful earnestness."[51] Douglass was among them. His autobiography proudly mentions that his first steady job was moving barrels of spermaceti at Joseph Ricketson's south side oil refinery, oil that would later be used for candle making.[52]

Even as he promotes New Bedford's prosperity, Ishmael exposes how implicated bourgeois culture was in the killing of whales. Taking us through the charming streets, he challenges readers to consider the origins of all that wealth:

> Go and gaze upon the iron emblematical harpoons round yonder lofty mansion, and your question will be answered. Yes; all these brave houses and flowery gardens came from the Atlantic, Pacific, and Indian oceans. One and all, they were harpooned and dragged up hither from the bottom of the sea. (32)

The passage eliminates all the processing and purchasing that makes a product out of the living whale. In *Clarel*, Ungar descries the "deflowering of every sylvan glade." In Ishmael's imagination, the gardens themselves are the pastoral product of environmental pillaging.

A few chapters later, Ishmael will mention the wealth more enthusiastically, touting the Nantucketer's history of "ploughing" the sea as if it were "his own special plantation" (64). Even as it invites comparisons to slavery, the plantation imagery builds off the association American whalers frequently made between the ocean's boundless open space and the Western prairie. The association conveniently presents an industry based on animal destruction as a pastoral, agrarian enterprise.[53] The New Bedford fences similarly conceal the industry's reality in the charm of commodities. The decorative harpoons may acknowledge the source of the dollars that purchased them, but they also make an ornament out of an economy built around extracting "the meat," as Colin Dayan has phrased it, "mutilated, bleeding, dead, rotting."[54] "Be economical with your lamps and candles!" Ishmael warns, "not a gallon you burn, but at least one drop of man's blood

162 THE PROSTHETIC ARTS OF *MOBY-DICK*

was spilled for it" (206). It is the gushing of whales' blood, however, that haunts the novel most.

Melville repeatedly ties this critique to marriage, perhaps the most sentimentalized institution in Anglo-American society. The *Jungfrau* may conjure images of virgin innocence (and terrible seamanship), but the success of the American whale fishery creates a more extravagant social world:

> In New Bedford, fathers, they say, give whales for dowers to their daughters, and portion off their nieces with a few porpoises a-piece. You must go to New Bedford to see a brilliant wedding; for, they say, they have reservoirs of oil in every house, and every night recklessly burn their lengths in spermaceti candles. (32)

Among the merry makings of bourgeois society, the "gay bridal" is the most joyous and productive of celebrations. And yet Ishmael's hyperbole twice asks us to think about the wedding in the context of the whaling industry, rhetorically placing the bride alongside Flask as he gruesomely kills the stump-finned bull. In the sexual terms of the chapter, there are no virgins on the wedding day because everyone has already been implicated in the hunt.

Agents of Terror, Pirates of the Sphere

Ishmael's revulsion toward Flask and his attention to the old bull's suffering expands our sense of how bodies matter in a capitalist society and how they do not. When he imagines the whale's voice "chained up" within him, when he considers the hunt from an underwater perspective, he briefly incorporates cetacean experience into the evolving consciousness of his text. As Ishmael presents it, Flask's extravagant violence is an undeniable part of American life, his cruelty silently absorbed into the cultural norms of dowries, weddings, and shops. What makes Ishmael's vision particularly radical is that he includes the whale in his argument, effectively expanding the body politic to encompass the leviathan who trembles—wounded and falsely prostheticized—under the *Pequod*'s boats. In this way, Ishmael both humanizes and nationalizes the creature that Flask has maliciously killed. Noting the stone lance head buried in the flesh, he gives the whale a history dating back to the indigenous peoples of the Pacific Northwest. The bull is neither a magnified mouse nor a water rat. He's an "old great-grandfather" (as Captain Bunger twice calls Moby Dick); his death deserves tribal respect (438).

And yet when we follow these environmental themes deeper into the text, we begin to see where Ishmael's and Ungar's environmental visions diverge, for as much as the narrator regrets the gratuitous destruction of sylvan and maritime life, he has an equally strong impulse either to bring rival human populations under American command or at least to exemplify their need for American technology, know-how, and values. (Amid the horror of the old bull's death, he maintains the comedy of the *Pequod*'s showing up the incompetent German ship.) Ishmael's democratic nationalism does not exist as an abstract appreciation for constitutional values: it seems inextricable from its connections to global commerce and power. The limits of his anthropomorphic imagination are not simply that he turns animals into people but that in doing so he turns people into a population that must be rendered and controlled.

The tension created by Ishmael's conflicting views arises in Chapter 87, "The Grand Armada," in which the *Pequod* encounters an immense caravan of whales occupying "at least two or three square miles" (387). "The Grand Armada" serves as a companion to the gruesome killing in "The Pequod Meets the Virgin." Unlike the earlier account, though, the chapter adds a sense of place to the sentiment and anthropomorphism that guided Ishmael's reflections on the old bull. The miles-long pod of sperm whales appears in the Sunda Strait, the narrow strip of water that divides Sumatra from Java and the Indian Ocean from the Java Sea. Ishmael points out that the large green promontories on both sides of the strait had long provided a natural gateway for Western ships sailing to China and the Far East. For centuries, pirates had haunted the area, intercepting ships in the midst of their profitable trade, and responding to popular accounts in the antebellum press, Melville supplies a ship of Malaysian pirates who begin chasing the *Pequod* midway through the strait.[55] Though they never amount to a serious threat, the pirates signal the *Pequod's* transition into the archipelago of islands that Ishmael associates with the ancient, dreamlike world of Fedallah, his Manilla oarsmen, and the Malaysian assassin he compares to Moby Dick.

In this oddly liminal, Islamicized place, the crew encounter an unforeseen danger when they lower their boats for the hunt. The fast-moving caravan suddenly stops, having fallen "under the influence of that strange

164   THE PROSTHETIC ARTS OF *MOBY-DICK*

perplexity of inert resolution, which, when the fishermen perceive it in the whale, they say he is *gallied*" (384). Rather than swim in tight protective columns, the whales become paralyzed with fright, swimming in circles and odd directions and yet, as a group, collectively remaining in place (385). This terrified response to predators puts the crew at risk, for they know that to strike a single whale could create such further agitation that it would pitch them into the sea amid the churning mass. When Queequeg harpoons a whale on the edge of the group, the victim responds by dragging Starbuck's boat "deeper and deeper into the frantic shoal" of writhing bodies where the sailors give up their "circumspect life and only exist in a delirious throb" (385). The experience provides an affective counterpart to Pip's losing himself in the wondrous depths or the wide-eyed Platonist falling from the masthead. Consciousness gives way to the herd-like sensation of distributed emotion and aggregated flesh.[56]

Surrounded by this tormented but paralyzed herd, the *Pequod* enters an extraordinarily peaceful domestic scene that the frenzy surrounding it protects. The passage builds off the bridal imagery Ishmael used six chapters before to contextualize Flask's killing of the old bull. Extending the metaphor, he now finds a nursery, a place of "enchanted calm" where the smaller cows and calves approach the boat with either "a wondrous fearlessness and confidence" or a "still becharmed panic" (387). Peering deeper into the water, the crew witnesses a dreamlike moment of mothers nursing their young, while the infants gaze up toward the surface. Starbuck, prompted by Queequeg, spies something even more profound—a newborn calf still attached to its mother:

> Starbuck saw long coils of the umbilical cord of Madame Leviathan, by which the young cub seemed still tethered to its dam. Not seldom in the rapid vicissitudes of the chase, this natural line, with the maternal end loose, becomes entangled with the hempen one, so that the cub is thereby trapped. Some of the subtlest secrets of the seas seemed divulged to us in this enchanted pond. We saw young Leviathan amours in the deep. (388)

The motherless Ishmael turns this primal moment into an elegantly effusive expression of the "tornadoed Atlantic" of his being and an understanding that while "ponderous planets of unwaning woe" revolve around him, he bathes in "eternal mildness of joy" (389). It is the kind of sentiment that,

THE UNNATURAL STUMP 165

among Melville's contemporaries, only Walt Whitman could express as convincingly.

And yet ominous signs abound. Ishmael reports that when the mothers' breasts are lacerated, they pour milk and blood into the sea. The whale line risks getting entangled with the umbilical cord, the prosthetic (as Flask jeeringly described it) threatening the natural link. "Predatory man," as Michael Rogin has put it, will soon take "the place of Madame Leviathan," drawing the infant from its peaceful sanctuary into the terrors of the human economy.[57] As they have been gazing into the origins of life, their shipmates have been darting whales on the outside of the caravan hoping to retrieve them later. Feeling the "extraordinary agony" of his tail wound, however, one whale frantically dashes among his comrades, endangering the mass with his frenzy:

> But at length we perceived that by one of the unimaginable accidents of the fishery, this whale had become entangled in the harpoon-line that he towed; he had also run away with the cutting-spade in him; and while the free end of the rope attached to that weapon, had permanently caught in the coils of the harpoon-line round his tail, the cutting-spade itself had worked loose from his flesh. So that tormented to madness, he was now churning through the water, violently flailing with his flexible tail, and tossing the keen spade about him, wounding and murdering his own comrades. (389)

The "appalling spectacle" reveals the "peculiar horror" of the industry (389). Flask's killing of the old bull was gratuitously cruel, but it reflected his will and achieved his intended result. What Ishmael describes in "The Grand Armada" is a violence that cannot be contained, as whales the *Pequod* had no intention of harvesting end up being slaughtered.

Writing about 1492, the year that Muslims were expelled from Spain and Europeans began colonizing the New World, Wai Chee Dimock has commented that "violence is reproductive rather than terminal, itinerant rather than stationary."[58] "The Grand Armada" envisions a similar dynamic in which environmental destruction breeds environmental catastrophe. Spurred by greed, the *Pequod* begins a cycle of indiscriminate killing and then cannot control the violence it has initiated. In an irony reminiscent of the old bull's treasures sinking to the bottom of the sea, crewmembers dart

166   THE PROSTHETIC ARTS OF *MOBY-DICK*

numerous whales, but they can only capture one.[59] The recklessness and waste might recall Ishmael's earlier comment that "there is no folly of the beasts of the earth which is not infinitely outdone by the madness of men" (385).

Dimock was not writing about *Moby-Dick*, but her comment resonates with Ishmael's decision to introduce his account of the terrorized whales with a discussion of geography and Western trade. He opens the chapter by characterizing the narrow passage and bold promontory of the Sunda Strait as an imposing entry to the "vast walled empire" of the Far East and its "inexhaustible wealth of spices, and silks, and jewels, and gold, and ivory, with which the thousand islands of that oriental sea are enriched" (380). Ships had traveled through the strait for centuries, using it as a link between the Indian and Pacific Oceans. But Ishmael wants to see the land resisting this traffic as if nature itself were attempting to guard these resources "from the all-grasping western world" (380). The comment anticipates Ungar's critique in *Clarel*, as Ishmael yearns for a buttress to capitalism's global reach.

Other narrators might present the Malay pirates as working with the landscape in forming another impediment to the extraction of Asian wealth. But rather than see them as allies in this environmental struggle, Ishmael turns them into threats to Western life. The Europeans built military fortresses on their principal straits, and the Danes demanded homage from foreign ships navigating between the Baltic and North Seas. The Malays, he tells us, have embodied that martial spirit unto themselves (Figure 10). They are "bloodthirsty pirates" and "inhuman atheistical devils" who lurk in the "low shaded coves and islets of Sumatra" (383–84). For generations, they have fiercely demanded tribute "at the point of their spears," so much so that European cruisers have had to take military action against them (381). And yet, despite "repeated bloody chastisements," the Malays audaciously return, "remorselessly" boarding and pillaging the English and American vessels that pass through the strait (381).

Ishmael was not alone in his concern about pirates in the region. Matt Matsuda writes that "accusations of violence and terror spread by marauders and pirates were accurate enough, and fearful traditions of unknown boats and sails are recorded in generations of tragic tales and oral accounts across archipelagos and coastlines." Eighteenth- and nineteenth-century Europeans increasingly objected to the presence of pirates in the Sunda Straits, but their "imputations of savagery" were "only part of the story."[60] The notion that Malays had a natural inclination to piracy

Figure 10 *Garay Warships of Pirates in the Sulu Sea*, circa 1850. Wikimedia.

developed in the late eighteenth century when European vessels began to increase their presence in the region. Differentiating them from other "Mahomedan populations" in the Philippines, Sir John Bowring claimed that the fierce Moros were "probably of Malayan descent."[61] Legends about the Malay pirates arose, in part, because locals objected to what Matsuda calls "the intrusion of empires into local seas."[62] As early as 1697, a sympathetic Englishman had described the piracy around the Strait of Malacca as a defense of local economies. "The Pirates who lurk on this Coast," he wrote, "seem to do it as much to revenge themselves on the Dutch, for restraining their Trade, as to gain this way what they cannot obtain in way of Traffick."[63] According to Stefan Eklöf Amirell, the rampant stories about Malaysian piracy grew in relation to the number of European and American ships that attempted to pull resources from this region.[64] Set in 1800, Melville's short story "Benito Cereno" features the American captain Amasa Delano, who nervously recalls the legendary tricks of "the Malay pirates" after he boards a "thinly manned" Spanish ship off the coast of Chile.[65]

Although they drop out of the narrative quickly, the Malays have a significant symbolic presence in the chapter in that they jeopardize the safety and profitability of Western commerce. The *Pequod* "sails primarily through Muslim territories," Nicholas Birns explains, and the appearance of these

168   THE PROSTHETIC ARTS OF *MOBY-DICK*

pirates, in the mouth of the Indian Ocean, puts the voyage "not only in the realm of religion and comparative mythology, but also the more contested sphere of history and politics."[66] Ishmael's emphasis on progressive democracy helps contextualize his hostility toward these populations in *Moby-Dick*. As Spencer Tricker has shown, the United States began to pursue a colonial presence in the region in the early decades of the nineteenth century. After Malay pirates killed the crew of two American ships in the 1830s, writers and readers gravitated to the figure of the treacherous Malay, a ghostly, heavily racialized sailor whose bloodthirsty violence impeded the nation's growing imperial aims. The presence of such pirates threatened the narrative that Western powers were bringing to the populations of Southeast Asia. Tricker concludes that the gothic trope of the timeless Malay disrupted the capitalist sense of progress that undergird US trade and military exploits in the region.[67]

In referring to the Malays as atheists rather than pagans, Ishmael echoes a charge that Christians have leveled at Muslims for centuries—that, coming after the resurrection of Christ, Islam does not establish a different faith as much as it denies the existence of God altogether. Although he never mentions Islam specifically, Ishmael's description of the pirates relies on some of the same slurs and accusations that have long been part of Islamophobic discourse in the West. The narrator known for his broad-minded views of different species and creeds perpetuates Orientalist stereotypes when it comes to a geopolitical rivalry. He reflects a practice that, according to Amirell, emerged in the first decades of the nineteenth century when Westerners began to define the Malays as a race, turning their economic opportunism into a reflection of "structural factors such as climate, geography, history, culture, and religion."[68] At the core of Ishmael's imperial vision is an incapacity to see himself as a potential enemy.[69]

As we saw in the image of Flask and Daggoo, the *Pequod*'s cosmopolitanism presumes that, despite racial conflicts, its international crew will serve the interest of its American owners and leadership. (The only crewmember to challenge Ahab's mission is the Nantucket-born Starbuck.) However fleetingly, the Malays offer resistance, and Ishmael's description echoes familiar clichés about the violent natives whose refusal to submit is a sign of their racial and religious intransigence (Figure 11). The situation recalls the way Ungar connected the phrase "*As cruel as a Turk*" with the trade-hungry colonialists who had dispossessed myriads of their land and rights: although condemned as bloodthirsty atheists, these Muslim seamen could easily be

THE UNNATURAL STUMP   169

Figure 11 Samuel Francis Marryat, Detail from *Illanoan Pirates of Tampassook* (Borneo), 1848, Pen and brown ink.
Image courtesy of the Paul Mellon Collection, Yale Center for British Art.

seen as defending the region's resources from the real "pirates of the sphere," the freebooting Anglo-Saxons.

This geopolitical setting clarifies *Moby-Dick*'s portrait of American whale hunters who produce extraordinary waste while trying to capture resources for their growing economy. Whatever sympathy Ishmael expresses for whales, whatever admiration he feels for the *Pequod*'s pagan harpooners, he

170   THE PROSTHETIC ARTS OF *MOBY-DICK*

projects the ship's environmental violence onto the Malays who try to impede their mission. For all its travels, the *Pequod* remains a strikingly insular craft. It neither engages in foreign trade nor enters a foreign harbor. In fact, although it pursues a different end, Ahab's monomania is a good representation of the industry's singular focus. Bound to its task, whale ships claim the ocean's resources to increase the economic capacity of Euro-American life, to lubricate the machines and light the cities that will bring further wealth to the West. As Flask exhorts his oarsmen, the bull whale is a bank; its "unnatural stump" and decrepit age making it easier and more lucrative prey than smaller, younger, more powerful whales. The mediocre Flask thrives in such a narrowly conceived environment, and it is no surprise that amid the tumult of the Grand Armada, he manages to kill a whale outright, without wounding it for later capture. Confusion and vulnerability are opportunities to Flask rather than deterrents.

In the end, the *Pequod* is an agent of terror in the Sunda Strait, spreading fear and panic to the caravan of whales and barely connecting the threats it encounters to its own violent intent. The chapter finds Ishmael in the perplexing situation of dehumanizing the Malays who are chasing the ship and yet humanizing the whales the crew is trying to kill. That paradox exposes the novel's repeated practice of making American violence a fearsome quality endemic to Turks, Berbers, Moors, Malays, and of course, to Fedallah, the fire-worshiping Parsee. Even the whales fall prey to these cultural associations. Caught amid the panicking herd, Starbuck's boat seems in grave danger until it shoots through "a narrow Dardanelles" of an opening and then, after a series of similar maneuvers, finds its way to safety (390). The scene already occurs in a strait that Ishmael claims is notorious for Muslim piracy. Alluding to the well-known strait separating Europe from Asia (and Greece from Turkey), the Dardanelles image reinforces the exotic danger of the setting. It subtly Islamicizes the herd's threat to the crew without acknowledging that, as a representation of the "all-grasping western world," the crew brought that threat into being.

An air of inevitability surrounds the *Pequod*'s progress through the Sunda Strait, as nothing appears capable of halting its voyage to the "Turkish-rugged waters" where it will find Moby Dick. Like the vaunted Spanish fleet, the Grand Armada of sperm whales seems destined to lose against the Anglo-Saxon quest for more resources and more commodities. The sense of inevitability extends to the demise of the species. With the cutting-spade flying about, wounding and murdering their comrades, the whales make a desperate effort "to pile themselves up in one common mountain" to protect the mothers and infants below. "The submarine bridal-chambers and nurseries vanished," Ishmael remarks, amazed at the herds' instinctual behavior (389). In that sudden vanishing, however, we can see something Ishmael could not: how the whales' naturally protective instincts would be no match for the unnatural violence inflicted on the oceans since the 1850s. Whether hunters, pollutants, plastics, or rising ocean temperatures, the effect has been similar: one species' bride disappears so another's can be illuminated.

From piercing the old bull to creating disaster in the Sunda Strait, the *Pequod* sails with the confidence that it should rightfully dominate whatever region or species gets in its way. These chapters provide us with a strikingly literal example of the debilitation of others in the name of profit and trade. The intent of Ishmael's anthropomorphism may be to create a more reflective population among the nations that live off the whaling industry, but he inevitably elevates the Anglo-Saxon mission above those who would resist their entry. When Ishmael Islamicizes the white whale, when he describes the caravan as the Dardanelles straits, he articulates a capitalist fantasy that the regions' inhabitants will ultimately welcome the West into their sylvan glades.

6

Eternal Hacking

Democracy's Lopped Limbs

In the final book of *Clarel*, five pilgrims meet a disabled Mexican man outside a convent in Bethlehem. While debating whether sinners want to be penalized for their sins, the pilgrims see a stranger coming toward them, evidently pleased by the topic of their conversation.

> In hobbling state
> He came among them, with one sleeve
> Loose flying, and one wooden limb,
> A leg. All eyes the cripple skim;
> Each rises, and his seat would give.[1]

The Anglican priest, Derwent, knows the man from London, and he joyfully introduces him as his "estimable friend" Señor Don Hannibal Rohon, a veteran who had won "great fame" on the battlefield in Mexico.[2]

With his missing arm and leg, Don Hannibal has spent the past years searching the Old World for a place to live, but wherever he goes—England, Norway, Egypt—he finds "cursed *Progress*" there to greet him. The illusion of advancement reminds him of the New World, and when Derwent tries to praise his military heroism, the effusively good-natured Don Hannibal abruptly cuts the compliment off:

> Hidalgos, I am, as ye see,
> Just a poor cripple—that is all;
> A cripple, yet contrive to hop
> Far off from Mexic liberty,
> Thank God! I lost these limbs for that;
> And would that they were mine again,
> And all were back to former state—
> I, Mexico, and poor Old Spain.[3]

The Prosthetic Arts of Moby-Dick. David Haven Blake, Oxford University Press. © Oxford University Press 2024.
DOI: 10.1093/oso/9780197780510.003.0007

The sunny demeanor belies profound regret, as the veteran links the separation of his country with the separation of his limbs.

Coming twenty-five years after the publication of *Moby-Dick*, Don Hannibal is the exhausted conclusion of the many dismembered characters that Melville created before him. He has something of Samoa's grace, Captain Boomer's cheer, and the man with the wooden leg's skepticism of progressive values. His empty sleeve recalls Horatio Nelson's reputation for valor, though unlike the admiral and his own countryman General Santa Anna, he will not allow his missing limbs to signify personal and national honor. Ahab tries to redeem his lost leg by making his prosthetic signify the righteousness of his revenge. Don Hannibal hops away from the site of his injury, turning his lost arm and leg into indictments against his idealistic past.

Melville wrote *Clarel* in the aftermath of the American Civil War, and the poem bears the heavy disillusionment of the period. Describing himself as a "reformado reformed," Don Hannibal has grown disenchanted with Mexican independence, and, more profoundly, he seems weary of the century's faith in democratic improvement.[4] Although praising the New World for contributing wine and tobacco to other nations, he has no faith in the political systems it has spread around the globe. Democracy, he contends, does not represent a better stage in the development of man. Creating turbulence out of stability, it severs colonies from empires, sinners from penalties, and the present from the past. Spurred by Mexico and the United States, it has ruptured the capitals of Europe, leaving London "too proletarian" and suffering from "too much agitation" for a peaceful life.[5] Don Hannibal had fought for reform only to see his nation fall apart. "But what's in this Democracy?" he challenges the pilgrims, before answering the question himself: "Eternal hacking!" *Battle-Pieces and Aspects of the War* (1866) was Melville's title for his book of Civil War poems. Don Hannibal takes that sense of fragmentation a step further. "Woe is me," he cries. "She lopped these limbs, Democracy."[6]

As it does with Captains Ahab and Boomer, the prosthesis becomes part of Don Hannibal's character. Culled from the species that injured him, Ahab's whalebone leg conveys his terrifying purpose. It physically straps vengeance onto his body and, with that, expresses the avenger's obligation to a well-defined narrative path. Don Hannibal's injuries cast him adrift, spurring him to roam the world in disappointment and disbelief. Walter Bezanson has described him as a "jolly monomaniac," but while the veteran

174   THE PROSTHETIC ARTS OF *MOBY-DICK*

has a sharp sense of humor, the label neglects the trajectory of his grief.[7] Although he blames democracy for his loss, the Mexican never fixates on a single goal or adversary, nor does he experience the all-consuming aggrievement that centers *Moby-Dick*. Don Hannibal may feel dismembered from his country, but the text treats his wooden peg more as an assistive device than as the physical manifestation of an obsessive concern. The slate on Ahab's prosthesis brands him with his cause. Seeking relief rather than payback, the disabled veteran moves around the planet without a calculated end.

Although they share a penchant for wandering, Don Hannibal retreats from the progressivism that Ishmael so vigorously acclaims. He travels to Asia, hoping to find a bulwark against the always-encroaching West. Ishmael dreaded the primordial energies that Fedallah and his boatmates seemed to represent, threatened by their countries' aversion to change. "*Even in these modern days,*" he writes, they "still preserve much of the ghostly aboriginalness of earth's primal generations."[8] Ishmael refers to the countries of the Malay Archipelago, but the same quality makes Palestine a promising place for Don Hannibal to assuage his woes. Whether political, philosophical, or theological, Melville often stages opposing views as conversations among his characters.[9] In *Clarel*, the character who most responds to Don Hannibal's disillusionment is Ungar, whose hatred of democracy hangs over the poem's Bethlehem cantos. Although wary of his cheerfulness, Ungar earnestly expands upon the fellow veteran's theme. He compares democracy to a "Harlot on horseback" who is accompanied through history by panderers, waste, and infamy. Like Don Hannibal, he takes comfort in believing that democracy will fall short of its imperial aims. "Asia shall stop her at the least," he says, "That old inertness of the East."[10] A rueful opponent of Anglo-American progressivism, he hates democracy's transience and its disregard for the past. When Don Hannibal describes his lopped-off limbs, he responds, "Ay, Democracy / Lops, lops; but where's her planted bed?"[11] Focused on his own experience, Ungar transforms an image of dismemberment into one of agrarian rootlessness.[12]

Jennifer Greiman has written that the darkness of Melville's post–Civil War writings stems from his conclusion that "democracy is a necessarily ungrounded, perpetually unsettled political practice."[13] The fear that democracy lacks stability, that its "foundations are always eroding and cracking and washing away," pervades such works as *Battle-Pieces*, *Clarel*, and *Billy Budd*.[14] If Melville's "democracy has any fixed meaning at all,"

Greiman writes, "it is that nothing about it can be presupposed: no territory, no community, no subjects."[15] Sorin Radu Cucu and Roland Végső have found similar sentiments in *Moby-Dick*. Ishmael describes "eternal war" as the basic condition of marine and human life, "the universal cannibalism of the sea" extending from the ocean to the relations between subjects, peoples, and states (209).[16] In Ishmael's description of Nantucket's "everlasting war" on the leviathan, Cucu and Végső perceive how the "imperial business of whaling" contributes to the persistence of global conflict. What Melville discovered in *Moby-Dick*, they contend, is that "perpetual war is the inherent condition of modernity."[17] "The war of Wrong and Right," as Melville called the rebellion, brought that enmity into stronger relief.[18]

Considering his interest in whaling's political impact, we need to acknowledge the overlap between Nantucket's "everlasting war" and the "eternal democracy" Ishmael mentions as being the product of American trade (64, 110). *Clarel* provides a revealing counterpoint on this theme. While Ishmael applauds the expansion of democratic capitalism, Don Hannibal laments the "Eternal Hacking" at its heart, asserting that, crudely and cruelly, the narrative of progress creates never-ending strife. The image draws upon the figure of amputation that had long been a part of Euro-American political rhetoric. Dating as far back as the Anglo-Dutch trade wars, English conservatives had portrayed republican government as a hydra, the implication being that without a monarch, the body politic had an infinite number of heads.[19] Republicans on both sides of the Atlantic inverted this image, using the hydra to argue that governments founded on public opinion would ultimately triumph over authoritarian regimes: "Opinion is power, and that opinion will come," Thomas Jefferson wrote John Adams in 1816. "The oppressors may cut off heads after heads, but like those of the Hydra they multiply at every stake."[20] When Don Hannibal refers to his lopped limbs, however, he foregrounds not the public's resistance to tyrants but the hazards of destabilized authority. Whether in the name of democratic reforms or popular sovereignty, the polis perpetually wounds itself. Unlike the hydra, its parts do not grow back.

Don Hannibal's wooden leg raises an additional set of questions that lead us back to Ahab's hunt for Moby Dick. If democracy generates universal instability, if it depends on the paradox of "groundless ground" (as Greiman describes it), then what do we make of those who, even in the steadiest conditions, struggle to stand, walk, or swim?[21] How does Melville's

176 THE PROSTHETIC ARTS OF *MOBY-DICK*

representation of dismemberment offer its own political critique? As Maurice Lee has cautioned, trying to pin Melville to a specific ideology is ill-advised, particularly because his texts buckle under the allegorical weight they often entice readers into placing on them.[22] And yet Don Hannibal's missing arm and leg can usefully convey one of the ironies Melville observed in the post-war years: the expectation that democracies would produce a functioning polis out of conflicting values and interests.

As numerous scholars have demonstrated, Melville grappled with this problem in the "Supplement" to *Battle-Pieces*, a prose essay in which he argued that reconciling the North and South must be the nation's top priority, even at the expense of temporarily denying suffrage to people who were formerly enslaved. The difficulty of reconciliation appears in the volume's dedication to "THE MEMORY OF THE THREE HUNDRED THOUSAND WHO IN THE WAR FOR THE MAINTENANCE OF THE UNION FELL DEVOTEDLY UNDER THE FLAG OF THEIR FATHERS."[23] The phrasing highlights the problem that Don Hannibal would identify in his lost limbs: the *war* to *maintain* the *Union* undermines the very condition it seeks to protect. The political ironies also troubled Melville's contemporaries. "We woo the South," Nathaniel Hawthorne wrote in the *Atlantic Monthly*, " 'as the Lion woos his bride.' "[24] Melville's dismembered veteran recalls numerous representations of the damaged body politic from Mathew Brady's battlefield photographs to Louisa May Alcott's *Hospital Sketches* (1863).[25] On a somatic, symbolic, and institutional level, however, Don Hannibal affirms that whatever union such wars achieve will ultimately require multiple prostheses. Melville gives the hero a crutch *and* a wooden leg as if neither were sufficient to secure his footing.[26]

What the image of limb loss contributes to a discussion of politics in *Moby-Dick* is the value of aggrievement in American democracy. Don Hannibal joins Captain Boomer as a revealing counterpart to Ahab's capacity to turn his sense of injury into authoritarian control. The veteran's wooden leg and empty sleeve convey his vulnerability, and using it as a brace, he comically wedges his body into a coffin that has been stockpiled in the monastery.[27] He exhibits the same gallows humor—ironic, self-effacing, drolly marking his distance from power—when he describes his crutch as the "sceptre" to a kingdom of limping, "refluent" men, each backward-flowing from the New World to the Old.[28] For Ahab, the despotism becomes increasingly real, his ivory leg a cudgel for public demonstrations of his will. In contrast to *Clarel*'s "one-legged pioneer," the captain extends his grievance across the ship, prosthetically turning thirty men into an integrated, mechanical whole.[29]

This chapter considers injury as part of the environment of democratic life. The groundlessness of American democracy may perpetually disrupt the body politic, but in Ahab's ivory leg Melville gives us the embodiment of grievance as a tool for domination and autocracy. As the case of Don Hannibal attests, Ahab should not be interpreted as Melville's representative vision of disability, limb loss, or physical and emotional difference. Rather, in his singular storyline, the captain illustrates how resentment can facilitate the rise of authoritarian personalities in the New World. Jefferson believed the hydra of public opinion would always grow back its head. Melville took the figure of hacking more literally, exploring the outsized role that wounding plays in the accrual and distribution of power.

The Jacksonian era provided multiple opportunities to see this dynamic at work. Americans, to borrow from *The Confidence-Man*, resembled the American Indian-hater par excellence, always alert to a "signal outrage" that would justify their violent quest for control.[30] In the name of a threatened white citizenry, Jackson oversaw the expansion of a federal government that committed itself to relocating indigenous peoples and further institutionalizing slavery.[31] The recourse to injury permeated the culture at large. Americans were difficult to insult, Tocqueville observed, but once insulted, they could be as vindictive as European aristocrats. "Their resentment is as slow to kindle as to abate."[32] In 1837, an English visitor noted that while Americans often tried to get around the law, they had an unusual fondness for lawsuits and cheerfully took each other to court.[33] The United States was a nation of aggrievement in which wound collecting was the inverse expression of self-reliance, an insidious, personal feeling of resentment that, in a destabilized, egalitarian society, one's sovereignty had been violated, slighted, undervalued, or simply ignored. What Tocqueville said of the government could apply to Ahab as well: "The least reproach offends it, and the slightest sting of truth turns it fierce."[34]

The effort to exoticize Ahab, to see him as reflecting Islamic forms of power, obscures the degree to which he represents American cultural traits and values. As we will see, Ishmael predicates his progressive vision in *Moby-Dick* on his removal from both historical complexity and an awareness that democracies can produce their own forms of totalitarian rule. Ahab and Ishmael do not respectively represent the terrors and promise of American democracy (as some readers have supposed), but rather

178 THE PROSTHETIC ARTS OF *MOBY-DICK*

constitute a symbiotic partnership in which demagogues gain a populist following from the public recollection of wounds. This final chapter situates Ahab's dismemberment in the context of *Clarel*, "Benito Cereno," and Melville's larger reflections on the New World. The wider perspective illuminates what the prosthetic arts of *Moby-Dick* can teach us about Ahab's power, Ishmael's progressivism, and our own critical priorities.

The Cold War Captain

Throughout this book I have presented Ahab as an authoritarian who turns others into prostheses and shifts accountability for his vengeance to the abstract concept of Fate. On the face of it, this reading may seem to reinforce the "Cold War Ahab" that dominated twentieth-century criticism from World War II through the Reagan and Bush administrations. "Cold War critics tended to believe that the challenge" of the novel lay in "figuring out how to name Ahab's power," Cucu and Végső recount, especially as it related to Starbuck, Ishmael, and their shipmates.[35] Such readings tracked historical events, persisting through the "generational shift from the antifascist politics of the 1930s...to the anti-Stalinist liberalism of the 1950s" and later, they argue, to the "defense of cosmopolitan populism."[36] The Cold War, as Donald Pease demonstrated in 1989, provided a "scene of persuasion" that framed the novel as a struggle between two sides—the autocratic Ahab who resembled foreign demagogues and the democratic Ishmael whose lone survival signified an American triumph over them. An "all or nothing" logic informed these readings, according to Pease, in which the novel's numerous oppositions were ultimately reduced to the simple formula of "'our' freedom versus 'their' totalitarianism."[37] As William Spanos explained, the implications of this binary reached beyond literary criticism. F. O. Matthiessen's reading of *Moby-Dick* inaugurated a critical tradition that treated "Ishmael's effort to free himself from the mesmerizing bondage of Ahab's totalitarian rhetoric of persuasion as the *canonical* (idealized) essence of the American nation."[38]

My focus on Ahab's vengeance emphatically does not seek to resurrect the Cold War paradigm, nor does it seek to resurrect the terms of the New Americanists who assessed it. Rather I see Ahab and Ishmael as key components in Melville's evolving critique of democratic life. The Cold War critics erred in projecting Ahab's power as a largely foreign threat when his aggrievement was cut from American wood and enacted on an American version of Shakespeare's stage. But even as they were transforming the Nantucket captain into a makeshift Stalin or Mussolini, the critics were earnestly offering Ishmael as an ideological counterweight, a neutralizing force who saw God's presence in the democratic principle of "divine equality" (117). And yet such a view neglects the racial and economic opportunism in Ishmael's global campaign. As the previous chapters explained, his Jacksonian rhetoric provides a rationale not only for colonizing other peoples but for using race to demonize their desire for autonomy. From *Typee* to *Billy Budd*, Melville would never create such a compelling and fully realized set of voices as he did in *Moby-Dick*. Indeed, part of what makes the novel so groundbreakingly heroic is witnessing the author explore his characters' astonishing discursive range. But to overlook how Ahab and Ishmael reflect their own versions of American arrogance is to submit to a nationalist rather than a critical agenda. The threats they expose are as homegrown as they are authentic.

The challenge is to liberate *Moby-Dick* from a Cold War context while continuing to think seriously about the novel's reflection on American wounding and tyranny. Melville did not need twentieth-century fascism to be concerned about the topic. As Elizabeth Duquette has shown, eighteenth- and nineteenth-century Americans regularly dwelled upon the ways in which their republic was vulnerable to authoritarian rule. "Not only were the educated schooled in the dangers of classical tyranny," she writes, but "its possible encroachment was a signal concern for the framers."[39] Duquette reminds us that what Tocqueville found "'most repugnant in America'" was "'the virtual absence of any guarantee against tyranny.'" Lincoln believed that, with increased prosperity, "the hateful paths of despotism" could reappear in the United States, and he somewhat hopefully praised the Declaration of Independence for enshrining the principle of equality as a "stumbling block" against that fate.[40] In these discussions, as Duquette demonstrates, white elites invoked tyranny to describe limitations on themselves, effectively accusing would-be tyrants of treating them like Black slaves. Discord over slavery only increased the references to tyranny. Abolitionists accused the South of practicing a race-based despotism, while the owners of enslaved people claimed they were the victims of "tyrannical overreach." Having been omitted from its principle of equality, Phyllis Wheatley, David Walker, and Frederick Douglass all condemned slavery as part of the tyrannical order of the United States.[41]

180   THE PROSTHETIC ARTS OF *MOBY-DICK*

Even in rejecting the Cold War paradigm, it is important to move beyond new critical binaries that position promising contemporary approaches to *Moby-Dick* against further investigations into Ahab's authoritarian will. Such binaries present a false choice between the insights of such fields as materialism, neuroscience, and disability studies and the frank acknowledgment that the American captain ruthlessly dominates his crew. Indeed, among the many lines of inquiry these fields help articulate, one is a reassessment of how Ahab grasps and wields his power.[42] *Moby-Dick* repeatedly alerts us to the importance of following this theme. In Chapter 20, Ishmael regrets joining such a long voyage "without once laying my eyes on the man who was to be the absolute dictator of it" (97). Eight chapters later, he describes the reclusive captain as the "supreme lord and dictator" of his crew (122). In Chapter 33, he explains how nautical hierarchies had contributed to Ahab's "irresistible dictatorship" over the three mates (147). The foreshadowing prepares readers for "The Quarter-Deck," in which Melville provides a master class in how to manipulate a crowd. Ahab enters with his "steady, ivory stride" (160). He asks "seemingly purposeless questions" as a way of soliciting a "fiercely glad and approving" response (161). His "animal sob" assigns blame for his lost leg onto a common enemy, the white whale (163). Enacting their solidarity, he choreographs the crew in a darkly communal rite. Such actions not only align the crew behind his "intense bigotry of purpose" but endow the captain with an extraordinary power (161). "Ahab does not want the crew members merely to *recognize* him as the commanding officer," Pease has written in a more recent essay. He wants to forge them into a "revolutionary" force and then "liberate themselves" from the industry's "disciplinary order so as to make Ahab their sovereign kingly captain."[43] To Pease, that disciplinary order is represented by Starbuck, the officer who most feels a sense of responsibility to the ship's capitalist owners.

While stagecraft and charisma may persuade the cheering crew, Melville depicts the three mates as requiring different kinds of convincing, and in that persuasion, we find a more subtle critique of American democracy. Holding their crossed lances, Ahab looks upon each of his mates "as though, by some nameless, interior volition, he would fain have shocked into them the same fiery emotion accumulated within the Leyden jar of his own magnetic life" (165). The image suggests the kind of distributive charge that demagogues hope to provide their followers, channeling their energy into dispersed citizens who use the charge to animate themselves. But the key phrase in the passage is "as though," for Ishmael quickly tells us that Ahab's Leyden jar experiment fails. The mates "quailed" before his "strong, sustained, and mystic aspect" as if it conveyed submission more than sparks. "Stubb and Flask looked sideways from him; the honest eye of Starbuck fell downright" (165–66). The charge never leaves the source. Although initially disappointed, Ahab welcomes the result, for he fears that the transmission would either expire his own charge or be so powerful that it would leave his subordinates dead (166).[44]

As I discussed at the beginning of this book, however, Ahab's power involves the depths of his affliction, and that affliction is what Starbuck finds difficult to oppose. One chapter later, when the first mate ruminates over the captain's command, he focuses less on magnetism than on his sense of injury. Feeling unmanned, he leans against the mainmast in the chapter "Dusk" and reflects on his confusing submission to the captain he loathes. The chapter provides a nuanced glimpse into what Timothy Snyder has called "anticipatory obedience."[45]

> I think I see his impious end; but feel that I must help him to it. Will I, nill I, the ineffable thing has tied me to him; tows me with a cable I have no knife to cut. Horrible old man! Who's over him, he cries;—aye, he would be a democrat to all above; look, how he lords it over all below! Oh! I plainly see my miserable office,—to obey, rebelling; and worse yet, to hate with touch of pity! For in his eyes I read some lurid woe would shrivel me up, had I it. (169)

Ahab's "lurid woe" repels and attracts, his grief so glowingly sensational that it would diminish almost anyone experiencing it. Even indirectly, through the wounded man's eyes, the woe elicits more sympathy than Starbuck can resist. Just as Ahab will die bound to Moby Dick, the first mate feels ineffably bound to his captain, and before the *Pequod* ever comes to crisis, he fears he will be incapable of cutting himself loose. Here at the quest's beginning, it seems inevitable that the captain will make Starbuck a prosthesis to both the wound and the wound collecting. "Oh now, I feel my topmost greatness lies in my topmost grief," he exclaims at the novel's end (571). In the context of Starbuck's unwilling obedience, the line seems almost exultant.

182 THE PROSTHETIC ARTS OF *MOBY-DICK*

Starbuck invokes the language of democracy to characterize Ahab's authoritarian power. From his introduction in Chapter 26, "Knights and Squires," Ishmael presented the first mate in the explicitly political terms of Andrew Jackson and the democratic dignity of the common man. After the spectacle on the quarterdeck, the chief mate returns to this theme, connecting the captain's disrespect for authority with his disrespect for the crew. Ahab "would be a democrat to all above," Starbuck observes, but "look, how he lords it over all below!" (169) The observation highlights the ease with which unchecked democracies can mutate into authoritarian rule.[46] Boosted by stagecraft, aggrievement turns the meanest mariners and steadiest men into accomplices of a despot who regularly humiliates them. Don Hannibal joked about leading a caravan of limping immigrants away from the New World. Raging against the consequence of his own economic pursuits, Ahab creates a feeling of collective dispossession that elevates his enemies and consolidates his crew. His vengeance seeks a more glorified stage than the colonial church where he was rumored to kill. Unlike Starbuck, Ahab expands to the size of his woe, wielding a sense of injury that rivals the whale in magnitude. He will strike the sun, punch through the mask, defy the trinity's lightning bolts. No one can stop the narrative from unfolding on these cosmic terms. As he predicts in "Dusk," Starbuck will shrink from shooting the sleeping tyrant, for the captain's aggrievement is too powerful for the first mate to resist.

The Marble Masthead

Ahab finds a useful counterpart in Ishmael, who cheers democratic progress and yet avoids the internal confrontations that democracies often demand. The problem Ishmael presents is how, amid rampant tyranny, he somehow maintains the "insular Tahiti" of his soul (274). Although generations of critics championed him as a democratic alternative to Ahab, others have questioned his detachment from the struggles he observes. Describing him as a "modern young intellectual" who "wavers constantly between totalitarianism and the crew," C. L. R. James accused Ishmael of being "enclosed in the solitude of his social and intellectual speculation."[47] Decades later, Michael Rogin compared Ishmael to Tocqueville's American who is "narrowly shut up in himself and from that basis makes the pretension to judge the world." Rogin concluded that by joining Ahab's hunt, Ishmael escaped the "diffuse longing for union" that his masthead reveries reveal.[48]

The masthead, of course, provides us with a ready-made image of how Ishmael's feelings of oneness could be dangerously remote not just from the exigencies of space and time but also from political complexity. Perched on his metaphorical masthead, Ishmael can neither see Fedallah outside Orientalist clichés nor muster a thunderous No against Ahab's disastrous chase. Although he is quick to endorse American progressivism abroad, he retreats from the politics of power and engagement, as if being "neither believer nor infidel" provided sufficient guidance for operating in society (374). Whales may be as scarce as hen's teeth when Ishmael goes aloft, but so apparently are thoughts about dispossession and the treatment of his fellow crewmembers. As James warned, Ishmael's spiritual search seems to leave him incapable of political action, let alone political conflict.[49] He avoids the hacking that led Don Hannibal to flee Mexico, but in the end, democratic nationalism is more persuasive to him than democratic practice.

Melville's fondness for associating the masthead with Islamic spiritualism adds to the complexity of this critique. *Moby-Dick* pictures Ishmael meditating on pantheistic oneness while he dangerously hovers above a Cartesian sea. In *Mardi*, Taji finds an equally mystical experience when he climbs the masthead and temporarily escapes "the brown planks of the dull, plodding ship." Looking abroad, he has an explicitly Islamic vision of ecstasy and peace:

> In the distance what visions were spread! The entire western horizon high piled with gold and crimson clouds; airy arches, domes, and minarets; as if the yellow, Moorish sun were setting behind some vast Alhambra. Vistas seemed leading to worlds beyond. To and fro, and all over the towers of this Nineveh in the sky, flew troops of birds. Watching them long, one crossed my sight, flew through a low arch, and was lost to view. My spirit must have sailed in with it; for directly, as in a trance, came upon me the cadence of mild billows laving a beach of shells, the waving of boughs, and the voices of maidens, and the lulled beatings of my own dissolved heart, all blended together.[50]

The masthead reveals an Andalusian heaven. The western sky produces airy minarets and palaces with the domes and arches the Moors brought to

184 THE PROSTHETIC ARTS OF *MOBY-DICK*

Spain. Taji feels his heart dissolve and blend with the mystic cadence of the ship. In *Moby-Dick*, this unifying "trance" becomes the enchanted state that "ebbs" Ishmael's spirit away and diffuses it through time and space (136). But as it does in *White-Jacket*, the threat of falling haunts *Moby-Dick*'s mast-head experience. In contrast, the mast in *Mardi* is a refuge where body follows spirit and West follows East. The vision motivates Taji who, unlike Ishmael, uses it to plot his escape from the ship.

Once again, *Clarel* can provide a revealing interlocutor for Melville's earlier work. In Book 1, a muezzin named Mustapha belatedly calls the faithful to their early morning prayers. The scene reconfigures Taji's experience by transforming the Jerusalem minaret into the masthead of a ship.

> Each turban at that summons shrill,
> Which should have called ere perfect light,
> Bowed—hands on chest, or arms upright;
> While over all those fields of loss
> Where now the Crescent rides the Cross,
> Sole at the marble mast-head stands
> The Islam herald, his two hands
> Upon the rail, and sightless eyes
> Turned upward reverent toward the skies.[51]

Taji's ecstatic vision, Timothy Marr explains, "subtly attests to the incapacity of traditional Western symbolism to strike a deep enough chord in expressing the fuller resonances of human experience." The scene dramatizes "the moment where language transcends the knowledgeable world to exude instead the romance of the mirage."[52] What Melville presented in *Clarel* was not an individual's transcendent vision but the calm of collective practice. Perched on the masthead-minaret, the muezzin exemplifies a reason why the crescent rivals the cross. In a sea of loss and uncertainty, he embodies the centering power of prayer. His cries roll across the city, leading the faithful in their observance.

With its evocation of monomania, a wandering Ishmael, and a prostheticized amputee, *Clarel* can sometimes read like an extension of *Moby-Dick*. Mustapha, for example, is reminiscent of Tashtego, who, as we saw in Chapter 4, calls his shipmates from the minaret of the sperm whale's head. But in a scene rife with disabilities (the handsome, humpbacked Celio has been locked outside the Martyr's Gate), *Clarel* transforms Tashtego's nimble athleticism into Mustapha's blindness and old age. The Ottomans preferred to give the job of muezzin to men who were blind, for they could not peer into the compounds from on high.[53] According to Marr, Clarel interprets this blindness as a symbol of God's distance from doubting Christians such as himself.[54] Though Clarel may lament it, that distance produces an admirable social effect. Ishmael nearly loses himself in the "inscrutable tides of God" and then withdraws from the problem of tyrants and the crowd (159). Taji's Moorish vision initiates his spiritual search, but moving from island to island, he regularly reflects on the contemporary world. Read from this perspective, Mustapha's disability signifies not a spiritual impairment but Islam's accessibility and strength. Reverently turned to the skies, his "sightless eyes" matter less than his impact on the population below. From Fedallah to the white whale, Ishmael invokes turbans to create a sense of menace and fear. With Mustapha crying from the minaret, the turban represents collective devotion and faith. Each time he calls Jerusalem to prayer, he contributes to the unity of Islamic civilization on earth. The "marble mast-head" stands as a beacon for the faithful, not a staircase to stolen truths.

As breathtaking as his reveries can be, Ishmael repeatedly downplays the significance of his actions in the world. He is an earnest egalitarian on land, but in the open sea he emphatically prefers the heights of philosophy to the complexities of power and democracy. He salutes Jackson on his "war-horse" and Nantucketers owning the "terraqueous globe," but he retreats from grappling with the political struggles on deck.[55] Think how rarely he brings his intellect to bear on the mass of men as they work through conflicting values, interests, and claims. As Rogin observes, Ishmael organizes his story around romantic rather than realistic social action, and that romance leads to his absorption in Ahab's quest.[56] He is so enclosed "in the solitude of his social and intellectual speculation," James contends, that he gravitates to men of action who do not contain "his own sense of homelessness and despair."[57]

Ishmael acknowledges this passivity at the novel's beginning. In "Loomings," he assigns responsibility for his joining a whaling ship to "the invisible police officer of the Fates, who has the constant surveillance of me, and secretly dogs me, and influences me in some unaccountable way" (7). Ahab justifies his pursuit of Moby Dick by claiming that, as the Fate's lieutenant, he is outranked: his actions have already been decreed.

186   THE PROSTHETIC ARTS OF *MOBY-DICK*

Ishmael enumerates the reasons why he might have chosen to hunt whales, but in the end, he concludes that the Fates cajoled him "into the delusion that it was a choice resulting from my own unbiased freewill and discriminating judgment" (7). That Ishmael would view the Fates as absolving him from decision-making is consistent with his preference to have others exert power over his life's trajectory. In a revealing image, he describes the Fates as cosmic police who have secretly compelled him to make the choices he thought he himself had made. The layers of humor in these passages come from Ishmael's fantasizing about submitting to the authorities. What motivates him, he jokingly reveals, is an awareness of surveillance, a fear of transgression, and a desire to align himself with regulatory power. Ishmael would have us consider that, between the grand contested presidential election and the bloody battles in Afghanistan, the police have selected him for visionary experiences that keep him conveniently aloft. His detachment recalls Eric Fromm's description of the modern democrat who is free "to act according to his will" if only he can determine what that will is. "He conforms to anonymous authorities and adopts a self which is not his," Fromm writes. Like Ishmael, modern man has "a veneer of optimism and initiative," but he is ultimately "overcome by a profound feeling of powerlessness which makes him gaze toward approaching catastrophes as though he were paralyzed." Fromm warned that such despair provided "fertile soil" for fascism.[58] Melville demonstrated how it fortified despots who expected others to become his arms and legs.

One of the qualities Ishmael prizes in the masthead is its removal from the responsibilities of history. He attributes this airy independence to others as well as himself. The first chapters of this book discuss the ways in which Admiral Horatio Nelson intersects with Melville's work, the dismembered mariner supplying an image of national pride, fierce valor, and calm acceptance of his traumatic wounds. But consider how Ishmael's praise for Nelson as he "stands his mast-head in Trafalgar Square" isolates the admiral from ethical and political concerns (155). Affixed to a column nearly fifty meters in the air, the statue of the dismembered hero towers so high over London that he does not "answer a single hail from below" (133; Figure 12). Like his compatriots Napoleon and Washington (who stand on their own mastheads in Paris and Baltimore), his spirit penetrates "through the thick haze of the future" and descries "what shoals and what rocks must be

Figure 12 Lord Admiral Nelson wearing his empty sleeve at the top of Nelson's Column, London.
Beata May, CC BY-SA 3.0. Wikimedia Commons.

shunned" (133). As Ishmael presents him, the empty-sleeved admiral seems a masthead visionary spotting the dangers ahead.

The passage says nothing, however, about Nelson's defense of British interests in the slave trade.[59] The absence would be less noteworthy if Melville himself had not movingly addressed the subject the year before in *Redburn*. The occasion for those comments was also statuary, this time the haunting Liverpool statue of Nelson "expiring in the arms of Victory"

Figure 13 Death reaches for the heart of Lord Nelson on the Lord Nelson Monument, Liverpool. Sir Richard Westmacott (sculptor) and Matthew Cotes Wyatt (designer), 1831.
Robert Freidus photographer. Image courtesy of the Victorian Web.

(Figure 13). The adolescent Redburn is struck by the spectacle of Death insinuating "his bony hand under the hero's robe, and groping after his heart."[60] But in shifting our attention to what surrounds the hero's demise, Redburn offers a counter-narrative that places the admiral in a fuller historical setting (Figure 14):

> At uniform intervals round the base of the pedestal, four naked figures in chains, somewhat larger than life, are seated in various attitudes of humiliation and despair. One has his leg recklessly thrown over his knee, and his

head bowed over, as if he had given up all hope of ever feeling better. Another has his head buried in despondency, and no doubt looks mournfully out of his eyes, but as his face was averted at the time, I could not catch the expression. These woe-begone figures of captives are emblematic of Nelson's principal victories; but I never could look at their swarthy limbs and manacles, without being involuntarily reminded of four African slaves in the market-place.

And my thoughts would revert to Virginia and Carolina; and also to the historical fact, that the African slave-trade once constituted the principal commerce of Liverpool; and that the prosperity of the town was once supposed to have been indissolubly linked to its prosecution.[61]

The statue prompts Redburn to ruminate about the English abolitionist movement and his father's friend, "the good and great Roscoe," who was an "intrepid enemy" of the slave trade, despite representing Liverpool in Parliament. Ishmael never addresses the subject in such a direct and detailed way.[62] "Who ain't a slave?" he asks at the opening of *Moby-Dick*, casually explaining his tolerance for abusive old sea captains (21). Redburn might have challenged his successor's jokey simplification, for the enslaved are not white men with the freedom to choose adventure over reasonable wages and good working conditions. In putting Nelson on the masthead, Ishmael gives him a visionary status that exempts him from the complexities of power, ethics, and commitment.

My point is not to castigate these masthead reveries but to suggest that Melville recognized his narrator's historical limitations. In November 1851, he wrote his editor, Evert Duyckinck, that the events of the novel took place "about fourteen years ago," putting the *Pequod*'s voyage at the end of the Jackson and (possibly) the beginning of the Van Buren administrations.[63] Ishmael's enthusiasm for the white working class, Western conquest, and the spread of US interests around the globe reflect a moment when the progress of democratic nationalism could seem to some adherents an ebullient, unqualified good. As a narrator, he records Stubb's cruelty to Pip, the racial conflict on the forecastle, and the humanity of his African and African American shipmates. Ishmael's changing perceptions toward Queequeg, Carolyn Karcher has argued, are meant to deliver "the final blow to his countrymen's ethnocentricism and color consciousness."[64] But the politics of slavery never troubles Ishmael, and in his joke about everyone's being a

Figure 14 Sir Richard Westmacott (sculptor) and Matthew Cotes Wyatt (designer), Figure of Slave at Base of Pedestal, Lord Nelson Monument, Liverpool, 1831.
Robert Freidus photographer. Image courtesy of the Victorian Web.

slave, we hear the complaints about tyranny that, as Duquette described, both exploited and affirmed the privilege of whiteness. Ishmael's zeal for Jackson and Nelson suits his masthead vision of power in which he withdraws into abstractions when political relations become difficult to sustain. Richard Chase, perhaps the most significant Cold War commentator on *Moby-Dick*, once described Ishmael as an American folk hero. That label obscures the degree to which he is also an ideological and historical type.[65]

ETERNAL HACKING   191

From Tommo and Redburn to Ungar and Don Hannibal, Melville's characters help raise the question whether Ishmael's "eternal democracy" is a mask for global conquest and the hacking it perpetuates.

The Islamicized Gaze

As if they were the pieces of a constantly changing puzzle, Melville returned to these themes in "Benito Cereno," his 1855 story that features an American sea captain, the quest for vengeance, the African slave trade, and yet another violently rendered body part. This time, of course, the victim was Babo, the Senegalese leader of a slave rebellion whose severed head haunts Lima's Plaza Mayor after his death. The image culminates the account of an American sea captain, Amasa Delano, who comes across a debilitated Spanish slave ship off the coast of Chile. Fooled by the passengers' elaborate deceptions and his own racist assumptions, Delano cannot see that the "cargo" of hundred and sixty Africans had taken control of the ship and that the terrified captain, Benito Cereno, only pretends to be in charge. Once Delano grasps the ruse, the Americans overtake the rebellion and deliver Babo to the colonial authorities who prosecute, convict, and execute him. "The body was burned to ashes," the narrator tells us, "but for many days, the head, that hive of subtlety, fixed on a pole in the Plaza, met, unabashed, the gaze of the whites."[66] Melville endows that decapitated gaze with as much significance as he did Ahab's ivory leg.

Adding to the commonalities with *Moby-Dick*, scholars have recently uncovered Islam's importance to "Benito Cereno" and the historical events upon which it was based. Greg Grandin has explained that the Africans on board the ship (the *Tryal*) came from the most Islamic sections of West Africa, and thus the story positions the Protestant Delano and the Catholic Cereno against the enslaved Muslim Babo.[67] As Kelly Ross has demonstrated, Melville explicitly introduces Islam into the scene in which Delano finally comprehends the mutiny. Having disarmed Babo on the bottom of his boat, the American looks up to the *San Dominick* and sees the slaves "not in misrule, not in tumult...but with mask torn away, flourishing hatchets and knives, in ferocious piratical revolt." Like "delirious black dervishes," six Ashantees "danced on the poop."[68] The image is revelatory. Coming out of the Islamic tradition of Sufism, the dervishes are members of a mystical order inspired by the medieval Persian poet Rumi. As nineteenth-century

192   THE PROSTHETIC ARTS OF *MOBY-DICK*

Orientalists understood them, dervishes worked themselves into states of religious frenzy through "music, dance, intoxication, and various kinds of hypnotic gestures."[69] Emerson joined writers on both sides of the Atlantic in praising the Sufi poets for their asceticism and mystical pursuit of oneness.[70] Taji's vision of the Alhambra, with its Sufi history and design, indirectly invokes this tradition as the site of cultivated mystical experience.

When Melville invokes "delirious black dervishes," though, he does not allude to the spiritual devotion and vows of poverty often associated with the sect. He depicts the revolt as a moment of Islamic ecstasy.[71] The dervish comparison explicitly anchors African resistance in a religious practice that may have appealed to transcendentalists, but also suggested a violent end to white control.[72] Although meant to warn against future revolts, Babo's decapitated head emits the spiritual intensity of the Ashantees dancing on the *San Dominick*. His power lies in the subtleties of perception—his visage meeting "the gaze of the whites," and yet it underscores a refusal to be incorporated into the system that has enslaved and executed him. This mystically engaged violence points toward an apocalyptic end and a reversal of the dynamics that Delano continually fails to understand. Promising deliverance, Babo combines what Ross has called an "imbrication of islamicism and messianic time." Depicted as both messiah and Antichrist, he practices a form of resistance that threatens to collapse the progressive sense of history that undergirds Christian conquest.[73]

Sterling Stuckey has shown that the story explicitly borrows from *Redburn's* meditation on the Nelson memorial in Liverpool. In a story haunted by the political meaning of bodies, Babo's head recalls the skeleton of the slave trader Don Aranda, which the rebels had substituted for a figure of Christopher Columbus on the ship's prow. With the ominous threat "Follow Your Leader!" chalked beneath him, Aranda's corpse explicitly warns the *San Dominick* crew that they must follow Babo's instructions if they want to remain alive.[74] Stuckey shows that not only did the memorial's figure of Death provide a model for Aranda's canvas-covered skeleton, but when Delano places his foot on Babo in the bottom of the whaling boat, he re-enacts the statue's representation of Nelson standing on top of a fallen adversary.[75] He reminds us that when Melville returned to the statue a year after the publication of "Benito Cereno," he recalled the "peculiar emotion" he had felt as a young man that *Redburn* recreates.[76] For all the heroism sailors ascribed to him, Lord Nelson figured prominently among the iconography of slave traders and enslavement that Melville developed across numerous works.

ETERNAL HACKING   193

Displayed on a pike, Babo's head ironically inverts the power dynamic that the colonial officers expected it to convey. Melville's conclusion situates the severed head amid carefully defined markers of Spanish control, as it meets

> the gaze of the whites; and across the Plaza looked towards St. Bartholomew's church, in whose vaults slept then, as now, the recovered bones of Aranda: and across the Rimac bridge looked towards the monastery, on Mount Agonia without; where, three months after being dismissed by the court, Benito Cereno, borne on the bier, did, indeed, follow his leader.[77]

The measured phrasing lays out the coordinates by which Babo's head exists in colonial space—the plaza, the buildings, the bridge, all establish a territorial relation to the proud remnant of this African man's life. Constitutionally shaken by the revolt, Cereno will soon follow Aranda's skeleton into the Catholic vaults, but Babo's head remains obstinately independent, its "hive of subtlety" openly suggesting defiant stratagems and religiously informed resistance. "Babo's head offers a warning," Christopher Freburg writes, "not just of one or more revolting slaves, but also of a future that cannot be mastered."[78] Even in death, his eyes assert the right to judge, oppose, and ultimately, bring their society to a crisis. The Founders took comfort in the hydra's capacity to grow new heads. In Babo's severed head, we can see the possibility that, like public opinion, his resistance will grow in numbers and in force. Dismemberment, to borrow a phrase from Peter Boxall, becomes integral to the "political anatomy of prosthetic life."[79]

Signaling both past and future vengeance, Babo's gaze reconfigures an important scene in *Moby-Dick* when, in fulfillment of his prophecy, Fedallah's tattered body rises from the ocean and looks Captain Ahab squarely in the eye. The two scenes employ a similar dramatic structure in which white Christians react to an Islamicized corpse:

> Lashed round and round to the fish's back; pinioned in the turns upon turns in which, during the past night, the whale had reeled the involutions of the lines around him, the half torn body of the Parsee was seen; his sable raiment frayed to shreds; his distended eyes turned full upon old Ahab. (568)

The passage cleverly denies Ahab the agency of spotting Fedallah first. The passive construction distributes the ghastly sight to everyone on ship, even

194 THE PROSTHETIC ARTS OF *MOBY-DICK*

as it alters the power between the captain and the corpse his vengeance has helped create. Earlier in the novel, Ishmael had described Fedallah's "wan but wondrous eyes" as appearing never to rest, and now, even in death, they seem to act under their own power, confronting Ahab directly (537).

The conclusion to "Benito Cereno" has earned nearly a century's worth of commentary, but grappling with Fedallah's waterlogged body has sparked less critical interest. And yet, twice in the period of four years, Melville turned to the image of an Islamicized corpse looking in the eyes of a shaken white power. At once visual, political, and meticulously arranged, the scenes resist ideological and allegorical certainty. As with Babo, there is meaning in Fedallah's gaze, his swollen eyes serving as a cosmic announcement that the prophecies were correct and that Ahab's reckoning nears. As with Delano, Ahab is fooled by a racialized other who speaks riddles he does not understand. Melville does not delve into either character's internal thoughts, and as he presents them, the significance of these characters (and their corpses) lies in what they say about the prospects of white men. And yet Fedallah's hair turban emerges from *Moby-Dick* as its own hive of subtlety, a symbol of ironies too enigmatic for the narrator to comprehend.[80]

Babo's head descends to us as the historical conscience of Melville's tale, the sober warning that rebellion will uncover the truth of the New World— that Columbus's discovery initiated an "an epoch of violence masked as progress" (as Dana Luciano has described it.)[81] That silent, unabashed gaze hints at the critique that Melville would more fully articulate in *Clarel* when Don Hannibal laments the lopped limbs and "cursed Progress" that democratic capitalists bring to the rest of the world—or when Ungar denounces the "pirates" whose Christianity and trade had left "myriads dispossessed." That such skepticism would come from conservative North Americans should not be surprising, for in Melville's vision, Jacksonian America had claimed the right to bring others under their control. Ishmael exemplifies this trait when he celebrates how the "just Spirit of Equality" and "great democratic God!" had produced both the "swart convict, Bunyan" and "the stumped and paupered arm of old Cervantes" (117).[82] Talent does not differentiate between the disabled, the poor, the condemned. Like the bull whale's fin, Cervantes's arm offers a subtle rebuke to Ahab's fixation on his prosthetic leg. And yet when Ishmael describes the political incarnation of this "democratic God," he touts Andrew Jackson, the self-proclaimed "Great White Father," who turned egalitarian whiteness and racial conquest into two sides of the same nationalist coin.

What happens when readers grant Fedallah the historical insight that they have given the Senegalese slave? His gaze confronts not just the aggrieved captain (whose death he literally oversees) but also the narrator who has textually brought that gaze into being, the Jacksonian sailor who has racialized his presence from his first appearance on deck. Those distended eyes should lead us to ask whether the marginalization of Fedallah is the fulfillment of a democratic vision that congenially accepts the value of others if they accept the supremacy of an American will. The Parsee may serve as a prosthetic to the narrative, but as we have seen, Ishmael repeatedly excludes him from the *Pequod*'s body politic.

Lawrence Buell has written that *Moby-Dick* is "an inquest into the state and possible fate of democratic society, American style, as it appears in the era of early industrial capitalism."[83] Chapter 24, "The Advocate," conveys how closely Ishmael identifies democratic nationalism with Western control. "I freely assert, that the cosmopolite philosopher cannot, for his life, point out one single peaceful influence, which within the last sixty years has operated more potentially upon the whole broad world, taken in one aggregate, than the high and mighty business of whaling." Like the "Egyptian mother, who bore offspring themselves pregnant from her womb," he explains, it has produced countless changes upon the world in "ferreting out the remotest and least known parts of the earth" (109–10). Ignoring the extraordinary violence that he will recreate in the *Jungfrau* and Grand Armada chapters, Ishmael reasons that whaling quietly opened doors that colonialists would have broken down more forcefully.

Even when we account for his humor and hyperbole, Ishmael's efforts to differentiate whaling from colonial conquest can seem far-fetched. When he argues that the industry has been crucial in opening foreign ports, he immediately highlights the military advantages it brings. "If American and European men-of-war now peacefully ride in once savage harbors, let them fire salutes to the honor and glory of the whale-ship, which originally showed them the way, and first interpreted between them and the savages" (110). Positing whaling as an anti-colonial force, he claims that whalemen "eventuated the liberation of Peru, Chili, and Bolivia from the yoke of Old Spain, and the establishment of the eternal democracy in those parts" (93). As we know, however, when Melville revisited that theme in "Benito Cereno," he considered how in recapturing the slaves on the *San Dominick*, the American sealer actively enforced what Ishmael calls the "jealous policy of the Spanish crown" (110). Ishmael's dream of a larger liberty is built on the extension of

196 THE PROSTHETIC ARTS OF *MOBY-DICK*

empire across the continent and into the Pacific. When he invokes "eternal democracy," he reveals his desire to identify American interests as being outside history and yet within progressive conceptions of time (93).

Along with his fellow stowaways and the Malaysian pirates who chase the *Pequod* through the Sunda Strait, Fedallah exemplifies the limits of Ishmael's egalitarian rhetoric. In *Mardi*, Melville touted the ship as a place of singular cohesion, an ecumenical paradise in which New Zealander, Persian, Christian, and Jew interpret no custom strange and no creed absurd. Taji memorably touts the "old tar" as a "cosmopolitan" who has found his identity and his language at sea: "Long companionship with seamen of all tribes: Manilla-men, Anglo-Saxon, Cholos, Lascars, and Danes, wear away in good time all mother-tongue stammerings. You sink your clan; down goes your nation; you speak a world's language, jovially jabbering in the Lingua-Franca of the forecastle."[84] The passage recalls Roger Williams's famous comparison of the commonwealth to a ship on which "Papists and Protestants, Jews or Turks" may all worship (or not worship) according to their conscience.[85] Although Taji elsewhere expresses considerable prejudice, here he explicitly includes the Manilla men in his roster of companions and, with that, offers an ethic born from experience.[86] Ishmael does not sink his clan or drop his nation, especially when addressing the Muslim-majority countries of Southeast Asia.

Fedallah's waterlogged gaze offers the beginnings of an Islamicized critique of how the rhetoric of democracy justifies the racialization of populations who resist American demands for change. Charles Olson understood the claims such arrogance made. "The American has the Roman feeling about the world. It is his, to dispose of," he wrote at the beginning of the Cold War. "Has he not conquered it with his machines? He bends its resources to his will." Olson was commenting on the way Ahab's solipsism resulted in the *Pequod*'s fate, but the lines also apply to Ishmael, whose cultural ambitions encompass the globe. "The pax of legions? The Americanization of the world. Who else is lord?"[87]

Ahab, Befooled

In the tragedy of *Moby-Dick*, Melville used the masthead only once as the setting for a Shakespearean soliloquy. Merging history, fiction, and the philosophical essay, Ishmael, of course, addressed the masthead in discursive rather than theatrical form. But Melville waited until the third day's chase to employ the masthead as an elevated stage upon which his tragic hero would speak. The speech gets little critical attention, perhaps because the distracted speaker continually interrupts himself, but it significantly articulates his thinking before the final carnage begins. Hoisted up the mast and barking orders to his crew, the captain takes "one more good round look aloft" at the sea, "an old, old sight" that had "not changed a wink" since he was a boy. "The same!—the same!—the same to Noah as to me," he cries, echoing an impression that Melville recorded after *he* nostalgically climbed the masthead in 1849 (565).[88]

Facing his possible death, Ahab addresses the mast not as a piece of nautical machinery but as a long-standing friend. The soliloquy reminds us that, after the previous day's disaster, Ahab now wears a wooden leg:

> But good bye, good bye, old mast-head! What's this?—green? aye, tiny mosses in these warped cracks. No such green weather stains on Ahab's head! There's the difference now between man's old age and matter's. But aye, old mast, we both grow old together; sound in our hulls, though, are we not, my ship? Aye, minus a leg, that's all. By heaven this dead wood has the better of my live flesh every way. I can't compare with it; and I've known some ships made of dead trees outlast the lives of men made of the most vital stuff of vital fathers. (565)

Marking him a brother to the mast, the wooden prosthesis draws the captain into a network of affiliations that he regards as enhancing his identity. Wood endures; wood adapts; it can host life forms that flesh and bone cannot.

The new prosthesis establishes the kind of mutuality that Ahab briefly found in Captain Boomer's ivory arm. In his terse syntax, the body and the ship take on each other's properties, each "sound" in their hulls with only a missing limb. The captain had once envisioned a cyborgian man whose tree-like legs had such roots that they would never retreat (470). Now, with another ivory leg in pieces, he views his dismemberment differently. Rather than lamenting his phantom pain, he proclaims, "This dead wood has the better of my live flesh every way." The feeling momentarily checks his aggrievement. The wooden prosthesis does not include an ivory slate, for there is no need to calculate his distance from Moby Dick. Vengeance awaits him "three points off the weather bow" (565). He no longer wears it on his body.

Preparing readers for the climactic surfacing of Fedallah's corpse, the speech grapples with the meaning of prostheses and prophecy. The corpse

198   THE PROSTHETIC ARTS OF *MOBY-DICK*

will show how the metaphysical assistance Fedallah has lent the captain has been as unreliable as a cord of whalebone legs. Both supplement the human limitations that Ahab bitterly contests. At this point, however, the Parsee's disappearance has done little to shake Ahab's confidence in his success. Still speaking to the mast, he shifts from the vitality of wooden legs to one of the "pledges" his pilot had made:

> What's that he said? he should still go before me, my pilot; and yet to be seen again? But where? Will I have eyes at the bottom of the sea, supposing I descend those endless stairs? and all night I've been sailing from him, wherever he did sink to. Aye, aye, like many more thou told'st direful truth as touching thyself, O Parsee; but, Ahab, there thy shot fell short. (565)

Even in his absence, Fedallah supplements Ahab's pride. The Parsee may have misjudged his own circumstances, but in helping find Moby Dick, he seems to have facilitated the retribution that the captain monomaniacally desires. As he imagines his own death at sea, Ahab believes that vengeance is at hand. Bidding the mast goodbye, he envisions Moby Dick "tied by head and tail" to the *Pequod*'s side (565).

In a passage filled with images of vision and sight (including the pun on "Aye"), Ahab fatally sees victory in what, in the end, are signs of his demise. He praises the wooden leg as an image of better-than-human life, but of course the carpenter has crafted that prosthesis from his boat's broken keel. Once dismembered, prostheticized, and reconstituted by whales, Ahab becomes a boat-made man who shares more of a relation with the *Pequod* than its prey. He likes the association, for the common hull of captain and ship imparts to him a sense of stability, control, and longevity. The "dismasted," "razeed" captain finds prosthetic assistance in the long piece of timber that holds together a whale boat's frame. As Ishmael has described him, Ahab is the crew's "one lord and keel," the tyrannical power that determines the direction in which they must head. The sense of self-definition pervades the confidence he conveys, for presumably miles away and under sea, the dead Fedallah will not appear before the day's battle with Moby Dick.

And yet, of course, the broken keel also attests to the community that has empowered Ahab's aggrievement and will be destroyed by his rage. To some, that spirit of destruction suggests the opportunity for new, more democratic forms of life; to others, the romanticization of destruction only leads to more destruction and fury. Ahab's nostalgic communing with the mast indicates that to him the wooden leg represents his Nantucket origins and his many years at sea. But what he does not consider—and cannot see—is that he goes into battle with the remnants of his "befooled" catastrophes (568). The broken whale boat, and the prosthesis its splintering helped make, anticipate not just the captain's death but the death of his shipmates. The smashed-up whale boat becomes the smashed-up *Pequod*, with everyone but Ishmael lost in the sea. Though Ahab understands it differently, the wooden prosthesis is both an origins story and a foreshadowing.

When he refers to the eternal hacking found in democracies, Don Hannibal laments the way that democracy pits communities against each other, with different factions and interests righteously pursuing their claims without the stabilizing effects of common values, traditions, hierarchies, and histories. Bent on a capitalist's version of progress, the New World not only severs itself from the Old: it also dismembers the body politic into warring factions, interests, and armies. But Ahab's story concerns the violence of men who have organized themselves behind an authoritarian who has little regard for their well-being. Ahab would not have the power of his prostheticized body if that body had not been both prostheticized and reconstituted in the crew. The drama of eternal hacking becomes the fate of tyrannically aggrieved men who forged themselves into a single, coordinated vessel without the ability to determine the direction in which they sail. Tyrants such as Ahab are not the individuals they claim to be: they are supplemented women and men, their incessant wound collecting a means by which others subordinate themselves to them.

Conclusion

Stuck on a Whale

"Bob Dylan's 115th Dream" offers an exhilarating mashup of American history. The 1965 song tells the story of a Captain A-rab who, leading the *Mayflower* into New York harbor, decides to "forget the whale" and claim America instead. The New World is not kind to the crewmember who narrates the tale. He stumbles as soon as he hits land and, as if suffering from injury himself, has difficulty standing up. The Captain, meanwhile, immediately gets to work—"writing up some deeds," setting up a fort, and "buying the place with beads." As Sean Wilentz has observed, the song collapses all sense of time, with Dylan's speaker narrating a tale that mixes 1620 with 1492, 1626, 1965, and, of course, 1851. In this surrealistic shaggy dog story, the crew gets hauled into jail for carrying harpoons, the Ishmaelean narrator gets robbed and threatened that he will be dismembered "limb from limb," the ship gets a parking ticket, and the captain gets "stuck on a whale." At the song's end, the bewildered speaker encounters Christopher Columbus and his three ships sailing into the bay. He wishes them "Good luck," for they have no idea what mayhem lies ahead.[1] The song portrays "an America that always has been and always will be," Wilentz points out, "a newfound land that is frantic, exasperating, jumbled, and irrational beyond the point of absurdity."[2]

That Dylan would frame this dream around *Moby-Dick* is hardly surprising, for by 1965, the novel was regularly seen as an icon of American life. (Indeed, three years earlier, Warner Berthoff argued that, compared to other writers, Melville had provided *the* exemplary response to "the presumptuous novelty of American experience.")[3] As one might expect, I find Dylan's decision to change Ahab's name especially intriguing, for the A-rab brazenly echoes the exoticization of the captain as a mogul, a sultan, and a "Khan of the plank." The Grand Turk of 1851 becomes the A-rab of 1965, the mispronunciation of "Arab" producing both the glibly irreverent rhyme and the construction of an insular, Know Nothing American whose slur

---

The Prosthetic Arts of Moby-Dick. David Haven Blake, Oxford University Press. © Oxford University Press 2024.
DOI: 10.1093/oso/9780197780510.003.0008

CONCLUSION 201

deliberately defies cultural conventions and respect. Dylan's captain may be the butt of Dylan's joke, but the speaker, too, seems imprisoned in his proudly provincial consciousness.

I do not propose the song as an elaborate gloss on *Moby-Dick*, and there is some reason to suspect that Dylan may have been inspired by John Huston's 1956 film more than Melville's text.[4] In what may be a misconception, the song puts its captain in Fedallah's place—"stuck on a whale"—instead of whisked from his boat and strangled by the towline. The erasure of the Parsee is consistent with Huston's film and a significant body of scholarship. Depicting Ahab as a foreign adventurer and a threat to democratic life, Dylan eliminates the character who repeatedly assists the captain's quest. From Voltaire to Daniel Webster, we have seen a pattern of eighteenth- and nineteenth-century intellectuals using Turks, Persians, and Malays to articulate forces that frustrate Euro-American aspirations at home and internationally. For Ishmael and Dylan both, Ahab seems so powerfully American that they feel compelled to present him as hailing from a Muslim-majority land. The prostheticization of Fedallah is the prostheticization of peoples who are rendered invisible in coming to signify America's most threatening characters and traits.

My analysis has focused on the numerous prostheses in *Moby-Dick*, from the series of medical devices that support people with missing and damaged limbs to the literary devices that help this story of dismemberment operate as a work of fiction. Scholars frequently use the word prosthetic to indicate artificial recreations of natural life, whether that be the simulating properties of language or the utility of virtual worlds. What is sometimes lost in the attention to artifice is that prostheses also convey a sense of assistance and support, a way to supplement bodily experience in the face of weakness, injury, or less-than-desired functionality. The discipline of disability studies has taught us that prosthetics are more easily incorporated into bodies than theorists sometimes admit. The pin inserted into an ankle, the crown covering a tooth, the cochlear implants embedded in aging ears, such prostheses often help individuals feel more human, more *themselves*, than they did before. No matter how awkward or painful it may seem, the artificial supplements the natural to the extent that, like tissue growing through surgical mesh, it can become pointless to fret about what is the implant and what is the flesh. When Ahab refers to "my leg," he can mean both the prosthetic and his missing limb.

202 THE PROSTHETIC ARTS OF *MOBY-DICK*

As we have seen, Melville reflected on disability throughout his career, so much so that he recasts the reader's sense of what "normal" or "desirable" means. ("I am, as I am," Babbalanja says in *Mardi*; "whether hideous, or handsome, depends upon who is made judge.")[5] Melville's particular interest in dismemberment found its fullest expression in *Moby-Dick*, which is unique among his novels, stories, and poems in placing profound emphasis on the prosthesis as the site of loss and revenge. I have argued that, although he continually reflects on his lost leg, Ahab emerges from *Moby-Dick*—not as a representation of disability—but as a wound collector whose charismatic sense of injury wins him control over the crew and commits them to the hunt. Ahab is not like the beggar by the London docks who paints "the tragic scene in which he lost his leg" for public regard.[6] Rather than recreate the past (visually, textually, or orally), he calculates his proximity to revenge on the smooth surface of his artificial leg, his figures transforming the reminder of his loss into the final, destructive battle with Moby Dick. Among Melville's disabled characters, Ahab cultivates a sense of injury so comprehensive that it results in "irresistible dictatorship." Contrary to Stubb's dream, limb loss does not spread through the characters in *Moby-Dick*, but submitting to the captain does.

Moby-Dick involves a story of American democracy as Melville imagined it in 1851, not the "ruthless democracy" he himself professed to practice in obliterating all sense of rank, but the democracy of parties, interest groups, and leaders seeking the power of other women and men. As Dylan did in 1965, we can see these concerns playing out in our own time. Melville recognized the role that injury played in democratic life, how it fused collective resentment into an abstraction that aroused enough terror to demand a tyrant's rule. As it did with Colonel John Moredock in *The Confidence-Man*, devastating loss triggers an all-out war against the white whale. But that war, in Ahab's mind, did not amount to just an act of retributive justice: it created a burden of righteousness, a "prouder, if a darker faith," that offered the promise of salvation itself. His character becomes inextricable from his aggrievement (497).

At a moment when leaders in Russia, Brazil, Italy, Spain, Hungary, Israel, Mexico, and the Philippines take comfort in the rise of authoritarianism in the United States, it seems imperative to acknowledge Ahab's vengeance as an explicitly American assertion of power. Amid calls for scholars to rethink Ahab's monomania, agency, and will, this book contends that we must use the insights of contemporary criticism to re-energize our attention to his

CONCLUSION   203

despotic rule. The Cold War critics followed Ishmael in casting Ahab as an external threat, a Soviet- or Turkish-styled tyrant outside democratic traditions and values. If the current moment has shown us anything, however, it is that the United States has no need to import examples of tyranny from abroad and that its greatest threats are its own fascist-leaning white nationalists. What binds these groups is a pervasive sense of aggrievement that, until the political rise of Donald Trump, lacked a figure capable of organizing it into legitimized federal authority. It should hardly be a surprise that the authoritarian Trump employs the same language of vengeance that Melville explored in *Moby-Dick*: "I am your justice," Trump told the Conservative Political Action Conference in 2023. "And for those who have been wronged and betrayed: I am your retribution."[7] The man who instituted a ban on immigrants from Muslim-majority countries continues to understand the value of cultural grievance in assembling a populist following.

Ishmael's antipathy to the novel's Asian characters contributes to Melville's meditation on US power. "If the [white] whale is more than blind, indifferent Nature unsubduable by masculine aggression," Toni Morrison wrote in 1988, "if it is as much its adjective as it is its noun, we can consider the possibility that Melville's 'truth' was his recognition of the moment in America when whiteness became ideology." To Morrison, the whiteness of the whale is the abstraction that Ahab assails, the "ideology of race" to which he madly loses "dismemberment and family and society and his own place as human in the world."[8] But like the greatest novels, *Moby-Dick* contains contradictory vectors and voices. While some may be convinced by the image of Ahab as the volcanic opponent of white supremacist rule, Ishmael remains a troublesome counterpart. The ideology of whiteness operates in Ishmael as a global force, his Jacksonian progressivism leading him both to racialize and denigrate peoples who resist the encroachments of the West. To the lethal force of Ahab we must also add the insidiously soft power that Ishmael represents, the power of commerce, the power of improvement, the power of the imperialist who appropriates the language of democracy. The years since 1851 have revealed another aspect of this ideology: that the hearses found in foreign lands and seas have often originated in the United States.

Morrison anticipated the extent to which white aggrievement would dominate the first decades of the twenty-first century.[9] It is illuminating to think of Ahab alongside Wendy Brown's analysis of the millions of Americans enthralled by Trump's authoritarian personality. Brown does

204   THE PROSTHETIC ARTS OF *MOBY-DICK*

not address Melville's work, but the contorted neoliberalism she finds in Trumpism reads like a primer on *Moby-Dick*. Ahab elucidates the contours of what she calls "aggrieved power," his "displacement" experienced not as economic decline but as a "lost entitlement" of humans over the nonhuman world.[10] When Ahab crushes the quadrant as the *Pequod* nears the white whale, we see his "nihilistic rejection" of expertise as an inconvenient threat to his cult of personality.[11] Like the white Americans who thrill to Trump's contempt for civil and constitutional norms, freedom for Ahab "becomes doing or saying what one likes without regard for its effects, freedom to be genuinely without care for the predicaments, vulnerabilities, or fates of other humans, other species, or the planet." It is a Flask-like freedom to, as Nietzsche puts it, "'wreak one's will' for the sheer pleasure of it."[12] "Behold the aggrieved, reactive creature fashioned by neoliberal reason and its effects, who embraces freedom without the social contract, authority without democratic legitimacy, and vengeance without values or futurity," Brown writes. "Its conscience is weak, while its own sense of victimization and persecution runs high."[13] Let me be clear: Ahab is too elevated, expressive, and philosophically heroic to be explained by the MAGA movement and the rise of the New Right.[14] And yet, amid all his complexity, the seeds of white aggrievement appear throughout his quest. "Spurred by humiliation and a thirst for revenge," Ahab may lament the immense burden that Moby Dick has thrust upon him, but when he inspires the harpooners, infects Starbuck, or tricks the crew with the lodestone, he revels in the "festive, and even apocalyptic" sense of his own destructive powers.[15]

I have suggested that Ahab's vaunted individualism is the prosthetic he leans upon to create his aggrieved self, the "queenly personality" that in the face of misfortune insistently demands its royal rights (507). Ahab's individualism makes his injury intelligible as a cosmic and ideological threat. It makes his grief political in the sense that it transforms an industrial accident into a profoundly collaborative and ruinous quest. In the end, we might consider injury itself as the first of Ahab's prostheses. In the unstable world of American democracy, the wound gives him an "overbearing dignity" that stuns and subordinates the crew (124). Ishmael comments on the "strange awe" he feels toward Ahab and the "cruel loss of his leg," "that sort of awe, which I cannot at all describe, . . . I do not know what it was" (80). Writing about white aggrievement, Juliet Hooker has argued that the "acceptance of loss is necessary for democracy" and that to be a citizen is "to cultivate the necessary democratic capacity of accepting the experience (true for all citizens) of frustrated sovereignty."[16] Ahab conceives of loss as the supplement that expands power, the deficit that makes him a "democrat to all above" and a lord to all below (169). *Moby-Dick* challenges its readers to think about the way loss "stirs up the lees of things," expanding our conception of our limits, our frustrations, and ourselves (184). To live in a democracy is to understand that loss is the condition of democracy—as long as it is accepted as loss.

Notes

Introduction

1. Herman Melville, *Moby-Dick or The Whale*, ed. Harrison Hayford, Hershel Parker, and G. Thomas Tanselle (Evanston, IL: Northwestern University Press; and Chicago: Newberry Library, 1988), 184. Future references will be made in parenthetical citations.

2. Before proceeding, it may be useful to differentiate my use of "grief" (an emotion responding to loss) and "grievance" (an articulation of that loss in a real or imagined appeal for justice) from "aggrievement" (a seemingly perpetual state of resentment over that loss, a condition of feeling unfairly treated). I have been particularly influenced by *Grief and Grievance: Art and Mourning in America*, a book accompanying the 2021 art show about the condition of Black grief at the New Museum in New York City. In an essay about the quest for racial justice in an American judicial system that is "complicit in the violence" inflicted upon Black men and women (12), Judith Butler writes about the political dimensions of grief and grievance. "Grievance is a complaint of some kind, a petition usually directed toward an authority to rectify a wrong or repair an injury" (13). "To be aggrieved is thus not only to be burdened but to be grieving some loss," she continues, explaining that "to turn that loss into a grievance is to make an appeal." Her sense of grievance looks toward "the advent of militant mourning, and the petition for justice" (15). Ahab's aggrievement, I argue, is distinct from the emotion he feels about his lost leg. When he says that his "topmost greatness" is his "topmost grief," he is asserting the burden of his condition, a quality of his character that remains all-defining for him and for everyone on ship. Ahab's aggrievement does not correspond to the historical situation that Butler addresses in *Grief and Grievance*. His sense of victimhood and the inability to accept material and symbolic loss is more akin to the white aggrievement that Juliet Hooker discusses in the same volume. See Judith Butler, "Between Grief and Grievance, a New Sense of Justice," in *Grief and Grievance: Art and Mourning in America*, ed. Okwui Enwezor, Naomi Beckwith, and Massimiliano Gioni (Phaidon Press, 2021), 11–15 and Juliet Hooker, "White Grievance and the Problem of Political Loss," 23–31. Butler's comments in *Precarious Life: The Powers of Mourning and Violence* may be more applicable to Ahab than her contribution to *Grief and Grievance*: "It is one matter to suffer violence and quite another to use that fact to ground a framework in which one's injury authorizes limitless aggression against targets that may or may not be related to the sources of one's own suffering." See Judith Butler, *Precarious Life: The Powers of Mourning and Violence* (New York: Verso, 2004), 4.

3. *Othello*, V.2.353 in William Shakespeare, *The Complete Works*, ed. Alfred Harbage (New York: Viking, 1969).

4. In using versions of the words "Orientalism" and "Orientalist" throughout this book, I refer to Edward Said's groundbreaking study *Orientalism*, which explicitly critiqued the discourse of Orientalism that emerged in the late eighteenth century and became the predominant "Western style for dominating, restructuring, and having authority over the Orient." "Without examining Orientalism as a discourse," Said writes, "one cannot possibly understand the enormously systematic discipline by which European culture was able to manage—and even produce, the Orient politically, sociologically, militarily, ideologically, scientifically, and imaginatively during the post-Enlightenment period." See Edward Said, *Orientalism*, 25th Anniversary Edition (1979; New York: Vintage, 2003), 3. Melville's writings participated in both creating and critiquing this discourse.

5. The Malaysian straits had been Islamic since the fourteenth century, largely influenced by Muslims from India and China. Wars between the Ottoman Empire and the Republic of Venice lasted from 1398 to 1798. For more information, see the essays in A. C. S. Peacock and Annabel Teh Gallop, eds., *From Anatolia to Aceh: Ottomans, Turks, and Southeast Asia* (London: Oxford University Press for the British Academy, 2015).

6. Bernard Stiegler, *Technics and Time*, vol. 1, *The Fault of Epimetheus*, trans. Richard Beardsworth and George Collins (Stanford: Stanford University Press, 1998), 115–16. The phrase "whole and entire about himself" is Stiegler's description of Rousseau, on 116.

208 NOTES TO PAGES 3–10

7. Alexis de Tocqueville, *Democracy in America*, ed. J. P. Mayer, trans. George Lawrence (New York: Anchor, 1969), 548.

8. Walt Whitman, *Specimen Days*, in *Complete Poetry and Collected Prose*, ed. Justin Kaplan (New York: Library of America, 1982), 712. Ralph Waldo Emerson had used a particularly ableist version of this image pattern decades before. "The state of society," he explained in 1837, "is one in which the members have suffered amputation from the trunk and strut about so many walking monsters—a good finger, a neck, a stomach, an elbow, but never a man." Ralph Waldo Emerson, "The American Scholar," in *Essays and Lectures*, ed. Joel Porte, (New York: The Library of America, 1983), 54.

9. Four artificial legs appear in *Moby-Dick*, three made of ivory and one of wood. I will address the differences between these prostheses later in this book, but for now we might regard them (as Ishmael often does) as a series of interchangeable devices substituting for Ahab's natural leg.

10. Toni Morrison, "Unspeakable Things Unspoken: The Afro-American Presence in American Literature," *Michigan Quarterly Review* 28:1 (1989), 18.

11. Tobin Siebers, *Disability Aesthetics* (Ann Arbor: University of Michigan Press, 2010), 20, 3.

12. Ibid., 4.

13. On Melville's improvisatory style, see Geoffrey Sanborn, *The Value of Herman Melville* (New York: Cambridge University Press, 2018), 19–27.

14. Leonard Kriegel, "The Cripple in Literature," in *Images of the Disabled, Disabling Images*, ed. Alan Gartner and Tom Joe (New York: Praeger, 1987), 35. See also Kriegel, "The Wolf in the Pit in the Zoo," *Social Policy* 13:16 (1982), 16–23.

15. Rosemarie Garland Thomson, *Extraordinary Bodies: Figuring Physical Disability in American Culture and Literature* (New York: Columbia University Press, 1997), 44. Since the publication of *Extraordinary Bodies*, Garland-Thomson has added a hyphen to her name. I include her full name throughout this study, but when I refer to the original publication, I do not include the hyphen.

16. Lennard J. Davis, "Who Put the 'the' in 'the Novel'? Identity Politics and Disability in Novel Studies," *Novel* 31:3 (1998), 328 n. 11, 330.

17. David T. Mitchell and Sharon L. Snyder, *Narrative Prosthesis: Disability and the Dependencies of Discourse* (Ann Arbor: University of Michigan Press, 2000), 17.

18. Ibid., 121. Although he does not discuss it as a disability, Jonathan D. S. Schroeder discusses Ahab's monomania as a medical diagnosis that legally establishes him "as an insane person who cannot be held criminally responsible, since he acts merely from a diseased heart and not a depraved one." See Jonathan D. S. Schroeder, "The Whiteness of the Will: Ahab and the Matter of Monomania," in *Ahab Unbound: Melville and the Materialist Turn*, ed. Meredith Farmer and Jonathan D. S. Schroeder (Minneapolis: University of Minnesota Press, 2022), 278–79.

19. Samuel Otter, "Melville and Disability," *Leviathan* 8:1 (2006), 9.

20. See Douglas B. Price, "Melville and Dismemberment: Obsession or Metaphor," *Perspectives in Biology and Medicine* 39:3 (1996), 384–86. John Bryant connects the siblings' disabilities to Melville's fiction throughout *Herman Melville: A Half-Known Life*, electronic ed., vol. 1 (Hoboken, NJ: Wiley-Blackwell, 2021). See especially 9, 260–62, and 395–96.

21. See Herman Melville, *Omoo: A Narrative of Adventures in the South Seas*, ed. Harrison Hayford, Hershel Parker, and G. Thomas Tanselle (Evanston, IL: Northwestern University Press; Chicago: Newberry Library, 1968), 127; Herman Melville, *Redburn: His First Voyage*, ed. Harrison Hayford, Hershel Parker, and G. Thomas Tanselle (Evanston, IL: Northwestern University Press; Chicago: Newberry Library, 1969), 190; Herman Melville, *Pierre or The Ambiguities*, ed. Harrison Hayford, Hershel Parker, and G. Thomas Tanselle (Evanston, IL: Northwestern University Press; Chicago: Newberry Library, 1971), 107; Herman Melville, "The Armies of the Wilderness," in *Published Poems*, ed. Robert C. Ryan, Harrison Hayford, Alma MacDougall Reising, and G. Thomas Tanselle (Evanston, IL: Northwestern University Press; Chicago: Newberry Library, 2009), 75; Herman Melville, *Clarel: A Poem and Pilgrimage in the Holy Land*, ed. Harrison Hayford, Alma MacDougall, Hershel Parker, and G. Thomas Tanselle (Evanston, IL: Northwestern University Press; Chicago: Newberry Library, 1991), 1.26.70–76.

22. As Rachel Adams, Benjamin Reiss, and David Serlin point out, contemporary activists have developed this idea into an acronym, TAB, or the Temporarily Able-Bodied. See "Disability," in *Keywords for Disability Studies*, ed. Rachel Adams, Benjamin Reiss, and David Serlin (New York: New York University Press, 2015), 5.

NOTES TO PAGES 10–14   209

23. Sari Altschuler, "'Ain't One Limb Enough?' Historicizing Disability in the American Novel," *American Literature* 86:2 (2014), 264.
24. Kriegel, "The Cripple in Literature," 34–35.
25. I am indebted throughout this book to John Kerrigan's *Revenge Tragedy: Aeschylus to Armagedon* (New York: Oxford University Press, 1996), and, in this passage especially, the discussion on 17.
26. See ibid., 15–17.
27. See, for example, Kim E. Nielsen, *A Disability History of the United States* (Boston: Beacon Press, 2012) and Susan Burch and Michael Rembis, eds., *Disability Histories* (Urbana: University of Illinois Press, 2014). These works build on the highly influential collection edited by Katherine Ott, David Serlin, and Stephen Mihm, *Artificial Parts, Practical Lives: Modern Histories of Prosthetics* (New York: New York University Press, 2002).
28. Sarah Jain, "The Prosthetic Imagination: Enabling and Disabling the Prosthesis Trope," *Science, Technology, & Human Values* 24:1 (1999), 32.
29. See Sigmund Freud, *Civilization and Its Discontents*, trans. and ed. James Strachey (New York: Norton, 2005), 74; Marshall McLuhan, *Understanding Media: The Extensions of Man* (Cambridge: MIT Press, 1994), 7; Donna Haraway, "Situated Knowledges: The Science Question in Feminism and the Privilege of Partial Perspectives," *Feminist Studies* 14:3 (1988), 583. I am indebted to Sarah Coffey's entry "Prosthesis" for the Keywords of Media Theory website, University of Chicago, http://csmt.uchicago.edu/glossary2004/prosthesis.htm.
30. Martin Heidegger, *Parmenides* (1942–43), trans. Andre Schuwer and Richard Rojcewicz (Bloomington: Indiana University Press, 1992), 80–81 and 85–86.
31. David Wills, *Prosthesis* (Stanford: Stanford University Press, 1995), 133.
32. Ibid. The OED cites the origins of prosthesis as a grammatical term in 1550 with the surgical term coming into effect in 1706. Oxford English Dictionary Online, s.v. "prosthesis (n.)," accessed July 2023.
33. Stiegler, *Technics and Time*, 152–53. The emphasis on mechanization in thinking about prostheses has led some readers to consider whether the ivory leg makes Ahab a cyborg. See, for example, Jake Bartolone's tongue-in-cheek essay "A Smart Dude Reads *Moby-Dick*: Episode 3. Enter Cyborg. We Mean Ahab," *Los Angeles Review of Books*, 9 October 2012, online. Another version of this theory is the Marvel Comics character Rory Campbell who, after losing his leg, is cybernetically transformed into the superhero Ahab. See www.marvel.com/characters/Ahab. Ishmael consistently does not present the captain as a mechanized man, though as I discuss in Chapter 2, Ahab himself envisions the ways in which the carpenter's prostheses could make him into an enhanced (and less human) being.
34. See, for example, Alison Landsberg, *Prosthetic Memory: The Transformation of American Remembrance in the Age of Mass Culture* (New York: Columbia University Press, 2004); Mark Wigley, "Prosthetic Theory: The Disciplining of Architecture," *Assemblage* 15 (1991), 7–29; and Diane M. Nelson, "Stumped Identities: Body Image, Bodies Politic, and the Mujer Maya as Prosthetic," *Cultural Anthropology* 16:3 (2001), 314–53.
35. Stephen L. Kurzman, "Presence and Prosthesis: A Response to Nelson and Wright," *Cultural Anthropology* 16:3 (2001), 375–76.
36. I am combining two points from Sobchack here. On the scandal of the metaphor see "A Leg to Stand On: Prosthetics, Metaphor, and Materiality," in *The Prosthetic Impulse: From a Posthuman Present to Biocultural Future*, ed. Marquard Smith and Joanne Morra (Cambridge: MIT Press, 2006), 21. On incorporating the prosthetic, see "Beating the Meat / Surviving the Text, or How to Get Out of this Century," *Body and Society* 1:3–4 (1995), 210.
37. Sobchack, "A Leg," 23; Kurzman, "Presence and Prosthesis," 381.
38. Stiegler, *Technics and Time*, 153.
39. Wills, *Prosthesis*, 11.
40. My use of prostheses to describe Fedallah's function in *Moby-Dick* may be objectionable to readers who reject seeing the character as an extension of the white, Christian Ahab. I understand this concern and have learned a great deal from critics such as Amirhossein Vafa who provide a backstory for Fedallah that gives him a more subjective presence. But if our focus is on the text as Melville wrote it, it seems crucial to acknowledge that Fedallah plays a more important role in making the narrative work than he does as an independent character himself.
41. Mitchell and Snyder, *Narrative Prosthesis*, 47.
42. Ibid., 47, 49.

210   NOTES TO PAGES 14–21

43. Peter Boxall, *The Prosthetic Imagination: A History of the Novel as Artificial Life* (New York: Cambridge University Press, 2020), 17, 186.
44. Ibid., 13, 11.
45. Ibid., 151.
46. Ibid., 29.
47. Peter Szendy sees prophecy and prosthetics in relation to Elijah. See *Prophecies of Leviathan: Reading Past Melville*, trans. Gil Andijar (New York: Fordham University Press, 2010), 23–28.
48. Boxall, *Prosthetic Imagination*, 219.
49. On the disability aspects of this story, see Daniel Diez Couch and Michael Anthony Nicholson, "Disability and Melville's 'Fragments,'" *Leviathan* 23:1 (2021), 7–23.
50. See "The Piazza," *The Piazza Tales: and Other Prose Pieces, 1839–1860*, ed. Harrison Hayford, Alma A. MacDougall, and G. Thomas Tanselle (Evanston. IL: Northwestern University Press; Chicago: Newberry Library, 1987), 1; Herman Melville, *White-Jacket or The World in a Man-of-War*, ed. Harrison Hayford, Hershel Parker, and G. Thomas Tanselle (Evanston, IL: Northwestern University Press; Chicago: Newberry Library, 1970), 318; and *Mardi and a Voyage Thither*, ed. Harrison Hayford, Hershel Parker, and G. Thomas Tanselle (Evanston, IL: Northwestern University Press; Chicago: Newberry Library, 1998), 7–8.
51. Melville comments, "Rascally priests demanding 'bakshesh.' Fleeced me out of ½ dollar; following me round, selling the fallen mosaics." Herman Melville, *Journals*, ed. Howard C. Horsford and Lynn Horth (Evanston, IL: Northwestern University Press; Chicago: Newberry Library, 1989), 59.
52. My thanks to my colleague Deborah Hutton, Professor of Art and Art History, The College of New Jersey, and Erin Hunt, Curator, Berkshire County Historical Society at Herman Melville's Arrowhead, for providing me with background information about this image. See "Herman Melville's Persian Tile" on the Arrowhead website for more detailed information: https://berkshirehistory.org/collection-sampling/, accessed 8 January 2024.
53. Stiegler, *Technics and Time*, 235.
54. Ronald Takaki, *Iron Cages: Race and Culture in 19th-Century America*, rev. ed. (1990; New York: Oxford University Press, 2000), 281.
55. Thomas Bender, *A Nation among Nations: America's Place in World History* (New York: Hill and Wang, 2006), 187. A helpful excerpt from Bender's book appears in "The American Way of Empire," *World Policy Journal* 23:1 (2006), 45–61. My thanks to Christopher Fisher, Interim Dean of the School of Humanities and Social Sciences, The College of New Jersey, for bringing these works to my attention.
56. Dennis Berthold, "Democracy and Its Discontents," in *A Companion to Herman Melville*, ed. Wyn Kelley (Oxford: Blackwell, 2006), 150.
57. Jennifer Greiman, *Melville's Democracy: Radical Figuration and Political Form* (Stanford: Stanford University Press, 2023), 4, 165.
58. Ishmael was not alone in applying the principle of manifest destiny to the expansion of American commerce into the Pacific. In his 1856 "Salut au Monde," Walt Whitman triumphantly believed that the technology that was closing the frontier would inevitably impose itself across the globe: "I see the tracks of the rail-roads of the earth, / I see them welding state to state, county to county, city to city, through North America, / I see them in Great Britain, I see them in Europe, / I see them in Asia and in Africa." Like Whitman and the railroad, Ishmael presents the whaleship as an expression of American power, a means by which the democratic nation extended its reach over "forbidden seas" and "barbarous coasts" (7). See Whitman, "Salut au Monde," in *Complete Poetry and Collected Prose*, ed. Justin Kaplan (New York: Library of America, 1982), 290–91.
59. Melville, *Clarel*, 1.15.38; 4:10.419; 4.10.186.
60. See Dorothee Metkitsky Finkelstein, *Melville's Orienda* (New Haven: Yale University Press, 1961), 203–5 and Timothy Marr, *The Cultural Roots of American Islamicism* (New York: Cambridge University Press, 1996), 243–44.
61. Melville, *Mardi*, 569–70, 574.
62. Ezekiel 37:7.
63. John Winthrop, "A Model of Christian Charity," in *The American Tradition in Literature*, 6th ed., ed. George B. Perkins, E. Scully Bradley, Floyd W. Beaty, et al. (New York: Random House, 1985), 22.

NOTES TO PAGES 25–31 211

Chapter 1

1. Herman Melville, *Moby-Dick or The Whale*, ed. Harrison Hayford, Hershel Parker, and G. Thomas Tanselle (Evanston, IL: Northwestern University Press; Chicago: Newberry Library, 1988), 160. Future references will be made in parenthetical citations.

2. Melville's *Acushnet* was registered as having a deck of 104 feet, 8 inches. Hershel Parker, *Herman Melville: A Biography*, vol. 1, *1819–1851* (Baltimore: Johns Hopkins University Press, 2006), 185. The deck of the *Charles W. Morgan*, the sister ship of the *Acushnet*, is 106 feet, 11 inches. See the Mystic Seaport website: https://www.mysticseaport.org/explore/morgan/, accessed 12 December 2023.

3. Herman Melville to Evert A. Duyckinck, 24 February 1849, in *Correspondence*, ed. Lynn Horth (Evanston, IL: Northwestern University Press; Chicago: Newberry Library, 1993), 119. *Mardi* was published in London on 15 March 1849. See Jay Leyda, *The Melville Log: A Documentary Life, 1819–1891*, vol. 1 (New York: Harcourt, Brace, 1951), 292.

4. F. O. Matthiessen, *American Renaissance: Art and Expression in the Age of Emerson and Whitman* (New York: Oxford University Press, 1941), 416.

5. Ibid., 419.

6. Michael Ralph, "Impairment," in *Keywords for Disability Studies*, ed. Rachel Adams, Benjamin Reiss, and David Serlin (New York: New York University Press, 2015), 107.

7. Matthew J. C. Cella, "The Ecosomatic Paradigm in Literature: Merging Disability Studies and Ecocriticism," *Interdisciplinary Studies in Literature and the Environment* 20:3 (2013), 578.

8. Thomas De Quincey, "On the Knocking at the Gate in Macbeth," in *Miscellaneous Essays* (Boston: Tickner, Reed & Fields, 1851), 9.

9. Arthur Frank, *The Wounded Storyteller* (Chicago: University of Chicago Press, 1998), 31.

10. Others join the normally jolly Stubb in being so unsettled. Part of the problem resides in the language Ishmael and his shipmates use to describe Ahab's condition. Alluding to the "dead stump," "ivory foot," and "leg," they frequently (but not always) refer to the same thing—the captain's thigh, knee, and upper calf as they are harnessed in an iron and whalebone prosthesis. The phrases convey the difficulty of talking about artificial limbs without referring to what they have replaced. As Mary K. Bercaw Edwards has noted, *Moby-Dick* is a notoriously inconsistent book. Melville includes contradictory information about the number of sailors onboard, whether they sleep in bunks or hammocks, and whether the *Pequod* has a whalebone tiller or captain's wheel. The novel surprisingly never clarifies whether the captain has lost his right or left leg. See Bercaw Edwards's discussion of the Charles Morgan on the Mystic Seaport website: http://educators.mysticseaport.org/scholars/lectures/morgan_tour/.

11. Rosemarie Garland Thomson, *Extraordinary Bodies: Figuring Physical Disability in American Culture and Literature* (New York: Columbia University Press, 1997), 45.

12. Michael Jonik, *Herman Melville and the Politics of the Inhuman* (Cambridge: Cambridge University Press, 2018), 32.

13. See Vivian Sobchack, "A Leg to Stand On: Prosthetics, Metaphor, and Materiality," in *The Prosthetic Impulse: From a Posthuman Present to Biocultural Future*, ed. Marquard Smith and Joanne Morra (Cambridge: MIT Press, 2006), 26, 18. On the animating aspects of prostheses, see Peter Boxall, *The Prosthetic Imagination: A History of the Novel as Artificial Life* (New York: Cambridge University Press, 2020), 2.

14. On Melville and Irving, see James C. Keil, "Melville's 'American Goldsmith': *Moby-Dick* and Irving's *A History of New York*," *Melville Society Extracts*, no. 102 (September 1995), 13–16. https://sites.hofstra.edu/melville-society-extracts/.

15. Hardkoppig Piet is Stubborn Pete. Washington Irving, *Knickerbocker's History of New York* (Chicago: W.B. Conkey Company, n.d.), chap. 6.

16. Russell Shorto, *The Island at the Center of the World: The Epic Story of Dutch Manhattan and the Forgotten Colony That Shaped America* (New York: Vintage, 2005), 7. For the coffin legend, see Maurita Baldock's lecture "How Did 'Peg-Leg' Peter Stuyvesant Lose His Right Leg?," New York Historical Society, accessed 22 October 2017.

17. On what is called "the Peter Gansevoort Chapeau," see Edgar M. Howell and Donald E. Kloster, *United States Army Headgear to 1854: Catalogue of United States Army Uniforms in the Collection of the Smithsonian Institution*, vol. 1 (Washington, DC: Smithsonian Institution, 1969), 3, online.

212 NOTES TO PAGES 31–39

18. The original illustration comes from French lithographer Nicolas-Toussaint Charlet. American Antiquarian Society. See Pendleton's Lithography, "The Soldier's Birth-Right," Boston, 1830–39. Collections of the American Antiquarian Society.

19. On *Moby-Dick* as a grail quest, see Christopher Sten, *The Weaver-God, He Weaves: Melville and the Poetics of the Novel* (Kent, OH: Kent State University Press, 1996), 201–2.

20. Jennifer Van Horn, *The Power of Objects in Eighteenth-Century British America* (Chapel Hill: University of North Carolina Press, 2017), 365–72.

21. James S. Baille, "Battle of Sierra Gordo. April 17th & 18th, 1847 Between Genl. Scott and Santa Anna: Capture of Santa Anna's Carraige, Cash, Papers, Dinner & Wooden Leg," Lithograph, 1848. Collections of the American Antiquarian Society.

22. For both the sketch and the song lyrics, see Andrea Tinnemeyer, "Embodying the West: Lyrics from the U.S.-Mexican War," *American Studies* 46:1 (2005), 68, 74.

23. See "View of the Barnum Property," *Yankee Doodle* 43 (1847), 168. Reprinted in Herman Melville, *The Piazza Tales: and Other Prose Pieces, 1839–1860*, ed. Harrison Hayford, Alma A. MacDougall, and G. Thomas Tanselle (Evanston, IL: Northwestern University Press; Chicago: Newberry Library, 1987), 447–48. On Melville's possible authorship of the article, see 788.

24. J. B. P., "The Old Boatswain," in *The Forget-Me-Not, For 1849*, ed. Alfred A. Phillips (New York: Nafis and Cornish, 1849), 200, 202. The illustration is by Edward Matthew Ward. Collections of the American Antiquarian Society.

25. On Nelson's amputations, see Dr. Harold Ellis, "Admiral Nelson's Above Elbow Amputation," *Journal of Perioperative Practice* 24:9 (2014), 286–87. For the details of Nelson's life, see N. A. M. Rodger, "Nelson, Horatio, Viscount Nelson (1758–1805)," in *Oxford Dictionary of National Biography*, Oxford University Press, 2004, online, May 2009, accessed 27 August 2017.

26. Herman Melville, *Omoo: A Narrative of Adventures in the South Seas*, ed. Harrison Hayford, Hershel Parker, and G. Thomas Tanselle (Evanston, IL: Northwestern University Press; Chicago: Newberry Library, 1968), 57.

27. Herman Melville, *White-Jacket or The World in a Man-of-War*, ed. Harrison Hayford, Hershel Parker, and G. Thomas Tanselle (Evanston, IL: Northwestern University Press; Chicago: Newberry Library, 1970), 319.

28. As the next chapter explains, the carpenter confuses things even more when he expresses relief that in making a new prosthesis for Ahab, he doesn't need to create a knee joint. Ishmael also reports in "Leg and Arm" that Ahab has a "solitary thigh" that he slides over the curve of a blubber hook on the *Samuel Enderby* (337).

29. James A. Berger, "Trauma without Disability, Disability without Trauma: A Disciplinary Divide," *JAC* 24:3 (2004), 574.

30. David T. Mitchell and Sharon L. Snyder, *Narrative Prosthesis: Disability and the Dependencies of Discourse* (Ann Arbor: University of Michigan Press, 2000), 137, 123, 120.

31. Berger, "Trauma without Disability," 574.

32. M. J. E. Neil, "Pain after Amputation," *BJA Education* 16:3 (2016), 107–12.

33. Herman Melville, *Mardi and a Voyage Thither*, ed. Harrison Hayford, Hershel Parker, and G. Thomas Tanselle (Evanston, IL: Northwestern University Press; Chicago: Newberry Library, 1998), 77–78.

34. See John R. Kirkup, *A History of Limb Amputation* (London: Springer, 2007), 2, 31.

35. Melville, *Mardi*, 77.

36. Ibid., 99.

37. Melville's indictment of flogging, a form of discipline that the United States outlawed during the War of 1812 but the navy later revived, contributed to Congress's banning the punishment six months after the book's publication. See "Brief History of Punishment by Flogging in the US Navy," Navy Department Library, online, accessed 8 January 2024.

38. Melville, *White-Jacket*, 249.

39. Ibid., 248.

40. Ibid., 257.

41. Ibid.

42. "Amputation," in *The Penny Cyclopaedia of the Society for the Diffusion of Useful Knowledge*, vol. 1, *A-Andes* (London: Charles Knight, 1833), 474. Internet Archive.

43. "Amputation," *Penny Cyclopaedia*, 473–74; Melville, *White-Jacket*, 259.

44. Melville, *White-Jacket*, 259.

NOTES TO PAGES 39–43   213

45. Nathaniel Hawthorne to Evert Duyckicnk, August 1850, in Nathaniel Hawthorne, *Selected Letters of Nathaniel Hawthorne*, ed. Joel Meyerson (Columbus: Ohio State University Press, 2002), 147.
46. Melville, *White-Jacket*, 261.
47. Ibid., 262.
48. Melville, *Omoo*, 11.
49. Eleanora C. Gordon, "The Captain as Healer: Medical Care on Merchantmen and Whalers, 1790–1865," *American Neptune* 54:4 (1994), 265, 273.
50. Ibid., 271.
51. Eric Jay Dolin, *Leviathan: The History of Whaling in America* (New York: Norton, 2007), 262–63.
52. Kirkup, "History of Limb Amputation," 25.
53. See Dr. Usher Parsons, *Physician for Ships; Containing Medical Advice for Seaman and Other Persons at Sea, on the Treatment of Disease and the Preservation of Health in Sickly Climates*, 3rd ed. (Boston: Little and Brown, 1842), 131. Published in 1820 and 1824, the earlier editions of Parsons's book (titled *Sailor's Physician*) curiously did not include a chapter on amputations. In cases in which amputation could wait, ships often sailed to the coast and brought a trained surgeon on board. National Library of Medicine, online, accessed 16 August 2017.
54. As described in Gordon, "Captain as Healer," 271, 274. Some manuals did not include chapters on amputations, such as Joseph B. Bond, *Master-Mariners Guide in the Management of the Ship's Company* (Boston: Wm. Crosby & H.P. Nichols, 1847), as many regarded the surgery as being routine. National Library of Medicine, accessed 16 August 2017.
55. Parsons, "Physicians for Ships," 132–33.
56. James Folsom, *The mariner's medical guide: designed for the use of ships, families, and plantations, containing the symptoms and treatment of diseases: also, a list of medicines, their uses, and the mode of administering, when a physician cannot be procured: selected from standard works* (Boston: J. Folsom, 1860), 110. National Library of Medicine, online, accessed 21 October 2017.
57. Melville, *White-Jacket*, 259.
58. Melville refers to Kemble as Mrs. Butler, using her married name, not her stage name.
59. Melville to Duyckinck, 24 February 1849, *Correspondence*, 119–20.
60. John Bryant, *Herman Melville: A Half-Known Life*, vol. 1, electronic ed. (Hoboken, NJ: Wiley-Blackwell, 2021), 271, 270. For Bryant's broader discussion of Kemble, see 270–76.
61. Herman Melville, "Mosses from an Old Manse by a Virginian Spending July in Vermont," in *The Piazza Tales: and Other Prose Pieces, 1839–1860*, ed. Harrison Hayford, Alma A. MacDougall, and G. Thomas Tanselle (Evanston, IL: Northwestern University Press; Chicago: Newberry Library, 1987), 244.
62. Ibid.
63. Ibid.
64. Bryant, *Half-Known Life*, 272–73.
65. Melville, "Mosses," 244.
66. Ibid., 245.
67. On Richard's "deformity," see William Shakespeare, *Richard III*, I.1.27, in *The Complete Works*, ed. Alfred Harbage (New York: Viking Press, 1969). On Shakespeare in America, see Lawrence Levine, *Highbrow/Lowbrow: The Emergence of Cultural Hierarchy in America* (Cambridge: Harvard University Press, 1990), 11–82. *Richard III*, the most popular Shakespearean play in the nineteenth century, was lampooned frequently in such versions as "Bad Dicky."
68. On the normate, see Garland Thomson, *Extraordinary Bodies*, 8–9.
69. Useful analyses include Michael Vannoy Adams, "Getting a Kick Out of Captain Ahab: The Merman Dream in *Moby-Dick*," *Dreamworks* 4:4 (1984–85), 279–87 and Chris Wiesenthal's Lacanian analysis in *Figuring Madness in Nineteenth-Century Fiction* (New York: St. Martin's Press, 1997), 149–53. Lacanian theorists might argue that the dream conveys the "aggressive disintegration" of someone who is regressing to an infantile pre-ego stage. But in Stubb's case, the fear is more corporeal and immediate. See Jacques Lacan, "The Mirror Stage as Formative of the / Function as Revealed in Psychoanalytic Experience Delivered on July 17, 1949, in Zurich at the Sixteenth International Congress of Psychoanalysis," in *Écrits: A Selection*, trans. Alan Sheridan (New York: Norton, 2006), 278.

214 NOTES TO PAGES 44–55

70. Chelsea Dornfeld et al. "Is the Prosthetic Homologue Necessary for Embodiment?," *Frontiers in Neurorobotics* 10 (2016), 21. PubMed Central. National Library of Medicine, accessed 29 September 2017.

71. Abby Wilkerson, "Embodiment," in *Keywords for Disability Studies*, ed. Rachel Adams, Benjamin Reiss, and David Serlin (New York: New York University Press, 2015), 68; Suzanne Bost, "From Race/Sex/Etc. to Glucose, Feeding Tube, and Mourning: The Shifting Matter of Chicana Feminism," in *Material Feminisms*, ed. Stacy Alaimo and Susan Hekman (Bloomington: Indiana University Press, 2008), 358.

72. As researchers have shown, many amputees feel a stronger connection to lifelike prostheses than more mechanical ones. See Dornfeld et al., "Prosthetic Homologue," 21.

73. To some readers, the dream represents Stubb's complete submission to Ahab; others see it as evidence that Stubb has achieved some wisdom in learning to reject the obsessive aggrievement that animates the captain's life. "On a ship where pride might well be the greatest sin," Alan Dagovitz writes, Stubb's "fatal lack of it probably isn't so bad." Alan Dagovitz, "*Moby-Dick*'s Hidden Philosopher: A Second Look at Stubb," *Philosophy and Literature* 32:2 (2008), 339. On Stubb's submission to Ahab, see Edward Rosenberry, *Melville and the Comic Spirit* (Cambridge: Harvard University Press, 1955), 120. See also Christine Stansell, "Dreams," *History Workshop Journal* 62:1 (2006), 241–52.

74. Garland Thomson, *Extraordinary Bodies*, 9.

75. Kim E. Nielsen, *A Disability History of the United States* (Boston: Beacon Press, 2012), 54, 56, 66. For an account of how this process also occurred with the development of asylums for people with cognitive disabilities, see Sarah F. Rose, *No Right to Be Idle: The Invention of Disability, 1840s–1930s* (Chapel Hill: University of North Carolina Press, 2017), 14–48.

76. The iconic reading of Pip and *King Lear* is Charles Olson's in *Call Me Ishmael: A Study of Melville* (San Francisco: City Lights Books, 1947), 59–73.

77. Jonik, *Politics of the Inhuman*, 37.

78. For a reading that focuses on incompletion and generosity, see Sharon Cameron, *The Corporeal Self: Allegories of the Body in Melville and Hawthorne* (Baltimore: Johns Hopkins University Press, 1981), 27–28. Commenting on this passage, Cameron writes, "Pip is the grief that completes Ahab's rage" (27). Writing before the rise of disability studies, Cameron focuses on the "incompletion" of Ahab's body. "The substitution for this wholeness would come in the form of analogy or relationship, in an acknowledged connection with other selves. In the generosity of Melville's image ('"do ye but use poor me for your one lost leg . . . I ask no more, so I remain a part of ye"') we see the lengths to which compensation can go" (29). Cameron ultimately sees Ahab as banishing Pip to the captain's chair, though the context suggests he is trying to protect Pip by keeping him below.

79. Melville, "Benito Cereno," in *The Piazza Tales*, 57.

80. Jonik, *Politics of the Inhuman*, 32.

81. Mitchell and Snyder present this scene as a sign of Ahab's unhealthy, monomaniacal perseverance rather than his adaptability and skill. See *Narrative Prosthesis*, 122.

82. Among numerous details, consider the serving dishes such as "wry-necked gourds; deformities of calabashes; and shapeless trenchers, dug out of knotty woods"; the menu comprised of "hunchbacked roots of the Taro-plant—plantains, perversely curling at the end, like the inveterate tails of pertinacious pigs; and for dessert, ill-shaped melons, huge as idiots' heads"; and the "numerous objects of vertu" presented to the guests to admire, including "bow-legged stools of mangrove wood." See Melville, *Mardi*, 573.

83. David Dowling, *Chasing the White Whale: The "Moby-Dick" Marathon; or, What Melville Means Today* (Iowa City: University of Iowa Press, 2010), 77.

84. Cella, "Ecosomatic Paradigm," 584, 574–75.

85. See *Moby-Dick*, 475, 490, 560.

86. As I discussed earlier in this chapter, the sentimental character of Boatswain Brace refers to his grandson as "my eyes and limbs," thus establishing a form of familial prostheses grounded in trust and devotion. Ahab is, of course, more threatening.

87. Frank, *Wounded Storyteller*, 35.

88. C. L. R. James, *Mariners, Renegades, and Castaways: The Story of Herman Melville and the World We Live In*, ed. Donald E. Pease (1953; Hanover: University Press of New England, 2001), 65.

89. In reviewing *The Whale*, the *Dublin University Magazine* implied the same distinction: "We will venture to assert that the immortal Nelson never hunted down a French frigate, in the heyday of his nautical reputation, with more determined energy than Ahab, commander of the

NOTES TO PAGES 57–67   215

Pequod, sailed after the white whale." See *Dublin University Magazine* 39 (February 1852), in *Herman Melville: The Contemporary Reviews*, ed. Brian Higgins and Hershel Parker (New York: Cambridge University Press, 1995), 415.

Chapter 2

1. This chapter is derived in part from an article published in *Textual Practice*, 19 August 2021, copyright Taylor and Francis, available online. https://doi.org/10.1080/0950236X.2021.1968179.

2. Herman Melville, *Moby-Dick or The Whale*, ed. Harrison Hayford, Hershel Parker, and G. Thomas Tanselle (Evanston, IL: Northwestern University Press; Chicago: Newberry Library, 1988), 470. Future references will be made in parenthetical citations.

3. On the "material differences of absences," see Sarah Jain, "The Prosthetic Imagination: Enabling and Disabling the Prosthesis Trope," *Science, Technology, & Human Values* 24:1 (1999), 40.

4. My examples are taken from Homer, *The Odyssey*, trans. Robert Fagles (New York: Penguin, 1996), Book 7, lines 289–311.

5. Cathy Caruth, *Unclaimed Experience: Trauma, Narrative, and History* (Baltimore: Johns Hopkins University Press, 1996), 4.

6. Robert D. Stolorow, *Trauma and Human Existence: Autobiographical, Psychoanalytic, and Philosophical Reflections*, e-book ed. (New York: Analytic Press, 2007), chap. 4, 19–20. Dereck Daschke makes a similar point in arguing that "trauma unsettles the assumed building blocks of meaning in the universe," disrupting "the storyline that makes up the narrative called 'past, present, and future.'" Dereck Daschke, "Apocalypse and Trauma," in *The Oxford Handbook of Apocalyptic Literature*, ed. John J. Collins (New York: Oxford University Press, 2014), 459.

7. David Wills, *Prosthesis* (Stanford: Stanford University Press, 1995), 12.

8. With its numerous qualifiers, some might read Ishmael's description as evidence of the carpenter's being neurodivergent. Ishmael senses that the carpenter has an unusual—and keen—intelligence, but he struggles to name and identify how it works. See Pilar Martínez Benedí and Ralph James Savarese, *Herman Melville & Neurodiversity, or Why Hunt Difference with Harpoons? A Primitivist Phenomenology* (New York: Bloomsbury, 2024), chap. 2 n. 22 for this interpretation.

9. On Ahab as a machine-man who seeks to be remade as technology, see Ronald Takaki, *Iron Cages: Race and Culture in 19th-Century America*, rev. ed. (1990; New York: Oxford University Press, 2000), 282–87.

10. See *Hamlet*, V.i.194–203 in William Shakespeare, *The Complete Works*, ed. Alfred Harbage (New York: Viking, 1969).

11. See Jennifer Van Horn, *The Power of Objects in Eighteenth-Century British America* (Chapel Hill: University of North Carolina Press, 2017), 342–65, especially 360–63.

12. In reference to the so-called Ugly Laws that began to appear after the Civil War, see Susan Schweik's *The Ugly Laws: Disability in Public* (New York: New York University Press, 2009). On the law's connection to Melville, see Yoshiaki Furui, "'Secret Emotions': Disability in Public and Melville's *The Confidence-Man*," *Leviathan* 15:2 (2013), 54–68.

13. Steven Mihm, "'A Limb Which Shall Be Presentable in Polite Society': Prosthetic Technologies in the Nineteenth Century," in *Artificial Parts, Practical Lives: Modern Histories of Prosthetics*, ed. Katherine Ott, David Serlin, and Stephen Mihm (New York: New York University Press, 2002), 288–89.

14. B. F. Palmer, A. S. Currier, and E. D. Hudson, *Palmer's Patent Leg Reporter, and Surgical Adjuvant* (Springfield, MA: G.W. Wilson, 1849), 13. Collection of the American Antiquarian Society. For background on the Palmer leg, see Katherine Ott, "Carnage Remembered: Prosthetics in the U.S. Military since the 1860s," in *Materializing the Military* (London: Science Museum, 2005), 52. For background on the Anglesey leg and its popularity in England, see Vanessa Warne, "Artificial Leg," *Victorian Review* 34:1 (2008), 29–31.

15. Douglas Bly, *A New and Important Invention* (Rochester, NY: Press of Curtis, Butts & Co., 1862). Collection of the American Antiquarian Society.

16. In a highly influential analysis, for example, Sharon Cameron memorably addressed this scene in *The Corporeal Self: Allegories of the Body in Melville and Hawthorne* (Baltimore: Johns Hopkins University Press, 1981). Focusing on Ahab's ambivalent desire to be as bodiless as air and yet take on a palpable form, Cameron analyzes the conversation as being rooted in philosophical questions about corporeality and identity, rather than the immediate subjects of amputation, prostheses, and phantom limbs. The analysis ultimately universalizes Ahab's

216   NOTES TO PAGES 68–71

experience and, in the process, obscures the material process, repeatedly claiming that the carpenter works with wood rather than bone (61–63).

17. Leslie Katz, "Flesh of His Flesh: Amputation in *Moby Dick* and S.W. Mitchell's Medical Papers," *Genders* 4:1 (1989), 4.

18. Michael D. Snediker, "Phenomenology beyond the Phantom Limb: Melvillean Figuration and Chronic Pain," in *Melville's Philosophies*, ed. Branka Arsić and K. L. Evans (New York: Bloomsbury, 2017), 156.

19. Pilar Martínez Benedí and Ralph James Savarese, "Neurological Crossings: Ahab, Pip, and Mirror-Touch Synesthesia," in *Ahab Unbound: Melville and the Materialist Turn*, ed. Meredith Farmer and Jonathan D. S. Schroeder (Minneapolis: University of Minnesota Press, 2022), 127–43. Martínez Benedí and Savarese offer an extended discussion of this phenomenon in *Herman Melville and Neurodiversity*, 65–87, especially 71–76.

20. Cassandra Crawford, *Phantom Limb: Amputation, Embodiment, and Prosthetic Technology* (New York: New York University Press, 2014), 52.

21. Herman Melville, *Mardi and a Voyage Thither*, ed. Harrison Hayford, Hershel Parker, and G. Thomas Tanselle (Evanston, IL: Northwestern University Press; Chicago: Newberry Library, 1998), 456.

22. The carpenter may be an unusually promising source for the acquisitive, ever-expanding sensation that Ahab describes, for unlike Dr. Bunger, he actually makes his captain's prosthesis.

23. Malcolm MacLachlan, *Embodiment: Clinical, Critical, and Cultural Perspectives on Health and Illness* (Berkshire, England: Open University Press, 2004), 111.

24. James Fenimore Cooper, *The Pioneers*, in *The Leatherstocking Tales I; The Pioneers, The Last of the Mohicans, The Prairie* (New York: Library of America, 1985), 73.

25. Herman Melville to Nathaniel Hawthorne, [1 June?] 1851, in *Correspondence*, ed. Lynn Horth (Evanston, IL: Northwestern University Press; Chicago: Newberry Library, 1993), 107. When Melville writes, "It seems an inconsistency to assert unconditional democracy in all things, and yet confess a dislike to all mankind—in the mass," his phrasing sounds very much like Ishmael's introduction of the carpenter in Chapter 107. Hershel Parker has questioned the dating of this letter and suggests that it was written in early May. See Hershel Parker, *Herman Melville: A Biography*, vol. 1, *1819–1851* (Baltimore: Johns Hopkins University Press, 1996), 841. Keeping with the editors of *The Writings of Herman Melville*, I will continue to cite the letter with its questioned date. My thanks to Jennifer Greiman for pointing out this discrepancy in *Melville's Democracy: Radical Figuration and Political Form* (Stanford: Stanford University Press, 2023), 293 n. 1.

26. Nathaniel Hawthorne, "Ethan Brand," in *Tales and Sketches* (New York: Library of America, 1982), 1058. Melville mentioned "Ethan Brand" to Hawthorne in the [1 June?] 1851 letter after the story appeared in *Dollar* magazine as "The Unpardonable Sin."

27. Guy R. Hasegawa, *Mending Broken Soldiers: The Union and Confederate Programs to Supply Artificial Limbs* (Carbondale: Southern Illinois University Press, 2012), xi.

28. See Silas Weir Mitchell, "The Case of George Dedlow," *Atlantic Monthly*, July 1866, online, accessed 27 October 2017.

29. S. Weir Mitchell, "Phantom Limbs," *Lippincott's Magazine of Popular Literature and Science* 8 (July 1871), 565–66.

30. V. S. Ramachandran and Sandra Blakeslee, *Phantoms in the Brain: Probing the Mysteries of the Human Mind* (New York: William Morrow, 1998), 23–28 and V. S. Ramachandran, *The Tell-Tale Brain: A Neuroscientist's Quest for What Makes Us Human* (New York: Norton, 2011), 26–28.

31. MacLachlan, *Embodiment*, 121. While early researchers saw the persistence of phantom limb pain as evidence of psychological denial, Ahab's situation more resembles what George Kolb suggested in the 1950s. As Crawford describes it, the syndrome reflected "the unconscious, primitively motivated persistence of the complete body scheme" (131).

32. Melville, *Mardi*, 78.

33. George Wilkins Kendall, *Narrative of the Texan Santa Fé Expedition*, as quoted in Christopher Taylor, "The Limbs of Empire: Ahab, Santa Anna, and *Moby-Dick*," *American Literature* 83:1 (2011), 33.

34. Across a diverse range of studies, in fact, researchers have found that the ability to visualize and commemorate the severed limb will often give the cortex an opportunity to adjust its body map and, in the process, ease phantom limb pain. See Ramachandran and Blakeslee, *Phantoms*

NOTES TO PAGES 71–80   217

in the Brain, 39–58. See also Monica L. Tung et al., "Observation of Limb Movements Reduces Phantom Limb Pain in Bilateral Amputees," *Annals of Clinical and Translational Neurology* 1:9 (2014), 633–38 and Katja Guenther, "'It's All Done with Mirrors': V.S. Ramachandran and the Material Culture of Phantom Limb Research," *Medical History* 60:3 (2016), 342–58.

35. Melville, *Mardi*, 78.
36. Ibid.
37. Mitchell, "Case of George Dedlow."
38. On Nelson's diagnosis, see William Gooddy, "Admiral Lord Nelson's Neurological Illnesses," *Proceedings of the Royal Society of Medicine* 63:3 (1970), 302.
39. Ramachandran and Blakeslee, *Phantoms in the Brain*, 22–23.
40. Oliver Sacks, *The Man Who Mistook His Wife for a Hat and Other Clinical Tales* (New York: Touchstone, 1993), 67.
41. Mitchell, "Phantom Limbs," 567.
42. Crawford, *Phantom Limb*, 197.
43. Herman Melville, *The Confidence-Man: His Masquerade*, ed. Harrison Hayford, Hershel Parker, and G. Thomas Tanselle (Evanston, IL: Northwestern University Press; Chicago: Newberry Library, 1984), 10, 14.
44. Ibid., 15.
45. The phrase comes from *The Confidence-Man*, 12.
46. Herman Melville, *Typee: A Peep at Polynesian Life*, ed. Harrison Hayford, Hershel Parker, and G. Thomas Tanselle (Evanston, IL: Northwestern University Press; Chicago: Newberry Library, 1968), 118.
47. See Harriet Hustis for an account of this scene in respect to monadic and dyadic bodies and narratives. "'Universal Mixing' and Interpenetrating Standing: Disability and Community in Melville's *Moby-Dick*," *Nineteenth-Century Literature* 69:1 (2014), 48.
48. John Bryant, *Melville and Repose: The Rhetoric of Humor in the American Renaissance* (New York: Oxford University Press, 1993), 223.
49. On the popular perception of surgeons as "bloody carpenters," see Keren Rosa Hammerschlag, "The Gentleman Artist-Surgeon in Late Victorian Group Portraiture," *Visual Culture in Britain* 14:2 (2013), 154–78.
50. Dickens edited *Household Words* from 1850 to 1859. Percival Leigh, "Some Account of Chloroform," *Household Words* 3:59 (1851), 152. *Dickens Journals*, online, accessed 21 April 2020.
51. Thomas Nickerson and Owen Chase, *The Loss of the Ship Essex, Sunk by a Whale* (New York: Penguin, 2000); see also David Dowling, *Surviving the Essex: The Afterlife of America's Most Storied Shipwreck* (Lebanon, NH: University Press of New England, 2016) and Nathaniel Philbrick, *In the Heart of the Sea: The Tragedy of the Whaleship Essex* (New York: Penguin, 2000).
52. On determinism, see David T. Mitchell and Sharon L. Snyder, *Narrative Prosthesis: Disability and the Dependencies of Discourse* (Ann Arbor: University of Michigan Press, 2000), 121.
53. Hustis, "Universal Mixing," 29–30.
54. Sari Altschuler, "'Ain't One Limb Enough?' Historicizing Disability in the American Novel," *American Literature* 86:2 (2014), 267.
55. Samuel Otter, *Melville's Anatomies* (Berkeley: University of California Press, 1999), 118. Otter's phrase echoes Michel Foucault's discussion of the medical gaze in *The Birth of the Clinic: An Archaeology of Medical Perception*, trans. A. M. Sheridan, Adobe eReader format (New York: Routledge, 1973), 107–23, especially 121.
56. On the medicalizable object, see the selection from *Power/Knowledge* in Michel Foucault, "The Politics of Health in the Eighteenth Century," in *The Foucault Reader*, ed. Paul Rabinow (New York: Pantheon, 1984), 282.
57. On bleeding as a treatment for hypertension, see L. A. Parapia, "History of Bloodletting by Phlebotomy," *British Journal of Haematology* 143:4 (2008), 490–95.
58. Lennard Davis, "Constructing Normalcy: The Bell Curve, the Novel, and the Invention of the Disabled Body in the Nineteenth Century," in *The Disability Studies Reader*, 2nd ed., ed. Lennard J. Davis (New York: Routledge, 2006), 5.
59. Jonathan D. S. Schroeder, "The Whiteness of the Will: Ahab and the Matter of Monomania," in *Ahab Unbound: Melville and the Materialist Turn*, ed. Meredith Farmer and Jonathan D. S. Schroeder (Minneapolis: University of Minnesota Press, 2022), 281–84. As Schroeder

218 NOTES TO PAGES 80–89

explains, the originator of the diagnosis, Jean-Étienne-Dominique Esquirol, chose a name "that pointed to the power of any passion—positive as well as negative—to engender a compulsive fixation on an object" (282). Melville's use of the term throughout his career—including in *Mardi, Redburn, Clarel,* and *Billy Budd*—was not restricted to characters who exhibited criminal or anti-social tendencies.

60. Herman Melville, *Clarel: A Poem and Pilgrimage in the Holy Land*, ed. Harrison Hayford, Alma MacDougall, Hershel Parker, and G. Thomas Tanselle (Evanston, IL: Northwestern University Press; Chicago: Newberry Library, 1991), 2.19.60–65.

61. Peter Boxall, *The Value of the Novel* (Cambridge: Cambridge University Press, 2015), 88.

62. W. H. Auden, *The Enchafèd Flood or The Romantic Iconography of the Sea* (London: Faber and Faber, 1951), 97–98.

63. Arthur Frank, *The Wounded Storyteller* (Chicago: University of Chicago Press, 1998), 6.

64. See the introduction for a discussion of the word "prosthesis."

65. John Kerrigan, *Revenge Tragedy: Aeschylus to Armageddon* (New York: Oxford University Press, 1996), 10–11.

66. Ibid., 17.

67. Susan McWilliams, "Ahab, American," *Review of Politics* 74:2 (2012), 257.

68. Alexis de Tocqueville, *Democracy in America*, ed. J. P. Mayer, trans. George Lawrence (New York: Anchor, 1969), 508.

69. McWilliams, "Ahab, American," 258.

Chapter 3

1. Herman Melville, *Moby-Dick or The Whale*, ed. Harrison Hayford, Hershel Parker, and G. Thomas Tanselle (Evanston, IL: Northwestern University Press; Chicago: Newberry Library, 1988), 442. Future references will be made in parenthetical citations.

2. Ishmael initially wonders about the figures in the dawn light, concluding that they couldn't be shadows in that kind of dark (98). In "The First Lowering," however, he refers to them as "mysterious shadows" (220).

3. The phrase "hair-turbaned" is confusing and can lead readers to assume Ishmael refers to a simple turban (231). My understanding is that Fedallah has long white hair that he has braided and "coiled" around his head, an arrangement that makes him appear to be wearing a "glistening white plaited turban" against his skin (217). Melville refers to "turbans" throughout his work, but I am not aware of other references to a hair-turban.

4. See the notes on Fedallah in Herman Melville, *Moby-Dick or, The Whale*, ed. Luther S. Mansfield and Howard P. Vincent (New York: Hendricks House, 1962), 729.

5. "Avenging angel," Edward F. Edinger, *Melville's Moby-Dick: A Jungian Commentary "An American Nekyia"* (New York: New Directions, 1975), 97–102; "bad angel," W. E. Sedgwick, *Herman Melville: The Tragedy of Mind* (Cambridge: Harvard University Press, 1944), 113; "diabolic infidel mystic," Dorothee Metkitsky Finkelstein, *Melville's Orienda* (New Haven: Yale University Press, 1961), 238; "shady genie," Timothy Marr, *The Cultural Roots of American Islamicism* (New York: Cambridge University Press, 1996), 230; "gothic symbol," Robert Milder, *Exiled Royalties: Melville and the Life We Imagine* (New York: Oxford University Press, 2006), 84; "duplication of self," Sharon Cameron, *The Corporeal Self: Allegories of the Body in Melville and Hawthorne* (Baltimore: Johns Hopkins University Press, 1981), 54; "spectre of barbarism," C. L. R. James, *Mariners, Renegades, and Castaways: The Story of Herman Melville and the World We Live In*, ed. Donald E. Pease (Hanover, NH: University Press of New England, 2001), 56; "a hateful figure," Rashā al Disūqī, "Orientalism in *Moby-Dick*," *American Journal of Islamic Social Sciences* 4:1 (1987), 123; "turban wearing handler," Nathaniel Philbrick, *In the Heart of the Sea: The Tragedy of the Whaleship Essex* (New York: Penguin, 2000), 35–36.

6. In an interview with the *Paris Review* in 2010, Ray Bradbury explained his decision to change the ending of *Moby-Dick*: "To adapt for the screen you've got to decide what to throw overboard. I didn't want Fedallah, the mysterious Parsi harpooner, because he's a terrible bore and he'd turn the whole thing into comedy. He's the extra mystical symbol that breaks the whale's back. If you're not careful in tragedy, one extra rape, one extra incest, one extra murder and it's hoo-haw time all of a sudden. So I got rid of Fedallah, and that leaves us at the end with no one to go down with the whale. So, hell, it's only natural that Moby Dick takes Ahab down with him and comes back up with all these harpoon lines, and Ahab gestures, so when the men

NOTES TO PAGES 89–93 219

follow him they are destroyed. Well, that's not in the book. I'm sorry, but I'm proud of that. Awfully proud of that." With many thanks to Ralph James Savarese for sharing this information with me. See "Ray Bradbury, The Art of Fiction No. 203," *Paris Review*, 52:192 (2010), online, accessed 15 December 2023.

7. On Huston, see John Bryant, "Rewriting *Moby-Dick*: Politics, Textual Identity, and the Revision Narrative," *PMLA* 125:4 (2010), 1046. See Franco Moretti, *Modern Epic: The World System from Goethe to García Márquez*, trans. Quintin Hoare (London: Verso, 1996), 33. My thanks to Amirhossein Vafa, who first discussed this dismissal in *Recasting American and Persian Literatures: Local Histories and Formative Geographies from Moby-Dick" to "Missing Soluch"* (New York: Palgrave Macmillan, 2016), 44.

8. David Wills, *Prosthesis* (Stanford: Stanford University Press, 1995), 133.

9. Sigmund Freud, *Civilization and Its Discontents*, ed. and trans. James Strachey (1930; New York: Norton, 2005), 76.

10. See Wills's discussion of this point in *Prosthesis*, 101–3.

11. Erich H. Fromm, *Escape from Freedom* (1941; New York: Henry Holt, 1994), 168.

12. Ibid., 168–69.

13. I borrow this phrase from Elisa Camiscioli's enlightening book *Reproducing the French Rage: Immigration, Intimacy, and Embodiment in the Early Twentieth Century* (Durham: Duke University Press, 2009), 75.

14. See Cyrus R. K. Patell, "Cosmopolitanism and Zoroastrianism in *Moby-Dick*," in *The Turn around Religion in America: Literature, Culture, and the Work of Sacvan Bercovitch*, ed. Nan Goodman and Michael Kramer (Burlington, VT: Ashgate, 2011), 31.

15. According to the view of one nineteenth-century Orientalist (Andrew Crichton in his 1843 book *History of Arabia*), Muslims perceived whiteness as a sign of "Satanic influence." See *Moby-Dick*, ed. Mansfield and Vincent, 733.

16. Wai Chee Dimock, "Hemispheric Islam: Continents and Centuries for American Literature," *American Literary History* 12:1 (2009), 47–48.

17. Rosemarie Garland Thomson, *Extraordinary Bodies: Figuring Physical Disability in American Culture and Literature* (New York: Columbia University Press, 1998), 44–45.

18. George Shulman, "Chasing the Whale: *Moby-Dick* as Political Theory," in *A Political Companion to Herman Melville*, ed Jason Frank (University Press of Kentucky, 2013), 87–88.

19. Benjamin Franklin, *The Autobiography of Benjamin Franklin*, ed. Edmund S. Morgan (New Haven: Yale University Press, 2003), 176.

20. Denise A. Spellberg, *Thomas Jefferson's Qur'an: Islam and the Founders* (New York: Vintage, 2013), 119.

21. See Paul Baepler, ed., *White Slaves, African Masters: An Anthology of American Barbary Captivity Narratives* (Chicago: University of Chicago Press, 1999).

22. Herman Melville, *Redburn: His First Voyage*, ed. Harrison Hayford, Hershel Parker, and G. Thomas Tanselle (Evanston, IL: Northwestern University Press; Chicago: Newberry Library, 1969), 5–6. Hilton Obenzinger identifies the traveler as most likely being John Lloyd Stevens, the author of *Egypt, Arabia Petrea, and the Holy Land* (1837). See Hilton Obenzinger, *American Palestine: Melville, Twain, and the Holy Land Mania* (Princeton: Princeton University Press, 1999), 63. For more on Stevens's presence in *Redburn*, see Bruce A. Harvey, *American Geographics: U.S. National Narratives and the Representation of the Non-European World, 1830–1865* (Palo Alto: Stanford University Press, 2001), 105, 128.

23. Finkelstein, *Melville's Orienda*, 34–36.

24. "Irving's Mahomet," *The Literary World: A Journal of Science, Literature, and the Arts*, vol. 5, 22 and 29 December 1849 (New York: Osgood & Co., 1849), 537–39, 560–61. "It is hardly possible," one reviewer wrote of the second volume, "to imagine a more stirring narrative." See "Lives of the Successors of Mahomet," *The Literary Gazette: A Weekly Journal of Belles Lettres, Arts, Sciences, &c*, no. 1734, 13 April 1850, 258. Google Books. American newspapers occasionally misspelled the title of Irving's work. The authoritative edition is Washington Irving, *Mahomet and His Successors*, ed. Henry A. Pochmann and E. N. Feltskog (Madison: University of Wisconsin Press, 1970).

25. Finkelstein, *Melville's Orienda*, 21, 52.

26. Herman Melville, *Journals*, ed. Howard C. Horsford and Lynn Horth (Evanston, IL: Northwestern University Press; Chicago: Newberry Library, 1989), 39. The book was most likely seized not because of its content but because it was a French edition of an English book.

220 NOTES TO PAGES 93–97

27. Melville, *Journals*, 144.
28. Herman Melville to R. H. Dana Jr., 1 May 1850, in *Correspondence*, ed. Lynn Horth (Evanston, IL: Northwestern University Press; Chicago: Newberry Library, 1993), 162.
29. For details of the event (including *The Berber*'s popularity), see Hershel Parker, *Herman Melville: A Biography*, vol. 1, *1819–1851* (Baltimore: Johns Hopkins University Press, 1996), 761–63; Marr, *American Islamicism*, 219; and Cornelius Matthews, "Several Days in Berkshire," in *Melville in His Own Time*, ed. Steven Olsen Smith (Iowa City: University of Iowa Press, 2015), 50–51. Melville's relationship with Mrs. Sarah Morewood has received a lot of commentary and speculation. See Michael Paul Rogin, *Subversive Genealogy: The Politics and Art of Herman Melville* (Berkeley: University of California Press, 1985), 183–86. Michael Shelden makes the entertaining (but unproven) conclusion that Melville and Morewood had a lengthy affair in *Melville in Love: The Secret Life of Herman Melville and the Muse of Moby-Dick* (New York: Ecco Press, 2017).
30. Ali Behad, "The Eroticised Orient: Images of the Harem in Montesquieu and His Precursors," *Stanford French Review* 13:2–3 (1989), 110.
31. Melville, *Journals*, 67. As Melville recorded in his brief journal entry: "Ladies pale, straight noses, regular features, fine busts. Look like nuns in their plaine dress, but with a roundness of bust not belonging to that character."
32. Edward Said, "Introduction to *Moby-Dick*," *Reflections on Exile and Other Essays* (Cambridge: Harvard University Press, 2000), 370.
33. In *White-Jacket*, the narrator praises a fellow sailor's poetry as possessing "a true Mohammedan sensualism," and in *Pierre* we learn that the main character is like Muhammad in being "very partial to all pleasant essences," or scents. Herman Melville, *White-Jacket or The World in a Man-of-War*, ed. Harrison Hayford, Hershel Parker, and G. Thomas Tanselle (Evanston, IL: Northwestern University Press; Chicago: Newberry Library, 1970), 383 and Herman Melville, *Pierre or The Ambiguities*, ed. Harrison Hayford, Hershel Parker, and G. Thomas Tanselle (Evanston, IL: Northwestern University Press; Chicago: Newberry Library, 1971), 94.
34. Melville, *Redburn*: "Moorish looking," 228; "Persian carpeting," "a bower," "oriental ottomans," 230; "whole place," 233.
35. See Sophia Rose Arjana, *Muslims in the Western Imagination* (New York: Oxford University Press, 2015), 138.
36. Ibid., 136.
37. Herman Melville, *Clarel: A Poem and Pilgrimage in the Holy Land*, ed. Harrison Hayford, Alma MacDougall, Hershel Parker, and G. Thomas Tanselle (Evanston, IL: Northwestern University Press; Chicago: Newberry Library, 1991), 2.27.44–48.
38. Malini Johar Schueller, *U.S. Orientalisms: Race, Nation, and Gender in Literature, 1790–1890* (Ann Arbor: University of Michigan Press, 1998), 136.
39. Dimock, "Hemispheric Islam," 41. See also Doyle Quiggle, "A Knickerbocker Prophet: Washington Irving's Americanization of '*Mahomet*,'" in *Washington Irving and Islam: Critical Essays*, ed. Zubeda Jalalzai (Lanham, MD: Lexington Books, 2018), 37–40.
40. Spellberg, *Jefferson's Qur'an*, 26–33.
41. Herman Melville, *Israel Potter: His Fifty Years of Exile*, ed. Harrison Hayford, Hershel Parker, and G. Thomas Tanselle (Evanston, IL: Northwestern University Press; Chicago: Newberry Library, 1982), 144.
42. Spellberg, *Jefferson's Qur'an*, 202.
43. Marr, *American Islamicism*, 186.
44. Ibid., 4.
45. Said quoted in ibid.
46. Herman Melville, *Mardi and a Voyage Thither*, ed. Harrison Hayford, Hershel Parker, and G. Thomas Tanselle (Evanston, IL: Northwestern University Press; Chicago: Newberry Library, 1998), 554.
47. Melville, *Journals*, 61.
48. Melville, *Clarel*, 1.16.94 and 1.31.66–80.
49. Melville, *Clarel*, 4.10.65–70. On the journal entry, see Melville, *Journals*, 84.
50. *Clarel* exemplifies this in the story of Nathan, the American Christian who falls in love with a Jewish woman, converts to Judaism, and then takes his family to Palestine to claim the land for Jews. See *Clarel*, 1.17.200–311. On Christian missionaries in the Middle East, see Melville, *Journals*, 81.

NOTES TO PAGES 97–104   221

51. The call to prayer is usually translated as "Prayer is better than sleep." Melville's departure may have come from his desire to follow the strict iambic tetrameter of the line, though the possibilities of "more" are intriguing. See Melville, *Clarel*, 1.18.75–77. "Did the Black Jew keep / The saying—*Prayer is more than sleep?* / Islam says that."

52. Melville echoed a central principle of Islam that Washington Irving's biography reinforced: Muhammad identified Islam "not as a new religion, but a purification of the message given to the Jews and Christians." See Zubeda Jalalzai, "An Introduction: Washington Irving and Islam," in *Washington Irving and Islam: Critical Essays*, ed. Zubeda Jalalzai (Lanham, MD: Lexington Books, 2018), xvi and xxii n. 29.

53. Melville, *Clarel*, 2.27.74–75.

54. Melville, *Clarel*, 3.16.115, 123.

55. Thomas Carlyle, "The Hero as Prophet. Mahomet: Islam," in *On Heroes and Hero-Worship, and the Heroic in History*, ed. John Chester Adams (New York: Houghton-Mifflin, 1907), 105.

56. David T. Mitchell and Sharon L. Snyder, *Narrative Prosthesis: Disability and the Dependencies of Discourse* (Ann Arbor: University of Michigan Press, 2000), 49.

57. Melville, *Clarel*, 1.4.12.

58. Herman Melville to Sophia Peabody Hawthorne, 8 January 1852, in *Correspondence*, 218–19.

59. Genghis Khan was not a Muslim and, in fact, viciously fought Muslim tribes. By 1290, however, his grandson had converted and built upon the Muslim faith of local tribes in spreading it to parts of India and China.

60. Aristotle, *The Poetics of Aristotle*, trans. S. H. Butcher (London: Macmillan, 1895), 43. Internet Archive.

61. On the complexity of Melville's vision of democracy and aristocracy, see Robert Milder, *Exiled Royalties: Melville and the Life We Imagine* (New York: Oxford University Press, 2006), 61–64.

62. Marr, *American Islamicism*, 227.

63. Arjana, *Muslims in the Western Imagination*, 69.

64. On the religious effects of the Greek War for Independence, see Cemil Aydin, *The Idea of the Muslim World: A Global Intellectual History* (Cambridge: Harvard University Press, 2017), 51–52. Timothy Marr comments that the image of the Turk as a ruthless power started to erode at the end of the Greco-Turkish war and gave rise to a softer, romanticized vision of seraglios and indolence. See Marr, *American Islamicism*, 12–13.

65. Daniel Webster, "The Revolution in Greece," 19 January 1824, in *The Great Speeches and Orations of Daniel Webster*, ed. Edwin Percy Whipple (Boston: Little, Brown, 1886), 68.

66. Carl W. Ernst, *Following Muhammad: Rethinking Islam in the Contemporary World* (Chapel Hill: University of North Carolina Press, 2003), 19.

67. Melville, *Journals*, 87–88.

68. Melville, *White-Jacket*: "doff their hats," 162; "Turkish code," 285; "judicial severity," 297; "Articles of War," 301. The spelling is the original.

69. Melville, *Redburn*, 293. Redburn's comments are echoed in *Moby-Dick* when Ahab rejoices in the "Turkish cheeks" of his pagan harpooners while leading them to their deaths (164).

70. Jonathan Schroeder notes similar rhetoric in the work of American abolitionists who often compared slavery to Asian despotism. See Jonathan D. S. Schroeder, "The Whiteness of the Will: Ahab and the Matter of Monomania," in *Ahab Unbound: Melville and the Materialist Turn*, ed. Meredith Farmer and Jonathan D. S. Schroeder (Minneapolis: University of Minnesota Press, 2022), 298 n. 24.

71. "Characteristics of the Mussulman," *The Knickerbocker, or New-York Monthly Magazine*, vol. 7, January 1836 (New York: Clark and Edson Proprietors, 1836), 81. Google Books.

72. Pierre Bayle, *Mr. Bayle's Historical and Critical Dictionary*, 2nd ed., vol. 5 (London: James Bettenham Printer, 1738), 631–32.

73. Bryant, "Rewriting *Moby-Dick*," 1047.

74. Ronald Takaki comments that "the significance of Asia in the irrational and demonic hunt for the great white whale may be seen not only in the location of the *Pequod* in the 'Japanese sea' but also in the relationship between Ahab and Fedallah. An Asian, Fedallah stands in Ahab's shadow as if he were the captain's extension." See Ronald Takaki, *Iron Cages: Race and Culture in 19th-Century America*, rev. ed. (1990; New York: Oxford University Press, 2000), 288.

75. Marr, *American Islamicism*, 230–31; Spencer Tricker, "'Five Dusky Phantoms': Gothic Form and Cosmopolitan Shipwreck in Melville's *Moby-Dick*," *Studies in American Fiction* 44:1 (2017), 2.

222 NOTES TO PAGES 104–111

76. Arjana, *Muslims in the Western Imagination*, 117–20.
77. William Beckford, *Vathek*, ed. Roger Lonsdale (New York: Oxford University Press, 1983), 22, 88, 111.
78. See Finkelstein, *Melville's Orienda*, 223–39, especially 227 and 235.
79. Melville, *Journals*, 144.
80. Ibid., 46–47.
81. Eleanor Melville Metcalf, ed., *Journal of a Visit to London and the Continent by Herman Melville, 1849–1850* (Cambridge: Harvard University Press, 1948), 166. Metcalf also comments on the possibility that *Anastasius* influenced the Ramadan chapter in *Moby-Dick*. See Metcalf, 143.
82. Thomas De Quincey, *Confessions of an English Opium Eater and Other Writings*, ed. Barry Milligan (New York: Penguin, 2003), 63.
83. Ibid., 63.
84. Ibid., 80–81.
85. Ibid., 81.
86. Ibid., 82. Chapter 5 will discuss the Malay pirates who chase the *Pequod* through the Sunda Strait.
87. Philip Armstrong encourages readers to consider the "networked form of agency that occurs at the climax of *Moby-Dick*" in which Ahab imagines "his relation to the crew in mechanical terms." I submit that a critical part of that networked agency is Fedallah. See Armstrong, *What Animals Mean in the Fiction of Modernity* (London: Routledge, 2008), 124.
88. "Thou must still appear to me, to pilot me still?" he beseeches the Parsee. "Well, then, did I believe all ye say, oh my pilot!" (499).
89. Tricker, "Five Dusky Phantoms," 19. There is some confusion over the image of rope in *Moby-Dick*. In "The Line," Melville says that the "Manilla rope has in the American fishery almost entirely superseded hemp as a material for whale-lines," and yet Ahab dies by hemp (278).
90. I Kings 22:19–23.
91. Peter Szendy, *Prophecies of Leviathan: Reading Past Melville*, trans. Gil Andijar (New York: Fordham University Press, 2010), 82.
92. *Othello*, V.2.349–55 in William Shakespeare, *The Complete Works*, ed. Alfred Harbage (New York: Viking, 1969).
93. "Either our history shall with full mouth / Speak freely of our acts, or else our grave, / Like Turkish mute, shall have a tongueless mouth, / Not worshipp'd with a waxen epitaph." See *Henry the Fifth*, I.2.31–34 in Shakespeare, *The Complete Works*.
94. M. Miles, "Signing in the Seraglio: Mutes, Dwarfs and Jestures at the Ottoman Court 1500–1700," *Disability & Society* 15:1 (2000), 118–19. Miles points out that Ottoman rulers enjoyed the novelty of having mutes in their courts, and that these men developed pioneering systems of sign language that taught visiting rulers and diplomats "some of the merits of signed communication" (129).
95. Beckford, *Vathek*, 35.
96. Uriel Heyd, *Studies in Old Ottoman Criminal Law*, ed. V. L. Ménage (Oxford: Clarendon Press, 1973), 262–63, 263n.
97. Finkelstein, *Melville's Orienda*, 229.
98. Ibid., 230.
99. Ibid., 234.
100. See ibid., 230–34. Commentators who follow Finkelstein's translation include Marr, *American Islamicism*, 230, and Bryant, "Rewriting *Moby-Dick*," 1047–48. The Orientalist association of hashish and the Ismaili assassins is extensive. See, for example, Chevalier Joseph Von Hammer's comment (among extensive etymological arguments): "A youth, who was deemed worthy, by his strength and resolution, to be initiated into the Assassin service, was invited to the table and conversation of the grand-master, or grand-prior: he was then intoxicated with henbane (hashish), and carried into the garden, which, on awakening, he believed to be Paradise: every thing around him, the houris in particular, contributed to confirm his delusion." Chevalier Joseph Von Hammer, *The History of the Assassins*, trans. Oswald Charles Wood (London: Smith and Elder, Cornhill, 1935), 137.
101. See Mansfield and Vincent, *Moby-Dick*, 733.
102. Some scholars dismiss Finkelstein, who survived the Holocaust as a girl and was a prominent Zionist in her twenties, as an unfortunate forebear in discussions about Melville's fascination

NOTES TO PAGES 112–119   223

with Islam. They charge her with fostering an image of Fedallah as a drug-taking, devil-worshiping terrorist that perpetuates anti-Muslim prejudice. One proponent of this interpretation concludes that Melville uses the name ironically. See Mukhtar Ali Isani, "The Naming of Fedallah in *Moby-Dick*," *American Literature* 40:3 (1968), 382–83. Jean-Francois Leroux objects to Finkelstein's participating in the "widespread cultural identification of Ahab with some despotic, irrational East." See Jean-Francois Leroux, "Wars for Oil: *Moby-Dick*, Orientalism, and Cold-War Criticism," *Canadian Review of American Studies* 39:4 (2009), 431. Vafa charges Finkelstein with being "by far the most cynical among her contemporaries" (78 n. 10).

103. On the whale's agency as a corrective to anthropocentric and non-materialist readings of Ahab's will, see Meredith Farmer, "Rethinking Ahab: Melville and the Materialist Turn," in *Ahab Unbound: Melville and the Materialist Turn*, ed. Meredith Farmer and Jonathan D. S. Schroeder (Minneapolis: University of Minnesota Press, 2022), 11.

104. Fedallah appears in just 16 of *Moby-Dick*'s 136 chapters, but ten of those appearances occur in the last 23 chapters, including each of the last 6.

105. Fromm, *Escape from Freedom*, 169–70.

106. Ibid., 168.

107. Ibid., 169.

Chapter 4

1. Herman Melville, *Moby-Dick or The Whale*, ed. Harrison Hayford, Hershel Parker, and G. Thomas Tanselle (Evanston, IL: Northwestern University Press; Chicago: Newberry Library, 1988), 201. Future references will be made in parenthetical citations.

2. Samuel Otter, "Reading *Moby-Dick*," in *The New Cambridge Companion to Herman Melville*, ed. Robert S. Levine (New York: Cambridge University Press, 2014), 73.

3. The editors of the Northwestern-Newberry edition of *Moby-Dick* felt so confident in the change that they cite it as an example of an "easily settled" correction. As G. Gordon Tanselle explains, the editorial assumption is that Melville originally (and mistakenly) had written "Yes" ("Note on the Text," *Moby-Dick*, 793). Otter highlights another editorial change in "The Chart" in the language of possibilities and probabilities in the same passage. See Otter, "Reading *Moby-Dick*," 75–77. On network theory and its relation to "The Chart," see T. Hugh Crawford, "Networking the (Non) Human: Moby-Dick, Matthew Fontaine Maury and Bruno Latour," *Configurations* 5:1 (1997), 14–16.

4. Some might argue that the mistaken "Yes" came from either Melville's wife, Lizzie, or sister Augusta, both of whom copied Herman's manuscripts for the printers and were perhaps not immune to mindless editorializing.

5. See Sharon Cameron, *The Corporeal Self: Allegories of the Body in Melville and Hawthorne* (Baltimore: Johns Hopkins University Press, 1981), 41, 65. For a Lacanian reading, see Russell Sbriglia, "Object-Disoriented Ontology; or, the Subject of What Is Sex?," *Continental Thought & Theory* 2:2 (2018), 42–47.

6. Gayatri Chakrabarti Spivak, "The Post-colonial Critic," in *The Post-colonial Critic: Interviews, Strategies, Dialogues*, ed. Sarah Harasym (New York: Routledge, 1990), 73.

7. A curious quality of *Moby-Dick* is that the only named characters who mention Fedallah in diabolic terms are New Englanders—Ahab, the three mates, and Ishmael. Captain Boomer and Dr. Bunger comment on his presence, but they do not respond to him as being out of the norm.

8. Amirhossein Vafa, *Recasting American and Persian Literatures: Local Histories and Formative Geographies from "Moby-Dick" to "Missing Soluch"* (New York: Palgrave Macmillan, 2016), 37.

9. Ibid., 49.

10. Ibid.

11. Ibid., 61.

12. Ibid., 49. Vafa (70–71) later contends that the Parsee tries to persuade Ahab to renounce his quest.

13. See M. Lamming, P. Brown, K. Carter, M. Eldridge, M. Flynn, G. Louie, P. Robinson, and A. Sellen, "The Design of a Human Memory Prosthesis," *Computer Journal* 37:3 (1994), 153–63; Susan Buck-Morss, "The Cinema Screen as Prosthesis of Perception: A Historical Account," in *The Senses Still: Perception and Memory as Material Culture in Modernity*, ed. C. Nadia Seremetaki (New York: Routledge, 1994), 45–62; and Bernard Steigler, "Derrida and

224 NOTES TO PAGES 119–123

Technology: Fidelity at the Limits of Deconstruction and the Prosthesis of Faith," in *Jacques Derrida and the Humanities: A Critical Reader*, ed. Tom Cohen (Cambridge: Cambridge University Press, 2002), 238–70.

14. Christopher Castiglia, "Approaching Ahab Blind," in *Ahab Unbound: Melville and the Materialist Turn*, ed. Meredith Farmer and Jonathan D.S. Schroeder (Minneapolis: University of Minnesota Press, 2022), 179–80.

15. Herman Melville to Nathaniel Hawthorne, [1 June?] 1851, in *Correspondence*, ed. Lynn Horth (Evanston, IL: Northwestern University Press; Chicago: Newberry Library, 1993), 192.

16. Ibid., 191.

17. *Spectator* [London], 24 (25 October 1851) in *Herman Melville: The Contemporary Reviews*, ed. Brian Higgins and Hershel Parker (Cambridge: Cambridge University Press, 1995), 360.

18. *Dublin University Magazine* 39 (February 1852) in ibid., 415.

19. *Athenæum* [London], 1252 (25 October 1851) in ibid., 356–57.

20. *Literary Gazette* [London], 1820 (6 December 1851) in ibid., 394.

21. Astley's was well known for its elaborate displays of horsemanship and its adaptation of literary narratives (e.g., Scott's *Ivanhoe*) to the ring. The *Illustrated London News* (29 January 1848) reported: "We this week give one of the most effective 'Scenes in the Circle' at this popular theatre—the daring feat of Jean Polanski [sic], on two fleet steeds, as 'The British Foxhunter.' Thus doubly mounted, Polaski chases a live fox round the circle, leaping over four gates in his course. There is something pretty national in the scene, and it has been received with great applause." One regrets *The Whale* was never brought to the hippodrome. See the entry for "Astleys" on Lee Jackson's Dictionary of Victorian London website, accessed 10 January 2022.

22. Exodus 16, 21.

23. Andrew Delbanco, *Herman Melville: His World and Work* (New York: Random House, 2013), xvii.

24. On the significance of this scene, see Vafa, *Recasting American and Persian Literatures*, 50–53.

25. Denis Donoghue, "Moby-Dick after September 11th," *Law and Literature* 15:2 (2003), 175.

26. The scene is so convincingly described that some Melville scholars treat the passage as a childhood memory, giving it a potential time (June 1825) and a potential place (33 Bleeker Place in New York City). See Jay Leyda, *The Melville Log: A Documentary Life of Herman Melville, 1819–1891*, vol. 1 (New York: Harcourt, Brace, 1951), 21–22 and John Bryant, *Herman Melville: A Half-Known Life*, electronic ed. (Hoboken, NJ: Wiley-Blackwell, 2021), 64–65.

27. Associating the chimney with the stepmother, Leslie Fiedler saw impotence, masturbation, and powerlessness in the appearance of the supernatural hand. *Love and Death in the American Novel*, rev. ed. (1960; New York: Norton, 1967), 374–75. Adopting a similar perspective, Samuel Kimball focuses on the uncanniness of the hand as representing the stepmother's ambivalence about her cruelty or the boy's masturbatory desires. "Uncanny Narration in *Moby-Dick*," *American Literature* 59:4 (1987), 531. Quoting Leo Bersani, Geoffrey Sanborn has argued that the scene blurs "the nonsexual sensuality of physical contacts, extensions, and correspondences." "Whence Came You Queequeg?," *American Literature* 77:2 (2005), 249. Christopher Looby has discussed the ways in which Queequeg and the counterpane offer Ishmael reparation for the sensory pleasure the stepmother's punishment had denied him. "Strange Sensations: Sex and Aesthetics in 'The Counterpane,'" in *Melville and Aesthetics*, ed. Samuel L. Otter and Geoffrey Sanborn (New York: Palgrave Macmillan, 2011), 80. Drawing on neurological research, Pilar Martínez Benedí and Ralph James Savarese explore how the passage depends on a synesthetic confusion that appears throughout the novel in *Herman Melville & Neurodiversity, Or Why Hunt Difference with Harpoons? A Primitivist Phenomenology* (New York: Bloomsbury, 2024), 68–71.

28. Peter Boxall, *The Prosthetic Imagination: A History of the Novel as Artificial Life* (New York: Cambridge University Press, 2020), 150. To Boxall, the supernatural hand is typical of the time period in emphasizing the "development of a new kind of interiority" (154) and Melville's singular interest in humanizing the nonhuman. He argues that the supernatural hand oversees the "contest between mind and matter" that is the narrative's "central concern" (187).

29. Nathaniel Hawthorne, "Ethan Brand," in *Tales and Sketches* (New York: Library of America, 1982), 1058. Melville mentioned "Ethan Brand" to Hawthorne in his [1 June?] 1851 letter after the story, then titled "The Unpardonable Sin," appeared in *Dollar* magazine.

30. In addition to Fedallah, Ishmael frequently associates gliding with ships, sea creatures, and Ahab.

NOTES TO PAGES 123–132   225

31. Castiglia, "Approaching Ahab Blind," 179.
32. Herman Melville to Nathaniel Hawthorne, 29 June 1851, *Correspondence*, 195.
33. Castiglia, "Approaching Ahab Blind," 179.
34. Tara Robbins Fee, "Irreconcilable Differences: Voice, Trauma, and Melville's *Moby-Dick*," *Mosaic* 45:4 (2012), 143. Fee argues that the narration indicates that "Ishmael neither reaches a state of unity between character and narrator nor achieves the coherence that marks a healed subject" (140).
35. See, for example, "Enhanced Phantom Limb Perception Improves Prosthesis Function, Study Finds," 4 December 2020, Johns Hopkins University Applied Physics Lab. Press release based on Luke E. Osborn et al., "Sensory Stimulation Enhances Phantom Limb Perception and Movement Decoding," *Journal of Neural Engineering* 17:5 (2020), online.
36. V. S. Ramachandran and Sandra Blakeslee, *Phantoms in the Brain: Probing the Mysteries of the Human Mind* (New York: William Morrow, 1998), 187.
37. Geoffrey Sanborn, *The Sign of the Cannibal* (Durham: Duke University Press, 1998), 128.
38. Branka Arsić, "Ambiental Cogito: Ahab with Whales," in Ahab Unbound: *Melville and the Materialist Turn*, ed. Meredith Farmer and Jonathan D. S. Schroeder (Minneapolis: University of Minnesota Press, 2022), 65–91.
39. Ibid., 87.
40. Sanborn, "Whence Come You, Queequeg?," 235–36. The full text can be found at [G. L. Craik], *The New Zealanders* (London: Charles Knight, 1830), Internet Archive.
41. On Queequeg as a composite nonwhite character, see Robert K. Martin, *Hero, Captain, and Stranger: Male Friendship, Social Critique, and Literary Form in the Sea Novels of Herman Melville* (Chapel Hill: University of North Carolina Press, 1995), 279. On Queequeg's eclectic faith practices, see Sanborn, "Whence Come You, Queequeg?," 254 n. 14.
42. Culled from a survey of Google Books, including *The Asiatic Journal* (London: Black, Parbury, & Allen, 1842), 157; Charles James C. Davidson, *Diary of Travels and Adventures in Upper India: With a Tour in Bundelcund, a Sporting Excursion in the Kingdom of Oude, and a Voyage Down the Ganges* (London: H. Colburn, 1843), 30; *A Hand-book for Travellers in the Ionian Islands, Greece, Turkey, Asia Minor, and Constantinople: Being a Guide to the Principal Routes in Those Countries, Including a Description of Malta; with Maxims and Hints for Travellers in the East* (London: J. Murray, 1845), 169; and Joachim Hayward Stocqueler, *The Oriental Interpreter and Treasury of East India* (London: James Madden, 1848), 200.
43. On Fast Day in Massachusetts, see "Here's How Patriots Day Became a Holiday in Massachusetts," 16 April 2023, on the Boston.com website. For an extensive collection of Fast Day sermons, see "Fast Day Proclamations," Online Book Page website, University of Pennsylvania, accessed 9 January 2024.
44. The Maori peoples did not develop a significant Muslim population until the end of the twentieth century. See Eva Nisa and Faried F. Saenong, "From Mahometan to Kiwi Muslim: History of NZ's Muslim Population," *The Conversation*, 25 March 2019, online, accessed 9 January 2024.
45. George Shulman, "Chasing the Whale: *Moby-Dick* as Political Theory," in *A Political Companion to Herman Melville*, ed. Jason Frank (Lexington: University Press of Kentucky, 2013), 79.
46. See my discussion of this topic in Chapter 3.
47. Ishmael notably rejects the Black church in Chapter 2, "The Carpet-Bag." The sermon about "the blackness of darkness, and the weeping and wailing and teeth-gnashing there" seems a "wretched entertainment" (10).
48. Herman Melville, *White-Jacket or The World in a Man-of-War*, ed. Harrison Hayford, Hershel Parker, and G. Thomas Tanselle (Evanston, IL: Northwestern University Press; Chicago: Newberry Library, 1970), 383.
49. The sentiment stems from the verse, which Child cites as "The whole world is a place of prayer." See Lydia Maria Child, *The Progress of Religious Ideas: Through Successive Ages. In Three Volumes* (New York: C. S. Francis & Company, 1855), 414.
50. Thomas Carlyle, "The Hero as Prophet. Mahomet: Islam," in *On Heroes and Hero-Worship, and the Heroic in History*, ed. John Chester Adams (New York: Houghton-Mifflin, 1907), 82.
51. Ibid., 106.
52. Child, *Progress of Religious Ideas*, 392–93. In Child's text, the much-admired verse reads "Oh earth, swallow up thy waters! And thou, oh heaven, withhold thy rain! And immediately the

226 NOTES TO PAGES 132–138

water abated, and the decree was fulfilled." For more information, see Adil Salahi, "Makkah in Pre-Islamic and Early Islamic Poetry," Muslim Heritage.com, 28 April 2021, online, accessed 12 December 2023: "Some poets became so famous because of the extra care they used with their poetry. It is said that when they composed a particularly important poem, they resorted to immortalize it by writing it on a scroll and displaying it on the wall of the Kaabah, for pilgrims to read."

53. Jeffrey Einboden, *The Islamic Lineage of American Literary Culture: Muslim Sources from the Revolution to Reconstruction* (New York: Oxford University Press, 2016), 129–31.

54. Ralph Waldo Emerson, "Manners," in *Essays: Second Series* in *Essays and Lectures* (New York: Library of America, 1983), 531.

55. Ralph Waldo Emerson, "Saadi," in *American Poetry: The Nineteenth-Century*, vol. 1 (New York: Library of America, 1993), 305.

56. Einboden, *Islamic Lineage*, 131–32.

57. Melville found the passage in John Harris's *Navigantium atque antium Bibliotheca; or, a Compleat Collection of Voyages and Travels*, vol. 1 (1705). The passage from Harris adheres to Leo Africanus's much-translated text but does include notable changes in diction and sequencing. John Leo, it should be noted, was writing about the town of Mesa on the Moroccan coast, but Ishmael removes that designation. On Melville's use of Harris's text, see John M. J. Gretchko, "New Evidence for Melville's Use of John Harris in Moby-Dick," *Studies in the American Renaissance* (1983), 303–11.

58. Walt Whitman, *Complete Poetry and Collected Prose*, ed. Justin Kaplan (New York: Library of America, 1982), 88.

59. Matt K. Matsuda, *Pacific Worlds: A History of Seas, Peoples, and Cultures* (Cambridge: Cambridge University Press, 2012), 4–8.

60. Elizabeth Schultz sees the phantoms as being reminiscent of twenty-first century refugees trying to migrate from their countries. See Schultz, "'The Subordinate Phantoms': Melville's Conflicted Response to Asia" in *Moby-Dick, Whole Oceans Away: Melville and the Pacific*, ed. Jill Barnum et al. (Kent, OH: Kent State University Press, 2007), 208.

61. Historians disagree about the degree to which there was a unified "Moro" resistance through the centuries, though the perception of that resistance remained strong among Spanish colonialists. For background, see Thomas McKenna, *Muslim Rulers and Rebels: Everyday Politics and Armed Separatism in the Southern Philippines* (Berkeley: University of California Press, 1998), 80–81; Victor Taylor, "Origins of Islam in the Philippines," Mackenzie Institute, 9 January 2017, online, accessed 12 December 2023.

62. When Ishmael refers to Ahab's Manillas, he most likely does not refer to the islands' mestizo or indigenous people, whose remote forest homes gave them little contact with the West. He refers to the Moro population who had frequent contact with American whaling ships.

63. Sir John Bowring, *A Visit to the Philippine Islands* (London: Smith, Elder, 1859), 165. University of Michigan Digital Collections.

64. Ibid., 347, 165.

65. Ibid.

66. Ibid., 346.

67. Ibid., 165.

68. Ibid., 308.

69. See Jo Marie V. Acebes, "A History of Whaling in the Philippines: A Glimpse of the Past and Current Distribution of Whales," in *Historical Perspectives of Fisheries Exploitation in the Indo-Pacific*, ed. J. Christensen and M. Tull (Dordrecht: Springer, 2014), 83–105.

70. Bowring, *Visit to the Philippine Islands*, 106.

71. Herman Melville, *Typee: A Peep at Polynesian Life*, ed. Harrison Hayford, Hershel Parker, and G. Thomas Tanselle (Evanston, IL: Northwestern University Press; Chicago: Newberry Library, 1968), 124, 196.

72. Schultz, "'Subordinate Phantoms,'" 199.

73. On Melville and Cuvier, see Richard J. King, *Ahab's Rolling Sea: A Natural History of "Moby-Dick"* (Chicago: University of Chicago Press, 2019), 173. It is notable that except for Fleece (who is feeding them over the bulwark), sharks are never attracted to Black sailors more than whites in *Moby-Dick*.

74. Dennis Berthold, "Democracy and Its Discontents," in *A Companion to Herman Melville*, ed. Wyn Kelley (Oxford: Blackwell, 2006), 155.

NOTES TO PAGES 139–145   227

75. Peter Szendy, *Prophecies of Leviathan: Reading Past Melville*, trans. Gil Anidjar (New York: Fordham University Press, 2010), 82.

76. Shoshana Felman, "Education and Crisis, or the Vicissitudes of Teaching," in Shoshana Felman and Dori Laub, *Testimony: Crises of Witnessing in Literature, Psychoanalysis and History* (New York: Routledge, 1991), 5. On Ishmael as the survivor of trauma, see Fee, "Irreconcilable Differences."

Chapter 5

1. Herman Melville, *Moby-Dick or The Whale*, ed. Harrison Hayford, Hershel Parker, and G. Thomas Tanselle (Evanston, IL: Northwestern University Press; Chicago: Newberry Library, 1988), 64. Future references will be made in parenthetical citations.

2. As Peter Coviello writes, Ishmael's "breezy and cheerfully digressive narrative consumes, then systematically dismisses or dissolves, each and every discursive precedent it lights upon." See Coviello, *Intimacy in America: Dreams of Affiliation in Antebellum America* (Minneapolis: University of Minnesota Press, 2005), 93.

3. It is possible to see these (and related) passages as Ishmael's satirizing an imperial mentality that his philosophic approach to whaling seems to undermine. Ishmael, such a reading would suggest, had turned the tolerance he had learned from Queequeg into a cogent stance against the power that American whalers were exerting around the globe. To arrive at such a conclusion, however, we would have to presume (1) that Ishmael had repeatedly elected to express that opposition not with candor but with irony and (2) that his stated enthusiasm for Pacific expansion had no connection to his racializing the diabolic presence he gives Fedallah and the Filipino oarsmen in his narrative. Coviello's discussion of Ishmael's style and nationalism is illuminating, and I would argue that, amid his "strangely voided nationalism" and interrogation of whiteness, when it comes to Asia, Ishmael also espouses the kind of racial preference and belief in (white) American progress that Melville questions. See Coviello, *Intimacy in America*, 93, 110–13.

4. As recorded in the author's journals, Perry visited Nathaniel Hawthorne in Liverpool in December 1854 and "soon introduced his particular business with me—it being to inquire whether I could recommend some suitable person to prepare his notes and materials for the publication of an account of his voyage.... I spoke of Herman Melville, and one or two others; but he seems to have some acquaintance with the literature of the day, and did not grasp very cordially at any name that I could think of." For more details, see Dorsey Kleitz, "Herman Melville, Matthew Perry, and the Narrative of the Expedition of an American Squadron to the China Seas and Japan," *Leviathan* 8:3 (2006), 25–26.

5. Herman Melville, *Clarel: A Poem and Pilgrimage in the Holy Land*, ed. Harrison Hayford, Alma MacDougall, Hershel Parker, and G. Thomas Tanselle (Evanston, IL: Northwestern University Press; Chicago: Newberry Library, 1991), 4.9.111–25.

6. I take the idea of four principal monomaniacs in *Clarel* from Walter E. Bezanson. On Ungar, see Walter E. Bezanson, "Historical and Critical Note," in *Clarel: A Poem and Pilgrimage in the Holy Land*, ed. Harrison Hayford, Alma MacDougall, Hershel Parker, and G. Thomas Tanselle (Evanston, IL: Northwestern University Press; Chicago: Newberry Library, 1991), 633. In order of appearance, the other monomaniacs include Celio, the humpbacked Italian Catholic who feels growing skepticism and despair the longer he lives in Jerusalem (617); Mortmain, the failed Swedish revolutionary whose will to self-destruction leads him to impulsively drink from the Dead Sea waters that he knows will kill him (626); and Agath, the Greek sailor whose constant traveling and extensive suffering make him a shipwrecked, nineteenth-century Job (614).

7. C. Vann Woodward, *The Burden of Southern History*, rev. ed (1960; Baton Rouge: Louisiana State University Press, 1968), 116.

8. Melville, *Clarel*, 4.5.140.

9. Jennifer Greiman, *Melville's Democracy: Radical Figuration and Political Form* (Stanford: Stanford University Press, 2023), 281.

10. Hilton Obenzinger, *American Palestine: Melville, Twain, and the Holy Land Mania* (Princeton: Princeton University Press, 1999), 141.

11. Brian Yothers, *The Romance of the Holy Land in American Travel Writing, 1790–1876* (New York: Ashgate, 2007), 131.

12. Melville, *Clarel*, 4.10.186.

228 NOTES TO PAGES 146–154

13. Bernard Stiegler, *Technics and Time*, vol. 1, *The Fault of Epimetheus*, trans. Richard Beardsworth and George Collins (Stanford: Stanford University Press, 1998), 116.
14. There's a significant history of scholars exploring the relations between empire, revolution, and prostheses. See Bill Brown, "Science Fiction, the World's Fair, and the Prosthetics of Empire, 1910–1915," in *Cultures of United States Imperialism*, ed. Amy Kaplan and Donald E. Pease (Durham: Duke University Press, 1993), 129–63; Heather Chacón, "Prosthetic Colonialism: Indian Removal, European Imperialism, and International Trade in Poe's 'The Man That Was Used Up,'" *Poe Studies* 50 (2017), 46–68; and Peter Boxall's discussion of *Oronooka* in *The Prosthetic Imagination: A History of the Novel as Artificial Life* (New York: Cambridge University Press, 2020), 79–83.
15. On the history of Franklin's image, see Chacón, "Prosthetic Colonialism," 50–52. A detailed discussion can be found at "Magna Britannia: Her Colonies Reduc'd, [January–February 1766]," Founders Online, National Archives, online, accessed 1 December 2023.
16. Eric Jay Dolin, *Leviathan* (New York: Norton, 2007), 206.
17. Lance E. Davis, Robert E. Gallman, and Karin Gleiter, *In Pursuit of Leviathan: Technology, Institutions, Productivity, and Profits in American Whaling, 1816–1906* (Chicago: University of Chicago Press, 1997), 4.
18. Dolin, *Leviathan*, 206. Charles Olson reports that in 1844 $120 million was tied up in whaling-related enterprises. See Charles Olson, *Call Me Ishmael: A Study of Melville* (San Francisco: City Lights Books, 1947), 18.
19. Mark Foster, "New Bedford—Whale Oil Refining Capital," *IA: The Journal of the Society for Industrial Archeology* 40:1–2 (2014), 51; Paul Lucier, *Scientists and Swindlers: Consulting on Coal and Oil in America, 1820–1890* (Baltimore: Johns Hopkins University Press, 2010), 152.
20. John D. Kelly, "New Bedford, Capital of the 19th-Century," *Anthropological Quarterly* 90:4 (2017), 1086. Kelly alludes to Benjamin's essay, "Paris, Capital of the 19th Century," both versions of which are published in Walter Benjamin, The *Arcades Project*, trans. Howard Eiland and Kevin McLaughlin (Cambridge: Harvard University Press, 1999), 3–13, 14–26.
21. Foster, "New Bedford," 53.
22. For a different interpretation of the *Pequod*'s activities, one that sees collection, rather than industry, as the best way to understand the whale fishery, see Yunte Huang, *Transpacific Imaginations: History, Literature, Counterpoetics* (Cambridge: Harvard University Press, 2008), 55–60.
23. See Alan Heimert, "*Moby-Dick* and American Political Symbolism," *American Quarterly* 15:4 (1963), 502 and Carolyn L. Karcher, *Shadow over the Promised Land: Slavery, Race, and Violence in Melville's America* (Baton Rouge: Louisiana State University Press, 1980), 81–82.
24. As interested as Melville was in disabled bodies, he also subscribed to the principle that nobility democratically expressed itself in character, intellect, and bodily form. He presents Flask's height as a sign of his limited vision and moral compass.
25. Foster, "New Bedford," 51, 53.
26. Michael Faraday to Jacob Herbert, 9 October 1845, *The Correspondence of Michael Faraday: 1841–1848*, vol. 3, ed. Frank A. J. L. James (London: Institution of Engineering and Technology, 1991), 411–19.
27. Sunaura Taylor, *Beasts of Burden: Animal and Disability Liberation* (New York: New Press, 2017), 43.
28. On the arm sling as a prosthetic device, see US Code of Federal Regulations 21CFR890.3640 "Physical Medicine Prosthetic Devices/ Arm Sling," Food and Drug Administration website, 27 October 2023, accessed 9 January 2024.
29. Lawrence Buell, *The Environmental Imagination: Thoreau, Nature Writing, and the Formation of American Culture* (Cambridge: Harvard University Press, 1995), 218.
30. Philip Armstrong, *What Animals Mean in the Fiction of Modernity* (London: Routledge, 2008), 100.
31. Robert Zoellner also sees a "covert affinity" between Ahab and the whale, arguing that, as an active participant in the hunt, the captain is "unable to detect the redemptive analogy or draw the saving parallel which the Medicare Whale represents." See Robert Zoellner, *The Salt-Sea Mastodon: A Reading of "Moby-Dick"* (Berkeley: University of California Press, 1973), 172.
32. William James, *The Principles of Psychology*, 2 vols. (1890; Cambridge: Harvard University Press, 1983), 1030–31. James addresses his contemporaries' effort to grapple with this instinct on 1031 n. 15.

NOTES TO PAGES 155–163   229

33. On William James and the historicity of emotion, see Phoebe C. Ellsworth, "Basic Emotions and the Rocks of New Hampshire," *Emotion Review* 6:1 (2014), 21–26.
34. I borrow this phrase from Michael D. Snediker, "Phenomenology beyond the Phantom Limb: Melvillean Figuration and Chronic Pain," in *Ahab Unbound: Melville and the Materialist Turn*, ed. Meredith Farmer and Jonathan D. S. Schroeder (Minneapolis: University of Minnesota Press, 2022), 148.
35. Davis, Gallman, and Gleiter, *In Pursuit of Leviathan*, 135.
36. Eric Fromm, *Escape from Freedom* (1941; New York: Henry Holt, 1994), 169.
37. See Elizabeth Schultz, "Humanizing Moby Dick: Redeeming Anthropomorphism," in *The Future of Eco-criticism: New Horizons*, ed. Serpil Opperman et al. (Newcastle upon Tyne, UK: Cambridge Scholars Publishing, 2011), 100–117, but especially 105–6 and an earlier version of this research in Elizabeth Schultz, "Melville's Environmental Vision in Moby-Dick," *Interdisciplinary Studies in Literature and the Environment* 7:1 (2000), 105–6.
38. On these points, see Taylor, *Beasts of Burden*, 31, and Richard J. King, *Ahab's Rolling Sea: A Natural History of Moby-Dick* (Chicago: University of Chicago Press, 2019), 250.
39. Schultz, "Melville's Environmental Vision," 102.
40. John Levi Barnard, "The Cod and the Whale: Melville in the Time of Extinction," *American Literature* 89:4 (2017), 854.
41. King, *Ahab's Rolling Sea*, 325.
42. Schultz, "Melville's Environmental Vision," 106. Discussing the chapter "Stubb Kills a Whale," Samuel Otter remarks that Ishmael frequently describes the whale's body, and especially the head, as a "container of value." See Samuel Otter, *Melville's Anatomies* (Berkeley: University of California Press, 1999), 141.
43. Ungar's disgust with the phrase "As cruel as a Turk" expresses a point that Carl W. Ernst makes: Christians have projected their own violence and hatred of Islam onto Muslims, depicting them with "sword in hand" for centuries. See *Following Muhammad: Rethinking Islam in the Contemporary World* (Chapel Hill: University of North Carolina Press, 2003), 44.
44. Rob Nixon, *Slow Violence and the Environmentalism of the Poor* (Cambridge: Harvard University Press, 2011).
45. Barnard, "The Cod and the Whale," 859.
46. On Ahab, see King, *Ahab's Rolling Sea*, 350; Randy Kennedy, "The Ahab Parallax: 'Moby Dick' and the Spill," *New York Times*, 12 June 2010, online, accessed 1 June 2020; Jean-Francois Leroux, "Wars for Oil: *Moby-Dick*, Orientalism, and Cold-War Criticism," *Canadian Review of American Studies* 39:4 (2009, 423–42.). Although now owned by the Saudi Arabian government, Aramco was founded in 1933 when the Standard Oil Company of California established a concession agreement with Saudi Arabia. See Aramco Americas, "Our History," online, 17 April 2020.
47. C. L. R. James, *Mariners, Renegades, and Castaways: The Story of Herman Melville and the World We Live In*, ed. Donald E. Pease (Hanover: University Press of New England, 2001), 53.
48. As Howard C. Horsford and Lynn Horth comment in their edition of the *Journals*, the Bank of England was "essentially the financial center of the nineteenth-century world" (275). Melville made frequent note of the recently renovated Bank of England during his December 1849 visit to London. See *Journals*, 15, 18, 40.
49. I am indebted to Sunaura Taylor's comments on ableism in the animal industries for helping me think through these issues. See *Beasts of Burden*, 59.
50. Frederick Douglass, *Narrative of the Life of Frederick Douglass, an American Slave, Written by Himself*, ed. William L. Andrews and William McFeely (New York: Norton, 1996), 41.
51. Ibid.
52. On New Bedford industries, see Foster, "New Bedford," 51–70. Frederick Douglass, *The Life and Times of Frederick Douglass*, in *Autobiographies*, ed. Henry Louis Gates Jr. (New York: Library of America, 1994), 656–57.
53. King, *Ahab's Rolling Sea*, 139–40.
54. Colin Dayan, "Melville's Creatures, or Seeing Otherwise," in *American Impersonal: Essays with Sharon Cameron*, ed. Branka Arsić (New York: Bloomsbury, 2014), 53.
55. On the Malay in antebellum periodicals, see Spencer Tricker, "'Five Dusky Phantoms': Gothic Form and Cosmopolitan Shipwreck in Melville's *Moby-Dick*," *Studies in American Fiction* 44:1 (2017), 3–6.

230 NOTES TO PAGES 164–174

56. Greiman suggests that the circular nature of the grand armada provides an image of nonhuman democracy, a cetocracy that creates "an entirely new view of what forms a collective agency and a political relation might take" (192). See *Melville's Democracy*, 192–97. In this, she argues, the grand armada remedies the failures of the *Pequod's* crew (199). This visionary democracy will soon, of course, be violated by the Pequod's hunt.

57. Michael Paul Rogin, *Subversive Genealogy: The Politics and Art of Herman Melville* (Berkeley: University of California Press, 1985), 114.

58. Wai Chee Dimock, "Hemispheric Islam: Continents and Centuries for American Literature," *American Literary History* 21:1 (2009), 44.

59. "The more whales the less fish," Ishmael remarks, citing an old fishermen's proverb that points to the gulf between species and commodity (390).

60. Matt K. Matsuda, *Pacific Worlds: A History of Seas, Peoples, and Cultures* (Cambridge: Cambridge University Press, 2012), 113.

61. Sir John Bowring, *A Visit to the Philippine Islands* (London: Smith, Elder, 1859), 165, 349–50. University of Michigan Digital Collections.

62. Matsuda, *Pacific Worlds*, 113.

63. As quoted in Stefan Eklöf Amirell, "'The Making of the 'Malay Pirate' in Early Modern European Thought," *Humanities* 9:3 (2020), 91.

64. Ibid.

65. Herman Melville, "Benito Cereno," in *The Piazza Tales and Other Prose Pieces, 1839–1860*, ed. Harrison Hayford, Alma A. MacDougall, G. Thomas Tanselle, et al. (Evanston, IL: Northwestern University Press; Chicago: Newberry Library, 1987), 68.

66. Nicholas Birns, "'Thickly Studded Oriental Archipelagoes': Figuring the Indian and Pacific Oceans in *Moby-Dick*," *Leviathan* 14:2 (2012), 14.

67. Tricker, "'Five Dusky Phantoms,'" 17.

68. Amirell, "Making of the 'Malay Pirate,'" 10.

69. I take this notion from Thomas Bender's comments: "At the core of empire as a way of life is precisely this incapacity to see oneself as a potential enemy. Confident in their ambition and desire, and sure of their own goodwill, Americans were strangers to self-reflection." Bender associates this trait with Ahab, but it is just as suited to Ishmael's nationalist enthusiasms. See Thomas Bender, *A Nation among Nations: America's Place in World History* (New York: Hill and Wang, 2006), 192.

Chapter 6

1. Herman Melville, *Clarel*, ed. Harrison Hayford, Alma A. MacDougall, Hershel Parker, and G. Thomas Tanselle (Evanston, IL: Northwestern University Press, 1991), 4.19.18–22.

2. Ibid., 4.19.55–56.

3. Ibid., 4.19.59–66.

4. Ibid., 4.19.76.

5. Ibid., 4.19.36–37.

6. Ibid., 4.19.117–19.

7. Ibid., 623.

8. Herman Melville, *Moby-Dick or The Whale*, ed. Harrison Hayford, Hershel Parker, and G. Thomas Tanselle (Evanston, IL: Northwestern University Press; Chicago: Newberry Library, 1988), 231, emphasis mine. Future references will be made in parenthetical citations.

9. On Melville's dramatizing political views, see Dennis Berthold's indispensable essay "Democracy and Its Discontents," in *A Companion to Herman Melville*, ed. Wyn Kelley (Blackwell, 2006), 154.

10. Melville, *Clarel*, 4.19.135, 142–43.

11. Ibid., 4.19.119, 4.19.126–27.

12. Following Ungar, scholars have sometimes subsumed Don Hannibal to the Turkish mercenary's views of the world. Hilton Obenzinger, for example, describes Don Hannibal as "the fool to Ungar's straight man." Calling him a "comic disfigurement" of the defeated Mexican rebels of 1846, Obenzinger comments that "drink and laughter serve as prosthetics for his amputated limbs and ideals." See Hilton Obenzinger, *American Palestine: Melville, Twain, and the Holy Land Mania* (Princeton: Princeton University Press, 1999), 151–52. Leaning into the metaphor of "lops," Jennifer Greiman centers Ungar's verbal transformation of Don Hannibal's limb loss into an image of the vertiginous, transient nature of democracy. See Greiman,

NOTES TO PAGES 174–178   231

Melville's Democracy: Radical Figuration and Political Form (Stanford: Stanford University Press, 2023), 206–7 and 254–55.

13. Jennifer Greiman, "Melville in the Dark Ages of Democracy," *Leviathan* 18:3 (2016), 14.

14. Ibid.

15. Ibid., 15. In *Melville's Democracies*, Greiman writes that "*Clarel* may well be Melville's masterpiece of groundlessness" (270). The book considerably expands on this theme on page 209 and pages 271–80.

16. Sorin Radu Cucu and Roland Végső, "*Moby-Dick* and Perpetual War," in *Handsomely Done: Aesthetics, Politics, and Media after Melville*, ed. Daniel Hoffman-Schwartz (Evanston, IL: Northwestern University Press, 2019), 25.

17. Ibid., 24. Cucu and Végső contend that one reason readers recognize themselves in *Moby-Dick* is that we have totally absorbed the modern conception of "life in the logic of war" (26).

18. Herman Melville, "Look-Out Mountain: The Night Fight," *Battle-Pieces and Aspects of the War*, in *Published Poems*, ed. Robert C. Ryan, Harrison Hayford, Alma MacDougall Reising, and G. Thomas Tanselle (Evanston, IL: Northwestern University Press; Chicago: Newberry Library, 2009), 65.

19. See, for example, John Dryden's comparison of fire to a hydra: "No help avails: for, Hydra-like, the Fire / Lifts up his Hundred heads to aim his way: / And scarce the wealthy can one half retire, / Before he rushes in to share the Prey." John Dryden, "Annus Mirabilis," *The Poems and Fables of John Dryden*, ed. James Kinsley (London: Oxford University Press, 1962), lines 993–96.

20. Thomas Jefferson to John Adams, 11 January 1816, *The Adams-Jefferson Letters*, ed. Lester J. Cappon (Chapel Hill: University of North Carolina Press, 1987), 460.

21. Greiman, *Melville's Democracy*, 209.

22. Maurice S. Lee, "Melville's Subversive Political Philosophy: 'Benito Cereno' and the Fate of Speech," *American Literature* 72:3 (2000), 500.

23. Herman Melville, "Preface," in *Battle-Pieces and Aspects of the War*, 2.

24. Nathaniel Hawthorne, "Chiefly about War Matters," *Atlantic Monthly*, July 1862, online, accessed 22 January 2019.

25. See Lisa A. Long, *Rehabilitating Bodies: Health, History, and the American Civil War* (Philadelphia: University of Pennsylvania Press 2004), and Megan Kate Nelson, *Ruin Nation: Destruction and the American Civil War* (Athens: University of Georgia Press, 2012).

26. *Clarel*, 4.20.161.

27. Ibid., 4.25.20–25.

28. Ibid., 4.28.27–36.

29. Ibid., 4.28.33.

30. Herman Melville, *The Confidence-Man; His Masquerades*, ed. Harrison Hayford, Hershel Parker, and G. Thomas Tanselle (Evanston, IL: Northwestern University Press and The Newberry Library, 1984), 149.

31. Michael E. Woods, for example, discusses the expansion of pro-slavery politics into American foreign policy positions during the Jackson and Van Buren administrations. See Michael E. Woods, "Building a Proslavery Lobby: The Domestic Politics of the *Encomium* Case," *Journal of the Early Republic* 44:4 (2024), forthcoming.

32. Alexis de Tocqueville, *Democracy in America*, ed. J. P. Mayer, trans. George Lawrence (New York: Anchor, 1969), 567.

33. "The Americans are fond of law in one respect, that is, they are fond of going to law," the English visitor "Captain" Frederick Marryat wrote in 1839. "It is a pleasure which they can afford, and for which they cheerfully pay." See Frederick Marryat, *A Diary in America: With Remarks on Its Institutions*, Volume 2 (Canada: W.H. Colyer, 1839), 231. Google Books.

34. Tocqueville, *Democracy in America*, 256.

35. Cucu and Végső, "*Moby-Dick* and Perpetual War," 14.

36. Ibid. Cucu and Végső cite the following representative texts: F. O. Matthiessen's *American Renaissance*, Richard Chase's *Herman Melville: A Critical Study*, and C. L. R. James, *Mariners, Renegades, and Castaways: The Story of Herman Melville and the World We Live In*.

37. Donald Pease, "*Moby-Dick* and the Cold War," in *The American Renaissance Reconsidered: Selected Papers from the English Institute*, ed. Walter Benn Michaels and Donald E. Pease (Baltimore: Johns Hopkins University Press, 1989), 113, 123, 117. As he put it in a later essay, with some variation, "The essentialized opposition between Ishmael and Ahab would

232 NOTES TO PAGES 178–186

dominate readings of the novel in the field of American literary Studies for the next fifty years." Donald Pease, "C. L. R. James, *Moby-Dick*, and the Emergence of Transnational American Studies," *Arizona Quarterly* 56:3 (2000), 95.

38. William V. Spanos, *The Errant Art of Moby-Dick: The Canon, the Cold War, and the Struggle for American Studies* (Durham: Duke University Press, 1995), 34.

39. Elizabeth Duquette, "The Fog of Tyranny in 'Benito Cereno,'" *Textual Practice* 35:11 (2021), 1855.

40. Tocqueville and Lincoln as quoted in ibid., 1856.

41. Ibid., 1855–56. See also Duquette's essay "Tyranny in America, or, the Appeal to the Coloured Citizens of the World," *American Literary History* 33:1 (2021), 1–28.

42. Citing a third wave of materialism, Farmer aims to establish a binary between Ahab as a "totalitarian dictator" and as a "sympathetic figure" in "Rethinking Ahab: Melville and the Materialist Turn," in *Ahab Unbound: Melville and the Materialist Turn*, ed. Meredith Farmer and Jonathan D. S. Schroeder (Minneapolis: University of Minnesota Press, 2022), 1–11. That binary, however, can be misleading. For example, Farmer's interest in examining "the importance, influence, and even agency of Melville's nonhuman actors," namely the white whale, leads her to conclude that "*Ahab is not a murderer*" (11). But we can value the scholarship surrounding nonhuman agency without disregarding the fact that Melville explicitly plants the idea of a murderous Ahab in Chapter 19 when Elijah alludes to the captain's having killed a Spaniard in a South American church before his dismemberment (92).

43. Donald E. Pease, "Ahab's Electromagnetic Constitution," in *Ahab Unbound: Melville and the Materialist Turn*, ed. Meredith Farmer and Jonathan D. S. Schroeder (Minneapolis: University of Minnesota Press, 2022), 261.

44. Other readings of the Leyden Jar scene include Inger Hunnerup Dalsgaard, '"The Leyden Jar' and 'The Iron Way' Conjoined: Moby-Dick, the Classical and Modern Schism of Science and Technology," in *Melville "Among the Nations": Proceedings of an International Conference, Volos, Greece, July 1997*, ed. Sanford E. Marovitz and A. C. Christodoulou (Kent, OH: Kent State University Press, 2001), 243–53, especially 245–47; Michael Jonik, *Herman Melville and the Politics of the Inhuman* (Cambridge: Cambridge University Press, 2018), 22; and Farmer, "Rethinking Ahab," 1.

45. Timothy Snyder, *On Tyranny: Twenty Lessons from the Twentieth Century* (New York: Tim Duggan Books, 2017), 18.

46. I borrow the idea of mutation from Greiman, *Melville's Democracy*, 177.

47. C. L. R. James, *Mariners, Renegades, and Castaways: The Story of Herman Melville and the World We Live In*, ed. Donald E. Pease (Hanover: University Press of New England, 2001), 40–41.

48. Michael Paul Rogin, *Subversive Genealogy: The Politics and Art of Herman Melville* (Berkeley: University of California Press, 1985), 110–11. On Ishmael's decision to seek an "an attainable felicity" in the comforts of domesticity, see Rogin, *Subversive Genealogy*, 151. For the entire quotation, see Tocqueville, *Democracy in America*, 430.

49. James, *Mariners, Renegades*, 37–42.

50. Herman Melville, *Mardi and a Voyage Thither*, ed. Harrison Hayford, Hershel Parker, and G. Thomas Tanselle (Evanston, IL: Northwestern University Press; Chicago: Newberry Library, 1998), 7–8.

51. Melville, *Clarel*, 1.15.33–41.

52. Timothy Marr, "Mastheads and Minarets: Islamic Architecture in Melville's Writing," in *Melville "Among the Nations,"* ed. Sanford E. Marovitz, Athanasios C. Christodoulou, and A. K. Christodoulou (Kent, OH: Kent State University Press, 2001), 477.

53. See Sara Scalenghe, *Disability in the Ottoman Arab World, 1500–1800* (New York: Cambridge University Press, 2014), 79.

54. Marr, "Mastheads and Minarets," 480.

55. On the withdrawal and return mythic pattern that Richard Chase saw in Melville's work, see Christopher Castiglia, *Practices of Hope: Literary Criticism in Disenchanted Times* (New York: New York University Press, 2017), 79.

56. Rogin, *Subversive Genealogy*, 109.

57. James, *Mariners, Renegades*, 41.

58. Eric Fromm, *Escape from Freedom* (1941; New York: Henry Holt, 1994), 254–55.

NOTES TO PAGES 187–193   233

59. All three of Ishmael's heroes were involved in slavery. Washington, of course, owned slaves throughout his life. After the National Convention had abolished the practice in 1794, Napoleon reinstituted the enslavement of Africans in the French colonies in 1802.

60. Herman Melville, *Redburn: His First Voyage*, ed. Harrison Hayford, Hershel Parker, and G. Thomas Tanselle (Evanston, IL: Northwestern University Press; Chicago: Newberry Library, 1969), 155.

61. Ibid., 155–56.

62. Ibid., 156.

63. Herman Melville to Evert Duyckinck, 7 November 1851, in *Correspondence*, ed. Lynn Horth (Evanston, IL: Northwestern University Press; Chicago: Newberry Library, 1993), 209.

64. Carolyn L. Karcher, *Shadow over the Promised Land: Slavery, Race, and Violence in Melville's America* (Baton Rouge: Louisiana State University Press, 1980), 69.

65. On Ishmael as a folk hero, see Richard Chase, *Herman Melville: A Critical Study* (New York: Houghton-Mifflin, 1949), 67–68.

66. Herman Melville, "Benito Cereno," in *The Piazza Tales and Other Prose Pieces, 1839–1860*, ed. Harrison Hayford, Alma A. MacDougall, and G. Thomas Tanselle, et al. (Evanston, IL: Northwestern University Press; Chicago: Newberry Library, 1987), 116.

67. Greg Grandin, *The Empire of Necessity: Slavery, Freedom, and Deception in the New World* (New York: Metropolitan Books, 2014), 8.

68. Kelly Ross, "Babo's Heterochronic Creativity," *Leviathan* 18:1 (2016), 16; Melville, "Benito Cereno," 99.

69. Dorothee Metkitsky Finkelstein, *Melville's Orienda* (New Haven: Yale, 1961), 190.

70. Grandin, *Empire of Necessity*, 171. Sufism had had a prominent presence in West Africa since the fifteenth century, and unbeknownst to its Concord admirers, many of the Africans originally brought to the Americas followed the tradition.

71. As Eric J. Sundquist observed in *To Wake the Nations: Race in the Making of American Literature* (Cambridge: Harvard University Press, 1993), Islam "was also a means to invoke the strength of a contrary source of revolutionary power; throughout parts of Latin America, Muslim teaching, assimilated to African and African American religions, had been influential in slave rebellions, and Islam in the New World was easily construed as a religion of resistance" (169).

72. Sterling Stuckey has shown how thoroughly Melville grounded this scene in Ashantee history and culture, drawing on such works as Mungo Parks's *Travel into the Interior Districts of Africa*, Joseph Dupuis's *Journal of a Residence in Ashantee*, and T. E. Bowdich's *Mission from Cape Coast Castle to Ashantee*. See Sterling Stuckey, *African Culture and Melville's Art* (New York: Oxford University Press, 2009), 13–14. On Ashantee practices relevant to the scene, see 60–62. Historians corroborate the connections, speculating that a number of slave revolts in both North and South America occurred on the last night of Ramadan, Laylat al-Qadr, which translates as the Night of Power. See Grandin, *Empire of Necessity*, 196. Interestingly, Melville's use of dervishes in this anti-imperialist fight anticipates the rise of the Dervish Movement in Somalia in 1899–1920, when Islamicist forces in Somalia sought an end to British, Italian, and Ethiopian control.

73. Ross, "Babo's Heterochronic Creativity," 16–17.

74. On the phrase "Follow your leader" or *Seguid vuestro jefe* as a reversal of the Middle Passage, see Ivy G. Wilson, *Specters of Democracy: Blackness and the Aesthetics of Politics in the Antebellum United States* (New York: Oxford University Press, 2011), 143–44.

75. On the Nelson statue as a model for both Aranda's skeleton and the masked satyr on the ship's prow, see Stuckey, *African Culture*, 37–38.

76. Ibid., 40.

77. Melville, "Benito Cereno," 116–17. On the head as an "ironic reversal" of the skeleton, see Dana Luciano, *Arranging Grief: Sacred Time and the Body in Nineteenth-Century America* (New York: New York University Press, 2007), 208. On Babo's voicelessness, see Sari Altschuler, "Babo's 'Mute'-ny: Deaf Culture and Black Testimony in Antebellum America," *PMLA* 138:5 (2023), 1149–64.

78. Christopher Freeburg, *Melville and the Idea of Blackness: Race and Imperialism in Nineteenth-Century America* (Cambridge: Cambridge University Press, 2012), 129.

79. Peter Boxall, *The Prosthetic Imagination: A History of the Novel as Artificial Life* (New York: Cambridge University Press, 2020), 188.

234   NOTES TO PAGES 194–205

80. Elizabeth Schultz has also discussed the similarity between these scenes, prompting her to see Fedallah as a slave and Ahab a slave master. See "The Subordinate Phantoms: Melville's Conflicted Response to Asia in *Moby-Dick*," in *Whole Oceans Away: Melville and the Pacific*, ed. Jill Barnum et al. (Kent, OH: Kent State University Press, 2007), 209.
81. Luciano, *Arranging Grief*, 207.
82. The author of *Don Quixote* lost the use of his left arm fighting the Ottomans in 1571.
83. Lawrence Buell, *The Dream of the Great American Novel* (Cambridge: Belknap Press, 2014), 360.
84. Melville, *Mardi*, 12–13.
85. Roger Williams to The Town of Providence, January 1654–1655, in *The Complete Writings of Roger Williams*, vol. 6, ed. J. R. Bartlett (New York: Russell & Russell, 1963), 278–279.
86. Redburn also speaks admirably of the Lascars and Malays and spends hours talking to a Lascar friend in Liverpool. See Melville, *Redburn*, 170–73.
87. Charles Olson, *Call Me Ishmael: A Study of Melville* (San Francisco: City Lights Books, 1947), 73.
88. Traveling as a passenger to London, Melville climbed the masthead his first morning out of New York (12 October 1849). "Retired early & had a sound sleep. Was up betimes, & aloft, to recall the old emotions of being at the masthead. Found that the ocean looked the same as ever," his entry flatly reads. See Herman Melville, *Journals*, ed. Howard C. Horsford and Lynn Horth (Evanston, IL: Northwestern University Press; Chicago: Newberry Library, 1989), 4.

Conclusion

1. Bob Dylan, "Bob Dylan's 115th Dream," in *Bob Dylan Lyrics, 1962–1985* (New York: Alfred Knopf, 1985), 170–71.
2. Sean Wilentz, "Bob Dylan, Historian," *New York Review of Books*, 19 June 2021, online, accessed 12 December 2022.
3. Warner Berthoff, *The Example of Melville* (New York: Norton, 1962), 21.
4. Although Dylan seems to have borrowed much of his Nobel Prize discussion of *Moby-Dick* from Sparks Notes, I refer to the song's description of the story's end: "Well, the last I heard of Arab / He was stuck on a whale," an image that corresponds to the conclusion of Huston's film more than to the text. On the Nobel Prize lecture, see Andrea Pitzer, "The Freewheelin' Bob Dylan: Did the Singer-Songwriter Take Portions of his Nobel Lecture from SparkNotes?," *Slate*, 13 June 2017, online, accessed 22 August 2020.
5. Melville, *Mardi and a Voyage Thither* (Evanston, IL: Northwestern University Press; Chicago: Newberry Library, 1998), 574.
6. Herman Melville, *Moby-Dick or The Whale*, ed. Harrison Hayford, Hershel Parker, and G. Thomas Tanselle (Evanston, IL: Northwestern University Press; Chicago: Newberry Library, 1988), 269.
7. Meryl Kornfield, "Trump Takes Victory Lap at Conservative Conference," *Washington Post*, 4 March 2023, online, accessed 4 March 2023.
8. Toni Morrison, "Unspeakable Things Unspoken: The Afro-American Presence in American Literature," *Michigan Quarterly Review* 28:1 (1989), 15–16.
9. Morrison's essay in the aftermath of Trump's election reads like an updated version of her comments on Melville in "Unspeakable Things Unspoken." See Toni Morrison, "Mourning for Whiteness," *New Yorker*, 13 November 2016, online, accessed 19 March 2023.
10. Wendy Brown, "Neoliberalism's Frankenstein: Authoritarian Freedom in Twenty-First Century 'Democracies,'" *Critical Times* 1:1 (2018), 67, 69, online, accessed 4 March 2023.
11. Ibid., 70.
12. Ibid., 71.
13. Ibid., 75.
14. By The New Right, I refer to the loose collection of thinkers, politicians, financiers, and tech entrepreneurs who are envisioning a post-democratic United States. Among many examples, see Andrew Prokop, "Curtis Yarvin Wants American Democracy Toppled," *Vox*, 24 October 2022 and Peter Thiel, "The Education of a Libertarian," *Cato Unbound*, 13 April 2009.
15. Ibid.
16. Juliet Hooker, "Black Protest / White Grievance: On the Problem of White Political Imaginations Not Shaped by Loss," *South Atlantic Quarterly* 116:3 (2017), 486.

Index

For the benefit of digital users, indexed terms that span two pages (e.g., 52–53) may, on occasion, appear on only one of those pages.

Adams, John Quincy 96, 110–111
"The Advocate" (chapter in *Moby-Dick*)
 143–144, 148, 195
"The Affidavit" (chapter in *Moby-Dick*) 99–100
Africanus, Johannes Leo 132–133
Ahab, Captain (character in *Moby-Dick*)
 aggrievement of 1–4, 9–11, 21, 26–27, 29,
  48–49, 55, 60–61, 82–83, 134–135, 146,
  150–151, 157, 176–177, 202–204
 assistive devices of 11, 29, 50–53, 55–56, 74–75
 Captain Boomer and 59, 74–75, 78, 197
 carpenter's fitting of a prosthetic leg
  for 57–68, 72–73, 82
 Cold War readings of 178–179, 202–203
 The Crusades and 99–100
 death of 109–110
 defiance of God by 50–51, 114, 120
 democracy and 177–182, 204–205
 disability studies and 8–10
 dismemberment and wounds of 1–4, 10–13,
  16–18, 21, 25–29, 31–33, 35–36, 41–45,
  49–50, 52, 54–56, 59, 74–76, 78, 81–82,
  91–92, 109–110, 119, 151, 157, 177–178,
  180, 204–205
 dominance over *Pequod* crew of 1–2, 6, 18,
  21, 26–29, 51–52, 54–55, 59, 74–76, 87,
  176–177, 180, 182, 198–199
 Fedallah and 14–15, 83–84, 87–91, 103–104,
  106–108, 112–113, 116–117, 127,
  134–135, 193–195, 197–198
 Flask and 35–36, 46–47, 79,
  148–150, 180–181
 Ishmael and 25–28, 36–37, 49–50, 57–58,
  62, 79–80, 99–100, 108–109, 116, 121,
  138–139, 178, 180–183, 198, 204–205
 masthead soliloquy of 196–199
 Ottoman imagery of power and 2–3, 13,
  100, 102
 pain and phantom pain experienced by
  18, 29, 35–36, 60–61, 67–73, 83
 prosthetic leg of 3–6, 9–13, 18, 21, 25–30,
  35–36, 43–50, 53–68, 72–75, 78, 81–84,

  107, 113, 119, 146, 173–174, 176–177,
  194, 197–199, 201–202
 Starbuck and 51–55, 90–91, 109, 112–113,
  121, 148, 168–169, 178, 180–182, 203–204
 Stubb and 27–29, 35–36, 43–48, 52, 90–91,
  125–126, 150, 153, 180–181
 theatrical leadership style of 114
 trauma and 35–37, 57, 60–61
 Trump and 203–204
 vengeance and 2–4, 6–11, 14, 25, 35–38,
  49–50, 58–61, 78–83, 87–88, 109–110,
  112, 127, 173, 178–179, 182,
  197–198, 201–203
 walking and pacing by 25–29, 45, 53, 119,
  123, 180
Ahab (king in Old Testament) 108, 111
"Ahab and the Carpenter" (chapter in
 Moby-Dick) 57, 62–63
"Ahab's Boat and Crew. Fedallah" (chapter in
 Moby-Dick) 46
Alcott, Louisa May 176
Alexander the Great 62, 143
Altschuler, Sari 9–10, 78
American Revolution 29–31, 46–47,
 96, 146–147
Amirell, Stefan Eklöf 166–168
amputation. *See also* dismemberment
 American Revolution soldiers and 29
 anesthetic chloroform and 41–42
 Civil War and 3–4, 69
 crisis of masculinity and 31–33
 gangrene and 40
 "guillotine amputation" and 37
 industrial, transportation and agricultural
  accidents as reasons for 29, 40, 54
 Mardi and 37–38, 70–71, 75–76
 ontology and 71
 Parsons's manual regarding 41
 Penny Cyclopaedia account of 38–39
 phantom pain and 68–69, 72
 White-Jacket and 38–40
Anastasius: Memoirs of a Greek (Hope) 93–94, 104

236 INDEX

Anglesey leg 64
Arabian Nights 93
Arjana, Sophia Rose 104
Armstrong, Philip 153–154
Arsić, Branka 126–127
Auden, W. H. 81
Australia 143–144
authoritarian personality (Fromm) 90–91, 113
Autobiography of Benjamin Franklin
(Franklin) 92–93
Aydin, Cemil 101

Babbalanja (character in *Mardi*) 20, 68–69,
96–97, 201–202
Babo (character in "Benito
Cereno") 48–49, 191–194
Baillie, James S. 34*f*
Barnard, John Levi 157–159
Barnum, P. T. 31–33
"Bartleby the Scrivener" (Melville) 8–9
Battle of Sierra Gordo (Baillie) 34*f*
Battle-Pieces and Aspects of the War
(Melville) 173–176
Bayle, Pierre 103
Becket, Thomas 99–100
Beckford, William 93–94, 104, 105*f*
Behdad, Ali 94
Bender, Thomas 18–19
"Benito Cereno" (Melville) 48–49, 166–167,
177–178, 191–196
Benjamin, Walter 148
Bentley, Richard 119–120
The Berber, or, The Mountaineer of the Atlas
(Mayo) 94
Berger, James A. 35–36
Berthold, Dennis 18–19, 138
Bildad (character in *Moby-Dick*) 78, 108, 148
"Bill for Establishing Religious Freedom"
(Jefferson) 92–93
Billy Budd (Melville) 8–9, 174–175, 178–179
Birns, Nicholas 167–168
Black Guinea (character in *The
Confidence-Man*) 73–74
Bly leg 64, 65*f*
"Bob Dylan's 115th Dream" (Dylan) 200–201
Boomer, Captain (character in *Moby-Dick*)
Ahab and 59, 74–75, 78, 197
amputation and 76
arm lost to Moby Dick by 57–58, 74, 78
assistive devices and 74–75
dismemberment and wounds of 75–76, 173
Fedallah and 87
fellowship with crew of 75–76
on Moby Dick as worthy combatant 78

prosthetic arm of 74–77, 82–83,
173–174, 197
on whaling industry's nobility and
violence 150–151
Bowring, John 135–136, 139, 166–167
Boxall, Peter 14–15, 81, 122–123, 193
Bradbury, Ray 89, 218–219 n.6
Brady, Mathew 176
Brown, Wendy 203–204
Bryant, John 42–43, 76, 103
Buell, Lawrence 153–154, 195
Bulkington (character in *Moby-Dick*) 124
Bunger (character in *Moby-Dick*)
Ahab and 78–80, 121
amputation of Boomer's arm by 76
Boomer's prosthetic arm and 76–77
Moby Dick and 163
providence and 77
scientific perspective of 77
on whales' digestion 77
Byron, Lord 93–94

"The Cabin-Table" (chapter in *Moby-Dick*) 82,
100, 102
"The Candles" (chapter in *Moby-Dick*)
50–51, 103–104
Carlyle, Thomas 97, 131–132
Caruth, Cathy 60
Castiglia, Christopher 119, 123–124
Catholics 95–96, 133–135, 191–192
Cella, Matthew 26–27, 50–51
Cervantes, Miguel de 194
"The Chart" (chapter in *Moby-Dick*)
115–117
Chase, Owen 77–78
Chase, Richard 189–191
Child, Lydia Maria 131–132
Christians
The Crusades and 16, 19–20, 98–100,
144, 158–159
European wars of religion (1522–1648)
and 95–96
Greek War of Independence
(1820s) and 101
imperialism and 144–145
Islamophobia and 95–97, 168
in Jerusalem 97, 101
"Cistern and Buckets" (chapter in
Moby-Dick) 130–131
Civil War
amputation and 3–4, 69
disillusion and 173
dismemberment and 176
phantom pain and 69

INDEX   237

political and civil rights for emancipated
  slaves and 176
prostheses and 63
Clarel (Melville). See also *specific characters*
  capitalism criticized in 148, 158–159,
    161, 168–169
  Civil War and 173
  The Crusades and 19–20, 98–99, 144
  democracy criticized in 144–145, 174–175
  imperialism criticized in 144–145, 168–169,
    174, 194
  Ishmael as character in 19–20
  Islam and 19–20, 97, 144, 184–185
  on Mosaic religions in Ottoman
    territories 97
  Native Americans compared to
    Muslims in 95
  Palestine as setting of 19–20, 144
Cold War 54, 178–182, 202–203
Columbus, Christopher 192, 194, 200
Confessions of an English Opium Eater
  (De Quincey) 104–106
The Confidence-Man (Melville) 16, 73–76,
    177, 202
Constantinople (Istanbul) 16, 17*f*, 94, 115
Cooper, James Fenimore 69
"The Counterpane" (chapter in *Moby-Dick*)
    121–122, 124–127
Craik, George Lillie 128–129
Crawford, Cassandra 68–69, 72
The Crusades 16, 19–20, 98–100, 144,
    158–159
Cucu, Sorin Radu 174–175, 178
Cuticle (character in *White-Jacket*) 38–42
Cuvier, Baron 137

Daggoo (character in *Moby-Dick*) 95, 134–135,
    137, 139, 148–150, 157–158
The Dardanelles 170–171
Davis, Lennard J. 8, 79–80
Dayan, Colin 161–162
Declaration of Independence 179
Delano (character in "Benito
    Cereno") 166–167, 191–192, 194
Delbanco, Andrew 121
De Quincey, Thomas 26–27, 104–106
Dickens, Charles 8, 122–123
Dimock, Wai Chee 91, 165–166
Disability Studies 180, 202
dismemberment. *See also* amputation
  Ahab and 1–4, 10–13, 16–18, 21, 25–29,
    31–33, 35–36, 41–45, 49–50, 52, 54–56,
    59, 74–76, 78, 81–82, 91–92, 109–110,
    119, 151, 157, 177–178, 180, 204–205

American Revolution and 46–47,
    146–147, 147*f*
  Babo and 191, 193–194
  bodies politic and 176–177
  Don Hannibal and 9–10, 172–177,
    182–183, 194
  Hope Leslie and 3–4
  imperialism and 146–147
  phantom pain and 18, 60, 67–73, 83,
    122–123, 197
  racialized politics and 7
  stigma and 27–28
Djalea (character in *Clarel*) 97
Don Hannibal Rohon Del Aquaviva
    (character in *Clarel*)
  democracy criticized by 173, 175
  dismemberment of 9–10, 172–177,
    182–183, 194
  as Mexican War hero 172–173
  Palestine and 174
  prosthetic leg of 173–176
  Ungar and 174
Donoghue, Denis 121
Dough Boy (character in *Moby-Dick*) 9
Douglass, Frederick 160–161, 179
Dowling, David 50–51
Dracula (Stoker) 104
Duquette, Elizabeth 179, 189–191
"Dusk" (chapter in *Moby-Dick*) 181–182
Duyckinck, Evert 39, 93–94
Dylan, Bob 200–202

Einboden, Jeffrey 132
Elijah (character in *Moby-Dick*) 9,
    36–37, 107–108
Eliot, George 122–123
Emerson, Ralph Waldo 132, 138, 194
"Enter Ahab; to Him, Stubb" (chapter in
    Moby-Dick) 27, 43, 45
Ernst, Carl W. 101
Ezekiel (Old Testament book) 21

Faraday, Michael 151–152
Faust (Goethe) 89
Fedallah (character in *Moby-Dick*)
  Ahab and 14–15, 83–84, 87–91, 103–104,
    106–108, 112–113, 116–117, 127,
    134–135, 193–195, 197–198
  Boomer and 87
  clothing and appearance of 88–89, 103, 108
  death and corpse of 6–7, 107–109, 117,
    120–121, 127, 197–198
  etymology of the name 111
  eyes and gaze of 125–126, 193–194, 196

238 INDEX

Fedallah (character in *Moby-Dick*) (*Continued*)
  as "ghostly aborigine" 98
  the gothic and 87–89, 104, 107–108
  Ishmael and 13–16, 19, 87–90, 98, 103,
    105–108, 114, 117–121, 123–124,
    127–129, 133–134, 136, 138–139,
    174, 195–196
  Islam and 6–7, 13, 15–16, 83–84, 89–91, 98,
    103–104, 129, 133–134, 136
  Manilla oarsmen and 103
  metaphysical insights and prophesies
    of 107–108, 116–117, 121, 134–135
  Moby Dick and 83–84, 87, 111–112, 117
  Orientalism and racialization of 14–15,
    88–92, 103–106, 117–118, 127, 133–135
  as Parsee 14–16, 87–91, 95, 98, 103–104,
    106, 112, 117, 120–121, 123, 127–128,
    134–135, 195, 198
  as phantom 123–124, 127
  as prosthesis and 13–15, 90, 107, 113,
    116–119, 124, 127, 195, 201
  romantic supernaturalism and 15
  Starbuck and 88–90
  Stubb and 88–90
  vengeance and 87–88
  whale watching by 107
Fee, Tara Robbins 123–124
Finkelstein, Dorothee Metlitsky 14, 111
"Fire-Worship" (Hawthorne) 93
Flask (character in *Moby-Dick*)
  Ahab and 35–36, 46–47, 79,
    148–150, 180–181
  capitalism and 151–160
  cruelty of whaling industry and 148,
    150–156, 158–160, 162–163, 165, 169–170
  Daggoo as prostheses for 148–150, 157–158
  doubloon scene and 159
  Fedallah and 88–89, 103
  Ishmael and 46, 148–150, 162–163
  mediocrity of 150–151, 169–170
  Starbuck and 154–155
Fleece (character in *Moby-Dick*) 25, 28
"The Fossil Whale" (chapter in
  Moby-Dick) 132–133
"The Fountain" (chapter in *Moby-Dick*) 58–59
"Fragments from a Writing Desk"
  (Melville) 16
Frank, Arthur 27–28, 54–55, 81–82
Frankenstein (Shelley) 104
Franklin, Benjamin 92–93, 130, 146–147, 147f
Freburg, Christopher 193
Freud, Sigmund 11–12, 90
Fromm, Erich 90–91, 113, 156, 185–186

Genghis Khan 99–100
Goffman, Erving 27–28
"The Grand Armada" (chapter in *Moby-Dick*)
  50–51, 163–166, 169–171, 195
Grandin, Greg 191–192
Greek War of Independence (1820s) 101
Greiman, Jennifer 18–19, 145, 174–175

Hagia Sophia mosque (Constantinople)
  16, 17f
Haman (king of Persia) 71
Hamlet (Shakespeare) 62, 64–67, 72–73,
  81–83, 91–92
Haraway, Donna 11–12
"The Hat" (chapter in *Moby-Dick*) 106
Hawthorne, Nathaniel. See also *specific titles*
  Civil War and 176
  gothic characters of 104
  Melville's interactions with 39, 93–94,
    143–144
  on *White-Jacket* 39
  Zoroastrianism and 93
Heidegger, Martin 11–13
Henry V (Shakespeare) 110
A History of New York (Irving) 30
Holmes, Oliver Wendell 63–67
Holy Sepulcher (Jerusalem) 101
Homer 58–59
Hooker, Juliet 204–205
Hope, Thomas 93–94, 104
Hope Leslie (Sedgwick) 3–4
Huston, John 89, 201

Illanoan Pirates of Tampassook (Marryat) 169f
imperialism
  Clarel and 144–145, 168–169, 174, 194
  Ishmael and 18–19, 117–118, 136, 143–144,
    146–147, 163, 166, 194–196
  Islam and 19, 95–96, 98
  Jacksonian America and 110–111, 117–118,
    143, 178–179, 189–191, 194
  whaling industry and 18–19,
    146–148, 195–196
Irving, Washington 30, 93, 95
Ishmael (character in *Moby-Dick*)
  Ahab and 25–28, 36–37, 49–50, 57–58, 62,
    79–80, 99–100, 108–109, 116, 121,
    138–139, 178, 180–183, 198, 204–205
  anthropomorphization of whales
    by 153–154, 156–157, 162–163,
    170–171
  Bulkington and 124
  capitalism and 157–158, 160–163, 166, 171

caravan of whales in Sunda Strait described
by 163–165, 170–171
on carpenter on *Pequod* 61
childhood memory of fear and guilt
of 121–126
chronological time on the *Pequod* described
by 58–59
The Crusades 98–99
democracy and 19–20, 163, 167–168, 175,
177–179, 182–183, 189–191, 194–195
environmental consciousness of 7, 145–146,
157–158, 161–163
Exodus predecessor of 120–121
The Fates and 185–186
Fedallah and 13–16, 19, 87–90, 98, 103,
105–108, 114, 117–121, 123–124,
127–129, 133–134, 136, 138–139,
174, 195–196
Flask and 46, 148–150, 162–163
Fleece and 28
impaired whale described
by 153–158, 162–163
imperialism and 18–19, 117–118, 136,
143–144, 146–147, 163, 166, 194–196
insularity and retreats of 182–183,
185–187, 189
Islam and 6–7, 13, 16, 19–20, 115, 129–134,
136, 138, 158, 168, 184–185
on Jackson 185, 189–191, 194
Malays and 166, 168–169
Manilla oarsmen and 87–88, 118–119,
129, 133–138
Moby Dick and 36–37, 111–112, 115–116
mystical experience on the masthead
of 183, 196–197
nationalism and 7, 145–146, 189–191, 195
on Nelson 35, 186–191
progressivism of 167–168, 177–178,
183, 203
prosthesis and 119
providence and 77
Queequeg and 88, 121–131, 133–134,
139, 189–191
Samuel Enderby and 74–76
slavery and 19, 189–191
Starbuck and 182
survival of 6–7, 15, 119–121, 137–139, 178
on Tower Hill whale artist 73–74
trauma and 123–124
on whales' skeletons and
anatomy 35–36, 59, 80
whaling industry violence and 18–19,
145–146, 148, 155, 162–163, 165–166

whiteness and racialized thinking
of 134–135, 137–138, 203
Islam
"Benito Cereno" and 191–192
capitalism and 150
Christian Islamophobia and 95–97, 168
Clarel and 19–20, 97, 144, 184–185
The Crusades and 16, 19–20, 98–100,
144, 158–159
dervishes and Sufism in 191–192
Fedallah and 6–7, 13, 15–16, 83–84, 89–91,
98, 103–104, 129, 133–134, 136
Founding Fathers of the United States
and 92–93, 96, 130
Greek War of Independence
(1820s) and 101
idol worship forbidden in 129–130
Ishmael and 6–7, 13, 16, 19–20, 115,
129–134, 136, 138, 158, 168, 184–185
Melville's interest in and understanding
of 2–3, 16, 92–97, 102, 104, 138
Native Americans and 95, 98, 131–132
Orientalism and 13, 91–96, 109, 131
Philippine Islands and 135
as prosthesis in *Moby-Dick* 13–18
The Qur'an and 101, 102, 131–132, 135
Ramadan and 15–16, 129–130
Redburn and 92–95
salaam (bowing) and 129–130
scholarship analyzing Melville's
interest in 14
Trump and 202–203
violence framed through references to 2–3,
13, 96, 108–111
Western imperialism and 19, 95–96, 98
Israel Potter (Melville) 49–50, 96

Jackson, Andrew 185, 189–191, 194
Jacksonian America
aggrievement and 177
democracy and 18–19, 189–191, 194
imperialism and continental conquest
in 110–111, 117–118, 143, 178–179,
189–191, 194
individualism and 91–92, 182
Native Americans targeted by violence and
removal in 177
racism and 178–179, 194
slavery's expansion in 177
James, C. L. R. 55, 159–160, 182–183, 185
James, William 154–155, 160
Japan 143–144
Jefferson, Thomas 92–93, 96, 175, 177

240 INDEX

Jerusalem 97, 101, 158–159, 184–185
Job (Old Testament) 153
Jonik, Michael 28, 48–49
Jungfrau (ship in *Moby-Dick*) 153–154, 159–160, 162, 195

Karcher, Carolyn 189–191
Katz, Leslie 68
Keats, John 93–94
Kelly, John D. 148
Kemble, Fanny 42–43, 47–48
Kendall, George Wilkins 70
Kerrigan, John 82–83
King, Richard J. 157
King Lear (Shakespeare) 42, 47–48
"Knights and Squires" (chapter in
    Moby-Dick) 182
The Koran. *See* The Qur'an
Kriegel, Leonard 8, 10–11
Kurzman, Steven L. 12

Lee, Maurice 175–176
"The Lee Shore" (chapter in *Moby-Dick*) 124
Le Fanatisme, ou Mahoumet le Prophète
    (Voltaire) 95–96, 102
"Leg and Arm" (chapter in *Moby-Dick*) 74–75
Leigh, Percival 76–77
"Loomings" (chapter in *Moby-Dick*) 185–186

Macbeth (Shakespeare) 26–27, 42–43,
    89, 107–108
MacLachlan, Malcolm 69–70
Magna Brittania or the Colonies Reduc'd
    (Franklin) 146–147, 147*f*
Malays
    Confessions of an English Opium Eater
        and 105–106
    Ishmael and 166, 168–169
    Islam and 168
    Orientalism and 108–109, 168
    as pirates in *Moby-Dick* 50–51,
        163, 166–168
    racialization of 168
    violence in *Moby-Dick* and 2–3, 169–170
    Western imperial and commercial interests
        threatened by 166–168
Manilla oarsmen (characters in *Moby-Dick*)
    Ahab and 87–88
    Fedallah and 103
    Ishmael and 87–88, 118–119, 129, 133–138
    Islam and 133–134, 136
    Orientalism and 103
    as phantoms 123

physical appearance of 88
    racialization of 88, 133–135, 137–138
"Manners" (Emerson) 132
"The Man That Was Used Up" (Poe) 64
Maori culture 128–129
Mardi (Melville)
    amputation in 37–38, 70–71, 75–76
    cosmopolitan identity at sea in 196
    Islam and 20, 96–97, 183–184
    Isle of Cripples in 20–21, 50
Margoth (character in *Clarel*) 80
Marr, Timothy 14, 96–97, 104, 184–185
Marryat, Samuel Francis 169*f*
Martínez Benedí, Pilar 68–69, 215 n.8,
    216 n.19, 224 n.27
Matthiessen, F. O. 26, 178
Mayo, William Starbuck 94
McLuhan, Marshall 11–12
McWilliams, Susan 83
Melville, Allan 94
Melville, Elizabeth 30, 94
Melville, Gansevoort 8–9
Melville, Helen Maria 8–9
Melville, Herman. *See also specific works*
    on challenges of writing
        Moby-Dick 119–120
    childhood of 29
    disability witnessed by 8–9, 29
    imperialism and 143
    Islam and 2–3, 16, 92–97, 102, 104, 138
    New York City home (1847–50) of 30
    Ottoman Empire travels (1856–57) of 16,
        17*f*, 94, 101
    US expansion into the Asia-Pacific and 18
Melville, Sophia 94
Metcalfe, Eleanor Melville 105–106
Mexican-American War (1846–1848) 31–33,
    34*f*, 70, 73
Mihm, Stephen 63–64
Milder, Robert 218 n.5, 220 n.61
Mitchell, David T. 8, 13–14, 35–36, 98
Mitchell, Silas Weir 69–72
Moby-Dick (Melville). *See also specific chapters
    and characters*
    Cold War readings of 178–182, 202–203
    collective work in 55
    contemporary reviews of 119–121
    democratic progress and 7
    disability aesthetics and 6, 123–124, 127
    disability studies and 9–10
    the gothic and 87–88, 114
    grievance and 1–2
    impairment of 7

INDEX 241

Islam and 16
Orientalism and 94–95
range of disabilities among characters in 9
supernatural hand metaphor and 122–123
vengeance and 1, 91–92
Moby Dick (film, 1956) 89, 201
Moby Dick (whale in *Moby-Dick*)
  Ahab dismembered by 36–37, 41, 108–109
  Boomer dismembered by 57–58, 74, 78
  dismemberment of 21
  humans wounded by 9
  Pequod sunk by 77–78
  Pequod whaling boat destroyed by 53
  as phantom 123
  as target of Ahab's revenge 10–11
  vulnerability of 18–19
  whiteness of 151, 203
Morewood, Sarah 94
Mormonism 96
Moro population (Philippine Islands) 135
Morris, Gouverneur 63
Morrison, Toni 6, 203–204
Mosses from an Old Manse (Melville) 42, 93–94
Muhammad, Prophet 93, 95–96, 102,
  120–121, 129–132
Muslims. *See* Islam
Mustapha (character in *Clarel*) 184–185

Nantucket (Massachusetts) 143, 148, 174–175
Napoleon Bonaparte 30–31, 101
Napoleonic Wars 33
Nelson, Horatio
  amputation of arm of 33–35, 55–56, 186–187
  battle wounds during 1790s of 33–35, 71
  Ishmael on 35, 186–191
  Liverpool statue of 187–189, 188f, 190f, 192
  military valor of 173, 186–187
  "The Old Boatswain" and 33–35
  Omoo and 35
  phantom pain experienced by 71
  slave trade and 187–188
  Trafalgar battle (1805) and death of 33–35
  Trafalgar Square statue of 186–187, 187f
  White-Jacket and 35
New Bedford (Massachusetts) 125, 148,
  151–152, 160–162
The New Zealanders (Craik) 128–129
Nielsen, Kim M. 46–47
Nietzsche, Friedrich 203–204
Nixon, Rob 158–159

Obenzinger, Hilton 145
The Odyssey (Homer) 58–59

"The Old Boatswain" 33–35
Olson, Charles 196
Omoo (Melville) 35, 40, 49–50
The Oresteia (Aeschylus) 82–83, 91–92
Othello (Shakespeare) 2, 108–109
Otter, Samuel 8–9, 79, 115
Ottoman Empire. *See also* Turks
  Ahab's command over crew compared
    to 2–3, 13, 100, 102
  authoritarianism in 2–3, 13, 96,
    102, 110–111
  British Empire compared by American
    colonists to 96
  capital punishment in 110
  gothic fiction and 104
  Greek War of Independence
    (1820s) and 101
  harems and 16, 94, 104
  Jerusalem and 97
  Melville's travels (1856–57) in 16,
    17f, 94, 101
  muezzin in 184–185
  Orientalism and 2–3, 13, 94, 104,
    109, 130–131
  White-Jacket and 102

Paine, Thomas 96
Palestine 16, 19–20, 95, 144, 174
Palmer leg 64
Paré, Ambroise 69
Parsons, Usher 41
Peale, Rembrandt 32f
Pease, Donald 178, 180
Peleg (character in *Moby-Dick*) 108, 148
Pendleton, John 31
Pequod (ship in *Moby-Dick*)
  Ahab's modifications to 49–52, 74–75
  caravan of whales in Sunda Strait
    and 163–165
  chronological time on 58–59
  coffin-taps on 53
  environmental destruction and 158–159
  insularity of 169–170
  international nature of crew of 148, 168–169
  physical dimensions of 25
  sinking of 6–7, 47–49, 77–78
  as stage 26
"The Pequod Meets the Rose-bud" (chapter in
  Moby-Dick) 58–59
"The Pequod Meets the Virgin" (chapter in
  Moby-Dick) 58–59, 151–163
Perry, Matthew 143–144, 227 n.4
phantom pain 18, 60, 67–73, 83, 122–123

242 INDEX

Philippine Islands 135–136
Physician for Ships; Containing Medical Advice for Seaman and Other Persons at Sea (Parsons) 41
The Pioneers (Cooper) 69
Pip (character in *Moby-Dick*)
　abandonment during *Pequod*'s sinking of 48–49
　Ahab and 25, 48–49, 54–55, 57–58, 90, 121, 150
　Fool from *King Lear* and 47–49
　laugh of 53
　madness of 9
　as prosthesis 150
　slavery as threat for 48–49
　wisdom of 48
Poe, Edgar Allan 6, 64, 93–94, 104
Polynesia 136, 143–144
Presbyterianism 130, 133–134, 138
prostheses
　Ahab and 3–6, 9–13, 18, 21, 25–30, 35–36, 43–50, 53–68, 72–75, 78, 81–84, 107, 113, 119, 146, 173–174, 176–177, 194, 197–199, 201–202
　American Revolution and 30–31, 146–147
　amputation implied by 11–12
　bodies politic and 18–20, 146
　Boomer and 74–77, 82–83, 173–174, 197
　Civil War and 63
　class-oriented concerns regarding 64–67
　Daggoo and 148–150
　design and 11
　disability and 4–6
　embodiment and 44
　etymology of 11–12, 16
　extension of human capabilities and 11–12
　fashion and 11
　Fedallah and 13–15, 90, 107, 113, 116–119, 124, 127, 195, 201
　Freud on 90
　images and photos depicting 5f
　indebtedness and 4
　Islam in *Moby-Dick* as 13–18
　loss of power and 3
　medical device industry in nineteenth century and 60, 63–64
　as metaphor 12–13
　narrative prosthesis and 13–14
　ontology and 68
　phantom pain and 124
　prosthetic imagination and 14–15
　racial embodiment and 4–6
　Santa Anna and 31–33, 63–64

Stuyvesant and 29–30
　trauma and 4–6, 18
　whalebone as material for 57, 59–60, 62–67, 72–76

Quakerism 78, 114
"The Quarter-Deck" (chapter in *Moby-Dick*) 50–52, 54, 112, 180
"Queen Mab" (chapter in *Moby-Dick*) 43, 153
Queequeg (character in *Moby-Dick*)
　caravan of whales in Sunda Strait and 163–164
　coffin of 117, 120–121, 125, 127
　as harpooner 148–150
　Ishmael and 88, 121–131, 133–134, 139, 189–191
　Islam and 129–130, 132–134
　Pacific Islander identity of 95, 127–128
　paganism of 124–125, 128–129
　racialization of 127
　Ramadan and 15–16, 129, 233 n.72
　Tashtego rescued by 130–131
　tattoos of 82–83, 117, 125, 151
　Yojo and 9, 129–130, 133
The Qur'an 101, 102, 131–132, 135

Rachel (ship in *Moby-Dick*) 117
Ramachandran, V. S. 69–71, 124
Ramadan 15–16, 129–130
Redburn (Melville)
　Hawthorne on 39
　Islam and 92–95
　Nelson statue in Liverpool and 187–189, 192
　Orientalism and 94–95
　slavery and 189
　Turks and 102
Revolutionary War Pension Act (1818) 46–47
Richard III (Shakespeare) 8, 42–43
Rogin, Michael 165, 182–183, 185
Ross, Kelly 191–192
Rousseau, Jean-Jacques 3
Rumi 191–192

Saadi Shirazi 132, 138
Sacks, Oliver 72
Said, Edward 94–97, 207 n.4
Salem leg 64
Samoa (character in *Mardi*)
　amputation of arm of 9–10, 37–38, 70–71, 75–76
　dismemberment of 146
　native culture and grace of 41–42, 70, 173
　wife of 37

Samuel Enderby (ship in *Moby-Dick*) 57–60, 74–76, 78, 80, 121
Sanborn, Geoffrey 125, 128
Santa Anna, Antonio Lopez de 31–33, 34*f*, 63–64, 70, 173
Savarese, Ralph 68–69, 215 n.8, 216 n.19, 224 n.27
"Schools and Schoolmasters" (chapter in *Moby-Dick*) 77–78, 94–95
Schroeder, Jonathan 79–80
Schueller, Malini Johar 95
Schulman, George 91–92
Schultz, Elizabeth 137, 156, 158
Schweitzer, Albert 54–55
Sedgwick, Catharine Maria 3–4
Seward, William 147–148
Shakespeare, William. See also *specific works*
    disability in the works of 43
    embedding of stage directions into character's lines in 57
    humor of misunderstanding and 61
    Kemble's public readings (1840s) of 42–43
    Melville influenced by 26, 29, 42–43, 47–48, 84
    Muslims and images of violence in the works of 2
Shelley, Mary 104
Siebers, Tobin 6, 123–124
Sierra Gordo, battle (1847) of 31–33, 34*f*
Smith, Joseph 96
Snediker, Michael 68
Snyder, Sharon L. 8, 13–14, 35–36, 98
Snyder, Timothy 181
Sobchack, Vivian 12, 28–29
The Soldier's Birth Right (Peale) 30–33, 32*f*
"Song of Myself" (Whitman) 133
Spain 135–136, 165–166
Spanos, William 178
"The Specksynder" (chapter in *Moby-Dick*) 100
Spellberg, Denise 95–96
"The Spirit Spout" (chapter in *Moby-Dick*) 25, 58–59
Spivak, Gayatri Chakraborty 117–119, 123
"A Squeeze of the Hand" (chapter in *Moby-Dick*) 126–127
Stamp Act of 1765 146–147
Starbuck (character in *Moby-Dick*)
    Ahab and 51–55, 90–91, 109, 112–113, 121, 148, 168–169, 178, 180–182, 203–204
    as assistive device 51–54
    capitalism and 148, 155–157, 180
    caravan of whales in Sunda Strait and 163–164, 170

    cargo on the *Pequod* and 78
    democracy and 181–182
    doubloon scene and 159
    Fedallah and 88–90
    Flask and 154–155
    Ishmael and 182
    Moby Dick and 111–112
    moral independence of 51–52, 159
    obedience of 181
Stiegler, Bernard 3, 11–12, 18, 146–147
Stoker, Bram 104
Stolorow, Robert 60
Stubb (character in *Moby-Dick*)
    Ahab and 27–29, 35–36, 43–48, 52, 90–91, 125–126, 150, 153, 180–181
    comedy and 27–28, 44–48
    doubloon scene and 159
    dream of 43–45, 52, 57–58, 68, 153, 156–157, 201–202
    embodiment and 44
    Fedallah and 88–90
    imperialism and frontier mentality of 156–157
    as prosthesis 150
Stuckey, Sterling 192
Stuyvesant, Peter 29–30
Sufism 191–192
Sunda Straits 163, 166–167, 170–171, 196
"Sunset" (chapter in *Moby-Dick*) 10–11
"The Symphony" (chapter in *Moby-Dick*) 112–113
Szendy, Peter 108, 138–139

Taji (character in *Mardi*)
    on cosmopolitan identity at sea 196
    Islam and mystical experience on the masthead of 183–185
    on Islam in Africa 96–97
    native culture and 70
    Samoa's amputed arm and 70–71
Takaki, Ronald 18
Tashtego (character in *Moby-Dick*) 57–58, 95, 116–117, 130–135, 139, 184–185
Taylor, Sunauro 152–153
Te Pehi Kupe 128–129
Thomson, Rosemarie Garland 8, 28, 43, 91–92
Tiny Tim (character in *A Christmas Carol*) 8
Tocqueville, Alexis de 3–4, 83, 110–111, 177, 179, 182–183
Tommo (character in *Typee*) 75–76, 136, 146, 191
Tricker, Spencer 104, 108, 167–168

244 INDEX

Trump, Donald 202–204
Turks. *See also* Ottoman Empire
  Henry V and 110
  Moby-Dick's images of violence and 2–3
  Othello and 108–109
  Ottoman imperialism in Jerusalem
    and 101
  Redburn and 102
  The Renaissance and European fears
    regarding 101, 108–109
  "Turkish mutes" and 109–110
  Vathek and 110
Typee: A Peep at Polynesian Life
  (Melville) 8–9, 75–76, 136, 178–179

Ungar (character in *Clarel*)
  capitalism criticized by 148, 158–159,
    161, 168–169
  as Confederate Civil War veteran 144–145
  democracy criticized by 144–145, 174
  Don Hannibal and 174
  environmental consciousness
    and 145–146, 163
  family history of 145
  imperialism criticized by 144–145, 168–169,
    174, 194
  Islamophobia condemned by 144, 158–159
  racism of 145
  as Turkish mercenary 144
"The Unpardonable Sin"
  (Hawthorne) 69, 122–123
Uxbridge, Lord 64

Vafa, Amirhossein 118–119
Van Horn, Jennifer 31–33
Vathek (Beckford) 93–94, 104, 105f, 110
Végső, Roland 174–175, 178
Venetians 2–3, 108–109
Vine (character in *Clarel*) 95, 97
Voltaire 95–96, 102, 201

Walker, David 179
Webster, Daniel 101, 110–111, 201
Westmacott, Richard 188f, 190f
"The Whale Watch" (chapter in
    Moby-Dick) 106
whaling industry
  bourgeois society and 18–19, 160–162
  capitalism and 148–163, 166
  consumer products produced by 147–148,
    151–152, 155
  economic scope of 147–148
  energy provided from sperm oil
    and 151–152, 157, 160–162, 169–170
  environmental destruction and 158–159
  global conflict and 174–175
  imperialism and 18–19, 146–148, 195–196
  industrial capitalism and 157, 169–170
  medical care for sailors employed in 40–41
  violence of 2–3, 18–19, 145–146, 148, 155,
    161–163, 165–166, 169–170
  whales' place in the body politic and 162–163
Wheatley, Phyllis 179
White-Jacket (Melville) 35, 38–40, 102,
    131, 183–184
Whitman, Walt 3–4, 133, 164–165
Wilentz, Sean 200
Williams, Roger 196
Wills, David 11–13, 60–61, 90
Winthrop, John 21
Wollstonecraft, Mary 122–123
Woodward, C. Vann 144
Wyatt, Matthew Cotes 188f, 190f

Yerger and Ord leg 66f
Yojo (Queequeg's idol in *Moby-Dick*)
    9, 129–130, 133
Yothers, Brian 145

Zamboanga region (Philippine Islands) 135–136
Zoroastrianism 15–16, 91, 93